Camilla
THE GREAT

JAKKI JELENE

"I remembered that the real world was wide, and that a varied field of hopes and fears, of sensations and excitements, awaited those who had courage to go forth into its expanse, to seek real knowledge of life amidst its perils."

– *Charlotte Brontë, Jane Eyre*

For my husband and friends who've walked with me through life's perils.

CHAPTER 1

"Do it, do it," her father urged. "Cast the net now!"

The young girl leaned over the small, weather-worn rowboat and dropped the makeshift net into the billowy sea, holding onto the edge with one hand so as not to fall in. The waves rocked the small vessel back and forth as she watched the net drop below the surface and into the dark, shadowy waters.

"We haven't much time before that storm rolls in," her father continued as he looked out across the gloomy horizon of the North Sea. He swiftly grabbed the line and began pulling the net back to the surface. "Hopefully we can get a catch for supper tonight, or else it's porridge again."

Camilla felt her stomach turn at the prospect. How she longed for something other than the mushy oat concoction to fill her belly. Not that she was ungrateful for what they had, but the promise of fresh fried fish made her mouth water after going without it for several weeks. Her mother and father had been hard at work in the field, preparing for the upcoming harvest, and had little energy left over at the end of the day to think of fish. It was lucky enough if they had a few fresh apples to warm by the fire and to sprinkle with sugar and cinnamon for an after-supper treat.

It's not that Camilla's parents didn't wish to have more strength for hunting and fishing, but they were both getting on in years and suffered from a host of physical ailments. As it was, they could barely put in a full day's work to eat through the winter without concerns over their provisions wearing thin by the end of the season. But now that Camilla was coming up in age, she was able to pitch in and help make up for the difference, which was lucky for Dob and Elsie Waller.

You see, Camilla's mother and father never believed they could have children of their own until suddenly the good Lord smiled down upon the unsuspecting pair and blessed them with an exuberant bundle of joy in the twilight years of most women's childbearing age. It was said that no baby was more eager to escape the womb than Camilla and that she must have jumped with joy the day she was to take her first breath, for she exited the birth canal expeditiously without giving much sorrow to dear Elsie Waller for the trouble of carrying her those nine restless months.

So how did the daughter of a poor field hand and his wife come to have such a noble name as Camilla, you might ask? As her dear mother often said, "You must always choose a name to suit a person's destined station in life." And somehow old Elsie believed her daughter would one day be a fine lady, though she neither looked nor dressed the part in the slightest, nor was it in her blood.

No, indeed, even at the age of sixteen, Camilla was the homeliest, skinniest little tomboy anyone ever did lay eyes on. Full of freckles that her mother referred to as "sun kisses" and a tangled mess of fair hair, she tied back into a messy knot to keep out of her eyes. Why, you never saw a girl who appeared less of a lady, and so her pa affectionately called her "Cami," and that suited her quite well. She loved being his little Cami and following him on any adventures to be found, just as if she had been an only son.

And so, little Cami was anxious to put the old rowboat to use and see about scaring up enough fish to feast on for the week to come. She watched eagerly, the boat rocking back and forth, as her father continued pulling at the net. To both their disappointment, it came up empty. They cast it once again, this time pulling up several medium-sized carp. The carp flapped hard against their fate to be supper to no avail, while father and daughter let out a victorious shout. The net was hauled in, and soon the pair was rowing back to shore, arriving home without absorbing so much as one drop of rain before the storm hit land.

Once inside the snug little wooden cottage, Cami kissed her dear mother on the cheek, then stoked the fire in the hearth by throwing another log on top of the diminishing pile. The fire roared back to life, so she rejoined her pa in the kitchen to help clean and prepare the fish for frying. It was a modest home, even among their humble neighbors, but it was full of memories of love, laughter, and warmth. Cami could not have asked for a happier childhood. Sure, there were times when they would have liked to have more food on the table or finer things to wear, but they were never lacking in love and cheer.

"You should have seen her!" Cami's pa said as he grabbed his wife up for a kiss. "She's a fearless one, that girl of ours. The waves ne'er scared her off for a moment. She was bound and determined to bring home a bundle of fish, and so here we are."

Elsie smiled with pride at her husband and daughter as she placed the fish in the fire. It wasn't long before the aroma filled the small house, and the Wallers were set for eating.

"I was thinking, Ma," Cami began after swallowing another bite of the salty filet, "Perhaps it's time I help you and Pa out in the fields full time. If we had another hand, then surely, we could hunt and fish more often between the three of us."

Dob and Elsie thought silently on the suggestion. For as long as possible, they did their best to let their little girl run wild and free, to enjoy the fleeting years of childhood. They were more than willing to do the hard work as there were just the three of them, but the last couple of years proved more difficult with Dob's bum leg, an injury he never recovered from after being thrown from a horse, and Elsie's wavering constitution from what she referred to as "the change of life."

"Perhaps," was all Pa said in reply.

"Griffin has been helping his parents out all this past year," Cami further pressed. "It seems only fitting that I should lend a hand too."

"But Griffin is a boy," her father continued. "And twice as strong as you, Cami."

"But I am twice as fast," she retorted. "And he has a whole year of labor on me now. I'm sure I could become almost as strong in time. Please, Pa, let me give you and Ma a rest."

"T'will be no resting for some time, my dear. Winter is coming, and we'll be working twice as hard through the rest of the season."

Cami jumped at the opportunity to further her proposition. "All the more reason for me to pitch in. I can see some of the crops need harvesting soon, and perhaps we can even work out a trade with some of the townsfolk to lighten our load in the years to come. We could work together and get everything we need with half the effort."

"And what's to come if we rely too much on one crop or another and by some misfortune it doesn't yield? What will we have for trading then? No, we need to continue being self-sufficient as we've always done."

Cami knew her father was right; she recalled the year Sal Brickell lost his entire crop of potatoes to blight and how his family nearly starved if not for the generosity of neighbors who were also struggling to put food on the table that winter. They still lost their youngest, Baby Lizzie, but she was always in poor health, and most expected her to pass months before she did. But even this sad recollection didn't stop Cami from trying to think up some way to make life easier for her parents in their old age. *If only I were a boy*, she thought. *I could care for them fine on my own, but one girl alone cannot easily support a farm.*

CHAPTER 2

The following morning, Cami awoke to a world still damp from the evening storm. The mist cast a bluish hue over the landscape, and a light fog rose over the hillside, causing the trees to look like grey silhouettes in the distance. She stepped onto the stone patio of the little cottage to drink in the promise of a new day when she noticed a figure emerging from the haze, heading her way at a rapid speed. It didn't take long for Cami to recognize the gait of the one fast approaching—it was Griffin.

Now what could he be in such haste about this early in the morning? She asked herself. Cami had known Griffin her entire young life, having grown up together as neighbors running the wild, rugged land. They had gone on many adventures and scared up plenty of trouble too. He was more like a brother than a prospect of the opposite sex, and Griffin had always treated Cami likewise, as she could run and play as hard as any boy he had ever known. And though they got on quite well for the most part, their kinship was not without trouble. They often bickered and fought hard, as siblings frequently do, never considering to hold back even the tiniest of grievances with one another.

This morning, Griffin walked on with purpose, his steps indicating he was on a mission. His shaggy copper locks looked especially unkempt, his shirt, half-buttoned, and his boots, unlaced. It was clear he had left the house without much fuss. "Hello, Cami, is your pa around?" he called out, waving.

"I believe he's in the chicken coop 'round back. Go see for yourself if you care to," she replied.

Griffin nodded and headed for the back of the cottage with Cami following close behind. Without much pause, he began to explain the reason for his early visit. "Bessie is about to calf. It must have started after we went to bed because she's close and with Pa feeling a little under the weather, he wondered if yeh pa wouldn't mind lending a hand."

Cami bit her lower lip. She knew a new calf would be a welcome blessing, but also another mouth to feed. Seemed a long time since they had a new calf themselves. The excitement of seeing the old cow give birth thrilled her. When they reached the coop, Dob Waller was nowhere to be found. Elsie, who was in the kitchen cleaning up the breakfast dishes, saw the pair from the window and popped her head out.

"Good morning, Griffin!" she called out in a sing-song

voice. "To what do we owe the pleasure of your visit so early?"

Cami was quick to answer before Griffin could respond. "Ma, Griff is here because Bessie is gonna calf any minute. He wants Pa's help but he's nowhere to be seen! Dae yeh know where he's gotten off to?"

Elsie frowned, "He went into town this morning to pick up some feed and won't be back for some time. He was in an awful hurry. Why don't you go and help, Cami?"

Both Griffin and Cami reeled at the suggestion. "Me?" she cried out.

"Of course, your pa has been teaching you to handle the livestock since you were able to walk. I'm sure between you and Griffin, there should be plenty of help to bring an old cow into the world."

Griffin and Camilla looked at each other with apprehension, then nodded to one another. After all these years as playmates, they had developed a secret form of communication that didn't always require words. They knew instinctively what the other person was thinking by a slight twitch of the eye or a subtle smile. After a moment of observation, they felt a confidence rise in one another so that together they felt certain they would get the job done.

Camilla acted quickly. She went into the house to grab her worn leather boots and put on her pa's old army jacket. Meanwhile, her mother packed a bit of bread and cheese to sustain her through the afternoon and reassured her once again that all would be well. Then together, Griffin and Camilla marched across the fields that joined their two properties and headed for the wind-beaten barn housing ol' Bessie.

They walked in silent determination for a time before Griffin gulped and asked, "Dae yeh really think we can do it without your pa, Cam?"

"Of course, we can!" she answered with false bravado. "If Ma thinks we're capable then it's sure to turn out okay. Let's just hope your pa agrees."

Griffin's pa, Gerald Felix, was known to be an anxious fellow who often had bouts from ulcers that flared up with his excessive worrying. Like many young men, he was called off to war at an early age, but his mind was not strong enough to handle the consequences of battle and the excessive carnage he was a witness to. He married Griffin's mother shortly before going off, but it was said he was never quite the same when he returned. Camilla had always known him to be a kind, but frail man. So unlike her own pa who was strong as a bear with incredible fortitude.

But Cami's mother and father had such tender compassion for Gerald Felix. Her pa always made an effort to befriend the quiet man. It made Cami proud to know her parents were such gracious and loving people. Secretly she did not envy Griffin in the least, but seeing her own father wind down after his leg injury, was humbling. She found it difficult to accept he was no longer the force she'd always known him to be. Though despite his diminishing health, her father rarely complained and continued his work as if nothing were the matter at all, aside from the occasional grimace which gave his pain away.

If Griffin was ashamed of his own father, it never showed. He was too good-natured a boy to worry much about such things. In fact, he always appeared to take his father's wisdom to heart. If there was one thing Gerald Felix taught his son, it was the importance of learning to read and write. He always had plenty of books on hand, which he pored over until the threads of the binding would come loose. And he was eager to discuss the many principles he gleaned from them with his family and neighbors. It was the one thing that made him light up, if anything could.

Griffin nodded at Cami's comment, "I'm sure Pa'll take whatever help he can get, at this point. We'd all but given up on Bessie after she lost the last two calves. She's getting up in age, and it's been a while since she's produced fresh milk. Pa thinks it might be a bull since she's taken a while longer than usual to give birth, but we're hoping for a heifer. We need a young cow for reproducing and milking. Anyhow, it's coming one way or another, and we'll soon find out."

By the time they reached the barn, Gerald was in position to assist the pregnant heifer and barely turned at the sound of his son's greeting. He was shaking a bit from nerves, but otherwise seemed to be focusing on the task at hand. The old cow moaned in labor as he worked to establish the position of the calf. Suddenly, Gerald Felix froze.

"What is it, Pa?" Griffin asked, a hint of concern in his voice, which caused Camilla to turn her attention from the cow to Mr. Felix.

His voice quivering, Gerald Felix replied, "I have the feet, but the dern head is turned the wrong way and won't budge. Dob, come give me a hand," he called out in sudden desperation to his old neighbor and friend.

"Pa couldn't make it," Camilla finally spoke for the first time. "Ma sent me instead."

Gerald turned in astonishment and stared at the young woman standing before him, dressed in her father's oversized coat, ready to assist. "How can *you* help? What do you know about it?" he replied, panic rising in his voice.

"Pa taught me everything he knows. I've seen him deal with this very thing a few times."

Gerald gave a look of doubt and began shaking his head fiercely at the prospect, but Griffin quickly interjected, fully confident in Camilla's ability, "Please, Pa, I really think she can help. I've seen Cami work with farm animals, and she's got real instinct."

Gerald was hesitant, but out of fear and desperation, he got up and moved out of the way to allow Camilla a chance to prove herself capable. Deep down, she was scared too. She had told the truth that she had seen her father face this very problem more than once, but she had never actually helped with the process. Still, she remembered how he was able to turn the head, so she stepped in confidently and got to work.

The first thing she noticed was that the calf was much larger than she was used to—and strong. Cami reached up and fought to turn its head, the way her pa did, but struggled to do so. If only she were stronger. Once more, she cursed herself for being a girl. The heifer moaned again and shifted its enormous weight, and Camilla lost her grip on the calf. She didn't want to reveal the growing doubt in her ability to help with the situation, something only Griffin could note from the look in her eyes.

Griffin jumped up and took hold of ol' Bessie, then called out, "It's okay, try again! I've got her. I won't let go—I promise. You can do this!"

Cami looked into her dear friend's eyes and drew strength from his unwavering faith in her. She managed to grab hold of the calf's head once again and grit her teeth, pulling until she finally managed to turn its head. From there, she easily walked the calf out slowly from the birthing canal, a sense of relief washing over them all.

When the moment of trauma had passed, they got the calf settled, and Camilla fell back into a pile of hay to catch her breath. Gerald Felix was still stunned at the sight of this tiny young lady taking control of the situation and successfully handling the calf, which turned out to be a heifer after all. Bessie carried the poor thing past term, which was the reason its size became a problem. But now both mother and baby bovine were healthy and recovering quickly from the whole ordeal.

"You're a remarkable young woman," Gerald said at last.

Camilla smiled, her loose, messy hair sticking to her face from sweat, "So I'm told." She gave a wide grin to Griffin, who was standing with his hands shoved into the pockets of his trousers, beaming.

CHAPTER 3

When Camilla's father heard the news about her heroic deed, he was bursting with pride. "Seems all that time hanging around the farm paid off," he said, feeling a bit justified in allowing his only daughter to run among the livestock as much as she did.

Little Cami knew her father actually deserved most of the credit. "I learned everything from you, Pa," she replied plainly, then added, "And Griffin helped too."

Nothing diminished the smile on his face as Mr. Felix recounted the story of how the kids helped bring the new calf into the world, with Camilla at the charge. For now, Mr. Felix called the baby cow Gretchen, but all his female cows became "Ol' Bessie" in time. The only person more proud of Cami than her pa was Griffin, though he said very little. He just continued beaming in admiration over his childhood companion.

It was getting late in the day, and Ma was eager to start fixing supper. Mr. Felix promised to have the entire family over for a meal soon, and they thanked him for the pending invitation as he turned to leave for home. Before following his father, Griffin turned to Camilla and said, "Hope you can come by tomorrow and see how Gretchen is getting along. Then maybe we can try to scare up some clams. Sure would be great for a chowder!"

"Sounds good, I'll be by sometime after breakfast if Pa doesn't need me for any other chores." She looked to her father for approval, to which he nodded his head.

Satisfied, Griffin skipped off toward the setting sun, creating a silhouette of his figure with each bounding step. For the first time, Camilla noticed he looked taller and more muscular than she remembered. It was the figure of a man, not the boy she once knew. It made her tummy ache at the thought of what it meant. Soon enough, he'd have to work around the farm full-time or look for work elsewhere. She wondered if their carefree days were coming to an end. The thought filled her with sadness, so she pushed it aside and headed into the house to help her mother prepare the table so they could eat dinner.

As she entered, she was filled with the warmth of the fire that chased out the early evening chill from her flesh. It was a modest home, but cozy and well-kept. Her mother had a knack for creating beauty out of little things. She always made sure there were fresh flowers in the vase on the table, plucked directly from her garden, which she enjoyed tending to when time permitted. The walls were adorned with other works of natural art made from twigs and rocks collected along the property. Camilla's favorite was a Christian cross made of tiny stones and wrapped loosely with a dried piece of vine. It had been there since before she was born and was lovingly made in honor of her grandmother, whom she had never met, but had been told many times she resembled in both looks and in spirit.

"She was a lady of excellence," her mother would say. "Though she never seemed to know it. She was full of passion and lived an extraordinary life." Camilla recalled the many stories she heard regarding her grandmother, Beatrice, and how she had survived a great famine when most others succumbed. She had bravely immigrated to their current land in search of food, despite weakness and hunger, saving twenty people in the process, whom she convinced to join her. They only lost two along the way, including an infant and an elderly gentleman who struggled to carry on and finally passed in his sleep during the journey.

Tales of her heroic deeds were legendary in their village, as many of the townsfolk were descendants of the families who made the journey. Most made their living farming or fishing, and aside from the rare dry season or intense winter frost, food supply was rarely a concern over the years. Still, it required hard work to survive in the rugged terrain, and even now, as Camilla looked over at her father, her heart ached over his tired frame. Like Griffin, he appeared older than she remembered.

After she finished setting the table, Camilla found a spot on the rug and sat at her father's feet. "How are you feeling, Pa?" she asked sweetly.

Dob placed a hand on his daughter's head and petted her messy hair affectionately. "Oh, just fine. It was a long day, what with going to town and the regular chores. I'm just looking forward to enjoying a nice meal."

Elsie had the inclination to fry up more of the fish they caught the day before. The sizzling aroma filled the room, making Camilla anxious to fill her belly as well. She felt spoiled. Normally, her mother would spread out their best meals to make them last in case there wasn't more fresh fish or meat in the near future. Camilla wondered what occasion had caused her mother to break her usual custom.

Before the thought could linger, her father began to speak. "You know, I might have to take you up on your offer to help more around here, Cami. I wish you could be a child forever, but we have no son to work the land, and everyone's predicting a long winter. I hope you can manage some new responsibilities."

Cami smiled up at her father, "Oh, I can, Pa, I promise I won't let you down. After tomorrow, I'll work alongside yeh 'til sundown. We'll be just fine."

"And what about Griffin, do you think he'll understand?"

Camilla bit her lip, "I'm sure he'll understand. 'Sides, he'll be helping out more around his own farm, I suspect. Especially now that they have a new cow to tend to. But I'll work twice as hard as him. You'll see Pa, I'll be every bit as helpful around here as any boy."

Her father's eyes were soft and adoring. "I don't doubt that for a minute, my darlin'. I've never seen a young one so strong and spirited as you. But let's hope this is temporary. In the spring, I'll see about hiring one of the orphan boys. Your ma worries that you'll lose sight of being a lady if we're not careful. And I think she's right. Women know about these things."

Camilla couldn't imagine anything she was less concerned about. "Oh, I love Ma, and she is the picture of a fine lady," she began, looking over at her mother who was listening intently, "But that's not me. I'm like you, I was meant for work, Pa. I don't mind, honest."

"But you'll be thinking about marrying soon, and for that you need to look at least a little part of a lady. Griffin is turning out to be a nice young man, yeh know."

Camilla's face scrunched at the suggestion, "Oh, Pa, Griffin is like a brother to me! And besides, I'm not going anywhere for a long time. So, please, let's not talk about it anymore. Ma is almost finished with supper, and I'm near starved. I've had a full day too, yeh know!"

Her father rubbed his hands together in anticipation of the hot meal, "You sure have—we both have! So, let's drop it for now and go eat!"

With that, they both stood up and lumbered over to the table to say grace and break bread together. The rest of the evening

23

was spent listening to Pa's story of going into town. How the shopkeeper's son, Henry, was recently engaged to Stella the schoolmistress, and that they were currently seeking her replacement. How he ran into Mr. Flanigan, the minister who was set on retiring soon and moving back to Ireland. And how the price of oats had gone up again. All signs of more changes taking place in Camilla's small world.

After dinner, her father pulled out his fiddle and played a couple of favorite ditties before settling down with his pipe and drifting off in his favorite chair. Cami loved it when her pa played his fiddle. She often danced and sang along, but on this night, she just laid her head on his knee and listened. His voice was strong, perhaps a tad gruff, but soothing to her soul. For the moment, Camilla felt at peace. The Wallers may not have had much, but Camilla felt rich.

CHAPTER
4

The next day, after eating breakfast and helping with a couple of chores around the farm, Camilla set off to see Griffin. Her father was fixing up the old plow in preparation for harvest season, which was always in need of mending. She waved to her father before leaving, asking once again if he needed anything else.

"All is well, little one," he called back to her. "You can start worrying about your ol' pa tomorrow." While Cami truly meant it when she said she wanted to do more work around the farm, she was glad for one last day of adventuring with her dearest friend. She was eager to see the new calf and romp in the sun, hunting for clams. However, she worried about how Griffin would take the news that their playdates were to come to an end.

As she approached the Felix farm, Griffin was already

halfway across the field, waiting for her under an old oak tree where they frequently met. He had a piece of straw hanging out of his teeth and was casually awaiting her arrival. "Wondered when you'd turn up, you ol' slug. I finished my breakfast an hour ago."

Camilla stuck her tongue out in response to Griffin's teasing. "I woulda been here much earlier had I not got stuck collecting eggs for Pa. Which reminds me, you're not gonna be pleased to hear this, but I'm not gonna be able to play with yeh anymore. At least not for the rest of the season. Pa needs me to help out around the farm. He's gettin' on and could use an extra hand."

Griffin didn't miss a beat. "Aye, me and Pa had the same talk last night. He said it was time for me to start acting like a man around the house. I told him it was a proper suggestion. So, I suppose we'll only have Sundays for rompin'. Better make the most of the day whilst the sun's still out, don't you think?"

All of Camilla's worst fears were coming true. They truly were growing up, and her childhood days were coming to an end. She thought it would be more gradual, not happen all at once. But the time had come, and her sense of duty to her parents overrode her selfish desire to while the days away. She was proud that Griffin would be doing the same. He was becoming a strong and capable young man, not that she thought much of him beyond that. As Camilla told her father, rightly. To her, Griffin was not much more than a pesky brother—you put up with them because they're your only playmate, but you love them despite their annoying ways.

Just then Griffin jumped up, grabbed Camilla's hand, and began running. "Come along you fool. I've got to show you how Gretchen is getting on. She's standing real strong now." Together they bolted through the tall grass, silently turning their running into a race, as children often do. They both worked to outdo the other, but in the end, Camilla reached the edge of the barn only slightly before Griffin. She may have beaten him, but not as easily as she once did. He was catching up in speed, which she didn't like. Camilla was known for her speed, but if she was honest, she had to push herself extra hard to get the better of him.

She took a moment to catch her breath before entering through the large barn door where the cow stall was. Before her stood the brown calf she helped bring into the world. "Good morning, girl." She spoke in a cheery tone, but the calf appeared only half-interested, seeming to already forget the one who brought her into the world. "My goodness!" she exclaimed. "This cow certainly has a short memory, even for a newborn." Still, she pet Gretchen's soft nose, and the baby cow seemed to warm up to Camilla quickly enough, pressing into her gentle caresses, but it wasn't long before she was ready to go back to her mama for feeding.

To those accustomed to country living, a cow is only mildly interesting for a short time, so after a few minutes, Camilla and Griffin were back to crossing the fields and heading toward the stream that led to the shoreline to see if they could dig up some clams. The ground was marshy, so when they reached the bank of the river, Camilla and Griffin removed their shoes and tramped through the mud to begin the hunt.

They slaved away for a time, finding a handful of good-eating clams, but the progress wasn't fast enough for Griffin's liking. "If we keep this up, it will be a month before we find enough clams for a decent meal. How 'bout we try by the tide pools in the cove?"

Camilla wasn't entirely unhappy with her findings, but didn't mind moving on to another location. "Oh, why not?" she answered, gathering her few prizes into the skirt of her well-worn shift.

The two playmates scampered along a cliff's edge toward the bay, whistling silly songs and arguing over who would make the better catch of the day. Camilla was already up by two, but Griffin knew the day was young and that he would have the better advantage when it came to climbing over the rocks of the tidepools and didn't mind saying so. Camilla knew he was right, but it didn't matter much, considering they usually split the gains between them evenly.

They were just about to head down the path to the shoreline when the sound of voices caught their attention. Just below the cliff, on the road leading to town, was a caravan of people accompanied by several wagons topped with long, red flags that flew wildly in the sea breeze.

Camilla was instantly intrigued. "Who do yeh suppose those people are, Griff?"

Griffin thought for a moment as he assessed the colorful paintings on the side of the wagons. Though he could not make out the images, he reached a verdict, "I believe they are circus performers. I remember seeing a similar-looking troupe in the city as a child. It appears as though they are headed for town."

Camilla stared in wonder. She had heard talk of circuses and carnivals, but never saw one in person. It was perhaps the most exciting thing she could imagine. "Should we follow them?" She asked at last.

"What about our clam hunt?"

"So what? We can hunt for clams anytime. But a circus! I want to get a closer look. C'mon, Griff, let's go watch."

Griffin would have perhaps protested, had he not been curious himself. His memory of the circus was fuzzy, at best, since he was a small child, but he remembered it being great fun and was told he talked of nothing else for days following. But his answer mattered very little either way, as Camilla was already picking up speed. "All right, let's go," he relented. "But of course you know that means this is how we are choosing to spend our last day of freedom. Not that I can think of a better way to do so."

Before he could finish his sentence, Camilla began sprinting along the cliff's edge toward the path that led down into town. She was certain the caravan would beat them there, but they were fast and wouldn't be far behind. Plus, they knew a shortcut through the woods heading southwest into town that would buy them time. Griffin didn't miss a beat and began running alongside her. As if reading her thoughts, Griffin began tramping through the grass and heading toward the wooded path even before they came upon it.

Once in the woods, they slowed their pace to a brisk trot to catch their breath. They had a couple of miles to go, but they knew the way well and saw no reason to rush, as the terrain would make it difficult to increase their speed by much. Even along the path, the ground was uneven from the many tree roots growing beneath it. This was an old forest, dense with craggy trees that blocked out much of the sun. Rarely did anyone take the shortcut in the late afternoon for fear of being trapped in the dark thicket with no additional way of escape but to press on until the end. And there were plenty of legends of the woods being haunted.

One such legend was about a young girl who thought to go to town after an early winter thaw to meet her pa on his way home from a day of trading. It was said she didn't emerge on the other side, and her body was never found by the searchers who went to look for her. Some suspected she was taken by wolves, while others wondered if she fell through some ice in the swampy marsh. But whatever the case, many told of having seen the figure of a young girl wandering the woods in the evening, crying.

Camilla would never admit to being afraid of ghosts, but while walking the woods she didn't care to think about it just the same. Nor did she ever suggest taking the shortcut late in the afternoon. Griffin didn't make the suggestion over the years either, so it was an unspoken understanding between them, as was the case with most of the townsfolk.

Today was not a day for legends and ghost stories, though. There were no long shadows in the woods, but the midday sun broke through at its peak. A light breeze brushed against the pair as they enjoyed a pleasant jaunt, talking and reminiscing about the many adventures they shared in these very woods. Childhood never seemed nearer, nor so far away. It was like saying goodbye to an old friend you'd never see again. Only, Camilla and Griffin were sure to see each other almost as much as ever, as their families were each other's closest neighbors and friends. Camilla wondered why then she felt uneasy about the future.

As they exited the woods, they followed the path over the hill and down toward town. Once on the hill, they could spot at least some of the caravan just on the outskirts. The pair began to pick up pace once again, realizing they might reach the wagons in time to see them enter town after all. And what fun it would be to see the look on everyone's faces as they realized that a circus had come to their own little village.

CHAPTER 5

T he procession was intoxicating to Camilla's young, callow senses. Each wagon that passed gave only a preview of the delights to come, but it was enough to illuminate her imagination with unlimited possibilities. Bright letters splashed across the side of the first wagon that spelled out *The Angelini Bros*. Never before had she seen such color, music, and fanfare—not to mention the animals in tow. She had heard of bears and wildcats, and even seen illustrations, but catching a glimpse of them in person only aroused her desire to get a closer look, as it was intended to do.

The man who sat at the head of the first wagon was a middle-aged, rotund gentleman who was sharply dressed in a top hat. Camilla wondered if he was one of the Angelini brothers, for whom the circus got its name. He greeted the townsfolk without reserve, calling out for the children to gather closer while throwing fistfuls of hard candy in their direction. It appeared as though the entire village had come to watch their spectacular entrance, most out of curiosity, and a few to voice their displeasure. The latter were drowned out by the excitement and music, so instead they stood at the edge of the crowd with arms crossed and shaking their heads in marked disapproval.

A strikingly beautiful woman in a pink tutu was introduced by the heavy-set man as a French dancer and tightrope walker named Fiona. She held a golden hoop, which she effortlessly spun and passed from one wrist to the other and then to her neck. She then performed an elegant pirouette and took a bow. Following behind her was a man waving who was as short as a child with a stout frame, along with a thin man walking on wooden legs who practically reached the sky, both dressed in a colorful striped suit and donning a tall cone-shaped hat.

There were so many wondrous things that Camilla could barely take in, but one act stood out above the rest. Toward the end, a dark gypsy-looking man in a grey leotard trotted by on a majestic white horse, riding bareback. He was introduced as "Frederick the Elastic Fantastic." He stopped just short of where Camilla and Griffin were standing and stood up swiftly on the horse's back, did a flip in the air, and then landed gracefully in place. Camilla was in awe of his great physique and command of the horse, as well as his white, toothy grin. As if he could feel her gaping up at him, the man glanced down, made direct eye contact with her, then gave a wink and a nod. Camilla's tummy did a little flip. *What was that about?* She wondered.

About this time, the crowd began to disperse, and Griffin felt he, too, had gotten his fill of theatrics. "C'mon, Cami, let's head back," he said, pulling her arm. "It's all very exciting, but if we leave now, we still have time to snatch up some clams before dinner. Besides, it will be dark soon, and then we'll have to take the long way back."

Camilla allowed Griffin to lead her away, looking back all the while. The thrill of the circus's arrival was dying down as the caravan ambled to the outskirts of the other side of town to settle in. Although a part of her deeply longed to continue following the procession, she managed to shake out of the reverie and began heading back over the hill and down to the wooded path. On the way back, she was quietly thinking to herself about all she had seen. Griffin seemed uneasy with her silence and tried to strike up a conversation, but Camilla was more annoyed than amused.

He babbled on, "So, who do you really think is going to get the most clams now? We lost at least an hour of time walking to town and back, but I still think I can outdo yeh. In fact, I would be willing to bet all my findings against yours that I gather up twice as many clams. What do yeh think of that? In fact, I plan to gather more clams this afternoon than I have all summer put together. In fact..."

"Shut your mouth, why don't yeh?" Camilla spat, "Must you go on and on so? I don't care about the stupid clams."

"Gee, I was only trying to lighten the mood with a bit of

friendly competition. Hey, what's got into you anyway?" he replied.

"Nothin', who said anything was wrong? I just don't feel like talking, that's all. Must we always chatter on as if we had no more sense than a canary?"

Griffin responded by walking ahead of Camilla on the path and not saying another word until they were out of the woods. Emerging under the late afternoon sun shifted the mood slightly, and Camilla began to return to her usual playful self by the time they reached the tidepools. They spent a happy time together gathering clams after all, filling the folds of the hems of their garments with shells and saltwater. When they tallied up their loot at the end of the day, Griffin pulled ahead as he predicted, but as always, shared his gains with his friend anyway.

As evening set, they skipped merrily home along the cliff's edge, looking out at the sea before the sun went down. Due to the heaviness of their gains, they decided to take a break to catch their breath. They found a soft spot in the grass to watch the sun as it dropped beneath the edge of the world. As it sank lower, the clouds displayed deep reds and violets, slowly darkening with every passing minute. It was a breathtaking sight, more colorful than the circus wagons and all their fanciful display. Rich or poor, such beauty was available to anyone willing to stop a moment to drink it in.

"So, this is it," Griffin finally spoke. "Our last day as free spirits."

"Speak for yourself, Griff, I was born a free spirit and so shall I die."

Griffin smiled at Camilla affectionately, "I have no doubt of it. You are a wild one, no one and nothing will ever change that. But promise me one thing."

"What's that?" she asked, raising an eyebrow.

"Promise me you'll never forget this day. That no matter what life brings, no matter the hardships or trials, no matter the riches or blessings, that this moment will always remind you of who you are and how life was meant to be."

Camilla gazed dreamily at the fading horizon. When she thought about it, life didn't get any better than this. "I promise," she said softly.

Camilla stepped up to the cottage cheerfully—barefoot, her hair a windswept mess, and her skirt soaked and full of clamshells. She couldn't wait to share her findings with her ma and pa, as well as tell them all about the circus coming to town and all the exciting things she had seen. She hoped her mother wouldn't be angry with her for coming home so late, but was sure all would be forgiven in light of the fact that she had plenty to show for it in the way of a hearty meal. Not to mention, she would be working hard alongside her father all the next day.

She grabbed an old wooden pail near the entrance and let the clams fall in, then opened the front door, calling out in a carefree manner, "I'm home!" It took a moment for her to notice how dark it was inside. The only light came from a single candle flickering near her parents' bedside on the other side of the room.

Camilla finally made out the figure of her mother sitting at its edge, her head bent down, and the sound of sobbing.

"Ma, what is it?" she called out.

Her mother turned to face her daughter, whom she could barely distinguish in the low-lit cabin. "My dear, where have you been? Griffin's pa and some of the other men have been out looking for you."

"I was in town part of the day, Ma. Why, what's going on?" she approached her mother slowly, a great feeling of doom washing over her. There lying on the bed was her beloved pa, his eyes closed, and his hands crossed over his chest. "Ma...what's wrong with Pa? What's going on?" The panic began rising in her chest.

"Oh, my dear girl," her mother replied, against tear-filled sobs. "Your pa is dead."

CHAPTER 6

*C*amilla's eyes widened with horror at the news of losing her father. She was in a daze as her mother did the best she could to explain what happened—that her father was testing out the plow when his heart gave way. He managed to hobble back up to the house before collapsing near the threshold. Elsie had to run to get Gerald Felix to help get her husband into bed. Before a doctor could be fetched, his breathing slowed, and he passed.

Even though she heard the words, Camilla could not fathom the reality of what was being said. Surely her father was just asleep—he needed rest, that's all. She went to his bedside and grabbed his hand, but it was cool to the touch and stiff, not strong and warm as it always was. He did not reach back to caress her hair and face and assure her that all would be well. There were no final words of affection, but she knew that's exactly what he would have said.

Camilla was then flooded with guilt. "I should have stayed and helped him today. It's all my fault. I was thoughtless and selfish. I knew he needed me." The tears now flowed hot and fast.

"No, no honey, nothing you could have done would have stopped this from happening. He hasn't been feeling well for a while. He never said, but a wife knows." Her mother paused. Camilla said nothing but continued sobbing softly. She continued as if reading her thoughts, "He knew you loved him, Cami, and he loved you so very much."

Camilla wasn't so easily consoled. It was a terrible night filled with a deep, heavy grief over the sudden passing of her beloved father. She slept very little, but even when she drifted off for a few moments, she would thrash and wake up in a cold sweat, her heart pounding wildly at remembering her great loss. It was as if her subconscious was wrestling to accept that her father was truly gone. It wasn't until the light of morning that she even began to consider the other implications of his death.

The Felixes came over first thing, a basket of food in tow as a token of goodwill to their grieving neighbors. "We sent for your sister," Gerald assured Elsie. "She'll be here this afternoon."

Elsie's sister, Meredith, lived on the other side of town where they both grew up. It was only a few miles away, but it may as well have been another world away for as often as they saw each other. Still, they had always been close as children, and their familial bonds were tight. Meredith wouldn't wait an hour upon hearing the news to go to her baby sister.

Camilla was glad for her mother's sake as it would give her someone to lean on. As for herself, she wanted nothing more than to continue her grieving in solitude.

Griffin watched her carefully, assessing her condition. He wanted to go to her, but could see by her closed-off disposition that now was not the time. "I'm real sorry for your loss, Mrs. Waller, Dob sure was a good man. Like a second father to me," was all he managed to choke out.

After exchanging niceties with the Felixes, Camilla headed to the barn to check on the livestock. Leaning up against the side of the shabby old building was Pa's weather-worn fishing boat. The net they used on their last fishing trip was hanging on a hook beside it.

Griffin, who had followed Camilla, unbeknownst to her, watched from a distance. After a time, he cautiously made his approach. Camilla, whose back was turned, did not hear him coming until he spoke. "Gee, Cami, I really am sorry. How are you taking all this?"

"How do you think I'm taking it?"

"Real hard, I imagine."

"That's an understatement. The only man I've ever loved is dead, and he won't be comin' back."

Griffin cringed at the words. "Is he really the only man you've ever loved?"

Camilla turned to face him, "You know I've never been

courtin' Griff, and I ain't had no brothers. Well, you were as close as it gets, so I guess you could say I love you that way. But my pa was something real special to me. We understood each other."

He eased slightly at this. "Yes, I know, he was a wonderful man. But you and your ma are not alone. I want you to know that. We're here for yeh, Cami, me and Pa, and Ma. We'll do whatever we can to help. Just tell me what you need."

"I sure appreciate the offer, but think I just need to be alone for a while, Griff. I hope that doesn't hurt yeh. It's just, I can't think straight right now." Her tone was tender even though her suffering was great.

Griffin nodded. "If that's what you think best, then you got it. I'll be around if you need anything else. You know where to find me." He hesitated, then turned to leave.

After spending a bit of time tending to the animals and thinking things through, Camilla headed back up to the house. Her Aunt Meredith had already arrived in her horse and buggy and had gone inside the house. Camilla entered quietly and saw her mother and aunt sitting at the table talking.

"I don't know, Meredith," her mother was in the process of speaking, "I just don't know if I'm ready, and this news would crush Cami even more after losing her father."

"What news?" Camilla interrupted.

Her mother was startled by the sudden appearance of her daughter. "Oh, it's nothing, dear," she waved her off. "We don't need to talk about anything right now. Come, have a bit of tea and relax."

Meredith jumped in, "Nonsense, my dear sister, Cami is old enough to handle it. The truth is, I think it's best—that is, your mother and I—think it's best if you leave the farm and come live with me until you get back on your feet. You were already struggling to keep this farm going even while poor Dob was alive, and with your mother getting on in years, and being two women alone, it just isn't practical to stay. I suggest we leave first thing in the morning and let the menfolk handle the sale of the property."

Camilla couldn't believe her ears. It never occurred to her that they would give up the farm, and so soon. "No, absolutely not!" she cried, "This is my home, this is my mother's home—this was my *father's* home. I am here to help now. We'll manage just fine, I'm sure of it. I'll do all the work myself if I have to!"

Her aunt scoffed at the idea, "Come, child, be realistic, the very idea that you could take care of a farm by yourself and feed both you and your dear mother, why that's just preposterous. No, we must be sensible, young lady. We leave tomorrow, so be a good girl and go pack your things."

Camilla had no intention of doing any such thing. "Ma! Please tell me you aren't going along with this. We simply can't give up the farm. Not after all the work Pa put into it. Please tell me you aren't seriously considering this."

Elsie put her head in her hands and began weeping, "I just don't know what else to do, my dear. Meredith has a point. I don't think we're strong enough to manage it."

"Ma, *please!*" she begged, but her mother couldn't muster the strength to fight the inevitable.

No further words were exchanged before Camilla flew out of the house and across the field to look for Griffin. She was grateful to find him on the porch, in his grandmother's old rocking chair. He seemed to be deep in thought, but she didn't care. She called out his name, "Griffin, Griffin, I'm so glad I found you. Please, you must help me!"

He sat up at the sound of her voice, then ran to be near her. Putting his arms around her, Camilla let her tears flow freely, without reserve. "It's okay," he assured her. "Whatever you need, I'm here."

She finally pulled away to look at him. "It's my Aunt Meredith; she wants us to give up the farm. She wants us to leave tomorrow. Oh, Griffin, I simply can't give up my home. I have to do something to convince her that we can manage. Please come with me and tell her how strong and capable I am. I know your pa will speak on my behalf, please."

Camilla's emotions heightened as she spoke, so Griffin made hushing noises to calm her. "Shh, shh, it's going to be okay. We'll figure this out." As she regained her composure, he looked into her sad, freckled face and was overwhelmed with compassion. "How about I help you take care of the farm?"

Camilla drew back in surprise. "What do you mean? You can't do that. Your own father needs you here. You can't possibly take care of both."

"Sure, I can, and I'll have you to help me."

"Oh no," she shook her head violently, "I couldn't ask you to do that. It's too much, Griffin. I have no right to expect so much of you. No, this farm belongs to me and Ma, and I'm going to tend to it. It's my responsibility."

Griffin paused to gather his thoughts then finally replied, "What if it was *my* farm...and *my* mother...and *my* responsibility?"

"What on earth are you talking about, Griffin Felix? Have you gone mad? I'm not handing my farm over to anyone."

"Don't you understand what I'm saying to you, Cami? Don't you get it? I'm asking you to marry me. I'm asking you to be my wife. That will solve everything!"

Once again, Camilla couldn't believe what she was hearing. "You *have* gone mad!" she exclaimed. "How dare you ask me this! You, my oldest friend. Is it possible you do not know me at all? Do you think I would consider marrying you to keep my farm? Oh, don't be absurd."

This wasn't the response Griffin had hoped for. "Cami, you can't seriously think I would ask you to marry me out of pity, do you? Of course, I know you would never agree to such a thing. I love you. I have loved you my whole life. And everyone has expected that one day we would marry. Sure, I would have liked to propose in a couple more years under better circumstances, but if it can't be helped, then why wait?"

Camilla could feel the shackles closing in on her with every word and began choking from the suffocation. *Love? Who could think about love at a time like this?* "I'm sorry, Griff, I simply can't consider it. I-I'm not the marrying kind. Besides, you are like a brother to me. I can't imagine marrying you any more than I can imagine marrying ol' Bessie. No, you've got to see it's impossible!"

Griffin wore a pained look from the harsh rejection of his proposal. "Really? You compare me to some dumb cow? Is that all I am to you?"

"No, of course not..."

"Don't you care for me even a little?"

"Oh, Griff, I told you, I *do* love you, I just can't marry you. And you're right, certainly not out of pity or to keep my farm. No, this is something I have to take care of myself."

Griffin sensed there was no use pushing the issue. When Camilla made up her mind, there was little anyone could do to combat her stubborn spirit, but he could be stubborn too. "Well, then I can't help you," he replied spitefully, crossing his arms.

"What are you saying?"

"You heard me, you can make a choice—marry me and let me help you, or you can figure this out on your own."

With that, Camilla's face darkened with rage, "How dare you, Griffin Felix. How dare you try to blackmail me into marrying you. I'll never forgive you for this, never, ever!"

Before Griffin could say another word, Camilla turned and ran back toward her house, curses flying from her mouth. The entire way, she swore never to speak to her friend again for as long as she lived. *I'll find some way to keep Pa's farm, and I'll do it without*

anyone's help. Not Ma's, not Aunt Meredith's, and most of all, not
Griffin's.

CHAPTER 7

*C*amilla tried with all her might to persuade her mother not to sell the farm, but Aunt Meredith had her very well convinced that leaving was the wisest decision to make under the circumstances. Fear had gripped her mother, and there was no changing her mind. Camilla went to bed that night, deeply frustrated at the prospect of leaving her home. The only one she wanted to talk to in the world was the very person she couldn't— her father.

Oh Pa, she prayed to herself, *What should I do? There has to be an answer.* She realized her father couldn't hear her pleas and decided to ask God instead. Still no answer. After a long, emotional day, she finally fell into a deep, restless sleep. Her dreams were a mix of voices from her mother, her aunt, and

Griffin, along with nonsensical imagery inspired by the sights and sounds of the circus—the music, the dancing, and swirls of color. It was shrouded in a fog of confusion she couldn't make sense of or escape. She was still lost in it all when she finally awoke before dawn.

Camilla sat up, relieved to find her mother and aunt still sound asleep. She slipped on her shift and her father's old army coat and wandered outside into the dark morning mist. She walked over to the barn and fed the chickens and the old cow, her dreams still plaguing her. But somehow, deep in her gut, she knew what she had to do. Was this certainty an answer to her prayer? She didn't know, but something drove her forward.

When the animals were fed, Camilla went back inside and quickly scrawled a note to her mother before she lost her nerve. She pinned it on a nail that was sticking out of the front door, knowing she was sure to see it first thing in the morning. She then slipped on her shoes, packed a light lunch, and headed out into the world.

Camilla didn't know exactly where she was going, but she knew the answers didn't lie in the old cottage or in Aunt Meredith's buggy. She knew the answers wouldn't come from Griffin either. In fact, the more she thought over his proposal, the angrier she got—especially how he refused to help her when she declined his offer.

"How could he?" she asked herself aloud. "Why on earth would he think I would agree to such a thing? And attempting to blackmail me? Some friend he turned out to be. Nothing but a backstabbing weasel."

She didn't really mean it, but the anger inside festered, and she fed it to bury the sorrow that lay beneath the surface to help spur her on. Never did she anticipate such a falling out with her friend, but neither did she prepare for any of these things to happen.

Camilla instinctively took the path that led to town. She had some idea that the answers she sought would be found there, though as her temper evened, she began to have second thoughts about her decision to leave home. The light of day was grazing the treetops, and she imagined her mother waking to find her letter on the door. It read...

Dear Ma,

I cannot let our farm go without a fight. Please go and stay with Aunt Meredith for the time being, but I beg you not to sell our land. I have left to find work to support you and will send everything I earn until we can live in the cottage together once again. All I ask is that you await my return before making any other decisions. I will return home when the good Lord allows.

Affectionately Yours,
Little Cami.

Thinking back on the note, Camilla decided it was too late to turn back. She must go forward with her plan, and certainly, she could never give Griffin the satisfaction of coming back and accepting his offer of marriage or begging for his help by any means. No, she was going to make her own way.

By the time Camilla reached town, the shops were just beginning to open. She walked through the dusty streets, observing any opportunities that called out to her. Most of the people she passed seemed tired and unfriendly. Were these the same faces that lit up only days before when the circus came to town? *The circus!* Camilla finally remembered her dream, and her curiosity about the traveling performers was piqued once again.

As she made her way to the edge of the village, she saw one large tent set up in a field, the wagons sitting alongside it with several small tents nearby. She meandered over for a closer look. No signs of stirring were coming from the encampment just yet. She wondered if this was a late-night bunch. It was evident that there was nothing intriguing to investigate, so she went back into town to enquire about possible positions.

Wherever she stopped, the owners were adamant that no help was needed. She offered to do any type of work at all, but one look at her skinny frame, and most scoffed at the idea of her doing hard labor. "Maybe if you were a boy," at least a couple said to her. Others ignored her inquisition altogether, waving her off and closing their doors.

She finally found herself entering a dress shop. A fine-looking lady dressed immaculately with her hair pinned up in the latest fashion approached her to see if she needed help. "Only help

I need is a job. Do yeh have any positions open for a hard-working girl?"

"Girl?" the lady gasped. "My goodness, you are a dirty little urchin, aren't you?"

Camilla looked down at her dingy dress and then back at the lady. She was a poor sight indeed. "Yes, ma'am, I suppose I would seem a bit shabby to a proper lady like yourself. But I'm willing to help in any way possible. Perhaps you need someone to help keep the place clean?"

The lady laughed delicately, "Oh dear me, you can't even keep yourself clean, little one. Tell me, do you know how to sew?" In her tone, Camilla detected a hint of mockery.

"My ma taught me how to stitch up a garment—I suppose I've torn plenty. I've done my share of patchwork, too. And I'm a fast learner."

The lady looked down at her with pity, "I'm afraid it will never do. I am in need of an experienced seamstress, and clearly, you've never handled fine clothing. I'm going to have to ask you to leave now. I have work to finish for a client and have no time to dawdle."

Camilla left the dress shop feeling more dejected than ever. Not only did she lose another prospect, but the lady made her realize just how poor her appearance must seem. It was becoming clear that there was no work to be found in her own village and that she might have to seek an opportunity elsewhere, perhaps on a farm. She was on the way out of town in search of other prospects when she passed the circus tent again. This time, she heard sounds of life coming from within the encampment.

She went in for a closer look. People were scurrying about, but no one seemed to take notice of her as she approached the larger tent. She boldly pulled back a flap and peeked inside and saw the one called Frederick riding the same white mare, bareback. They swiftly made their way in a circle, jumping hurdles that increasingly grew in height. Once again, she was mesmerized by the sight of him and didn't notice when a man approached her from behind. He was a burly, sweaty man in a stretched-out tank top, with rough hands that grabbed her arm mercilessly.

"Alright, kid, what are you doin' here?" he growled. "If you want to see a show, come back tonight and pay for it like everybody else."

Camilla loosened herself from his grip and stumbled backward, nearly falling on her behind. "I-I-I wasn't meanin' any harm. I…"

"Sure, kid, why don't you get on home before I remove you myself?"

"I don't have a home to go to just now," Camilla managed to choke out. "I'm looking for a job. Please, is there anything here I can do?"

The gruff man looked her up and down then scoffed, "Oh sure, we got works for yeh. How 'bout we dress yeh up in some fancy clothes and put yeh on a trapeze? Hey Rocco," he called to one of his fellow thugs. "Come get a load of this dirty little canary poking around the place. She wants to get in on the act. Maybe we can help her."

The menacing man named Rocco ambled over, clearly up for a bit of sport. The two began pulling at her messy hair and dirty dress, laughing at what a homely little thing she was, when suddenly a voice like a bell rang out from behind. It was a woman with a French accent.

"Hey, knock it off, you lugs. Why don't you leave the poor thing alone and get back to work before I tell Max how you good-for-nothings have been slack in your work all morning?"

The two men released their grip on Camilla and grunted at the pretty lady whom she remembered from the day the circus came to town—the one wearing the pink tutu. As they left to return to their duties, the lady turned to leave as well when Camilla spoke up, "Thank you, ma'am, really. I appreciate it. I don't know what would have happened had you not been here."

The lady turned and smiled, her eyes wide with thick, dark eyelashes and a face full of rouge, "Oh, think nothing of it, little one, you mustn't mind these brutes. They were just looking for a bit of amusement. They wouldn't have hurt you, I'm certain. You just need to know how to handle that sort."

Camilla was touched by the lady's kindness as she had experienced so little of it all morning. "Well, thank you just the same. Please, Miss, can you tell me, is there a job available here? You see, my pa died and we're going to lose our farm if I don't find work and..."

The French girl shook her head, which was full of bouncy yellow curls, "Oh, Cher Moi, I couldn't say. You would have to speak to Max about such things, and I wouldn't recommend it if he is in a mood this morning."

"Max?" Camilla asked.

"Oh yes, Maximillian Angelini, the owner of the circus and our ringmaster. His tent is over that way," she said, pointing to a red-striped tent standing alone in the distance. "But you must understand, he is not to be disturbed if he has not yet risen. When he drinks, Mon Dieu, he is a bear. So, tread lightly, little one."

Camilla felt anxious at the thought of approaching the tent alone, "Would you come with me, please? Let him know what I'm here for, see if he is in 'a mood', as you say?"

Again, the lady shook her curl-filled hair, "Oh, non, non, I couldn't think of getting involved."

Camilla hung her head dejectedly but knew she must summon the courage to go alone. "Well, thanks anyway, I will give it a shot," she said before walking cautiously toward the tent. She stopped at the entrance and stood paralyzed.

After a time of watching Camilla's hesitation, out of pity, the lady finally intervened. "Oh, come, I'll see if he'll speak to you. Max! Max!" she called out from behind the tent entrance.

"What is it now?" A voice boomed just before the heavy-set man popped his head out from behind the tent flap. His face had a look of aggravation, but when he saw who called for him, his lips curled into a smile which said he didn't mind the

56

disturbance after all, "Oh, Fiona, it's you. What can I do for you this fine morning?"

Fiona put on her most charming smile, "Oh, Max, this young girl would like to speak to you about any work you may have available. Be a dear and have a talk with her, would you?"

Max noticed Camilla standing there for the first time and frowned at her appearance. "Now what work would I have for such a weakling of a girl? I'd find more use from a stray cat."

"I'm not weak," Camilla finally spoke up. "I'm a strong, hard worker, and I'm fast. Please, sir, I'll help in any way I can."

Fiona lent her support, "Look, she is such a determined little thing. C'mon, Max, couldn't you find something for her to do? She is so desperate, and we always need extra hands around here."

Max did not seem pleased but appeared to be thinking it over a bit, which brought hope to Camilla's heart. "I don't know, what could she possibly be good for?"

"Anything at all," was Camilla's quick reply.

"Well, can you cook? We need someone to help get meals ready around here."

"Yes, sir, my ma taught me how to cook well. I make a mean chowder and can prepare a hunt, no problem."

"And how about live animals, are you afraid of them?"

"No, sir," she responded confidently. "My pa taught me to care for all the livestock. I even just helped a heifer give birth to a stubborn calf. The mess didn't bother me none either."

"Well, no need for all that," his face scrunched up at the thought. "We need someone to feed the animals and clean their cages from time to time. If you can do all that, I'm sure we can find something for you to do."

Camilla clapped her hands together and nearly leapt in the air like a gazelle, "Oh, thank you, sir, thank you, I won't let you down, I promise!"

The man's face scowled, "And be sure you don't either. The minute you fall behind in your duties or slack off, you're outta here. Understand?" Camilla nodded. "You start tomorrow morning. Now, go, before I change my mind."

With that, the man went back to his tent, and Camilla was left grinning ear to ear. She turned to her advocate, but the kind lady was already prancing away. "Thank you, Miss," she called out.

"Think nothing of it, my dear," she said without turning around.

CHAPTER 8

C amilla contemplated whether she should go home and tell her mother about the job she secured with the circus, but the more she considered it, the more she was against the idea. Her mother would probably only try to talk her out of it, and at this point, she was determined to see it through for the sake of their farm. *Besides, Ma has likely gone with Aunt Meredith by now, and even if she hasn't, they might even try to force me into going with them.* She thought to herself.

Instead, she decided to stay put and watch the final performance night of the circus in her town. So many people filled the seats, it seemed as if the whole village must be in attendance. For that reason, Camilla did her best to stay out of sight, in case someone she knew happened to be there. She eventually managed to find a good view beneath a small section of the bleachers where no one was sitting. She surveyed the scene through the slats of the steps and was mesmerized. It was even more thrilling than she could have imagined. Never had she seen such a spectacle, and the roar of the crowd was intoxicating.

Nor had she ever seen anything like Frederick the Elastic Fantastic. A feeling of rapture washed over her as she watched him perform. Not only were his equestrian stunts brilliantly executed—far more impressive than the little demonstration he gave as he rode into town—but his acrobatic feats were nothing short of astounding. And the crowd loved him.

He was clearly the star of the show, with Fiona not falling far behind. Though taken by her kindness that afternoon, she was now astounded by her grace and beauty. No question, she had many years of training and was deserving of all the admiration she received.

After the show, Camilla found an inconspicuous place to sleep in a fresh pile of hay near the circus tent. That way, she'd be ready to start work bright and early, before shoving off to the next village. As she settled into her makeshift bed, she thought back on the night and marveled to think that such a thrilling life would soon become her own. It was with these exciting thoughts that she finally drifted off into a deep slumber, the most peaceful rest she had enjoyed in two days.

The next morning, she was up before the rooster's crow. Despite the coolness of night, she rested comfortably in the warm pile of hay, her father's coat wrapped tightly around her. Camilla stared at the moon still high in the sky and considered her next move. She wasn't exactly sure who she was to report to, but figured she'd at least wait to enquire about her duties when some of the others were up. To her great fortune, the first stirring she heard was from one of the clowns she recalled from the night before, who appeared to busy himself preparing food for breakfast. She was only able to recognize him without his makeup because he was notably short—the shortest person she ever laid eyes on, aside from a child.

Camilla brushed off the excess hay from her skirt and approached him cautiously. "Good morning," she began, startling him as he hadn't noticed her approach. "I believe I am supposed to help prepare meals—which appears to be what you're doing."

The small man looked up at Camilla and replied with a hint of scorn, "Oh, so you're the girl they've stuck me with. Lucky for you, we lost one of our best hands. Drown himself in the sea after a cliff dive broke his neck. A damn shame. I hate training people, so I hope you don't like cliff diving." The little man's good humor from the night before seemed to have worn off in the light of morning.

"No sir," she answered.

"Good." Was all the man said as he handed her a sack of oats almost as big as himself. He then told her to throw them in the pot near the fire and add some water to make porridge for breakfast.

The sack was heavy, but Camilla did as she was asked.

Shortly after the oats began cooking, the rest of the troupe began to awaken. The burly men she ran into the day before were the first to claim their breakfast. It was their duty to take down the main tent and pack up other structures to prepare the circus for departure. Both the man who accosted her, whom she heard the short man refer to as Wolfie, and his buddy Rocco, seemed astonished at the sight of Camilla. She quickly doled out the porridge into their bowl and avoided further engagement.

Shortly after feeding the bulk of manual laborers, the performers started to make their entrance. They were a colorful bunch of characters who knew each other well. Some had friendly banter while others argued vehemently over the performance the night before and whether there was a better order to present their acts. Camilla took in as much as she could, eager to learn about the life she had in store.

A thin man with a long mustache and a thick foreign accent was the first to take notice of her and introduce himself. "Hello, I see you are new here. I am Benito, the fire eater." Camilla recognized him and though it was difficult to make out his words, she was glad to know he was friendly. Fiona also smiled when she entered and was excited to tell the others how she was responsible for bringing in the new help. Camilla was enjoying all the interactions when Frederick came in. She then suddenly became shy and withdrawn, against her own wishes.

She was a bundle of nerves as he approached with his bowl. He smiled kindly as she scooped out some of the now-hardening porridge into it. "So, you're the new girl, huh? Is it Cami?" She nodded, though Camilla was surprised he was even aware of her existence, let alone her name. "Fiona told me all about what happened yesterday. I'm glad it all worked out, but listen," he leaned in closer to her, "Don't let these animals push you around. They are all bark and no bite for the most part. You'll see in time."

Camilla blushed at his nearness and instinctively smoothed the skirt of her dress. "Thank you," she said quietly. "I shall do my best."

"And here's a tip," He leaned in closer with a stage whisper, "If you work hard and learn to laugh at everyone's jokes—even the bad ones—I have no doubt you will win over the whole lot of us in no time!" Camilla nodded. "We performers love nothing more than to be encouraged in our antics," Frederick winked, then walked back out of the tent from where he came. Camilla couldn't understand why her cheeks were so hot, but was impressed with how welcoming Frederick and the others were.

Once breakfast was over, everyone got to work packing up their belongings and props and taking the rest of the tents down. Some of the bigger acts had assistants to do much of the manual labor, but still had tasks of their own. This was a routine they were all familiar with and had become quite proficient at.

The short man, whose name she finally learned was Dominick, led her to the animal cages and showed her how to feed each of them accordingly. The sad, pathetic creatures no longer seemed the great, imposing beasts she took them for the night before. Most didn't even bother to look up as she approached, but stayed curled in place on the dirt floor of the cage.

She finished with the feeding, and realizing she still had an hour or so before their departure, decided to write her mother a letter to send off so she wouldn't worry. *It's the least I can do*, she thought. *Not to mention, it will reassure her that our land will be taken care of as promised so she won't feel pressured to sell.*

As she was approaching the post office, she looked up and saw Griffin, who had already spotted her and was running in her direction, waving. "Cami!" he called out frantically.

Camilla wanted to turn and run, but there was nowhere to go. She had already been spotted, and there was no getting out of this discussion. She waited for Griffin to catch up, still feeling angry with him for all that had transpired when they last met.

"Cami, I am so glad I found you," he said breathlessly. "I was hoping you hadn't gotten far off. I must admit, we all thought you were bluffing when you said you'd left town. We thought for sure you'd be back, but when I heard you were still gone this morning, I had to come looking for you. Look, I'm real sorry about what I said. I've thought a lot about it, and you were right to be angry with me. I still want to help you, just come back and we'll work all this out."

Camilla stuck her chin in the air, unable to accept his apology just yet. "I'm sorry, Griffin, I simply can't. I've already got other plans, so you can just go back and tell everyone I'm okay and that it's all taken care of."

"Plans? What plans? What are you talking about?"

"I have joined the circus. We are leaving any minute now. So, you see, I can't go back with you." Pride welled up in Camilla as she revealed how she had been successful in securing a job so quickly.

"The circus? You can't be serious!" Griffin said in astonishment.

"Of course, I am serious. Didn't you believe me when I said I'd find a way? Now please, I must go."

Camilla attempted to walk away, but Griffin grabbed her arm. "What are you talking about? Don't you know how crazy this sounds? You can't expect me to believe you're actually going through with this."

"Oh, but I am. You can stay and see me off if you don't believe me. There's a front row seat just on the edge of town."

Griffin was getting angry now. "Cami, I demand you stop this nonsense and come home with me. I told you we'd work it out. I can't let you do something so foolish. 'Sides, you don't know a thing about circus people."

"Oh, and I suppose you do?" Camilla said indignantly.

"A little, and I know they are known for being low characters. You could be in real danger."

"Well, that's where you're wrong. I think they are just lovely people. All bark and no bite," she repeated Frederick's words.

Finally, Griffin's shoulders slumped in defeat. "Would you honestly rather go off with these strangers than marry me, your oldest and dearest friend?"

Camilla's pride got the best of her, and she spat back, "Yes, and that's exactly what I plan to do, now let me go." She released herself from his weakening grip.

Griffin sighed both from renewed heartache and exasperation. "Well, if there's one thing I've learned about you, Cami, once you set your mind to somethin' there's no stoppin' yeh. So, I suppose there's nothin' more I can say."

Tears began stinging Camilla's eyes, so she didn't respond but instead remained stone-faced. After a moment, she finally spoke, "I have to go," then turned to leave. But in a moment of regret over leaving her friend under such bitter circumstances, she turned back, gave him a swift hug, and handed him the letter. "I'm sorry. Please give this to my mom," she choked, then ran in the direction from which she came.

Griffin stood watching as she disappeared into the crowd, calling out, "Please, don't go…" But Camilla was long gone.

CHAPTER 9

Camilla had been on the road with the circus for two weeks now. In that time, she learned a lot about the world she didn't know. They'd been through five different villages, difficult to discern one from another, but it was the troupe that had done much to enlighten her. At first, she was shocked by their bawdy humor, but laughed anyway, as Frederick suggested. They didn't pay her much mind at first, but her laughter wasn't unpleasant to their ears, so they let her hang around.

She also saw how much hard work went into the rehearsals for the nightly shows. When she wasn't working, Camilla would sneak a peek at the performers, who always seemed to be intent on reinventing their act because the competition for the spotlight was fierce. They were companions after hours, but competitors by day.

Fiona continued to be the picture of grace and beauty, and Camilla admired her all the more as the days passed. She handled the unruly menfolk assertively, but toward Camilla, she sweet as pie in their brief interactions. Every morning at breakfast, she was sure to give her a smile and a word of encouragement, as if she herself were responsible for the young girl.

The acrobats and tightrope walkers were never tiresome either. Camilla watched breathlessly in awe of every death-defying stunt. And though each performer was impressive in their own right, none captured her attention, or her heart, quite like Frederick the Elastic Fantastic. He said very little to her at all, but would often give a smile when passing by, which melted Little Cami's heart. She didn't know what to make of these feelings, but it gave her cause to rise each morning and face another day with enthusiasm.

She attended the nightly shows, when her duties allowed, and took note of how all the girls would swoon alongside her. When the shows were over, small crowds would gather around the performers, asking for autographs and peppering them with questions about their acts. Frederick and Fiona were never short on attention from the opposite sex. They humored their fans quite nicely, which often made Camilla feel jealous, but it also began to awaken a longing to experience the thrill of applause for herself.

So late at night, after the crowds died down and the troupe began to settle in, Cami would lie awake dreaming of being a great performer like Fiona. She knew absolutely nothing of juggling and tightrope acts, having no natural grace about her whatsoever, but she wondered if perhaps she, too, could discover some talent hidden within herself that would make people cheer.

She would then drift off, missing her mother and even Griffin. After a time, she wrote them both letters letting them know she was still doing well and even exaggerated a little where Griffin was concerned. She was no longer angry with him, but pride motivated her to emphasize every good thing she could think of about the circus. She purposely left out how much drinking and carousing went on and how the boss and ringmaster, Max, would often wake up in a cranky mood and yell at her for not being fast enough at preparing his breakfast.

Despite Max's occasional complaints, everyone assured Camilla that she was doing a fine job and not to take his insults to heart. The truth was, Cami was gaining a reputation for being a hard worker and had already seen an increase in her responsibilities as she earned the trust of cranky ol' Dominick. She was tending to the animals more and even given the privilege of being trained to groom the horses for the performances. But no matter how well everything was going along, she was continually warned to avoid Max when possible.

His temper was something legendary among the troupe, as he was known for his excessive cursing and throwing things in a fit of rage. His unpredictable nature caused him to fire people at a moment's notice, though if the offense was not too great, he would then rehire them after he calmed down. But there were times when he was perfectly jovial with a booming laugh that everyone wanted to be the recipient of. The clowns worked especially hard at it, because making Max laugh meant getting a special slot in the side show. But once given such an honor, Max demanded a certain level of crowd reaction from all his performers and would not hesitate to revoke someone's privileges and give them to someone he deemed more worthy.

Therefore, the warnings made sense to Camilla when she began picking up on cues of his "being in a mood", as Fiona originally put it. But what confused her more than anything was how many of the girls spoke emphatically of avoiding him when he was in *too good* of a mood. No one would explain what that meant, they all just seemed to know. Camilla hoped never to find out what that experience entailed, so she mostly avoided Max altogether, keeping out of his way to the best of her ability. Lucky for her, aside from the occasional bouts of angst, he didn't seem to pay her much attention. He was a busy man, after all.

On a particularly humid afternoon, Camilla decided to withdraw to the stable in an effort to take some initiative on the grooming she was being trained to do. She picked up the horse brush and began gliding it along her favorite horse of them all— Frederick's white mare, Sugar, whom she now knew was named by him personally. She was a playful, but graceful creature with a pure white coat and flowing mane to match—made for the spotlight.

Sugar and Frederick had a special bond wherein they

developed several routines, including one where she would pretend not to let him ride her as he made several attempts to mount her for his act. Sugar would pull away, and the crowd would laugh hysterically. It was only when he presented her with a carrot, complete with lush greens hanging from its top end, that the horse would relent and allow him to get atop her. The crowd would then cheer loudly, as the pair proceeded to give them their money's worth in feats and then some. Not a night went by that the two weren't a hit, so Max was wise to always withhold his angst from Frederick for fear he might join a competing circus.

As Camilla continued her grooming, her thoughts wandered to home. She wondered how her little cottage and land were faring. Had they been abandoned altogether? What about the farm animals? No, she suspected Griffin would still tend to things as best he could in his spare time. She still regretted the way in which they parted, but was glad there was at least some minor reconciliation.

Camilla was sure he had received her letter by now and began to second guess her need to be so pompous about her experience. It really had been largely positive, but the truth was, she missed home—she missed her father and mother, and she missed Griffin. For as long as she could remember, they had been terrific playmates, and hardly a day passed in their lives that they didn't see each other. They shared everything with one another. And despite their occasional bickering, they always made up quickly. But with being on the road now, there was little chance of receiving word from him. So, she wondered what he might be doing and how he felt at receiving her letter.

Suddenly, the gate to the stall opened, startling Camilla a bit. "Hello," a velvety voice with a light accent tickled her ears. It was Frederick. Camilla's heart began to beat a little harder against her will as he approached. "Taking good care of my girl, I see?" he said warmly, observing her as she continued mindlessly brushing Sugar's coat.

"Why, yes," she replied simply, turning to hide the rising flush in her cheeks.

"And where is Dominick this afternoon?" he inquired.

Camilla shrugged, "I don't really know. He has been training me to care for the horses, so I thought I would take the opportunity I had to get an early start. Besides, I love being around the animals."

Frederick approached Sugar with ease and caressed her nose, the horse pressing into his affectionate touch. "Yes, and horses are especially wonderful creatures. They are both sweet and intelligent. A truer companion cannot be found in all the earth." He leaned forward to plant a kiss on his beloved mare's nose.

"Yes," Camilla replied, surprised by the sound of her own voice when inside she was full of nerves. "The only horse we ever had was a work horse, but my dad considered him a friend. And I loved him too."

Frederick smiled in response at the young girl, "Your father, is he a farmer?"

"He was a farmer. He died shortly before I came here. That's why I needed a job. To keep up the payments on our land. My mother is too old, and I don't have any brothers."

Frederick was about to inquire into the matter further when Dominick suddenly approached, a look of surprise at the sight of the two. "Hello, Mr. Frederick. I do hope this young girl is not bothering you this afternoon?"

"Oh no, this young girl…Cami, is it?" she nodded. "She was just telling me how well you are training her to care for our horses, Sugar in particular. I think she is doing a beautiful job at that. You have done well, indeed."

Camilla blushed and Dominick beamed, "Yes, well, she is a fast learner, but she has arrived much too early, I'm afraid. She doesn't know that you often like to take an afternoon ride without distraction."

"Well, this was a most pleasant distraction. Cami and I were having a lovely conversation. But I suppose if you'll saddle up my girl here, I'll be on my way."

Dominick quickly obliged Frederick, not because he was under any obligation to, but because it was considered an honor to be of assistance to the popular performer. Dominick worked quickly, and in no time at all, Frederick was mounted on the beautiful creature and was ready to trot off to a nearby field, but not before giving Cami a quick smile and salute. She felt warm all over and knew their interaction, their first formal conversation, would consume her thoughts for the rest of the day and night.

CHAPTER IV

"Here, sweep up this sawdust, and after that you can start peeling potatoes for lunch." Dominick shoved the sweeper into Camilla's hand, then walked off toward the tent where the other clowns were congregating for rehearsal.

While it was taking her some time to get used to the gruff manner in which some of the circus folks spoke, Camilla didn't mind the odds-and-ends chores she was given. She was just thankful to have a job, and the variety kept her on her toes.

Sweeping also gave her time to think. On those days, she spent most of her time daydreaming about Frederick and keeping an eye on his wagon to see when he would emerge. She had become quite familiar with his schedule by now. Usually, the last to wake up for the day, Frederick would make an appearance around 9 am to pick up his breakfast and take it back to his wagon.

He wasn't as sociable as the other performers, which made him all the more mysterious and in high demand.

Frederick would remain in his wagon most of the morning, doing strength-building exercises that kept him lean and fit. After a small lunch, he would go for a ride to warm up Sugar for their nightly performance. He would then return to the stables and run through a few routines with the rest of the horses. If Camilla were lucky, she would finish her afternoon chores early enough to watch from a distance, her appreciation for his physical prowess growing by the day. To her, there was no greater performer in all the world. But what did she know of the world?

The rest of the afternoon would be spent promoting the show in town. Frederick and several of the main acts would set up a makeshift stage and give demonstrations of their great feats. Crowds would always gather in fascination, a few to send out jeers. Children especially loved the circus, which always caused some adults to be concerned about the influence such frivolity might have on the future generation, but Frederick won them over if anyone could.

Upon return, all the performers convened to their quarters to get ready for the big show. They would then emerge, fully arrayed in costume and makeup, and head to the big tent for a quick warm-up with old Max at the helm. He was usually in a jolly mood, as he fed on the rising anticipation of the whole event. Camilla would often be called upon to help prepare the grounds by sweeping and picking up trash left behind by the troupe. She was then often called on to run a ticket booth or one of the food carts selling popcorn, hot nuts, and sweetcakes.

The warm aroma filled the air with anticipation, but when the triumphant music began, oh, how it thrilled her. Camilla longed to be a part of it all, but she had a job to do. Once the crowd settled in and the line died down a bit, she would sneak to the tent flap and watch as much of the show as time would allow. Night after night, she surveyed her surroundings in awe, and rather than her interest waning from the effects of diminishing returns, her fascination only increased, along with her desire to participate at a greater level. But what did a homely little thing like her have to offer that could satisfy the demands of the crowd? Though the wheels turned continuously in her head, Camilla couldn't identify any skill of significance. So instead, she returned to her duties in an attempt to quiet the growing desire in her heart.

Once the show was over, Camilla took her time with the cleanup, dawdling as an excuse to watch the loitering after-crowd surround Frederick as they swooned. He was a great showman and knew how to please his fans. He was charming, light-hearted, and would often plant a kiss on every lovely girl's cheek, making them blush wildly. Some would present him with a rose as a token of admiration, but no one received more roses than Fiona. That was her claim to glory. Her wagon was always well-stocked with fresh flowers, the scent of which could be detected from outside its perimeter.

Max usually drew in the children because of his larger-than-life personality. He knew they were certain to dream of fantastical men and beasts for days to come, and played to their curious nature with exaggerated accounts of circus life. He also never seemed to mind fielding their adolescent questions and relished their wide eyes and laughter—they were his intended audience, after all. Max would often say, "Children make the best patrons because they still believe in fairy tales." In other words, they were easy to impress. And the wonder on their faces proved it to be true.

Camilla contemplated if that made her a child still, for she, too, had a look of wonder on her face every night, and by the time all the excitement died down, she was ready to fall right into dreamland. For that reason, she never managed to stay awake long enough to see what the performers got up to after hours. She knew many would begin drinking. The chatter and music would sometimes drift over the grounds, waking her from time to time, but mostly she slept through the night, knowing she would have a few moments of solitude before dawn and would then be ready to do it all over again.

On this late afternoon, Camilla had nothing particular on her mind while sweeping at Dominick's request. He was a cantankerous little man, but Camilla learned it was more of an act he kept up to deal with his own displeasure at being pushed around by some of the other larger crew members, so she took it in stride, trying her best to obey his orders with a pleasant attitude. Sometimes she sensed he was beginning to warm up to her as a result, but other times she wasn't so sure.

Suddenly, she heard a shriek from Fiona's tent that startled her. The beautiful dancing acrobat was shouting many words in French, and though Camilla did not understand most of them, it was obvious she was in great distress. Several of the nearby workers ran promptly to her aid, only to find her assistant, Bella, had fallen ill and fainted dead away from heat and exhaustion.

After Bella awakened, she appeared quite dizzy and held her head, exclaiming that it ached something awful. Fiona did her best to console poor Bella, but the strongest of the men scooped her up and carried her off to another location where she could be tended to by their traveling physician. Fiona stood watching them, her hands on her pretty face, an expression of deep concern for both the girl and herself. "Oh no," she said in English now, still revealing her French accent. "Whatever will I do? That girl is so faint of heart. It simply cannot be helped."

It was then that she spotted Camilla, who had just finished sweeping the area. "Hello, my dear," she waved frantically, "You there, Cami, is it? Please, could you be of service to me? As you can see, my assistant is not feeling too well, and I just don't know what I will do without her, as there is much to be done before the show tonight."

Camilla looked at Fiona, stunned by her request and unsure of how to answer. "I would be glad to help you," she said finally. "But I am afraid Dominick will be expecting me to help prepare dinner soon."

Fiona waved her hand in the air, dismissing any concern, "Oh, not to worry, my dear, I will speak to Monsieur Dominick and explain the whole thing. Now hurry, we must get started right away."

Camilla wasn't sure whose authority ranked higher, but since Fiona was such an integral part of the show, she thought it best to serve her in whatever way she needed. She set the broom against a nearby tree and followed Fiona into her wagon.

"Now wait here, little one. I will go find Dominick right away and let him know you will not be available this evening." And with that, she hurried away. This left Camilla a few moments to observe her surroundings. She had never been in a ladies' room before. Though her mother was certainly a great lady in her own right, there was no real comparison. Camilla always noted that her mother pulled her hair back neatly and wore one of three hand-stitched dresses, one with a touch of lace, but she didn't have a room to herself for dressing and never had fine things. No, she was more of a lady in how she carried herself and treated others. But this was a whole new world to Camilla.

Camilla observed the various silk scarves, leotards, and tutus strewn over a tri-fold dressing screen and draped across a small wooden stool. There was a matching wooden table with a mirror atop that was littered with various cosmetics and tonics, as well as hair ornaments. She picked up a hair comb adorned with pearls and admired its delicate beauty. Never could she imagine owning something so elegant. Deep down, she both adored and envied Fiona.

Looking into the mirror, she saw her own reflection and, for the first time in her life, really saw what a messy, unkempt creature she was. Her freckles seemed darker than she remembered, her hair nothing more than a matted mess, and her dress, shabby with several patches to cover the holes she created playing along the rocky shore of her homeland. She gazed at herself with a sense of realization of what a far cry she was from the beautiful Fiona. Touching her face, she turned from her own reflection in shame.

At that moment, Fiona returned, startling Little Cami. She set the comb down quickly and turned her attention to the starling. Fiona did not seem to notice, but instead proceeded with her frantic talk in an accent that was difficult to discern at that speed. Finally, the puzzled look on Camilla's face told her she needed to slow down, and she began again.

"Dominick said all would be well without you tonight, my dear. You will help me. And to start, I need you to mend my stockings. Do you know how to sew?"

"A little..."

"It will have to do. Please," she handed Camilla a pair of silk stockings and a case holding a needle and a thread, "There is a hole in the toe, which is a disaster. The slightest imperfection is sure to throw me off my game. Would you please see to it that it's taken care of and then fluff my tutu?"

Camilla was learning fast that everything was a bit

dramatic where Fiona was concerned, but it didn't make her admire her any less. Mostly, she couldn't believe she was trading the physical labor she had grown accustomed to for such menial tasks, but who was she to complain? "Yes, I can do that." She replied and went to work immediately.

Fiona, in the meantime, worked on her stretches and pirouettes, something that she explained was absolutely vital to her daily routine to maintain control of her balance. "It could be the difference between life and death," she emphasized. Camilla only nodded and would occasionally look up in awe at the delicate creature before her.

They went on in similar fashion until it was time for supper. Fiona picked up the stocking and surveyed it with satisfaction, "You did very well on such short notice, my dear." She then remarked on how well she had prepared her costumes for the night, exactly according to the way she had requested. Camilla beamed with pride at her ability to please the lady.

Having completed any immediate tasks, they exited the wagon together, but not before Fiona told Camilla she must return as soon as she had finished her meal to help her get ready for the show. It suited Camilla just fine. She was being exposed to a whole new world, and spending time with Fiona somehow made her feel significant. *If only I could assist her always. Perhaps then I, too, could learn to be a lady.* She thought to herself as she headed to the tent for supper.

CHAPTER 11

*C*amilla continued to assist Fiona for the next two nights, and when the circus wagons pulled out of town, Bella did not join them. She still had not fully recovered from her fainting spell, and since she was just a short ride away from her native town, she decided to go home. There were whispers that the timing was all too convenient and perhaps she staged the whole thing because she didn't have what it took to sustain life on the road. Though sweet and accommodating to Fiona, she was a slight girl prone to bouts of exhaustion and homesickness.

Camilla began to wonder how she might fare in time. She certainly felt homesick some days, but her curiosity about how the events of the day would unfold always kept her interest piqued. And before she could ever get too comfortable, they were off to the next town. Besides, she knew circus life was never meant to be a permanent arrangement for her; she was simply trying to do what was necessary to provide for her mother and save her farm so she could reclaim it without having to rely on the charity of others. Once she saved enough money to buy the farm outright, she too would be on her way home.

One unintended benefit of constantly being on the move was not having to face her father's death head-on. In her mind, she could pretend he was still sitting in his old chair, smoking a pipe and playing his fiddle. She ached at the very thought of it not being so. Her greatest comfort was knowing how proud he would be of her courage to step up and try to make her own way. Camilla was pondering all these things as the wagons ambled along the dusty road when she laid her head against its wooden frame and drifted off.

⚜⚜⚜

The next town was a day's ride, so the troupe stayed overnight in a field so they could make their grand entrance the following afternoon. Even while traveling, Camilla had her chores. She rose from her slumber just as the party was coming to a stop. Exiting the wagon, she immediately began to tend to the animals to provide them with fresh food and water and to make sure they had a chance to relieve themselves. Sugar appeared restless as she awaited Camilla's approach. This was a horse that was born to be free. It saddened Camilla that such a magnificent creature should be held captive, even if she was better cared for than all the other animals put together.

Frederick approached with a light-hearted gait to greet his precious mare. "How's my girl?" he said, rubbing her nose. Camilla shrank into the shadows, not wanting to draw attention to herself. Why was she always so shy in Frederick's presence? He gently led his horse away without noticing her at all. Camilla wasn't sure if she was disappointed or grateful, but continued tending to the rest of the hungry beasts.

It wasn't long before Dominick joined her, but instead of barking orders at her, as he usually did, he relieved her of her duties. "Well, as I'm sure you know, Bella will no longer be with us, which means Fiona needs a new assistant. She specifically requested you for the job, and it turns out Max okayed it. It's a wonder that she would choose a scrap of a girl like you, but I told her you'd work hard anyway. So, if you're okay with the new arrangement, I guess you're done here."

Camilla's mouth gaped open in surprise at the sudden turn of events. She had only dreamed such a thing would be possible, but she assumed one of the other girls would easily be chosen over her. "Why y-yess…" she stammered, "It would be an honor."

"Well, then, you'd better get out of here. Seems Fiona will be wanting you to start right away to help her get ready for the grand entrance tomorrow." Did Camilla only imagine the look of disappointment on Dominick's face?

"Sure thing, right away!" she replied. "And Dominick, thank you for all you've done to help me get started. I'll never forget your kindness." She threw her arms around the tiny, gruff man. He didn't return the embrace, nor did he pull away from it. And Camilla was off to report to her new boss...the beautiful, elegant Fiona.

⚜⚜⚜

Fiona had made a mess of her wagon as she dug through piles of costumes looking for the exact tutu she planned to wear the next day. Camilla tapped lightly on the open door before entering. Fiona was too distracted to look up, "Be a dear and help me find my pink tutu and matching tights, would you?"

It wasn't exactly the formal greeting Camilla expected for the official start of her new position, but she jumped in to assist. She eventually found both garments behind the dressing wall in the corner. Fiona gave a huge sigh of relief. "Oh my, I feared I left them behind. I don't always keep track of my things the way I should. I suppose that is where you come in," she said, smiling at the proud girl.

"I will serve you in whatever way my lady requires," was

Cami's prim reply.

"Oh, no need for such formalities, my dear. You will be a big help to me, no doubt, and I do yell from time to time, but don't take it personally. I never mean any harm. I want us to be good friends." She grabbed Camilla's hands, which Camilla noticed were soft and neatly manicured. "Now sit for a moment and let's talk, you and I."

Camilla took a seat on the little stool in front of the vanity while Fiona sat in a small mauve-tufted velvet armchair across from her. "Tell me a little about yourself. How did you come to join our circus again?"

Camilla took a deep breath and explained the whole story leading up to her arrival in town and her need to find a job that fateful afternoon. She spoke about her father's passing, her Aunt Meredith's arrival, and even Griffin's proposal. Fiona nodded at the recollection of finding Camilla in the presence of Rocco and Wolfie and how she helped to secure her the job by talking to Max. "That's pretty much the whole story," Camilla concluded.

Fiona frowned and gave the girl a compassionate pat on the hand. "You poor dear, losing your father and your home. Poor little lamb. Why did you not want to marry this Griffin? It seemed like a very good offer. Is he not a very nice boy?"

Camilla squirmed in her seat at the mention of Griffin. "No, he is a very nice boy. It's just...he is like a brother."

"I see! We certainly wouldn't want to be marrying our brother, would we? Well, no matter, you are with us now, and as long as you work for me, I will take very good care of you. No need to worry. But my dear, this simply won't do." Fiona picked up one of Camilla's messy braids and held it out in front for her to see. "And these clothes—we must certainly do something about that. But we'll talk more about such things tomorrow. For now, I need you to help me pick up this mess."

Camilla soon learned that to "help" Fiona meant to do it alone. She was a great lady after all and had more important things to tend to—such as her beauty sleep.

CHAPTER 12

*T*he next town they pulled into was expected to be a week-long stay, something Camilla was quite pleased to learn. Sometimes they would only stay in a town for three nights and be right back on the road. Not that she minded terribly, but it left little time to look around as she would be working practically every waking hour. A week in one place meant there would be a little downtime as well, which the entire cast and crew were looking forward to.

But before anyone could even think about taking a break, the tents and structures needed to be set up for their Friday night show, as well as getting the animals settled in. Camilla was no longer responsible for that, but it didn't stop her from wanting to pay the animals a visit on the way to fetch Fiona a pitcher of water.

Dominick was spreading out fresh piles of hay with his

new assistant—one of the newer clowns to join the troupe who appeared not much older than Camilla. "So, you came to beg for your old job back, I see." Dominick barked. "Well, I ain't havin' yeh. Chuckles over there is outperforming your duties three to one, and well, I wouldn't take yeh on again if you got down on your knees wailing like a banshee."

Camilla looked over at "Chuckles", who was lazily resting against a tree with his arms crossed and his eyes closed. "Oh yeah? Looks like you sure got a live one there."

Dominick looked over and couldn't help but let out a chuckle of his own. "Yeah, well, he had a long night—of drinking. So, what brings you over to us rabble? I thought now that you're working for that superstar you wouldn't have time to go slummin' no more. How is the big star treating yeh anyhow?"

Camilla smiled affectionately at her former boss, which made him look away, for fear he might reveal his soft side, but it was too late. His reddening cheeks gave him away. "She's treating me very well, but nothing could keep me away. I'd still like to visit the animals from time to time, if you don't mind."

"Yes, well, just see to it you don't make a mess or distract Chuckles from getting his work done."

"What is his real name, anyway?"

"Beats me," Dominick shrugged. "He hasn't been awake long enough for me to ask him. I suspect he won't be around long if he keeps that up." Chuckles continued to snore loudly through their light banter.

While Max never discouraged the troupe from having a good time on their off hours, Camilla knew he wouldn't tolerate laziness when there was work to be done. Dominick walked away to continue with his chores, so Camilla approached the once-astonishing, but now-familiar beasts. She took turns giving each of them a moment of her time, along with a little treat, before getting back to work herself. She wondered if she might cross paths with Frederick, but no luck. He hadn't come out of his wagon all morning.

When Camilla returned to Fiona's room with the pitcher of water, the performer was in a hysterical state as she couldn't seem to find her favorite lipstick. "I was sure I put it here in this drawer," she wailed. "Oh, Cami, please be a dear and help me look for it! I simply must have it for tonight's show."

Camilla set the pitcher of water down on a small table next to Fiona's bed and proceeded to dig around the vanity where she kept most of her cosmetics. Finally, she found it in a different drawer, buried under a pile of other strange beauty products that were unfamiliar to Camilla.

Fiona gave a huge sigh of relief—she was never short on dramatics. "Merci beaucoup, my dear!"

Camilla wasn't sure, but based on the tone, she assumed that meant 'thank you'. She nodded, then proceeded to watch Fiona apply a dab of the crimson wax to her pouty lips and then smack them together in satisfaction. Camilla had never known anyone to wear color on their lips and wondered if someone had to be rich to possess such a luxury. It certainly gave them allure.

Fiona noticed Cami watching her curiously and smiled. "Would you like to try a little, my dear?" Camilla shook her head in embarrassment at being caught staring. "Oh, come, it will do wonders for your pretty smile. Stand in front of me, little one." Camilla slowly approached the lady but was too bashful to look up. "No need to worry, my dear, just stick your lips out like this." Fiona gave an extra-pouty look as she jutted both of her lips out.

Camilla did her best to imitate Fiona's pucker, but felt ridiculous. She stood still as the colorful wax was lightly applied to her bottom lip and then her top lip. When the task was complete, Fiona leaned back and exclaimed, "Will you look at that!" Before Camilla could turn around and look in the mirror, Fiona had grabbed her rouge kit and a brush and began applying it to Camilla's pale, freckled cheeks. "Oh mon!" she cried, "What an incredible transformation. Don't you agree?" With that, Fiona grabbed Camilla by the shoulders and spun her around to gaze upon the reflection of her newly painted face.

Camilla was stunned by what she saw. She barely recognized herself at all. Her hair was still a mess, but she looked much older, and so much more womanly—so much more like Fiona. She touched her cheek and wondered at the transformation. It only took a couple of minutes to make her utterly unrecognizable.

"Well, what do you think, my dear?"

"I...I...I'm not sure what to think. I don't feel like

myself."

"Well, that's the point, little one. Who wants to look like themselves? Non, you want to look magnifique!"

"Mag-ni-fique?" Camilla attempted to repeat the word, "And do I look mag-ni–?"

Fiona cut her short. "Not quite. That will take some work. But in time, perhaps. Come, let's finish prepping my costumes for tonight, then you can help me with some of my training, and I'll have you help pin my hair a little later. And maybe soon we can work on the rest." Camilla smiled at the suggestion, took one more look at her reflection, and smoothed her hair back.

"Magnifique," she whispered.

The humidity of the previous week was lifting, which cleared the atmosphere so that the evening stars shone brightly through the sky overhead. It had been a small gesture on Fiona's part, but Camilla felt electric, as though a page in her book had been turned and major changes were ahead. She still wasn't sure she wanted anyone to see her face, but neither did she want to wipe away the lipstick and rouge. She mostly tried to keep to herself and turned away from anyone who might look her way.

No longer in charge of manning any booths, Camilla now

waited in the wings of the big tent to assist Fiona with her quick costume changes. She was a bit nervous about performing these new duties, but the two of them had run through practice routines enough times that Camilla felt confident she could do the job efficiently. In the meantime, it simply gave her more time to watch bits of the show—most notably, Frederick.

Her view was significantly closer now than when she had to hide way in the back by the tent's entrance. She could feel the wind from the momentum whipping her face as sugar ran past, Frederick carefully balancing himself upon her steady back. They were followed by several other riders—secondary performers—who did their own share of feats. None of them nearly so impressive as Frederick the Elastic Fantastic, but that was by design. He was the star of the show, and the biggest part of his act was always saved for the grand finale. He would then jump through hoops of fire, sometimes while doing a flip. Though the danger of the stunt took Camilla's breath away, along with everyone else in the audience, he never failed to land perfectly on Sugar's back once on the other side.

Tonight, there was an addition to the act that Camilla was unfamiliar with. All the riders worked to make a pyramid formation while simultaneously riding two horses running side by side. It looked incredibly perilous, yet Frederick stood confidently at the top with his hands on his hips, yelling out "Ole'!" The crowd cheered with a roar, which he only encouraged by lifting his hands high in the air and yelling out, "Ole'!" once again, with even more vigor.

Camilla's heart beat wildly in her chest at the sight. She now knew exactly what this effect he had on her was. There was little room for doubt after that night. "I think I must be in love," she said out loud, only for herself to hear.

CHAPTER 13

*T*wo more nights of shows and the troupe finally had a day of rest. Camilla had been so consumed with helping Fiona that she wondered if she wasn't made to work harder than when she did manual labor for Dominick. Still, she very much enjoyed Fiona's company, despite her occasional dramatics, and studied her every move. She so admired the performer that she wished to be more like her in every way.

She saw very little of Frederick as he, too, was rehearsing longer hours than usual to improve his act. Camilla thought it must be paying off as he seemed more dazzling with every nightly performance. She wasn't sure if it was just her imagination, but it seemed to be reflected in the audience's enthusiasm as well. Camilla overheard a great deal of chatter at breakfast, and some speculated whether he wasn't preparing to join a better circus. She feared it might be true, but tried not to think about it.

Even though it was her day off, Camilla decided to check in with Fiona that morning to see if she needed any help. She was becoming quite proficient at helping the starlet and enjoyed feeling needed. She knocked lightly on the wagon door, not wanting to wake her in case she was still sleeping, but a soft voice called to her from the other side. "Come in, deary."

Camilla opened the door and found Fiona wide awake and ready for the day, sitting at her vanity. "I thought it might be you," she said kindly. "Come on over here, little one."

Camilla did as requested and noticed Fiona had most of her cosmetics splayed out across the table in front of her. "What's all this for?"

"Oh, I just thought I'd go through my belongings while we have a break. My room is getting overcrowded, so I think it's time to pare down to the essentials. Well, at least rid myself of the *non-essentials* anyway."

Camilla figured Fiona liked having lots of pretty things and would have a difficult time making the decision to let go of much, but she offered to help just the same.

"Yes, dear, I would very much like your assistance. In fact, I was hoping you'd help me unload some items. How much room do you have in your sleeping quarters to store things?"

Camilla couldn't imagine what Fiona was up to, but she replied, "I have some space under my bed and that's about it. But as you can see, I don't own very much to begin with."

"Well, that's just perfect, here take this…" Fiona grabbed a pile of clothing on the floor and thrust it into Camilla's arms. Camilla couldn't even fathom what exactly she was being given, but a glance at the jumbled mess of lace and ribbons told her it was far better than anything she'd ever dreamed of owning. "Now be a good girl and go try those on so we can see how you look."

It took a moment for Camilla to collect her thoughts before doing as she was told. She ambled over to the dressing screen in the corner of the room. She set the clothing down on the floor and stripped down to her well-worn shift, then called to Fiona on where she might begin.

"I have a feeling this is going to be a long afternoon," Fiona replied, walking over to assist the poor, hapless girl.

After an hour-long changing session, the two of them managed to put together three full outfits that were more than presentable, along with a couple of other pieces to mix and match and some basics. Fiona was quite pleased with herself as she assessed the young girl's ensemble. Camilla, however, was uncomfortable and felt unable to breathe in the girdle that tightly squeezed her mid-section. She had yet to see herself, as Fiona wanted to complete the look before revealing the final outcome.

Once again, Fiona pulled out a few cosmetics and went to work on Cami's face. This time, she began by powdering her down excessively before applying rouge and lipstick. Once satisfied, she took a comb to her hair and worked through the matted tresses that always appeared so unruly. As she raked the comb through them, Camilla gave a little yelp of pain, but they got through it together. Fiona then proceeded to pin her now-smoothed hair up into a loose bun on top of her head, as was the fashion among most civilized women. Cami's hair had a bit of natural wave that Fiona managed to work with to frame her face and at the nape of her neck.

"It will have to do." she said finally. "I think we should work on your hair a little more some other time, but this should do well enough for now. Go see for yourself."

Camilla already felt the alteration before she saw it with her own eyes and tried to imagine what she might look like. Try as she may, she could not have prepared herself for what she was about to see. She approached the mirror and gasped at the sight of her unrecognizable reflection. *Could this really be me?* It didn't seem possible. The girl standing before her was no longer the ratty tomboy who ran through the farm and spent her days by the tidepools. This was a full-grown woman, with even a hint of beauty, if she did say so herself.

"Could it be?" she finally breathed.

"How joyous! You do like it then?" Fiona couldn't be more pleased with her skills in helping the poor girl blossom before their very eyes.

It took a few silent minutes for Camilla to accept what she was seeing. "I can't believe that's me. I never knew such a thing was possible. If Mama and Papa could see me now…" The painful recollection of her father's death affected her momentarily before she regained her astonishment.

"Well, let's wait to show the others. It will surely take them by surprise. We'll keep you hidden until suppertime and then see who recognizes you." Camilla was slightly disappointed that her plans for a walk into town were thwarted, but she agreed to go along with Fiona's plan, even though she couldn't bear the thought of wearing that girdle all afternoon.

"What will I do in the meantime? What about lunch?"

"Nothing to fret, my dear. I will get your lunch for you and bring it back here. Oh mon, can you hardly believe it? I will be waiting on you for a change. Who is the lady now?" she winked, humoring the girl.

Camilla felt it was much more than she deserved, but she allowed the starlet to do as she pleased.

"Now," Fiona continued, "You must have a comb of your very own, a bit of makeup, and some perfume. I got this little bottle from a traveling salesman I once fancied myself to be in love with, but he turned out to be a real boor. As you can imagine, I have no attachment to it whatsoever, so it's yours now." And with that, she hit the pump attached to the round bottle and sent a spray across Cami's neck.

Camilla hadn't prepared for the gesture and coughed as she inhaled some of the perfume. Fiona couldn't help but giggle as a result, though she was admittedly charmed by the girl's naivete.

Already, little Cami was beginning to feel the nerves of

her big reveal. She was suddenly self-conscious and wondered if anyone would even notice and what they would think. Or rather, she was concerned about the reaction of one person in particular. It wouldn't be long now. She just had to find a way to steady her breath in the meantime.

CHAPTER 14

By dinnertime, Camilla was feeling quite ready to get the whole thing over with. She had gotten somewhat used to the girdle, but she was eager to feel normal again. She knew it would all take some getting used to, but once the initial reveal was over, that would be plenty of practice for one day.

Fiona was sure to refresh Camilla's lipstick and rouge before they made their way to the food tent. Fiona handed Camilla a pair of silk shoes with a slight heel. "Here, put these on."

It made the look complete, but when Camilla stood up in the shoes for the first time, she found them to be a little tight and difficult to walk in. Going down the steps of the wagon proved particularly difficult.

"What if I fall?" she asked, carefully working her way

down the wooden steps to the soft earth below.

"Nonsense," Fiona retorted, flipping her hand in the air to dismiss the young girl's concerns. "You will do fine. Just follow me and you will have nothing to fear. We will get our food, then take a seat, and all will be well."

Camilla wondered who her first spectator would be. Would they think she was nothing more than a fraud? Perhaps she would fit in better with the clowns. She looked over the grounds and saw no one nearby, which was a relief. The two of them slowly made their way to the food tent, seeing more people coming their way as they drew nearer.

Cami hid her face behind Fiona, beginning to lose her nerve. Now, at the moment of truth, she dreaded anyone taking notice of her. If only they could turn back, but she knew there was little chance of Fiona letting her off the hook. Thankfully only a couple of people murmured a hello, but they didn't stop to assess the two girls, most likely because they were focused on satisfying their appetite. Once in the tent, it was another story.

Dominick was the first to spot Camilla. It took a moment, as he habitually dropped a ladleful of stew into her bowl as though she were just another member of the troupe. It was only after she thanked him by name that he recognized her voice. Looking up, he couldn't believe his own eyes. His mouth gaped open in response. "Could it be…?" he finally uttered.

"Yes, Dominick," Cami whispered. "It's me."

"What did she do to you? Well, it sure didn't take long for

you to turn into one of them, did it? Got you all gussied up I see, and soon you'll be acting the part. I suppose that means you'll be too good to be seen with the likes of me. I know how certain circus folk stick together and the clowns and grunt labor stick to themselves."

"Not at all, nothing has changed, I swear it." Camilla felt terrible to be accused of becoming a completely different person just because of a little rouge and perfume.

"Well, we'll see about that. I must say, I didn't suspect you'd clean up so well at that. I'd say you're just about as pretty as any gal in the troupe. And I don't just say these things, you know."

Camilla blushed but could hardly believe it to be true. Fiona was too busy talking to one of the other trapeze artists to catch any of the conversation. Suddenly, two thug-like figures approached the ladies, addressing Fiona first.

"Hey Fifi, who's your new friend? Aren't you gonna introduce us?"

Fiona's face turned red with irritation, "Wolfie, how many times have I told you not to call me Fifi? Only my dearest friends have the right to call me that, and you, sir, are most certainly no friend of mine."

The big man laughed heartily at that, "Oh come off your high horse, you silly broad. Stop playing games and introduce me to this here lady friend of yours. Is she a new performer or what?"

Fiona rolled her eyes, unaffected by the familiarity in which they spoke crudely to one another. "I'll have you know, this young lady is my new assistant. You may recall that Bella fell ill and had to leave us with such short notice, so Camilla here was gracious enough to take her place. And she's doing a fine job, at that!"

The name meant nothing to the ape-like man who still scared Cami. He gave her a sickening grin. Though the smile communicated a more friendly discourse than their first encounter, it made her skin crawl no less.

His friend Rocco was with him and interjected, "Hey, haven't I seen you somewhere before?"

Camilla didn't dare say a word. Wolfie spoke up instead, "Nah, I think we'd remember a face as nice as that, even if she is just an assistant. Hey, girly, how about spending a little time with me and my friend here after dinner? We could have some drinks and a few laughs. What do you say?"

Camilla was petrified at the thought of being alone with either of these men, let alone at the same time. She shook her head, unable to speak.

"Oh, she's just shy, is all," Rocco said, grabbing her by the arm to pull her closer.

Camilla yelped at his sudden grip, and Fiona stood up quickly in her defense. "Let her go, you brutes, or I'll be sure to tell Max where you've been getting those bottles of liquor you suck down night after night."

Wolfie made a sour expression at her. "You wouldn't dare. Why do you keep interfering any time we want to have a little fun?

You prima donnas are all the same—you think you can push everyone around, but let me tell you, we're not letting some little ballerina tell us who we can and can't talk to." He then grabbed Camilla's other arm. "You want to spend some time with us, don't you, girly? Why don't you come sit with us at our table instead of hanging around with this cheap floozy of a tight walker?"

Camilla tried to resist, but the two men started to pull on her against her will. Suddenly, a voice called out from behind. It was strong, but calm. "How about you two leave these girls alone before it becomes necessary to make a scene?" The men released their grip with a grunt. Camilla turned around to see that her savior was none other than Frederick.

"Thank you, dear Frederick," Fiona replied. "These two are harassing my poor assistant. Please make them go away."

Frederick merely nodded in their direction, and they began to walk away. For all their antics, they really didn't want to be on the outs with the performers or have the scuffle getting back to Max. Not to mention, they were beginning to attract the attention of everyone else.

"Don't worry," he said to Camilla, who still looked a bit shaken up. "Those guys are idiots. They just go berserk when they see a pretty face. What is your name anyway?"

Did Frederick the Elastic Fantastic just call me pretty? She could hardly believe her ears. Never in her whole life was she ever called pretty, least of all by one so 'magnifique'. "My name is Camilla," she said finally.

"Camilla?"

"Most people call me Cami."

It suddenly dawned on the premier equestrian. "My word. You're the girl I met in the stables, no?"

Camilla nodded quietly.

"Well, I'll be. Fiona must have done a number on you. She certainly has the magic touch." He looked the girl up and down with his flashy eyes, which caused Camilla to blush deeply. "But I'll tell you what. You ladies enjoy your dinner in peace, and hopefully, I'll see you around soon. I have to eat quickly and then do a bit of training on a new act that me and the guys are working on."

Fiona thanked Frederick again, who assured them that Wolfie and Rocco would not disturb them further. But having overheard the exchange themselves, it finally dawned on the thuggish pair that this was the same dirty little girl they picked on when she first came looking for a job. They nudged each other at the realization, shocked and amused, but went to take a seat at the far corner of the tent to avoid further altercations.

Fiona and Camilla decided to take their dinner back to the wagon after all, which was a relief to Camilla, whose feet were already aching from the short time of wearing heels. Her entire experience since joining the circus had temporarily taken the spirit out of her. She was tired at the moment and began missing the safety and security of home.

When they got back to the room, Fiona helped her out

of the fancy clothing so she was finally able to eat—and breathe. This made Camilla feel a tad rejuvenated, so they sat together laughing and talking until nightfall. "You sure showed them!" Fiona proclaimed with glee.

Camilla was certainly shocked by the reaction she received, but ultimately wanted to spend her time thinking of nothing except Frederick's great entrance when he rescued her from the grip of those surly crew members. And once again, she recalled his words that made her tummy swirl with ecstasy. *He said I was pretty.* Her dreams were sure to be sweet that night.

CHAPTER 15

*C*amilla awoke the next morning, relieved to have the day to herself. She planned to go exploring a bit to get some fresh air and some time away from the circus atmosphere. Much as she loved the excitement, mentally she needed a break. As she considered what to wear, she felt torn as her old clothes no longer seemed sufficient, and the new clothes that Fiona gave her seemed too much for a casual outing. She finally settled on a simple linen dress that didn't require a girdle and would breathe in the heat. She ran the comb Fiona gifted her through her hair and pinned it up to the best of her ability, as she was taught. She then shoved some paper and pencils into her satchel and headed out into the world.

Getting into town only required a short walk. It was very much like her own village, perhaps slightly bigger. Camilla was beginning to realize that one town was very much like another, with the usual shops and the usual cast of characters. She stopped by a market for some fresh fruit and a small loaf of bread. There were times when she almost imagined she saw people from back home, but a double-take always confirmed she had been mistaken. The experience both comforted her and made her long for familiar faces.

But rather than wallowing in nostalgia, Camilla chose to live in the here and now. She especially enjoyed perusing the shop windows at pretty things but was careful not to indulge her every whim as she planned to send as much of her earnings to her mother as possible. Having received several weeks of pay now, plus the increase she received from being promoted to Fiona's assistant, she felt confident it was enough to make a real difference in paying down the farm if she stayed disciplined.

One item in the dress shop window particularly her eye though. It was a simple cornflower blue gown adorned with crisp, white lace on the neck and hems. There was something very becoming about it that appealed to Camilla's newfound interest in her appearance. A closer look revealed that the price was higher than she anticipated. She considered the amount she set aside to live off of in the coming weeks and realized it would require dipping into the money she intended to send home. She carefully weighed if she should make a sacrifice that would allow her to satisfy an impulse purchase, but finally decided against it. She walked away with a touch of sadness in her heart, but determined not to lose sight of the reason she sought employment to begin with.

The humidity increased as the morning progressed, leaving Camilla slightly exhausted and ready to rest. She helped herself to some water at a nearby well, then headed over to a field just outside of town where she found a large shady oak tree to rest under. She leaned back against the rough texture of its trunk. It reminded her of the tree she and Griffin often met at. She contemplated what Griffin might be up to at that very moment and whether he still sat beneath the old tree on his time off. Did he think of her too?

Sitting quietly for a time, Camilla took in the sounds of nature. The birds were still chirping, and a light breeze rustled gently through the heavy branches overhead. She closed her eyes and gave in to the wistful longings of home. She imagined she was under that familiar tree, in a time gone by, and for the moment, it tricked her senses. A feeling of peace washed over her that she hadn't experienced since losing her father.

Camilla thought back to the last time they went fishing together and how excited they were to bring in the haul for dinner. She recalled the electricity of the storm rolling in and the smell of the salty sea. How she missed the sea right at that moment. It was something she took for granted, just a part of daily life, but now she ached to be standing on the cliff's edge looking out at the vast horizon—the same horizon she and Griffin watched the sunset on the day her life would be forever changed.

Rather than dwell on these sad memories, Camilla pulled out the paper and pencils in her satchel and began to write a letter to her mother. She assured her all was well and that she was enclosing the funds to help care for the farm, just as she promised. She briefly filled her in on the sudden change in her role at the circus. She was certain it would put her mother's mind at ease knowing that her daughter was assisting a lady performer and no longer doing manual labor. She left out her recent transformation, though not entirely sure why. She mostly kept things matter-of-fact to convince her mother that all was well and that there was nothing to worry about.

Camilla then decided to write Griffin once again. Along with her mother, she knew he would be anxiously awaiting news of how she was doing. She considered telling him where the circus was heading next so he could write her back and fill her in on all that was going on back home, but decided against it for fear he would pass the information on to her mother and they would be waiting there to talk her into returning home. Or worse—to Aunt Meredith's. As much as she would love to receive a letter from Griffin, she couldn't risk it at this time. Especially when things were going so well. For now, it would just have to remain a one-way communication.

She initially decided to keep the letter brief, but it wasn't long before words poured out onto the page as Camilla couldn't help but share everything she was experiencing with her oldest friend. She told him all about Dominick, the animals, how she came to help Fiona, and even described many of the circus acts she witnessed on a nightly basis. As with her mother, she left out her recent makeover. Somehow, she felt Griffin wouldn't understand or even care about such things.

Once the letters were complete, she folded the papers and tucked them in her bag, planning to mail them out before heading back to the circus grounds. She decided to rest a while longer, staying under the shade of the oak tree and making a light lunch of the food she purchased in town.

She was savoring some wild blackberries when the sound of hooves came thundering across the field. She looked up to see Frederick and Sugar whipping wildly through the tall grass at lightning speed. It seemed they were enjoying their time off as well, for there was nothing of work in their ride, only pleasure.

For a moment, they disappeared from sight as they ran behind a cluster of trees in the distance. A short while later, they reemerged, running off in the opposite direction, and then appeared to be heading her way. Camilla was sure Frederick had not seen her but wondered how long it would be for him to take notice of the girl watching him from under the giant tree. He made a quick approach as Sugar nearly set the field on fire with her blazing speed.

As they came nearer to the tree, they slowed down to a trot, and by now Camilla was sure she had been spotted. Frederick was wearing a white linen shirt that clung to his chest from the rising heat of the day. Beads of sweat lined his forehead, making his jet-black hair wet with perspiration. "Hello there!" He called out, coming closer with every trot. "Are you enjoying your afternoon off?"

Camilla waved hello in return. Standing to her feet, she replied, "Yes, very much." She could hardly manage to say more.

"It is nice to get a break now and then. Max would work us seven days a week if he could, but even he likes a little time off to unwind. So, what are you up to this pleasant afternoon?"

Camilla looked down and patted her satchel. "I was just writing home. I don't want my mother to worry about me."

"I see. Well, she most certainly would worry if she knew what kind of characters you were keeping company with these days," he said with a wink, then continued. "I say, I suspect those ruffians haven't given you any more trouble?"

"No, not at all—thanks to you." Camilla blushed slightly at the memory of Frederick coming to her rescue. Little did she know how attractive her pink cheeks made her look.

Frederick smiled at the idea of being a hero to this young, naïve girl. "Well, I'll tell you what—should they try something like that again, you send them my way. Though I don't expect them to make much trouble. The truth is, they are okay guys. They just get restless on the road and feel the need to scare up some mischief now and again. I doubt they would have hurt you, especially with Fiona around. They know she has a good relationship with Max."

"I don't know Max very well. From stories I've heard, I thought it best to avoid him."

"Yes, I suppose that's just as well. Circus people are strange and unpredictable. Nothing is what it seems. But stick with Fiona, she is a good girl and will watch over and guide you. She barely remembers a time when she wasn't on the road. Her parents were circus performers as well, so she's very used to this life."

"Oh? And how about you? How did you come to embrace this life?" Camilla could hardly believe how forward she was in asking such a personal question of a relative stranger. The star of the show, no less.

But Frederick never hesitated to speak of himself. "Me? I've been on my own since I was twelve years old. I was taken on as a hired hand by a rancher who happened to be a former Equestrian. He taught me everything he knew, and I took it from there. This is the third circus I've performed with, so I suppose you could say I am working my way up in the world." His smile was cocky but charming.

This made Camilla giggle softly as warmth spread across her belly once again. How was it possible that this skilled showman was taking time out of his day to converse with her, a simple farm girl? "I enjoy watching what you do very much."

"You like the act, do you?"

"Well, I love animals, especially horses, and yours is pretty remarkable." She felt turning her praise to Sugar was a pretty good save from appearing to fawn over Frederick alone.

"I've noticed you with the animals, and you do seem to

handle Sugar well," he returned in kind. "Tell me, would you like to ride her yourself some time?"

Camilla was breathless at the offer. "I'd like nothing better."

"I am very particular about who I let handle my star performer, but in your case, I will make an exception since you seem to have such a deep appreciation for her. I am about to head back to the circus to work on some stunts with the other guys, but we will arrange it soon. How does that sound?"

"That sounds perfectly delightful!" she sighed. "But yes, I have to head to the post office now myself to mail out these letters."

"Well, at least let me give you a ride back into town." Frederick offered quickly. Before Camilla could respond, Frederick jumped down off his beloved mare and put his hands around her waist, lifting her light as a feather into the air and setting her on the back end of his beloved horse. He then hopped back on quickly, sitting in front of her and taking the reins. "Put your arms around me and hold on tight, little Cami," he said before flying toward town at breakneck speed to show off Sugar's riding abilities.

Camilla had ridden many horses in her life, but none so swift. The ride was nothing short of exhilarating. No further words were spoken between them, but Camilla pressed herself as snugly against Frederick's back as her little arms could muster. He felt strong and capable.

Her heart began beating in time with Sugar's hooves, but it wasn't long before they arrived in front of the little post office, and Frederick dismounted the horse once again. He reached up to help Camilla down, set her gently on her feet, then hopped back up on Sugar, gave a wave and a wink then took off. Camilla felt a little dizzy but somehow managed to regain her senses enough to take care of the business at hand. Walking back to the circus grounds, her steps were noticeably lighter, and the old oak tree back home was forgotten.

CHAPTER
16

*A*nother week in a new town and Camilla had not crossed paths with Frederick in a significant way. He kept busy, and when he wasn't working, he liked to be alone. Camilla thought back to their last interaction numerous times, wondering if she had only dreamed up the moment he let her ride Sugar with him back to town. And did he mean it when he said she could ride Sugar by herself sometime? She didn't dare pursue it but hoped he would offer again when the time was right.

To keep busy, Camilla spent her time tending to Fiona's every whim. As lovely a girl as Bella was—a fine companion for a bit of light cleaning and sharing the latest gossip—she did little to help the starlet stay organized. For as small as the wagon was, Fiona still amassed enormous amounts of attire and other trappings, which she crammed into every nook and cranny, so that she could never find a thing. Camilla decided to spend their last days off helping to get her belongings in order. Fiona was ever so grateful and as a result, parted with several more items as a gift to Camilla for all her help.

Among them was a dress that reminded her of the one she eyed in the shop. It wasn't quite cornflower blue but more of a sky blue, which was no less pretty, and the fashion was similar. It too, was adorned with delicate lace, more cream than white. She explained to Fiona what a gift it was and hugged it tightly, only hoping that it would be a good fit. A quick change of clothes, and she found it only needed some slight adjusting, but was otherwise very flattering. Fiona jested that if she had realized how pretty the dress really was, she might have thought twice about disposing of it. But ultimately, she affirmed it was made for Camilla and brought out her eyes.

Receiving such a wealth of fine clothing, Camilla was now compelled to throw her worn clothes out for good, with the exception of her father's old army coat. Not only was it deeply sentimental, but she felt it could come in handy during the colder months. But to wear it now would be rather absurd. Looking at herself in Fiona's mirror, Camilla still could not believe her recent transformation. She was even growing accustomed to the radical new her. Throwing her old clothes away became almost a symbolic act of shedding her previous life and her former, shabby self.

Fiona was even patient enough to teach her how to style her hair properly, something Camilla did not take to easily, but she was working on it. Though the fashionable updos were becoming, she still preferred to let her hair hang long and loose. Only now she kept it combed neatly, securing the sides with pins or a pretty comb to ensure it would remain tidy.

Today was such a day to let her hair down. After checking in with Fiona to see if she needed anything, she had a little time before lunch to pay Dominick and the other animals a visit. Dominick was in a surly mood, but that was nothing new. Still, he seemed glad to see the young girl.

"Came to check in on old Dominick, did yeh? Well, I guess you kept your word after all," he said.

"Of course, and I just had to see how the animals are getting on too."

Dominick pretended to be disgruntled that she should come for any reason besides seeing him, but then replied, "Go on, they've missed you too."

Camilla wandered over to the freshly cleaned cages. She always marveled at how the animals seemed far less fearsome when they were pent up than during the performances. She had gotten to know them a bit during her time working under Dominick and found most to be friendly, if not a little timid. She knew she must always proceed with caution when dealing with the bear and even the leopard, but as long as they were well fed, they remained mostly docile and enjoyed her attention. The dogs were always happy to have a visitor and jumped with delight at the sight of Camilla, barking happily and slobbering all over her as she opened the gate of their cage. The pot-bellied pig, Calliope, was the source of many gags in the animal performances but was currently unmotivated to rise from her sleeping position.

Camilla then moved onto the horses, but not before grabbing a handful of oats to give them as a treat. They neighed on her arrival and nuzzled her hand aggressively with their soft, wet noses. She spoke gently to each of them, missing her old workhorse, Clive, who served her family well for many years. How sad her father was when it came time to put him down. It was Camilla's first real experience with death. Sure, she had seen plenty of farm animals put down, even did the job herself a couple of times, but Clive was a friend.

Camilla's thoughts turned to her father once again, and the pain of losing him came flooding back. Tears began to well up in her eyes as she longed for one more moment in his presence. *I wonder what he would think of me now. Would he still muss my hair and call me his little Cami?*

Just then, she heard the crunch of the grass to indicate someone was approaching. Already she could feel him. It must be Frederick. She glanced behind her quickly to check. *It is!* Her heart began steadily beating in her chest as he walked up to the gate where Sugar was patiently waiting her turn for Camilla to share the oats. This was a noble creature who did not feel the need to push her way in to get her portion but knew it would come to her in time.

"Well, hello, Cami! How are you this fine day?" Frederick

said with a smile.

She answered quickly, afraid she might lose her words altogether, "Splendid. Just came by to say hello to my friends. I was planning to give some of these to Sugar, if that's okay?" She held out her hand and showed him the oats.

"How thoughtful, I'm sure she would be very appreciative to receive a treat about now." Frederick walked with her to where Sugar stood, raising her head high with an air of dignity. Even as Camilla offered the oats to the showy mare, she took her time nibbling them from her hands. When the treat was finally consumed, Camilla brushed the excess crumbs from her hand and gave Sugar a pat. The horse leaned her head into Camilla's hand as an affectionate gesture as if to say, "Thank you."

"She sure seems taken with you," Frederick observed. "I'd say she's just about ready for a warm-up. If you don't have any plans at the moment, I'm sure she'd be pleased to have you join her for a run."

And there it was. He really meant it when he said she could ride Sugar. "Oh, yes, I would take great pleasure in a ride." Dressing like a lady was even making Camilla talk like one. "Are you certain Max won't mind?" she added, suddenly concerned that as a mere assistant, she might be out of line riding one of the star performers.

Frederick waved off her concerns. "Not to worry, Cami, Sugar is my horse, and I know her best. Besides, Max has been gone since we pulled into town yesterday. Who knows when he'll be back."

Camilla suddenly realized she had not heard his booming voice yelling at anyone the day before or all morning. It was curious to her that he should leave the circus grounds as she hadn't known him to do so before. "Do you know where he went?"

"Max is always up to something, but he never tells us anything," he said with a wink.

"What about his brother?" Camilla inquired. She had never met the other half of the *Angelini Bros.*

"Huh?" Frederick seemed confused, and then his face lit up with understanding. "Oh, you mean the name? Yeah, that's a long story. The short version is that many years ago, before I joined this particular circus, Max and his brother, Lorenzo, started this circus together, but as rumor has it, there was a great deal of trouble between them. They had a serious blowout, and Lorenzo left and they never spoke to one another again."

"But why keep the name then?"

"Well, one thing you must have learned about Max, he is a very spiteful and shrewd man. And when he learned what it would cost to change the name of the circus on the wagons and all the banners and posters, well, if you can believe it, he decided to keep the name out of principle—and to stick it to his wayward brother."

Camilla chuckled at the notion, "I can believe it."

"Now about that ride…" Frederick proceeded to saddle up Sugar, who was becoming more restless by the minute. Sensing she would soon be free from the makeshift stable, she was working herself up for a run. "There, that should do it," he said as he tightened the last strap on her harness.

Despite Frederick's breezy nature about letting Camilla ride his treasured filly, Camilla was a bundle of nerves. Never had she mounted an animal so spectacular in stature. Sugar pranced in place, kicking up a bit of dirt and flicking her long, white mane with a shake of her regal head.

"Up you go," Frederick said, grabbing Camilla by the waist and setting her firmly on the horse's saddle with ease. It took a moment for her to adjust the skirt of her dress, but soon Camilla was sitting proudly, ready to exit the stall. Frederick grabbed the reins and gently led her to the open space just beyond the circus grounds. Sitting high atop the stunning creature, she felt like a special attraction in a procession. *So, this is how it feels to be a star*, she thought.

A couple of people working on the grounds took notice of the unusual sight, but Camilla kept her head lifted and her gaze fixed forward as if what she was doing was perfectly natural. A cool confidence washed over her as the special guest of the great Frederick the Elastic Fantastic. The star performer had offered her this special privilege, for what reason she didn't know, but she felt strengthened by his validation. Not because of how he was perceived by everyone else, but because of how she perceived him—his name was well earned, as there was none so fantastic in all the world in her eyes.

Once in the field, Camilla had shaken her nerves and was ready to go. She was not an experienced rider by any means, but she had ridden her fair share of livestock, so she was familiar with basic commands. Frederick proceeded to explain them anyhow, and with a click of the tongue and a shake of the reins, the two were off, trotting through the open field at a moderate pace. She went on that way for a while until she eventually worked up enough courage to canter a bit, though she wasn't quite ready to get the horse up to a gallop as Frederick had done.

Camilla may have been eager to ride Sugar, but in no way was she ready to test Sugar's full speed. The jolly canter was well enough to thrill her little heart for a year, and she hollered to display the elation she felt as they jetted back and forth through the field. Frederick's eyes twinkled with delight at the sight of Camilla's apparent joy. There was something infectious in her spirit that he found himself mesmerized by.

Every part of Frederick's being was so consumed with Camilla that he didn't notice Fiona, watching him from a distance. She, too, was taken by the unbridled enthusiasm Camilla displayed and recognized the infatuation in Frederick's eyes. It was a fetching sight indeed, but she couldn't help but feel uneasy at the potential implications.

CHAPTER 17

*C*amilla awoke the next morning to quite a commotion taking place outside. Most of the performers should have been sleeping for at least another hour, but even they began to emerge from their quarters at the booming sound of Max shouting, along with several other workers. The master had returned home and did not come alone. He had something enormous to show for his journey, the likes of which blared like a trumpet—another reason for the ruckus.

Whips cracked as Max tried to take control of his new prized possession, its large body resistant to being brought into submission. Again, it blared, raising its trunk high and lifting its colossal feet from the earth. Camilla stared in wonder—she had never seen anything so imposing in all her life.

"He went and done it," Camilla overheard someone in the crowd say. "He went and got him one of those elephants."

Another shook his head. "We'll be sunk for sure now."

One of the female tightrope walkers squealed gleefully, "Have you ever seen anything so marvelous?"

Camilla had no idea what to make of the development, but a tingle went up her spine with every trumpet blast. Apparently, this was to be a new addition to their circus, but clearly Max was having a difficult time reigning the animal in. The whips cracked again, and the elephant bucked, but somehow the crew of men managed to lead it back into the giant wagon that it arrived in.

"We'll worry about it later," Max said to the men. Then, turning to the gathering crowd and waving them on, he yelled out, "Sorry, folks, everything is under control. You can go back to your work." No one dared question the ringmaster, and they all began walking away, whispering in astonishment over the new development.

Camilla looked back at the wagon, seeing it shake from the still-furious beast. She had heard of elephants but had no idea what one looked like. She was equally fascinated and terrified by its enormity. She decided to head to Fiona's wagon to get her take on this when she caught sight of the performer lingering outside, another spectator in the crowd. Fiona waved Camilla over to join her back in the wagon, which she obeyed without hesitation.

Once they closed the door, Fiona began spouting off in

French endlessly, as if Camilla could understand a word. "Mon Dieu!" she finally called out. "What did Max go and get himself into this time?"

"I don't know…" Camilla replied weakly.

"This is all he or anyone else will think or talk about for weeks to come. We'll all suffer for it too. Impetuous little man. There is no reasoning with him once he's gotten something in his head. Well, I'm just not going to give it another thought. We'll go on as usual."

Camilla was greatly confused as to what all this meant. "Is it not a good thing?"

"Oh, for business, sure. We're sure to pack 'em in now. That is, if he can do anything with the poor beast. But what about *me*? Oh, it's hard enough to get time in the show. We'll have to cut back once again. Well, I'm not having it. He's simply going to have to cut somebody else!"

It was beginning to dawn on Camilla what the problem was where Fiona was concerned. "Oh, I see. Having a new act will certainly infringe on everyone else's?"

Fiona, still in a hot rage, continued, "Yes, and this time he may even lose some of us for good! Frederick will not stand for it either. Trust me. And then what?"

"You think this would cause Frederick to leave the circus?" Camilla hadn't thought of that.

Fiona snapped out of her tantrum and looked at the girl. "The truth is, Frederick will be the last one he cuts. I hate to admit it, but he's our biggest draw at the moment. He may spare me as well, but someone has to take the cut. What's going on with you and Frederick, anyhow?" Fiona eyed the girl carefully, reading her expression at the inquiry.

"Nothing." Camilla looked down. "Why do you ask?"

"I saw you riding Sugar yesterday. No one, and I mean *no one*, rides Sugar except Frederick."

Camilla's face began to get hot. She hadn't realized how unprecedented the move was. "He just knew I liked the horses and offered me a ride, that's all."

Fiona lifted a brow in suspicion but didn't press further. "Well, you just better hope that Max doesn't find out. He is extremely protective of his stars—they are his money makers after all."

The last thing Camilla wanted was to be the target of Maximillian Angelini. She had avoided his ire since becoming Fiona's assistant and hoped to keep it that way. "I'm sure it won't happen again," was all she managed. Instead of changing topics, she proceeded to help Fiona pick out the perfect costume for the show that night. It didn't take much to distract the starlet. It was as simple as putting the focus back on her.

No one came near the elephant's wagon for the rest of the day. It lay dormant once the beast settled down after finally accepting its fate to be caged. Out of curiosity, Camilla walked by a couple of times to see if there were signs of stirring, though nothing but silence came from its chambers. It seemed content to be left alone.

Word quickly spread that Max was in a foul mood, but by evening his spirits had slightly lifted with the rising anticipation of opening night in a new town. It was too irresistible not to get swept up in the excitement of preparing for a new crowd of spectators to entertain.

Just the same, Camilla kept herself busy and out of his line of vision, as did most of the cast and crew. But now he was out among the troupe, barking orders as the crew prepared the big tent and the performers went about their rehearsals.

Frederick was absent all morning until late afternoon when he finally emerged from his wagon to rehearse. Sugar had not been taken out for her usual afternoon jaunt, but she seemed content to have the day off. Now Camilla watched through the tent flap as they ran through their act, seeing it through new eyes now that she had the pleasure of riding Sugar. It also made her think back to what Fiona said, and she wondered why Frederick had broken protocol for her sake. Could she actually be special to him? She didn't dare entertain the possibility. Instead, she just watched, full of admiration for the performer.

Meanwhile, the sight of the man named Rocco caught her eye as he ambled his way over to Max with a look of mischief. He whispered in the ringmaster's ear and said something to perk his interest. They both looked at Frederick and continued talking at a faster pace.

Camilla was trying to make out what they might be saying when she was suddenly interrupted by another performer making his way to the tent to rehearse his own act. It was Benito the Fire Eater. They had only crossed paths briefly, but Camilla always found him to be a pleasant, polite, if not slight, man.

"Excuse me, my dear," he said in a thick accent. He was holding several torches that were used in his routine, along with a can of fuel. Camilla stepped out of the way to let him pass. He began walking past her when he turned around. "Cami, isn't it? I must say, you are gaining quite the reputation here."

Camilla couldn't imagine what on earth he was referring to. "What do you mean?" she asked.

"Oh, we circus folks always talk. But not to worry, all good things, all good things." And with that, he continued to walk on. Camilla looked once again to see what Rocco and Max were up to, but they were no longer anywhere in sight.

CHAPTER 18

*C*amilla was on her way to see Fiona when Max stopped her, stepping out of seemingly nowhere. "Good morning, my dear. And where are you off to, if I may ask?"

"To see Fiona. I am her assistant. She likes me to be punctual, so I always try to arrive a little early.

Max smiled eerily at the young girl. "Oh, I think Fiona can wait a few minutes. May I have a word with you?" Camilla couldn't imagine what Max would have to say to her, but she nodded silently. "In my office, if you please," he added, gesturing toward his wagon.

It was a short walk, but even one minute felt like a long time to be alone with her thoughts. There was something foreboding about the way in which Max accosted her, though she couldn't imagine for the life of her what she had done to garner his attention.

Once in the office, Max offered Camilla a seat on an old stool while he took a seat behind a craggy wooden desk. He didn't speak at first, but instead, allowed an uncomfortable silence to hang in the air.

Camilla shifted in her seat, unsure of what to do. She looked around at the assortment of circus posters hanging on the wagon walls and other paraphernalia strewn about—a shrine to Max's life's work. Looking back at Max, she saw he was staring at her intently. "I'm sorry," she finally blurted out. "Am I in trouble for something?"

Max chuckled, "Not at all. I just wanted to talk to the girl everyone has been making such a fuss over. I had to see for myself what all the hullabaloo is about."

"Oh? What have they been saying?"

"Well, for starters, I wouldn't have believed in a hundred years that you are that same scrap of an urchin I hired some weeks back. It's utterly astounding what a miraculous turnaround you've made, my dear. Enough to catch my star performer's eye, I hear." Max's sick smile returned.

Camilla blushed deeply.

"Oh, think nothing of it, darling. Frederick has always had a way with the ladies. That's nothing new. But then I've heard some rumors that are quite troubling."

"What sort of rumors, sir?"

"Is it true that you were seen riding our prized show horse,

Sugar?" Max's eyes began to narrow.

"Y-y-yes, sir. Only for a moment. You see, I-I-"

"Save it. You are nothing more than an assistant. Do you understand me?" Max pointed a finger in Camilla's face as the volume of his voice began to rise. "You will not risk me losing one of this show's most important assets because of some silly flirtation taking place. Do you hear me, missy?"

Camilla nodded, dumbfounded.

"And yes, I am aware that Frederick allowed it. Can't say that I blame a man for having a lapse of judgment where a pretty dame is concerned, but that's not the point. I am in no position to make demands of him; however, I can certainly make demands of the likes of you."

Despite her best efforts to remain stoic, tears began welling up in Camilla's eyes.

"Oh, stop crying. I don't go for tears. Just listen up and listen good. If he ever offers to let you ride that horse again, you refuse. Do you understand?"

Camilla was frozen with fear.

"I said, do you understand? Answer me!"

"Y-y-yes," she finally stammered.

"Good, then there is no reason to speak on this again. In fact, if I were you, I would avoid going around the animals at all. No need to invite temptation."

As much as this situation seemed unfair to Camilla, and as much as it pained her to never see the animals she had come to love, she didn't dare question Max. Instead, she apologized and promised it wouldn't happen again, just as he demanded.

After the altercation was put to rest, Max softened and lowered his tone. "Okay, that's all. I'm glad this didn't have to get unpleasant." He stood to walk Camilla out, putting a hand on her shoulder as she stood and squeezed lightly. "For all the shenanigans, I wouldn't want to lose a hard worker like you. And you certainly aren't terrible on the ol' eyes as it turns out. So, let's be friends, alright?"

Camilla shivered; she couldn't get out of there fast enough. She reassured Max once again that he would have nothing to worry about, then wished him a good day. She sensed that on another day, he may have tried to engage her longer, but he had other things on his mind, so he let her go.

⚜ ⚜ ⚜

Once she made her escape from Max's presence, Camilla ran straight to Fiona's wagon. She gave her customary knock but didn't wait for a reply before opening the door. Fiona was awaiting her arrival. "Where have you been, my dear? And why are you crying?"

Camilla's tears were now trickling down her cheeks, which reddened with embarrassment. "Oh, Fiona, I'm so sorry I'm late. I was on my way to see you when Max took me to his office to have a talk with me."

"Mon, mon. I worried about that," she said, shaking her head.

"How did you know?"

"Oh, dear, all anyone ever does around here is talk. They have nothing better to do."

"But what did I do wrong?"

"Oh, nothing, little one. You did nothing wrong at all. But there is an order to things. Come, tell me all about it." Fiona reached out to take Camilla's hand, led her to the edge of the bed, and handed her a handkerchief to dry her eyes.

Camilla wiped the tears away and then relayed the whole conversation to Fiona, not leaving out a single detail, including the final comment from Max that made her skin crawl. Fiona was very understanding, but she couldn't hide the look of concern on her face.

"Is everything all right? Did I mess up that badly?"

"Non, non, you couldn't have known. It's just that Max is very particular about things. He has to be careful with Frederick. He doesn't want to lose him, but he also likes to control everything. It was easy to make you his target, but what I am most concerned about is that now you have drawn attention to yourself. Do all you can to appease him, and hopefully, he will forget you. Besides, he has plenty on his plate right now, so I doubt he'll seek you out any time soon if you give him no reason to."

Camilla didn't understand this, but then she didn't understand so many things. She really was a naïve girl, so unaware of how the world worked. She ached for the safety of home. But there was no home to go back to, not the way she knew it anyway. If only she could return to the way things used to be, when she was wild and carefree. But then, she would never have known Frederick.

"Fiona," she began timidly, "What about Frederick? Why did he let me ride Sugar in the first place if he knew Max wouldn't like it? Is it possible he cares for me?"

"Listen, Cami, I would stay away from Frederick, too, if I were you. He's a fine person and all, and I'm sure he likes you well enough. You are a lovely girl, but circus people—this way of life—is not what you think. I don't want to see you get hurt."

Cami's spirit was fully deflated by now. She had felt so good the day before, so special. But what did she expect? Of course, Frederick could never care for her really—she knew that. But somehow, she had a small flicker of hope, and feeding that hope caused it to become a blazing fire. Now fully extinguished, Camilla nodded to Fiona and asked to be excused for a few moments. She stepped outside of the wagon and shed a few more tears, hoping no one would take notice of her, then stepped back inside and proceeded with her work for the day.

I am lucky, she told herself; *I am doing what I came here to do—save my land—and that's what I need to stay focused on. I can't blow it on silly girlhood fantasies.* Still, her heart fluttered at the prospect of seeing Frederick's performance that night, but she kept the thought quietly to herself.

CHAPTER 19

Two weeks passed, and every day since the elephant arrived, Max attempted to tame the beast to no avail. By now, everyone suspected the thing was too wild and would never be of any use to the circus. Max was determined to prove them all wrong and increased the hostility toward the animal as his crew surrounded it with whips and staffs.

Camilla couldn't bear to watch. She winced at every crack that echoed over the circus grounds as the poor creature trumpeted its cries. Fiona assured her that this was normal protocol for training new animals, but it didn't sit right with the young, sensitive girl. What did she know of such things? Still, her own farm animals never required such brutality and they never seemed to have trouble minding.

All this, of course, put Max in the foulest of moods, and

no one dared to come near him or inquire about how it was going. Even opening night in a new town had no positive impact on his stormy disposition. It all seemed a gigantic waste of resources, at least that's what everyone was saying.

This aside, Camilla was in fine spirits. The previous trouble with riding Sugar had subsided, and she did well to keep her head down, as Fiona suggested. She and Frederick crossed paths often, and each time they did, he would stop and ask how she was doing. Camilla enjoyed these minor interactions, and thankfully, he never brought up riding Sugar again. Camilla didn't care to tell him about her interaction with Max either, as she didn't want to create any more controversy than there already was, since she needed this job. She wondered if word had already gotten back to him yet. She was quickly learning that secrets were not easily kept among the troupe.

On this particular sunny afternoon, Camilla finished her chores early and decided to walk into town to mail off a few letters she had written. She also carried a stack given to her by Fiona, one of her many chores. She kept her correspondence fairly brief this time, feeling less inclined to share her experiences with anyone back home. Instead, she kept them light and was sure to include the money she had saved to send to her mother. It still pained her not to be able to receive word from her or Griffin, but she knew it was ultimately for the best.

On her way back, she once again spotted Frederick riding Sugar a ways off in a nearby field. He saw her and waved, so she waved back. This prompted the equestrian to call out, "It's a beautiful day! How about a ride?"

Internally, Camilla felt panic wash over her. "No, thank you. I mean, thank you, but I have to get back right away. Sorry!" With that, she began to hustle away, not even daring to look in Frederick's direction.

Frederick continued calling after her without success. Camilla was determined to avoid the situation at all costs. She eventually went from a trot to a sprint as she could hear Frederick coming, not far behind. "Hey, Cami," he called again. "I want to ask you something, wait..." but she refused to turn around.

To her relief, she approached the grounds before he could catch up and ran to Fiona's wagon. Fiona was standing outside talking to one of her fellow tightrope walkers, but Camilla didn't stop to say hello. Instead, she ran inside, closing the door behind her, doing her best to avoid a confrontation. Her hastiness took Fiona by surprise, but as she noticed Frederick's approach, it began to make sense. He tied up Sugar to a nearby post and seemed unsure what to do next.

"What's gotten into that girl, anyway?" he said more to himself than anyone.

Fiona abruptly ended her conversation with the other performer and approached Frederick delicately. "Hey, what's going on here?"

"I have no idea. I wanted to talk to Cami, and she just took off. Is she mad at me or something?"

Fiona crossed her arms. "What are you doing, Frederick? Why don't you leave the poor girl alone?"

"What do you mean? I haven't done a thing to her. I just wanted to talk to her, and she took off."

"Then it's probably just as well."

Frederick looked incredulous. "What do you mean?"

"You know just what I mean. Leading the poor girl on like that."

"Look, Fiona, I haven't done a thing. I only…"

"But of course you did. Why did you let her ride Sugar? What were you thinking?"

Frederick gave a toothy, confident grin. "Because she likes horses. I don't think there's any harm in that."

Fiona leaned in to lower her voice so no one around could hear her. "Of course there is, when the girl thinks she's in love with you."

"In love with me? Oh, what nonsense. Nothing more than a slight infatuation. Happens to all young girls."

"I don't think so, Frederick. I think she really believes you care for her. Look at the lengths you were willing to go for her. You even got Max's ire up, and he dressed down the poor thing. How will she feel when she finds out she is nothing to you?"

"I never said she was nothing to me."

"But we both know she's not. You've been through this with a hundred girls before, Frederick. Don't start with this one. Cami is a nice girl, and she doesn't have a friend in the world—

except me. And I warned her to stay away from you, so just back off, okay?"

"Fiona, you had no right—"

"I said, lay off," Fiona replied sharply. She then turned on her heel and went to her wagon, where Camilla sat waiting, on the verge of tears.

"I didn't know what to do, Fiona. He offered me another ride, and I didn't want to cause any more trouble with Max. I had no choice but to walk away. I hope he doesn't think I'm mad at him. Maybe I should talk to him." Camilla began to rise, but Fiona put out a hand to stop her.

"No worries, my dear. I already talked to Frederick. You were right to avoid the situation. Everything is okay. Now let's work on my stretches before showtime."

The following morning, Camilla went to the food tent to pick up breakfast for Fiona and herself. She was surprised to see Frederick already there, waiting. It was not like him to be up so early. "Can we talk?" he asked gently.

"Where, here?"

"No, let's go outside."

Camilla looked around to see who might be watching

them. No one seemed to be paying attention, but still, she was nervous. "I don't think it would be a good idea to go for a ride or anything..."

Frederick grabbed her hand. "No riding. Let's just take a walk."

The warmth of Frederick's touch rose to her cheeks, hot and tingly, as they walked off together. Once outside, he released her hand and placed his hands behind his back as they trekked a path that led beyond the circus grounds. Once they were well out of earshot, they walked slightly off the path to a nearby tree for some privacy.

Camilla leaned against a tree and looked up at the leaves quivering in the breeze. It reminded her of the day she saw Frederick out in the field riding Sugar, only not nearly so hot and humid. Frederick stood in front of her as if reading her thoughts. "It was a beautiful day that time I ran into you, and we rode back to town together."

Camilla looked down, afraid to meet Frederick's gaze as if she might melt under it. "It sure was." The memory of holding him tightly came rushing back to her.

"Listen, Cami, whatever Fiona told you about me, it's not true. I mean, yes, maybe I do have a reputation for being a fun guy, but I am not playing games. I genuinely like you. I didn't mean to get you into trouble with Max or anything."

"She told you about that?" She said, finally looking up. "I really wish she hadn't. I didn't want to cause any issues, is all."

"It's okay," he reassured her. "I'm glad I know. But don't worry, I won't get you into any more trouble. On my word, my motives toward you are sincere. There's something different about you. I don't know exactly what it is, but I'd like to find out."

"But I'm just an assistant. And you...you're a great performer...you're Frederick the Elastic Fantastic. The star of the show."

Frederick blushed slightly at her admiration of him. "Oh, dear Cami, you think much too highly of me. You are right, though—you're not like me. There is something honest and true about you. I can see it in the kindness you show the animals and the crew, even when you think no one is watching. But I notice. You see, it's so very lonely on the road, and the last thing I need is the company of another competitive performer. I need a true friend."

This caused a smile to spread wide across Camilla's sincere, freckled face. "I'd be happy to be a friend in whatever way I can," she said. "I just don't know where to start."

Frederick lifted a hand to caress her cheek, then gazed intently into both her eyes, looking back and forth, down at her mouth, and then forth and back. The feeling this elicited caused Camilla's world to spin in place. She suddenly felt dizzy. "Here's one way you can start..." he breathed tenderly, then softly brushed his lips atop hers, causing the earth to tremble. Was this really happening, or was it her imagination?

CHAPTER 20

*I*t was only a short while ago that Camilla knew nothing of love, nor did she desire it. She never daydreamed about such things, as was typical of girls her age. Frederick was the wild card she never expected. She only wanted to do right by her mother and honor her father's memory. The last thing on her mind was finding love, but love found her anyway. And it made her into a woman overnight.

Now, knowing such feelings, she reflected once again on Griffin and his untimely proposal. How odd it seemed to her then that something as prosaic as marriage should be on the lad's mind when the world was falling apart around her. But in that same crumbling world, Camilla discovered that love was a great rejuvenator. She was never more alive with hope since losing her father than she was at the moment.

Marriage was still far from her mind, though. For now, she just wanted to think on the memory of her first romantic kiss, for never did she imagine the sign of affection so casually bestowed upon her as a child could be so thrilling in other conditions. Never had she experienced such sensations coursing through her veins, and she longed to experience them once again. But something gave her pause.

Both Max and Fiona alluded to the idea that Frederick was no stranger to making such advances. And Frederick himself admitted as much, though he also expressed sincerity where she was concerned. She wanted to believe that somehow, she was different in his eyes, but what had she ever done that would warrant his favor? Since joining the circus, she had made little of herself, aside from a physical transformation. Was that enough to win the heart of the "fantastic" performer, or should there be more?

All Camilla knew was that she didn't want Frederick to share these experiences with anyone else. Hadn't her mother and father only ever belonged to one another? She wished she could ask her mother about such things. She knew what felt right, but could her feelings be trusted when she had proven so ignorant of the world, time and time again?

Camilla decided it was a good idea to follow Frederick's suggestion of spending time together to learn more about each other. It seemed a reasonable proposition, but who was she, after all? She wasn't sure anymore. Back home, she was carefree and full of spirit, but now she was out of her element, and it left her feeling timid and insignificant, like one of the caged animals at the mercy of their master, Max. Under her father's care, she had never known such feelings of insecurity, even as a girl no more desirable than a rag doll.

Today may be a new beginning—for both of us, she said to herself. After their kiss, she and Frederick had walked back to their tented city together, but not before he asked if she would join him for a picnic lunch the following day. Time alone and away from the spying eyes of the meddling troupe sounded ideal. Perhaps this would allow her the opportunity to figure out where she stood in Frederick's eyes.

As Camilla tended to her chores the following day, she found herself whistling the morning away, which began to arouse Fiona's suspicion. Despite her inquisitive looks, Camilla thought better of sharing the cause for her happy mood or her afternoon plans. Somehow, she knew Fiona wouldn't approve and might try to talk her out of it. But Camilla was already determined in her heart to go.

Instead, she worked quietly and swiftly, mending two leotards and a frayed tutu. She also added new laces to the dancer's favorite boots as the old ones were brittle and broken. She lovingly admired the boots as she brought them back to life with the new laces and a fresh shine. What would Frederick think of her in a pair of boots as brilliant as these? Maybe one day she would have a pair of her own. How smart they would look with the frilly blue dress given to her by Fiona!

Camilla sighed with longing, finished the rest of her morning tasks, took a quick peek in the mirror of Fiona's vanity to ensure she still looked presentable, and then took off with hardly a goodbye. Fiona, who was in a contorted pose, barely took notice, except for the closing of the wagon door, which broke her concentration. "Now where is she off to in such a hurry?" she asked herself, though she had her suspicions.

Frederick was still in his wagon when Camilla came looking for him. They hadn't picked a particular meeting place, so she decided to wait near the food tent as it was a central location on the circus grounds where you could see people coming and going. While pacing the grounds, she happened to notice that Max and his select crew were at it again with the elephant, Rocco and Wolfie among them. She looked away, not wanting anything to spoil her lovely thoughts, as it pained her to see the unfortunate animal the object of their relentless scorn.

Frederick soon approached. Camilla was relieved and greeted him with a smile. He seemed in good spirits too, which she needed right then. They entered the food tent to fill a wicker basket for their picnic, and the pair was on their way.

As they walked, Camilla tried to shake her troubling feelings regarding the elephant, but couldn't get it off her mind. "Frederick," she finally asked, "Do you suppose Max will ever tame that elephant?"

"I certainly hope so—for all our sakes."

"Why do you say that? Fiona seemed to think it was a threat to bring it here."

"Well, she is right in one regard—it would be sure to take attention away from the other performers, at least for a time—but now that it's here it's absolutely imperative that they find a way to put the darn thing to use."

Camilla nodded but still didn't fully understand. Frederick led her by the hand through a nearby meadow and over to a shady grove, ideal for their lunch date. He set down the basket and spread out a blanket he'd been carrying. They turned to face the rolling meadow, blanketed with tall, feathery grass dotted with delicate white wildflowers. Against the horizon were layers of cascading hillsides, perfectly framing the picturesque landscape. They took a moment to drink it in, satisfied with their place of refuge.

Once comfortably seated, Frederick spoke again, "You see, Camilla, Max sunk everything he had into that beast. He was so convinced that this would be our bread and butter that he took a huge risk in purchasing it. If he doesn't make it work, well, the entire circus is 'finito.' Do you understand?"

She did. "Well, I can see why it's made Max insufferable.

I avoid him at all costs."

"Yes, he can be quite a bear, but this is not Max's first major risk, though it may be his biggest—and his riskiest. But let's not talk of unpleasant things. Let's enjoy this beautiful day. The air will soon turn cool, and we'll have fewer of them."

Camilla couldn't agree more. Fall was close at hand, and she wanted nothing more than to draw her focus on this warm, sunny afternoon alone with Frederick. How beautiful he was. His dark, wavy hair fell slightly over his eyes, which sparkled at her obvious admiration.

"What is it you see in me, little one?" he asked.

"Are you kidding me? I've never known anyone like you in all my life. You're strong, you're brave, incredibly talented, kind..."

"Am I not handsome?" he grinned playfully.

"Yes, I suppose you are." Camilla looked down, feeling her face get hot.

"Don't you know, all these things are illusions? It's just a show. If you knew me, the real me, I doubt you would maintain such a high opinion."

For the life of her, Camilla couldn't imagine what she would ever find out about Frederick to change her good opinion of him, but it did pique her interest in getting to know him better—and for him to know her. "I'm not much to speak of either, yet here you are with me. Of all girls."

Frederick scooted closer. "Some people, you just get a

good feeling about." He took Camilla's hand and kissed it lightly, sending shivers through her. "Now, let's eat. I'm famished."

They ate together, talking away. He sure knew how to make her laugh. He was quite the performer off stage as well as on. He teased her a bit, too, especially how she had changed so much since their first meeting, but not in any way that made her feel bad.

"You were kind to me even then," she said.

"Well, see, I knew you were a nice kid."

"I'm not always nice, you know. You could ask Griffin. He'd tell you. I can have a real temper!"

Frederick raised an eyebrow. "Oh, and who is this Griffin? Someone I should be concerned about?"

"Not at all. He is just my old friend back home. We've known each other since forever. I was actually pretty mean to him when I left. I'm not sure he would even talk to me again if I saw him."

"I can't believe you'd be mean to anyone." Frederick grinned at the thought and scooted even closer.

"Well, not that I'm proud of it. I'm working on being more of a lady. Fiona is helping me."

Frederick chuckled, "Oh, Fiona, Fiona. She is a great girl, as far as they go, but I wouldn't necessarily classify her as a lady. No, that is one area you have up on her."

Camilla couldn't believe her ears. How could anyone see Fiona as anything but a great lady? And she certainly had been a good friend, something she emphasized in response.

"Oh, I have no doubt you make a nice pet for dear Fiona. But just remember, she is a performer like all the rest, and the spotlight will always be her first love."

Camilla didn't want to talk badly about Fiona. The look of sadness on her face pained Frederick, so he apologized and promised to stop talking Fiona down. "Let's get back to you then," he continued. "I refuse to believe you were ever anything but sweet and pleasant. This Griffin is going to have to answer to me if he says otherwise."

Now it was Camilla's turn to chuckle. "Oh, no worries. I doubt you'll ever meet him. Home is a million miles away."

"Good, because I don't need any additional competition."

"No one could ever compete with you, where I'm concerned, Frederick." Camilla's boldness was returning to her. This time she looked him square in the eyes—eyes that penetrated her soul, just as before.

Again, Frederick inched closer to Camilla. She leaned back slightly, teasing him a bit, which only tempted him to pursue her all the more. And before either knew it, they became a tangled mess, locked in a passionate embrace.

Camilla could barely catch her breath as she and Frederick slowly walked back to the circus grounds. Frederick was a perfect gentleman—almost. Sure, they may have given in to the moment a bit, but they stopped short of anything that would be considered truly scandalous. Still, she was glad no one was around to see the amorous display and add to the steadily increasing gossip about their relationship.

Even as she was filled with warmth at the thought of her lips being locked with Frederick's for the better part of their time together, these lovely reflections came to a screeching halt with the sound of the elephant, once again trumpeting its displeasure and stomping against the ground.

Camilla and Frederick followed the sound, almost beyond their own will, to find Wolfie whipping the animal mercilessly while Rocco hit him with a long wooden rod, both laughing all the while. "You stupid pachyderm, we'll teach you." Max was nowhere to be seen, but the elephant was tied in several places against the tree, fighting against their brutality with all its might, with no success.

Crack! The whip flew again, this time landing across the animal's face, causing a slash mark across the cheek near its eye, a trickle of blood beginning to spill. Laughter came from the men once again as Rocco landed the rod hard against the elephant's knees, causing it to cry out in pain.

Horrified at the sight, and without thinking, Camilla screamed, "Nooooo!!!!" and rushed between the two men.

Frederick tried to stop her, but she was as wild as the elephant. Without fear for her own life, she grabbed the rod from Rocco with ease, as he was taken off guard, and began swinging it toward Wolfie with abandon. "Stop it! Stop it this minute, you brute! Stop it!"

Wolfie, gathering his bearings, stood firm with the whip in his hand. "Don't do anything stupid, girly. You don't want to get hurt now, do you?"

Camilla couldn't have been less concerned about her own safety at the moment. She was about to lunge at the man with the rod when Frederick stood between them with his hands in the air. "Look, Wolfie, let's not get carried away. What in the world do you two think you are doing anyway?"

"We're on Max's orders," the man growled.

"Oh, and would Max be pleased to know that you are marring his future star's face? Is that part of his orders?"

Both Wolfie and Rocco were quiet.

"I'll tell you what, you leave now and we won't say a word. But you need to get out of here, or this will be the end for you both."

The men were anything but pleased, being pushed around by the privileged performer, but they also knew he was right. Max would not take well to Frederick telling him what they had been up to—abusing the animal, though it posed no immediate threat.

"Fine," Wolfie said, throwing the whip down, "But this isn't over. All you stars think you'll shine forever, but your star will

160

fall like they always do, and then you're gonna get it good."

Rocco nodded in agreement, and the two men walked away, just as before. For now, Frederick's word held sway.

Camilla threw the rod down and collapsed to the ground, weeping. Frederick put his arms around the forlorn girl and helped her back to her feet. "It's okay, everything is okay. Those guys were really out of line this time. It's a good thing we got here when we did."

Camilla began to approach the beast, but it quivered with terror, still in shock from the abuse it suffered. Frederick pulled her away before any more harm was done. "Come on, Cami, let's get out of here." But she looked back at the elephant, her heart overflowing with compassion as Frederick pulled her along back to the wagons.

CHAPTER 21

Frederick dropped Camilla off at Fiona's wagon after lunch, but not before making sure she had calmed down from the incident with Wolfie and Rocco. "I admit I was wrong about those two, but don't worry, everything will be okay," he reassured her. She wanted to believe him, but those two thugs had always put her on edge, and now they were making threats.

Camilla tried to settle her nerves and spent the rest of the afternoon helping Fiona prepare for the nightly show. The tightrope walker was too distracted with her own troubles to notice Camilla was not her usual talkative self. She had ripped a parasol and was fretting over the possibility that she had put on a few pounds, as her costume was feeling a little snug. Camilla did well to reassure her she was the picture of perfection, but Fiona continued to whine about it for the rest of their time together.

Despite the dramatics and her declarations to go on a diet immediately, it didn't stop Fiona from heading over to the food tent to get dinner before warming up for the show. Camilla was emotionally spent and thankful to be alone again. Her tummy ached too much to get dinner. Instead, she snuck across the grounds, determined to see how the poor elephant was doing.

Surprisingly, the animal was still tied to the tree, unable to move. Camilla stood observing it, considering what to do next. It was a pathetic sight. Out of compassion, she finally made a slow approach, unsure if it would lash out at her with its enormous trunk. It didn't move at all, as if it were finally defeated. Camilla cautiously worked her way closer, just as she would a wild horse or a moody cow. She had dealt with her fair share of animals and could easily read the signs of danger, but the elephant was giving off none.

Even as she came to its side, the elephant stood stock still. She reached out to untie the ropes that were hugging it the tightest around the large oak tree. The elephant finally flinched at the first sign of touch, but Camilla hushed it, speaking in tender tones, "It's okay, I won't hurt you. I'm here to help."

Camilla got to work loosening all the ropes, daring to untie another with each success. She didn't have the faintest idea of what she was going to do once the thing was finally free, but something deep in her soul compelled her to continue on.

Unbeknownst to her, Wolfie was outside securing pegs on the circus tent when he caught sight of them both. Without hesitation, he went in search of Max to inform him of what Camilla was up to, hoping to gain favor with the ringmaster. Meanwhile, Camilla finally got the elephant untied, leaving only the rope around its neck. In response to freedom, it raised its feet high in the air, causing Camilla to back away. She fell on her backside, a bit unsure of what it would do now, but once it landed back on the ground, it stood still once again.

After sensing she was not in danger, Camilla got up and then dared to approach the elephant once more. She gently laid a hand on its face where it had been cut with the whip. "You poor, poor thing," she spoke gently. The elephant nodded but showed no signs of aggression. She patted it again, and it lifted its trunk as a sign of pleasure at the sign of affection.

Max marched toward the scene with Wolfie, full of rage at what had been reported. "How dare she cross me. That little dog is out of here!" he screamed. But as he approached, he stopped short at what he saw.

Now was the true moment of boldness. Camilla gently grabbed the rope that was tied around the pachyderm's neck and began to lead it. To her great surprise, it followed with little resistance. She eventually got it into a nearby empty stall, stroking and assuring the compliant creature that it was a "good elephant." Again, it raised its trunk, patting Camilla gently on the head as a gesture of gratitude.

She then looked around to find something for the poor thing to eat but could find nothing nearby. She decided to go to the main stable to see what she could scrounge up when Max fast approached. "Why, hello there, my girl. How are you this evening?" He greeted her in a sickeningly sweet tone.

Camilla was hesitant, unsure if she was about to get reamed. "I'm fine."

"And what are you up to, my dear?" Camilla was silent. "Never mind that," he said. "You have nothing to fear. I saw you with that elephant. Tell me, how did you get it to obey you so well?"

Camilla was caught in the act, and there was no getting out of it, so she simply shrugged. "I don't know. It just did."

"Well, come." he grabbed the girl's arm. "Show me!"

Max and Camilla approached the stall where the elephant stood awaiting her return. As the two drew closer, it immediately showed signs of being erratic once more. "I think you should back away," the girl said. Max didn't like taking orders from anyone, but with so much on the line, he decided to do as she requested.

With Max far enough back, Camilla was once again able to approach the animal with ease. It was calm and lowered its head in response to her touch.

"Well, I'll be..." Max said, a new plan brewing in his business-minded little head.

Fiona was none too happy when Camilla delivered the news. "Why, you little traitor!" she spat.

"Honest, Fiona, I didn't want to betray you. What was I supposed to say? Max told me if I don't do it, the whole circus could go under."

Fiona crossed her arms, sticking her nose in the air. "I just can't believe you're abandoning me when I need you most. After all I have done. Have I not been good to you?"

"Of course you have, I couldn't be more grateful. But Max was very insistent. Can you please try to understand? I promise I'll make sure you have an even better assistant than I was. Please don't be cross, your friendship is so important to me, and I need it now more than ever!" Camilla pleaded.

Though she had a bit of a temper, Fiona was never one to stay mad for long. Hearing the girl's pleas and her predicament to please Max, she let up, despite her own troubles. "Yes, I do understand, but I'm not happy. Mon dieu! Whatever will I do now?"

"I don't start training until tomorrow, so I will still help you with whatever you need done today. Just say you forgive me."

"Enough of that, little one. Yes, I forgive you. But I don't know of what help I can be to you. You belong to Max now, and there is nothing more that can be done. I tried to warn you, but now you will see. Oh, mon, let's just enjoy our last day together. Come, have a drink with me. I save it for special occasions."

Fiona pulled out two long-stemmed glasses and a bottle

of wine. She poured the drink liberally into each glass, handing one to Camilla. Having never tasted wine before, Camilla was eager to try it, but the taste was bitter on her tongue, and she could not take more than a couple of sips. Fiona, however, downed hers without a second thought, then took the glass from the inexperienced girl and downed hers too. "Well, I guess that's it," she said, raising the empty glass. "To show business!"

Camilla could hardly believe it herself. Max had asked her not only to train the elephant, but if she proved her ability to do it successfully, she would become a part of the nightly shows. Just imagine, Camilla, Little Cami, sharing the stage with Frederick and Fiona! It was beyond her wildest imagination. She couldn't wait to share the exciting news with Frederick. *Hopefully, he'll be more receptive than Fiona.*

CHAPTER 22

*F*rederick was flabbergasted. The sudden turn of events with Camilla going from Fiona's assistant to training the intended main attraction of the circus was beyond anything he anticipated when she said she had to talk to him. He had worried that perhaps the whole incident with Wolfie and Rocco had gotten back to Max, and he had taken out his rage on the young girl again. But this news left him utterly speechless.

"I know, it's crazy. I had no idea things would turn out this way. And who knows, maybe it will all blow up in my face in the end. I'm really scared, Frederick. But I feel like I have no choice." Camilla was rubbing her hands and pacing.

"You are right—you have no choice but to comply or leave. At this point, Max is desperate, and you may be his ticket to breaking even in this whole fiasco. But what do you know about training an elephant? It could be dangerous."

"Isn't everything in the circus dangerous, though?" Her courage was building.

"Well, yes, but we have years of training. You're going into this with absolutely no experience whatsoever."

"That's not true! I have worked with animals my whole life. My pa taught me everything I know. Did you ever think maybe that's why I was able to approach the elephant when no one else could?"

Frederick shook his head, "I don't doubt you have a way with them. I've seen it myself, but I'd be lying if I didn't say that I am concerned about your safety. Only you can decide if you can handle it or not, though. Just know that if you fail, it will certainly put an end to your employment here. And what will you do about your farm then? You need to think about that. Because no question, Max will be rid of you if you don't succeed."

Camilla trembled at the thought of being separated from Frederick so soon into their budding romance. "Yes, I am sure you are right, but at this point, he'll be rid of me if I don't try. I've got to give it a shot, Frederick. It's the only way, and I believe I have a good chance at doing this. I am the only one the elephant seems to trust at this point, so I must be doing something right."

Frederick couldn't argue with her. They both knew she couldn't say no. Although the conversation didn't go quite the way Camilla imagined it would, she now had the resolve to face the situation head-on. Strength was rising within her after weighing her options, and she was utterly convinced of what she had to do. She could very well fail miserably, but she was sure to walk away with nothing if she didn't give it a shot. And success would change everything for the better. Perhaps now she would feel worthy of Frederick's affections. There was no dissuading her determination now.

The next morning, Camilla rose early to get breakfast and headed over to where the animals were kept. She had eaten little the past couple of days and didn't want to start on an empty stomach. Feeling satisfied and full of nervous energy, Camilla made her way over to where the elephant was kept. Dominick was up and standing around as if waiting for her arrival.

"So, you're really gonna do it, huh?" Apparently, he was fully informed of what was expected of the young girl.

Camilla nodded with a look of fortitude. "I'm certainly going to give it my best shot."

"Well, your best had better get the job done. We're all depending on it."

"Gee, no pressure," she replied, rolling her eyes.

"Hey, we're friends, right? I'm just telling you the truth. But if it makes you feel any better, I'm rooting for you. You are our best hope."

Camilla smiled. "Thank you, Dominick. I needed to hear that."

Dominick walked over to the elephant's wagon with her to unlock the door. "Better stand back," she warned. "The fewer people standing here when I open the door, the better."

"Are you sure you'll be all right?"

Camilla nodded, "Let's hope."

Dominick walked away but continued watching from afar as the girl slowly opened the wagon door. The elephant was in a sitting position, as if waiting for the girl. In reality, it had little room to do much else but sit and stand. Camilla's first priority was to get a read on the elephant's temperament—it seemed unprovoked by her presence.

Slowly, she entered the wagon, speaking words of assurance in a hushed voice. As she drew closer, she reached her hand out, placing it gently on the upper region of its trunk, between the eyes. It shook its head in reaction to the touch, so Camilla pulled away, then tried again. This time, the animal didn't flinch.

Continuing to speak softly, she encouraged the animal to get on its feet. Surprisingly, it obeyed and stood at full attention. Within the confines of the wagon walls, it seemed unlikely to lash out or do anything incredibly unpredictable, so Camilla decided this would be the best opportunity to check its sex.

She walked carefully to the side, never releasing her hand from the elephant's large body. Once in full view, she crouched down to look beneath the trunk and spotted two breasts underneath the front legs. "You're a girl!" she proclaimed. She didn't know much about the anatomy of an elephant, but from the looks of it, it seemed she may have given birth recently. Satisfied,

Camilla decided not to examine further. She could only imagine what came of the offspring, and it caused her to wonder if that didn't contribute to her distress.

"Poor girl." She said sweetly. "Now to give you a proper name." Camilla thought of her mother's philosophy on such things: *You must always choose a name to suit a person's destined station in life.* "You are a regal creature," she said, determining its fate. "How about Duchess?"

The elephant raised its trunk in agreement.

"Then Duchess it is!"

The next challenge was to get Duchess out of the wagon. The rope that hung around the elephant's neck was still there. Camilla took the rope gently and began to back slowly toward the wagon door. Duchess didn't budge at first, so Camilla waited before trying again. "C'mon, dear, you can do it," she said, picking up the rope and trying again.

This time, Duchess began walking toward her as she carefully walked backwards, making her way down the broad wooden steps of the wagon. It took a moment, but the elephant began to follow suit. Eventually, she managed to coax Duchess all the way out, and she was now standing perfectly docile upon the dusty earth. Dominick could not believe his eyes.

Camilla then led Duchess to the stall, gently opening and closing the gate to avoid alarming the skittish creature. Once inside, Cami leaned against the rail to catch her breath. She couldn't believe she managed to do so well on her first day. By now, Max had joined Dominick to watch the girl do the seemingly impossible. A small crowd gathered behind them to watch as well. Some sighed in relief, others were skeptical she would be able to do much with it beyond this point, and others were visibly distressed that the animal would become the star of the circus that it was intended to be.

Camilla was unaware of all these things though. Her focus was squarely on Duchess. She was too busy reading her mood, careful not to upset her in any way. She then began to lead Duchess slowly around the stall with relative ease. Though the crowd of observers had grown, no one dared come close or call out to Camilla. Mostly, they just watched in stunned silence that this was the same wild beast that was unlikely to ever be tamed. It now seemed as harmless as a bovine.

They went on this way most of the morning, Camilla's main goal was to get the elephant some exercise, though still mindful of the injuries it may have sustained at the hand of Rocco's rod. After some time of responding to simple leading, she worked on getting Duchess back into her wagon so she could go to lunch. By now she was emotionally and physically spent and in need of rest and sustenance. Dominick assisted her in locking the door, and off she went, in hopes of seeing Frederick to share all the details about her first morning as an elephant trainer.

Max was still beside himself at the unbelievable turn of events. Once Camilla was out of sight, he urged one of the animal trainers, a husky man named George, to try and re-engage the pachyderm. In a show of bravado, he approached the elephant's wagon, with the key in hand, and attempted to unlock the door. But before he could even turn it, the elephant began stomping around erratically once again. Duchess was having none of it.

CHAPTER 23

*T*he next few days consisted of more of the same type of mild exercise for Duchess. Camilla knew it was important to ensure that the animal grew more accustomed to her and to also gain strength and confidence before pushing it beyond that point. Easy walks around the stall, along with working on hand feeding, kept them both busy enough. Trust building was Camilla's first aim. The progress would have to be gradual, but as long as there was indeed progress, she was satisfied. She only hoped Max would also be satisfied and would not try to rush the process.

Frederick was encouraging, if not a bit overly concerned. Not that he didn't believe Camilla was capable, but he also knew what was at stake. The crowds would soon diminish as they went into their slower season, and financially, the circus was already struggling to get by. Max was pushing the performers harder than ever to work on improving their acts, to show more enthusiasm as they rolled into a new town, and to drum up more interest in the side shows.

But such is the life of a traveling circus. As exciting as living on the road seemed to Camilla, it was also very cyclical in nature; the grand entrance into town, the build-up of the nightly shows, the grand finale of the final performance, and then off to the next town to do it all over again. In many respects, one day seemed very much like another.

That didn't bother Camilla much. The setup of the circus grounds was very much the same from one town to the next, so even though they were constantly on the move, it very much had a feeling of home. It was as though within this perimeter, life was completely static. The outside changed, but the inside stayed the same.

She now understood the familial bonds that were formed among the troupe. So, too, did she understand why some people who had glamorized a life in the circus ultimately found it to be monotonous. But those who truly loved it, and most of them did, created their own excitement. It was a great incentive for developing one's act. The clowns had worked out several routines, which they changed up nightly to keep things fresh for the crowds, as well as themselves. Camilla had pretty much memorized them all by now, but still found much pleasure in watching them just the same.

Settling once again in a new town, Camilla and Frederick

made plans for a long lunch. Both having the flexibility to set their own hours, Frederick's offer to take her away for the afternoon proved far too great a temptation for her to stay behind and work. Besides, she mentally needed the break. She had thought of nothing but elephants for days—they even invaded her dreams.

A book on the topic that she happened across in a bookshop a couple of towns back didn't help keep the continuous thoughts of elephants at bay, as it taught her a great deal about Duchess. For instance, she was what they called an Asian elephant. More specifically, an Indian elephant. The more Camilla discovered, the more she felt confident in her ability to work with the animal. In fact, she was feeling brave enough to start taking their training to the next level.

But for now, she was looking forward to a break. Tempting as it was to take it with her, she left the book under her pillow. No thoughts of pachyderms this afternoon.

Frederick seemed content to not talk about circus life either. The good news for everyone was that Max had returned to his enthusiastic self. This meant he was less testy with the troupe—though he was never completely void of the occasional tantrum. Toward Camilla, he was sweet as pie. She held the promise of the lucrative opportunity he dreamed of, so for now, he did his best to accommodate her.

Camilla's demands were few, but she was more than a little overjoyed when the ringmaster revoked his command that she not ride any of the horses, including Sugar. After proving herself to be quite proficient with animals, especially Duchess, he saw no reason not to trust her, or so he said. And speaking of Duchess, he loved the name so much he chose to make it her official moniker. Yes, Camilla was quite satisfied at the moment with how things were developing.

Frederick was also pleased about the news regarding Sugar. He took the first opportunity to exercise their renewed privilege and invited Camilla for a ride. They intended to put some distance between themselves and the circus grounds and find a spot to enjoy their lunch together in solitude.

The two of them rode on for several miles before finding a perfect location to stop for a bite. Once again, Frederick laid out the blanket for them to set up their picnic. Both feeling famished, they decided to eat right away. The moment was peaceful, with a few clouds drifting in the sky. It was a telltale sign of rain to come, but for now, there was no concern of it interfering with their day.

After lunch, Frederick leaned against the tree trunk they sat under, while Camilla rested her head in his lap dreamily. It seemed their most beautiful times together were under a tree. This one was set snugly near a babbling creek, the sound of which tickled their ears like music. The setting was like something out of a storybook, which soothed their weary souls.

"Frederick," Camilla began after some silent dreaming, "Do you consider yourself lucky? I mean, to have lived this life?"

Frederick thought about it for a moment, then said, "No, I don't think I ever considered myself lucky. I did what I had to do to survive."

"But you do love it, don't you?"

"I suppose I do. I'm good at it, and it's always ideal if you can make your way in the world doing something you're good at. I *love* the applause. But I don't know if it's what I would have chosen had I been given the option."

"What do you mean?" Camilla propped herself up on one elbow to get a better look at his face.

"Well, I told you I left home when I was twelve. I suppose you could say I was lucky that I found someone kind enough to take me on and teach me a new trade, but I guess I wish things had been different in the first place."

Camilla searched his expression, noting the brooding nature behind his eyes. "Please tell me."

"Oh, everyone has their sad stories. Are you sure you want to hear mine? It's not that interesting, really."

"Yes, I want to know," she replied simply.

"Well, my mom, she died when I was nine. My memory of her has mostly faded, but I do remember that no one loved me better in all my life. But my dad. Well, he was taken to drink and had a mean temper. Once my mother died, it only got worse. I ran away from home because I couldn't take it anymore. I thought he'd kill me, or I'd kill him first. It wasn't good anyway."

Camilla lifted her hand and softly caressed Frederick's cheek. "I'm so sorry, you deserved better." While Camilla certainly had her own sad story, she had a wonderful father, and it hurt her to know Frederick did not have such a luxury. "Where is he now?" she finally asked.

"I don't know, dead I suspect. I left and never looked back."

It was Camilla's turn to make a move. She sat up straight and leaned in to bestow a soft kiss on Frederick's lips. A desire sprang up in her to give him the sincere love and affection he had gone without since the passing of his mother. For the first time in her life, Camilla thought of marriage. *If he ever asks me to be his wife, I'll give everything I have for his happiness.*

CHAPTER
24

Once again, Camilla was up with the sun and ready to take on the day. After her little break in the country with Frederick, she was energized and ready to take her training with Duchess to the next level. One good place to start was teaching the elephant to sit. Cami tried to look around for some good treats to entice Duchess with. There was always plenty of hay around the circus. Still, the elephant seemed especially fond of willow tree branches or apples, and right now Cami was ready to utilize any motivational tools at her disposal. So, she gathered up a nice-sized pile of her favorite treats, throwing in a few carrots and sweet potatoes for good measure.

It took a little coercion, but with a bit of patience, Cami was able to successfully train the elephant to sit by late afternoon.

Duchess was surprisingly eager to please when handled in a calm, gentle manner. Camilla figured it would take some consistent training to get any of the new commands to stick, but for now, Duchess was showing herself to be an eager learner, which excited the young girl.

The following morning, they did more sitting exercises, but then Camilla began teaching Duchess to stand on a wooden platform with her enormous front feet. It wasn't remarkably entertaining to anyone passing by, but making so much progress in training technique, trust building, and effective communication laid the foundation for the regal beast to easily transition into learning feats suitable for a spectacular circus act.

Sure enough, Camilla's instincts and steadfastness were paying off quickly, and the two became quite inseparable. Most of Cami's time was spent working with the elephant, and when she wasn't in direct training, she was reading books about elephants that she picked up in bookstores in towns along the way. Her mind was constantly focused on the next course of action.

Even with Frederick, Cami could barely contain her excitement. He was patient and kind, but she began to sense that her nonstop obsession was starting to take a toll on his attention span. "I think it's wonderful how far you've come, my little one." He would reassure her, but then he would kiss her hand and suggest they talk of other things.

Camilla would blush and make a genuine effort to turn her attention back to the star she so lovingly admired. He was no less brilliant in her eyes; it was just nice to have something of her own to share. She also hoped that being more than an assistant would elevate her in Frederick's eyes; that perhaps they might have more in common.

As the weeks passed, Cami also found herself thinking of home less and less. It was a far-off dream to her now. Circus life had become her normal. She often began to lose sight of why she joined the circus in the first place. All she could think of was getting Duchess ready for their big debut. Max seemed to understand the time it would take to train a wild animal while still insisting they show Duchess to the world as soon as possible. He hoped it wouldn't be long before he could begin recouping some of the money it cost to keep the elephant well-fed. "Everyone here has to earn their keep, animals are no exception," he would boom. Cami understood and promised to do her best to prepare quickly for an exciting entry into the circus.

The big challenge would be getting Duchess to allow Cami to ride her. Sure, there was much camaraderie building between the two, but that was one feat she had yet to attempt. In truth, Cami was nervous at the prospect. The animal had calmed considerably, but could still be a bit skittish at times. And though she rarely acted in such a way with Cami, any other person who tried to approach Duchess was usually met with hesitation, bordering on aggression, especially where the surly crew was concerned. The elephant had not soon forgotten their acts of cruelty.

But it was the obvious next step. Their livelihood depended on it. In truth, Camilla couldn't help but fantasize about their grand entrance into the first town they would appear in, sitting high above the crowd as they ambled regally through the dusty streets, waving her hand with the trunk in unison to a cheering crowd. She would finally experience the sensation of arousing an applause. And it didn't seem an impractical dream, but there was still much work to be done to attain it. Fantasizing about that moment gave her ample motivation to get to work.

Learning to mount such a large animal would prove challenging, of course, but Camilla was up to the task. She received some instruction from one of the books she picked up, complete with hand-drawn pictures. She began by gently tying a rope around the elephant's torso. Duchess only shifted slightly during the process. Once knotted and secured, Cami knew the most difficult part was still to come. While Cami had successfully bonded with Duchess and was permitted to place her hands on the elephant's body at will, she was unsure of whether Duchess would willingly go into a kneeling position so that she could climb atop her head and get to the neck.

The first step was to attempt to lead the elephant toward the ground, but Camilla was met with much resistance. Such a submissive position would take some time to achieve, so Cami spent the better part of the day working Duchess into a kneeling position, enticing her through tasty treats, verbal commands, and exercising much patience. By the end of the next phase of training, she was able to finally get the elephant on its knees and to press its trunk to the ground when she would say "down", but she still didn't dare go further just yet.

Several days passed before Camilla had worked up the courage to attempt to mount the elephant. Duchess was quite obedient by now in responding to the command to kneel, but Cami wondered if she would hold steady as she tried to climb her enormous head. With the elephant close to the ground, Cami approached cautiously, placing both hands on top of her head. Duchess immediately rose in protest, clearly confused at this new development. Cami stepped back, demonstrating her willingness to give space.

After gently getting the animal back on its knees, she made another approach. It was met with a similar response but with slightly less hesitancy. Cami knew it was going to be another long day. It wasn't until late in the afternoon that she had built enough trust to heave herself up on the elephant's head.

The first attempt was unsuccessful. Camilla hesitated and didn't get enough momentum, so she quickly slid back down and landed on her behind in the dirt. Duchess remained on her knees but looked up to see what became of the girl. Cami quickly got back on her feet, placing a hand on the elephant's head to get her back down to the ground. She tried again, this time with more gusto, and got high enough to hang there with her feet dangling off the ground, but did not achieve the elevation necessary to grab the rope on the elephant's back. She jumped off backward and landed on the ground once again.

After several more tries, Duchess finally kicked her head back, which gave Camilla the boost she needed to grab the rope. She was then able to pull herself up on the elephant's neck, but she still needed to turn around to face forward. Duchess rose quickly off her knees, which jolted the girl who was holding on for dear life.

In the distance, a small crowd had gathered, Max among them, watching to see what would happen next. They tried to suppress their laughter as Camilla sat backward, holding tightly to the rope as the elephant began to lumber around. It was awkward, but there seemed to be no immediate threat. Finally, using the established verbal command to "stay", Cami got the elephant to stop moving, which allowed her to maneuver her body around to face frontways. Her success was met with cheers by the onlookers.

Feeling a sense of achievement, Camilla was now high in the air, looking out across a cornfield and feeling larger than life, sitting atop the gigantic beast. She felt no sense of danger, yet she didn't dare breathe for fear of startling the animal. Instead, she thrust forward to see if the elephant would pick up on the cue to begin walking again. Duchess seemed to understand and began moving forward, walking slowly around the pen. Camilla could already taste the triumph of knowing their grand entrance was now imminent.

Frederick and Fiona had joined the crowd in time to witness Camilla's achievement and were astonished by the sight of the young girl riding with ease upon the elephant that no one else would dare approach. Seeing the growing number of spectators only made Cami raise her head higher, enjoying her moment of victory. Still, it wasn't long before she began to feel anxious at the thought of getting back down. That was something she had not yet attempted and knew could be disastrous. The last thing she wanted was to make a fool of herself in Frederick's presence.

"Stay, Duchess." She called out with false confidence, hoping to get the animal to stop once again. To her great surprise, the elephant obeyed again. Now was the moment of truth. "Down, Duchess," she said, trying out one of the newer commands, hoping it would stand the test. Sure enough, Duchess went to her knees as she had before, allowing the young girl to clumsily climb back down.

Camilla's heart was still in her throat, but she pretended for everyone else's sake that things had gone just as she expected. Deep down, she knew she was fortunate that there were no further complications. Duchess had learned well, and for that, she made a show of giving her a reward in the form of a tasty apple. The elephant took it gently from her hand and devoured it with its massive teeth while the crowd of bystanders cheered. Among them was Frederick, who was showcasing a broad grin as he joined in their applause.

Camilla couldn't believe her success and decided not to push it any further. That was enough for one day.

CHAPTER
25

Several weeks had passed, and Max felt it was finally time to debut Camilla and Duchess. For the fire time in her life, Camilla experienced the pleasure of having her portrait done by a real painter. She did her best to sit still so that her image could be properly captured sitting high atop Duchess. She wanted to ensure it would turn out right, as the commissioned artwork was being used on the side of the wagons and also on new posters used to advertise the up-and-coming stars.

Once completed, Camilla could hardly believe her eyes at how majestic she and the elephant appeared in the colorful illustration. It didn't seem possible that this was happening—that she was worthy of such an honor. But it was all everyone in the circus talked about. Most had come around to the inevitable and were looking forward to the crowd's reaction as they strolled into the next town.

Camilla should have been thrilled with all this attention, but despite the excitement building, Cami was feeling a bit uneasy about the grand entrance the next day. She had worked diligently to prepare the elephant for the show, but it was a massive responsibility to ensure nothing went wrong. So much seemed to be riding on her shoulders, and though outwardly she seemed sure of herself that she was ready for opening night, secretly she wondered if she had what it took to pull it off.

To establish greater confidence in her success, Camilla was wise to spend a great deal of time acclimating Duchess to being around other people. As long as Camilla was nearby, she was not easily roused, though she still became irate whenever Wolfie or Rocco dared approach. They seemed to keep their distance, but it didn't stop them from sneering at Cami when she caught their eye. Knowing Duchess would now be the bread and butter of the circus, they knew better than to taunt the new moneymakers as Max made no secret about the great expectations he had for his prized possession.

This kept Cami safe from Max's ire as well, being the only one who could work effectively with the elephant. Though Max's temper continued to be legendary, toward her, he was sweet as pie. Without a doubt, he made sure she still knew who was boss, but since Cami was making such excellent progress, there was little reason for conflict. She did well to please the ringmaster, not to mention she wanted to taste the success of her hard work as much as he did.

As for Fiona, she had begun to pull away from Camilla. She rarely said hello when passing her on the circus grounds and seemed quite impatient with her new assistant, who couldn't seem to do anything to appease the glamorous starlet. If Cami had more time on her hands, she would have worked harder to mend things between them, perhaps even teaching her new assistant a few things. But as it was, she barely had time for Frederick, whom she loved with all her heart.

Frederick, who was used to being the center of her world, was now the one trying to pin Camilla down to make time to steal away. No one had ever seen the "fantastic" performer chase any girl. This turn of events was not lost on Frederick, and he began to grow frustrated. But their time together was always splendid, which made up for it. Camilla seemed to affect him as no woman ever had. There was no question of her love, and everyone could see that Frederick had fallen for the girl in return. So, he endured, knowing the ebb and flow of circus life and how things would calm down after a time.

Not anytime soon, however. This day, Camilla was entirely consumed with what would be the biggest moment of her young life. Never did she imagine she would be in such a position, and her tummy fluttered with nerves.

She paced the floor of the wagon Max had gifted her for all her hard work. They didn't get any new wagons, so she couldn't help but wonder what poor chump was forced out of this one, but she didn't have time to think of that just then. For now, she went over the entire process in her mind, reminding herself of every command and sorting through her costumes in hopes of finding the perfect ensemble for her and Duchess's grand debut.

Her wardrobe was growing considerably, not only with the clothing Fiona had gifted her, but after receiving a small raise, Camilla began skimming her paycheck to buy herself pretty little things before sending the rest to her mother. Max promised much more if she delivered the goods where Duchess was concerned, so she figured she'd make up for the difference later.

Thoughts of fine clothing, admirers, and bouquets of roses filled her fantasies as she imagined herself now in Fiona's place. It wasn't that she wanted to topple Fiona, but she did want to be like her in every way.

After contemplating everything that was on the line, Camilla decided to go check on her prized companion. Duchess was lazily eating hay and looked unconcerned with the events of tomorrow. After all, she had no idea what was in store, only that she was content and had a reliable friend in Camilla. Cami found comfort in her laidback stature, a reminder that all was well. She pressed her head against the elephant's trunk in a show of true affection.

"Oh, Duchess, please do well tomorrow. I need you to help me succeed. Everything is dependent on this moment."

The elephant answered back by placing its trunk on top of her head in a return show of affection. Cami smiled at the warmth of their growing intimacy. She was beginning to understand Duchess on a deeper level, almost as if she were a person herself. "I promise I will always take care of you if you take care of me," she added, certain they already had an understanding between them.

⚜⚜⚜

This was it; the moment of truth had arrived. Camilla sat nervously on top of Duchess, waiting for Max to give the cue to the troupe to move toward town. Everything was set, but no one was as nervous as Camilla at that moment—the others had done this dozens of times before. She was dressed in a glittering red leotard and her face covered in rouge and lipstick. Though many in the troupe complimented her glamorous look, Camilla felt anything but confident or beautiful. She felt scared and self-conscious.

I don't deserve this, she told herself. *I don't belong here. I'm an imposter!* But it was too late to turn back now.

Max raised his baton, and the caravan of performers began to move in the direction of the town before them. Duchess seemed calm as they began ambling together as one with the rest of the troupe. Again, the elephant's calm demeanor helped steady Camilla's nerves. The pair was toward the back, so they had a good view of all that was taking place. Max had specifically placed them in the rear because he wanted to save the best for last, something that the other performers did not much appreciate, but understood.

Frederick had been kind to give Camilla an encouraging word before they took off. He kissed her hand and reassured her she would do well. The thought of his well-wishes stayed with her even now. The greatest confidence she had was in knowing that an incredible performer such as himself would believe in her. It was all she had to cling to as the voices in her own head told her otherwise.

She silenced these voices by focusing on the road ahead and estimating how far she had to go to get through this. *It will all be over soon*, she reminded herself. She couldn't even think of the night show just yet. Thankfully, Max wanted to take it slow with Duchess, so the tricks were simple, but Camilla—Little Cami—had never been in the limelight before.

The time had finally come. The rest of the caravan had made its way through town and quite a crowd had assembled along the street to gawk at so many strange and wonderful things. The onlookers pointed at Camilla and Duchess from afar, as they caught first sight of them. Children squealed at the prospect of seeing a real-life elephant that they had only seen in picture books and dreams.

Duchess was sure to impress, too. She had grown strong under Cami's care but also carried herself with a sense of dignity.

Yes, she earned that name of hers—she was royalty. And to prove it, a custom-made tiara sat upon her noble brow, Camilla wearing one to match.

Max's booming voice carried over the town as he announced each spectacular act. Frederick rallied the crowd with his usual charm and antics with Sugar. The onlookers cheered! Fiona was the source of many oohs and ahhs as she flexed some of her acrobatic abilities. Benito inspired gasps of awe from those who couldn't believe a person could survive eating fire. And then Cami heard her name.

"And next," Max began, "We have Camilla the Great, riding the colossal, the exotic, the one-of-a-kind, Duchess the Royal Elephant."

The crowd roared as the two worked their way through the heart of town. Children stood in awe, their mouths gaping open as they looked up at them in wonder. The reaction gave Camilla a sudden boost of confidence. Her spine straightened as she took on the character of one who was doing what they were born to do. She smiled brightly and waved at the assembly before her. Duchess raised her trunk and trumpeted, which caused the crowd to applaud once again. It was as if they were both made for this.

Camilla tingled at their reaction, and a hunger was born in her. She now understood for herself what it was that drew Frederick and Fiona to this life. She had tasted it and determined in her heart to make it last. Even as the procession came to an end, the heat of the moment still burned inside Little Cami. If only her father could see her now!

Her father. She hadn't thought of him for some time, but at this moment, she could almost think of nothing else. Even though he was gone, she wanted to make him proud. But this was only the beginning. The real test was still to come that night.

CHAPTER 26

"It was a disaster, Frederick, I'll never be able to show my face again!" Camilla was still shaking.

"Nonsense, my dear," he reassured her. "It was only a slight hiccup. No one will remember. It happens to all of us at some point. The main thing is that you kept going."

Camilla cringed at the memory of her first nightly performance. Nothing seemed to go as it had in rehearsal. Duchess suddenly became obstinate, ignoring many of the commands they had worked so hard to establish, and she behaved quite erratically. All was fine before they entered the tent. Camilla was able to mount Duchess with ease, but once in the dimly lit, closed space and surrounded by strangers, she was no longer working with the elephant she came to know.

Her first, and most daunting task, was to dismount the

animal. This was the initial indicator of how their act would go. Duchess wouldn't stop pacing the sawdust floor, despite Cami's repeated commands to "stay." This caused several workers to try to intervene, which only made Duchess more uneasy. Being surrounded, she eventually froze in place, so Camilla shouted "Down!" but the elephant refused to go into a submissive position with all these unfamiliar people surrounding her. Camilla did her best to try to shoo them away. "I have it from here," she called out. "Stand back, please." They finally got the hint, backed off. Only then did Duchess reluctantly go to her knees.

Camilla then attempted to climb down the elephant's massive head, but the people began to cheer. This startled the nervous pachyderm, so she lifted her head, and 'Camilla the Great' came sliding down ungracefully, falling on her rear. The crowd laughed, which stung the poor girl's pride, but she thought, at least they were being entertained. She played it up a little by pretending to scold the poor beast.

They clumsily worked their way through the routine from there, eliciting more laughter when things didn't go as planned, which was often. Camilla continued to pretend the incidents were intentional, as though they were part of the act, but Camilla knew better. And what's more, so did Max. The audience seemed to buy it, or at least they played along, but Camilla's ego was badly bruised. Inside, she wanted to run and hide.

"Max is sure to send me packing now. How can I ever go out there again after this?" The tears came flooding now.

Frederick wrapped his arms around the trembling girl, "Oh, it was not as bad as all that, you'll see. Max wouldn't dream of letting you go after all the progress you've made with his prized elephant. What choice does he have? Besides, you handled everything like a pro. It doesn't matter if the act goes according to plan; it only matters that the audience has a good time. And Cami, you had them eating out of the palm of your hand. You handled everything as you should. That's what counts."

Camilla was amazed by what Frederick said, the tears drying up somewhat. "Really? You think it will be okay then? I sure felt like a failure tonight."

"Believe me, little one, we all have these moments, especially when we start out or are trying something new. It's expected. But what matters is how you handled it. You didn't give up but pressed on and made the best of the situation. Besides, you don't have to worry about what the people in one town think. That's the best part of being in the circus—there is always a new audience waiting for you in the next town over. Let this be an opportunity to work on your act and figure out where you can improve for next time."

Camilla couldn't believe her ears. Frederick's pep talk sure was working. Although it didn't seem possible ten minutes earlier, she suddenly began to see the turn of events in a new light. Courage began to well up in her once again. "Thank you, Frederick," she said. "You have no idea what this means to me. I just hope Max echoes your sentiments."

Frederick wiped away her remaining tears and hugged her tightly. "I'm actually jealous," he added.

"Of what? Me?" Camilla was incredulous at such a remark.

"Yes, of course. You get to experience all the ups and downs of performance life for the first time. This is when everything is so exciting and new. You really figure out so much about yourself and what you're good at—the first taste of rousing an audience, even the first disappointments. It teaches you what you're made of. If you allow it to challenge you rather than defeat you, then you will have earned your place. And with that comes a sense of pride in knowing you conquered your greatest fears and failures. Then you will be unstoppable. That's when you really feel on top of the world."

Camilla bit her lip. She was reignited by Frederick's speech, but didn't know if it was enough to overcome all this adversity.

As if reading her mind, Frederick added, "But we all need people to believe in us along the way. Without that, most of us would certainly give up. And I believe in you, little one. I will not let you falter."

Camilla wrapped her arms around his neck, showing her gratitude with a series of pecks all over his now blushing face, "Thank you, thank you," she said, finally landing on his lips, Frederick's kiss reciprocating her great affection. At least for the moment, everything was set right in the world.

It turned out that Max shared Frederick's outlook for the most part. He wasn't thrilled with how the act went down, but seemed optimistic about future performances. As Frederick did, Max credited the young girl with holding it together when faced with the unexpected. As long as the audience was happy, Max could overlook just about anything. Still, he was stern that Camilla would have to work harder than ever to ensure the act took less unpredictable turns in the future. She agreed wholeheartedly, thanked him, and promised not to let him or the circus down.

The following night went much more smoothly. There weren't quite so many laughs, but the audience was no less responsive. Indeed, they were enchanted. The tent was filled with the echo of their gasps as the elephant went through the feat of showing off its enormity and strength. The tricks were simple, but effective. And doing their routine live gave Cami a chance to see where the act needed improving. *We need a bigger finish*, she noted to herself. That would be her next order of business in the weeks to come.

In the meantime, she was content to know the joy of performing and receiving accolades from the audience, cast, and crew. Children were eager to ask her questions about elephants, which she found she could answer quite easily, having read many books on the subject by now. The other performers encouraged her, as Frederick had, to say that she had done well in the short time she had worked with the exotic animal. And the crew merely admired her beauty and poise—when she wasn't falling on her behind, of course.

Her success grew with each performance, and Camilla was quickly learning the art of working the stage. She and Duchess were fast becoming the toast of the entire troupe, having single-handedly saved the show from bankruptcy. There was one who had not yet approached her, though—Fiona. The starlet carefully watched from the sidelines, her arms crossed, with a twisted expression on her pretty face.

Camilla tried approaching her more than once, but if Fiona saw her coming, she'd quickly turn and walk away. This pained Camilla greatly. She wanted to ensure that all was well between them, but for now, she chose to bask in her accomplishments and soak in the increasing praise she received. Perhaps they could work things out another day.

As for home, she reminded herself that she must write to her mother soon and send more money to help cover the farm. Money was sure to come in more than ever. That also meant more pretty dresses, but the farm must be paid off—eventually, anyway.

CHAPTER 27

S pring had arrived and, much to Max's delight, the circus had managed to keep its head above water through the winter months. More than that, they were thriving as word spread about Camilla the Great and Duchess the Royal Elephant. People in the towns they settled in were already familiar with their troupe and cheered their arrival. Never had any of the performers experienced such a welcome.

Gone were the days when crowds of protestors would congregate to air their grievance over the wicked performers desecrating their villages. Now they were greeted with open arms. Curious children and adults alike gathered in droves to get a first look at the enormous elephant they had received word of.

Camilla, who was still positioned at the back of the procession, thrived on the rising anticipation of their arrival. She trained Duchess to raise her trunk high in the air to get the attention of onlookers, even as other acts were being highlighted. It seemed a harmless way to work up a crowd, and they loved it. However, she was sure to keep a lower profile when Frederick was up. He was still a fan favorite—and hers as well.

Camilla and Fiona had yet to mend fences, though they were cordial with one another in the dinner tent or when practicing for the nightly shows. They mostly did well not to step on each other's toes, though more than once Camilla intentionally used Duchess to get the crowd's attention during Fiona's introduction, much to the starlet's chagrin. It seemed a small offense compared to withholding the friendship she once cherished, but Camilla, having truly loved Fiona, felt a twinge of guilt and decided she would no longer enact this petty mode of revenge on her former friend.

It was a particularly beautiful early April morning. The crisp, fresh air felt good as it brushed against Camilla's skin. The trees surrounding the plot of land where they set up for the week were heavy with fresh apple blossoms. The scent wafted over them with each passing breeze. The sun counteracted the coolness in the air and felt warm on Cami's face. It was sure to be a rare sort of afternoon and one she didn't intend to waste.

The entire circus was taking two days off to rest after a long journey to the current town. They were all in need of a break. She and Frederick had plans to go for a ride in the country. She had spent so much time working with Duchess that it seemed only right to give him her full attention. Not just for his sake—she too longed for a moment to focus on him alone, so no talk of circus life or elephants would be on her lips.

Camilla was just heading over to the food tent to grab breakfast before their afternoon ride when she spotted Fiona going in. It was still early, so she was surprised to see the starlet out and about at such an hour. She hesitated briefly before deciding to follow her into the tent. Fiona was stepping up to the food line when Camilla approached and took her by surprise. A bit startled, the French girl quickly regained her composure but said nothing.

"Good morning, Fiona," Camilla said softly.

Fiona merely nodded her head in response.

Camilla wasn't giving up just yet. "Looks like it will be a beautiful day. Any big plans for your day off?"

"Non," Fiona said sharply, clearly not interested in keeping the conversation going.

The awkward tension rose between them, and Camilla didn't know what else to say, so she stayed silent as she heaped piles of food on her plate. Fiona eventually took her own plate, and to Camilla's surprise, took a seat at one of the tables rather than taking the food back to her wagon. Camilla saw another opening and decided to try again.

She approached the table where Fiona sat, her eyes cast down on her plate. "May I sit with you?" she asked sweetly.

"Whatever you like. Anything for the big star," she spat

bitterly.

Despite the hostility in her tone, Camilla sat just the same. They ate awkwardly for a few moments when Camilla could keep silent no longer. "Fiona, what has come of us? Why are we no longer friends?"

Fiona looked up. "Were we ever friends?"

"I thought we were." Camilla's face felt hot.

"I don't believe so. Circus people don't have friends. We only have assistants and competitors."

"Why does it have to be that way, Fiona? I am your friend. At least, I want to be. I will never forget your kindness to me…"

Fiona cut her off quickly, "Oh, you want to be friends, do you? You will never forget my kindness? Did you think of these things when you ditched me to be Max's new star? Did you think about how you had repaid me for such 'kindness', as you say? Non. I believe you only thought of yourself. That is what circus people do. And I would have done the same—we all would. That is how this business works."

"Fiona, you know I had no choice in the matter. Besides, there would be no circus if I didn't—"

"There you have it, you think you saved the whole circus from ruin. And maybe you did, but you didn't save all of it. Thanks to you, I am ruined. I have lost my good assistant and am no longer Max's prized performer. You have that honor, but don't be mistaken, little one. It never lasts. Max is always looking for something new and shiny, and soon enough, you and your elephant will also be old news."

Camilla shook her head, "How can you say you are ruined, Fiona? You are a great dancer and tightrope walker. You are beautiful. The people love you. And so did I—I still do," she corrected herself.

Fiona's face softened slightly at Camilla's tender words. "I believe you think those things, but believe me, no one is special in this business. We all fight to stay on top, but it's just a matter of time." Fiona paused, then added, "But there are ways to slow down the inevitable. Perhaps you should know, I am leaving."

"Leaving?"

"Yes, I am a vain creature, you know that. I cannot be second to anyone. I am joining another circus where I am desperately needed."

Camilla couldn't believe her ears. "Surely it isn't as bad as all that. You are a big star here! As for me, I have barely made a name for myself. We need you—I need you. I hope you will reconsider."

"Your star, little one, has only begun to rise. You are Max's little pet. As long as you have leverage, you will do well, but you do not yet know what it's like for the other girls. What it is like to be at his mercy. I will not go back to being merely one of Max's girls. I hope you know what you've gotten yourself into. Perhaps Frederick will even protect you for a time, but as for me, I am on my own."

Camilla wasn't sure she understood all that Fiona was

referring to, but she had seen Max's sickening smile and could imagine his intentions with the girls were anything but pure. "You are not alone. If I have 'leverage' as you say, I will protect you, Fiona. I won't let anything happen to you. It's the least I could do."

Fiona laughed sarcastically, "Oh, you are naïve, my dear. I do appreciate your intentions, but you have much to learn. When it comes to this life, there are simply no guarantees. You will keep busy enough looking out for yourself. Now, go, and don't worry about me. My worthless assistant will have to fend for herself, too. I wish you well, my dear."

Camilla was desperate now with the thought of losing her friend for good. "Please, Fiona, what will I do without you? And what will the circus do without you? You are one of the best acts we've got!"

Fiona stood up to leave. "Cami, I hate to admit it, but dancers like me are a dime a dozen in this world. Max will have no trouble finding my replacement. You? Well, let's just say, elephant trainers are not so easy to come by. That will buy you some time. You will do fine without me, you'll see." Fiona began to walk away, then stopped, turned around, and hugged the young girl. "I wish you all the best, little one." With that, she disappeared into the bright light of day beyond the tent's opening.

Camilla enjoyed her afternoon ride with Frederick, but was still troubled over her conversation with Fiona. She had promised herself earlier that she would not discuss circus life with him today, but it was difficult to suppress her emotions under the circumstances.

Frederick allowed Camilla to ride Sugar while he rode a brown mare named Maple. Sugar was the faster horse, but Frederick was a skilled rider and had no problem keeping up. It truly was a beautiful spring day, and he seemed to be basking in the brilliance of their surroundings so that he didn't notice the brooding look on Camilla's face immediately.

It wasn't until they stopped by a spring to let the horses drink some water that it finally occurred to him that something was a bit off with Camilla. "What is it, my dear?" He asked. "You look as though something is troubling you."

Camilla looked away to hide her sad eyes, "I'm sorry, Frederick, this is our special day. I didn't want to upset you at all. Let's talk of other things."

"No," he replied, grabbing her hand. "Tell me what is on your mind. Maybe I can help cheer you."

Camilla sighed and then proceeded to tell him about her interaction with Fiona. "It saddens me, Frederick. Fiona was my first and only friend for a time. And now she is leaving on account of me. I didn't even realize I had made such trouble for her."

Frederick gave a soft, inoffensive chuckle, "Is that all, my dear? You have nothing to worry about. Fiona is a bit of a drama queen—we all know that. I have no doubt that she doesn't appreciate you stepping on her pirouetting toes, but she'll be fine. She was right, girls of her caliber may be a dime a dozen, but Fiona is a rare breed in that she doesn't easily buckle under pressure. All will be well. Max may even talk her out of leaving altogether."

"I don't know, she seemed pretty set on her decision. And Max, well, she seems to think…"

Frederick hushed the worried girl. "Now, don't get all concerned about Max right now. Yes, he is a hard taskmaster. We are all aware of how he can be. And yes, he takes a liking to certain girls, but you have nothing to fear. Fiona was right, he can't afford to lose you. And he knows you're my girl. He wouldn't dare cause a stir. Everything will be fine. Now, do you feel better? If so, let's walk the horses over to that shady patch and enjoy the rest of our day together. Sound good?"

Camilla was anything but fine, but the day was simply too beautiful to waste on worrying over the situation further. Instead, she decided to take Frederick's advice and put all these troubling thoughts out of her mind. Besides, it wasn't often that the two of them had the luxury of so much uninterrupted time together. And maybe that was for the best.

When alone, they often found themselves in a passionate embrace and this afternoon was no different. Admittedly, Camilla enjoyed the affection he lavished on her, and the temptation to succumb to Frederick's delicious kisses was increasingly difficult to resist.

CHAPTER 28

*W*eeks passed, and the summer heat was bringing out the crowds. Fiona had made good on her promise to leave the circus, and all Camilla had to remember her by were the few costumes she had in her trunk that were given in kindness to a messy, hopeless girl. She shed a fair number of tears over her departure, but she was right. It took Max no time at all to replace the starlet with a new French dancer and tightrope walker named Isabelle. Not only was the new performer younger, but some argued that her act was much more polished.

Camilla found Isabelle to be superficially friendly, but haughty and even more ill-tempered than Fiona. She didn't suspect they would be good friends. The men, however, fawned over the new beauty on-site, a great novelty with the troupe, who welcomed anything to break up the usual routine. Camilla didn't even mind that attention was being taken from her own beauty for the time being. She was happy to have moments of peace where she and Duchess could continue working on their act without distraction.

And work, they did. Camilla had now taught the elephant several new tricks to work into the nightly act. The best of all, in her opinion, was getting Duchess to raise her front feet high in the air, demonstrating the massive stature of the animal. The crowd absolutely loved it and gasped at the thrilling sight. She had also begun to incorporate the use of a giant rubber ball. She would place it on the end of the elephant's trunk, which Duchess managed to balance with considerable ease. Duchess would then raise it high in the air, over her head, garnering plenty of cheers at the accomplishment.

Max was all too happy with Camilla's progress and praised the girl through words and another wage increase, but not without an expectation of greater things to come. With the summer months before them, the circus was doing better than ever. Word continued to spread about the girl and her royal elephant, Camilla marveling at their increasing notoriety. Yet, she never saw it coming.

She had just finished another successful performance. Duchess, having grown accustomed to circus life, was becoming quite reliable in responding to commands and even tolerating the crowds of people that would surround them after a show. Camilla took cues from Max and the others on how to appease the fans.

Children were especially fun, so she worked out some minor tricks to give them a final taste of circus magic before they headed home for the night.

Everyone had just about scattered when she looked up and saw a figure in the shadows watching her from a distance. She thought nothing of it to start, but then, as if being flooded with some memory, she froze into place as the specter approached. When it finally came into the firelight of the torches, her heart leapt to her throat.

"Little Cami. Can it be?" The voice spoke.

Camilla could hardly find her words, but finally choked out, "Griffin, is that really you?"

The smile that spread across the young man's face told her all she needed to know. Suddenly, she was transported to another time and place. The past she had spent little time reflecting on these days, suddenly came flooding back as though it had never left her. Griffin, her oldest and dearest friend, wrapped his arms around her in a big, tight embrace. In an instant, she was home.

"How is it possible? How did you find me?" she cried.

Laughter, mixed with tears of joy, sprang forth. "I saw your poster," he replied. "It didn't look like you, but I knew it must be you with that name. I had to come and find out for myself. And here you are." Griffin grabbed Cami's hands and pulled back to get a better look at her. "I'd never have recognized you if I didn't know you as if you were my own kin."

Camilla grinned brightly at the comment and did a full

turn, "Do you like it?" she asked, referring to her radical transformation.

Griffin wrinkled his nose, "You look so much like a girl now. Excuse me, a lady. But how? How did this all happen?"

"It's a long story. Oh, Griffin, I have so many things to tell you."

"You haven't written in so long. I've worried about you, and so has your ma."

Camilla was now filled with shame. She certainly had been negligent these past months. "I'm sorry, Griffin, truly. My life...well, you can imagine. I suppose I've been caught up in everything that I've neglected to write as often as I should. Please forgive me. And please, tell me how my mother is and everything on the farm."

Griffin smiled, "Of course I forgive you, you little fool. But let's not talk about all these things tonight. I plan to be in town for a couple more days. Can we meet and talk sometime?"

Camilla had plans to have lunch with Frederick, but figured he would understand. "Yes, tomorrow at noon would work for me. How does that sound?"

Griffin nodded, then embraced Camilla once more. "Yes, the sooner the better." His strong arms were familiar, yet foreign.

The following morning, Cami went to Frederick and explained to him about her surprise visitor. He pretended not to be jealous, having recalled all she had told him about her past, but was understanding as to why she needed to break their lunch date.

"We will make up for it later this week," he promised, then kissed her cheek. "Now, don't you let him talk you into leaving us. This is your home now."

Camilla blushed. Frederick had not yet proposed to her, but she wondered if that wasn't at least a small hint of his intentions where she was concerned. "Don't worry, I have no thoughts of running off. I want to be where you are, always." She wrapped her arms around Frederick's waist and then took off for town to meet her old friend.

Camilla sat on a bench outside the inn Griffin told her he was staying. It was still five minutes to noon, but she somehow expected him to be there when she arrived. He was nowhere to be seen. She waited patiently, chewing on a nail as she anticipated news from home. She had done well to keep up the payments for the farm, even throwing in extra at times, but not being able to hear from anyone in so long left her wondering how everyone was managing in her absence.

Finally, Griffin emerged from the door of the Inn just as the town clock sounded the time. Getting a better look at him in the light of day, Griffin appeared more like a man than the boy she knew. He was indeed stronger, which indicated he had been working the farm, but his usually messy auburn hair was now combed neatly, and he wore brown pinstripe pants and a matching vest. These were a far cry from the usual torn trousers he wore as a child. He was handsome, even.

"Well, look at you," she said. "It seems I am not the only one who has undergone a transformation."

"This is new," he admitted. "As you know, Father has always been fond of books and wants me to get an education. Of course, my parents couldn't afford to send me to school, but I am here to meet with a gentleman who is willing to apprentice me with the hopes of one day hiring me on as his full-time bookkeeper."

Camilla had lost track of where she was geographically. "That's wonderful, Griffin, but how far are you from home now?"

"About twenty miles off. Don't you know where you are?"

Camilla laughed, a bit embarrassed. "I don't really think about it anymore. We've been everywhere, and most days are like a dream."

"I can't imagine what stories you must have to tell," Griffin smiled. "Let's go find a place to talk. How about a stroll through the park on the edge of town?"

Camilla nodded, and they began to walk together slowly, neither knowing where to begin. They simply enjoyed the peace that came from being in each other's company once more. Finally, Camilla broke the silence. "Please tell me about home. How is Ma? And the farm?"

Griffin turned away wistfully, "The farm is intact. I did

everything I could to ensure your mother didn't sell the land before the funds you sent came in. We did have to sell off the animals as there was no one to tend to them, but the land was preserved. My family scraped to take what livestock we could, but the rest was sold to the locals. I am sorry for that, but there was no other way."

Camilla understood. What mattered was that the land was still in her family's possession. "And what about Ma?"

"Well, your ma, she hasn't been doing well. Don't get me wrong, it's not critical, but with you leaving and losing her husband—your father—well, she has often taken ill. She is pale and thin. She worries constantly about what has become of you. She is living with her sister, as planned, but she asks after you regularly. She made me promise to find you. Of course, I didn't know where to begin to look for quite some time, but when I saw the poster…"

Tears welled up in Camilla's eyes, "I am so very sorry, Griffin, for any pain I have caused either of you. It's just—I wanted to do what I could to save my father's farm. I thought it would be the best thing for everyone. And I was blind with fear and grief. What can I say?"

Griffin wrapped an arm around Camilla's shoulder, "It's okay, Cami. We understand. We just miss you."

After wiping the tears away, Camilla thanked her dear friend for seeking her out and coming to bring news. "Please tell my ma that everything is going well for me. Honest. She has nothing to worry about, and it won't be long before I pay off the farm. I am making good on my promise, and everything is working out just fine."

"I can see that." Griffin took another look at his old friend. "How on earth did you ever find such clothing...and is that makeup? The Cami I knew would never have been caught dead in such a fine dress."

Camilla pretended to be a bit offended, "Excuse me, but a lady never tells her secrets. Besides, I don't even know that girl anymore. Was I ever so wild and free?"

"I suspect you still are. Circus life doesn't strike me as being exactly tame, Cami."

"Yes, well, it's also not as thrilling as one would imagine. It's hard work, and we stick to a very strict routine. But the people, I admit, are quite strange. Then again, I'm already used to that." She nudged Griffin playfully.

"Won't you come back with me?" Griffin asked boldly. "I know you still have a way to pay off the farm, but I am working hard to make a better living. And Cami, my offer still stands."

Camilla's eyes widened with surprise at the overture. "Griffin, I can't..."

"I know you have a life here, but your home is with us. Camilla, I know the life I offer isn't nearly as exciting as this one, but it will be stable for both you and your mother. And besides, it won't be long before I'll be yearning for a family of my own. There is a girl who expects me to ask her, but I haven't been able to. Not knowing you were out here doing God knows what..."

Camilla's temper flared, "Excuse me? Griffin, have I ever seemed inept to you? When did I ever beg you to come and rescue me? You came here on your own, but I'm doing just fine. Great, even! I am the star of the show, I'll have you know."

Griffin was beside himself. "I'm sorry," he began.

"You should be! To think you could come here and insult me once again. And just to inform you, I, too, hope to be married soon. So go ahead, go back to your other girl. Marry her and have lots of babies, because I am not interested. I thank you for coming," she spat, then turned on her heel and walked away.

Griffin called after her, but it was no use. Camilla was fleeing rapidly when she came upon a man with a small carriage and asked for a ride to the other side of town. He helped her up, and they were gone.

CHAPTER
29

*G*riffin didn't give up so easily. He had not come all this way to end on a sour note with Camilla once again. Though he gave her some time to cool off, he eventually made his way to the circus grounds. Camilla sat stewing in her wagon. She was angry, but her rage soon turned to tears once she had returned. Frederick had asked what the matter was, but she needed to be alone to think.

When Griffin approached, he didn't begin to know where to look. He saw a small man tending to the animals and decided to ask him. "Hello, my name is Griffin, and I am looking for one of your performers, Camilla."

The short man turned to look Griffin up and down, then snorted, "Yeah, you and everybody else. The show is at seven. You can wait in line with the rest of them."

"I'm sorry, you don't understand, I am a friend of Camilla's, and I need to see her."

Again, the short man scoffed, "Yeah, you and everyone else. Beat it."

Another man was watching carefully and approached. The dark Italian walked up to Griffin and greeted him, "What's this I hear? You are looking for our Camilla? And who may I ask is calling?"

Griffin was thankful to speak to someone a little more pleasant in demeanor. "Please tell her Griffin is here to see her. I'm an old childhood friend. I'm afraid we got off on the wrong foot, and I'd like to speak to her before I leave."

The Italian man patted Griffin on the back. "I'll see what I can do."

A few moments later he returned and offered to escort Griffin to Camilla's wagon. "By the way, I am Frederick. I am a good friend of Camilla's as well."

"Oh?" Griffin looked Frederick over, impressed by his svelte physique and good looks. "Are you the one she plans to marry then?"

Frederick was surprised to hear this. "Who, me? We are good friends, to be sure, but marriage? I don't know."

Griffin said no more and once led to Camilla's wagon, he gently knocked on the door.

Camilla answered, her face clearly tear-stained. "Come in," she offered. She was surprised that Griffin had found her so easily, but was even more surprised when she peered over Griffin's shoulder at Frederick, who smiled and shrugged.

"I'll wait here," he said softly.

Griffin entered the wagon and was astounded by all the pretty things Camilla had strewn about. It didn't look unlike Fiona's wagon when Camilla had first arrived.

"Where did you get all of this?" he asked, clearly in awe.

"Oh, this? It's for my act. I have to keep up an appearance."

Griffin picked up a jeweled tiara sitting on the vanity, "I don't believe I've ever seen so many fine belongings. Your mother would be astonished."

Camilla turned red, but didn't reply. She had thought so little of her mother in light of all she was going through. Perhaps she was more bitter than she realized that her mother was willing to sell her father's farm so quickly after his death.

"Anyway," he continued, "I came to apologize. I didn't mean to upset you. Cami, you know how much I care for you. We are like family. Please say you'll forgive me. I can't stand the thought of parting ways on bad terms again."

Camilla sighed, "Of course I forgive you, Griff. I don't know why I got so upset. Nothing has been right since my father died. Can you forgive me, too? I know my temper sometimes gets the best of me."

Griffin happily returned the offer of forgiveness. "I'm pretty used to it by now. Anyway, I can see this is where you intend to be for the time being. But Camilla, I want you to know that you can come home any time you want. Never feel like this is something you have to do."

"Thank you. It's good to know I still have a home to come back to when that day comes. But Griffin, don't let me stand in the way of your happiness. As you said, we will always be like family, you and I, but you don't owe me anything. I want you to be free to pursue all the things in life you want. I can't ask you to make sacrifices on my behalf. Do you know what I mean?"

Griffin looked at Camilla, really looked at her. Yes, the girl he knew was still in there. The one he played in the tidepools with, catching crabs and climbing trees. The one he fell in love with. But it was clear that she did not love him the way he loved her. "I believe I understand," he sadly replied. "I promise not to make you such an offer again. I only wish you well."

It was what she wanted to hear, but somehow Camilla grieved at the prospect of Griffin walking out the door and into a new life without her. She couldn't imagine life without him, but neither could she leave Frederick. It was right to let him go. "And I wish you well," she said, grabbing his hand.

They embraced once more before Griffin turned to leave the wagon.

"Wait!" Camilla called out. She grabbed the tiara from her vanity and handed it to Griffin. "Please give this to my mother. Tell her I love her, and I will return as soon as I am able. In the meantime, she needn't worry."

Griffin took the jeweled crown from her hand, kissed it, and then said goodbye. Frederick was still waiting outside the door as Griffin exited. Neither man said a word but merely nodded in each other's direction. After Griffin was out of sight, Frederick entered Camilla's wagon to see how everything went.

"He's gone. I don't believe I'll be seeing him again," she said sadly.

"And did he try to convince you to go with him?"

"Yes. But as you know, my place is here—with you."

CHAPTER
30

*T*he pressure was on. Camilla's star was on the rise, just as Fiona had predicted. Never before had the troupe worked so hard to keep up with one of its star performers. And as word spread about Camilla and Duchess, people began coming out in droves to see the "royal" pair. If another act didn't hold their attention, the people would shamelessly chant "Duch-ess, Duch-ess, Duch-ess!" Then Max would urge the two from the sidelines to reclaim the stage to perform one of the encore acts they had developed for such an occasion.

Everyone else was beginning to feel like filler, except Frederick, who was still holding his own quite well. It didn't stop him from putting in extra hours with the other equestrians to keep things fresh and exciting. He was still competitive after all.

Toward everyone else, Max was harsher than ever,

pushing the entire troupe to put in more hours to take their act to another level to drum up more reaction from the audience. The last thing he wanted was to be labeled a one-act show. This greatly displeased the other performers, as they were already exhausted with the schedule they were keeping due to the demand from more towns that were eager to get a look at the famous elephant.

Where once Camilla was hailed as the savior of their traveling circus, she was fast becoming an object of scorn. Even the crew was turning on her as they were made to work harder to set up and tear down the grounds so they could move on rapidly. Frederick did his best to shelter her from most of these harsh critics, but Cami sensed a change in demeanor from even her closest allies.

She eventually caught wind of the fact that the wagon she was gifted by Max belonged to none other than Benito the Fire Eater, who was now left to bunk with the clowns. He was too kind a soul to ever let her know, but certainly, the loss had greatly bruised his ego. Though he was still cordial when they met, he no longer greeted the girl with his winning smile as he once did. His spirits were crushed by the events unfolding, and he too was now under an enormous amount of pressure to up his routine.

Even Dominick would barely offer her more than a friendly hello when they ran into each other during her training sessions with Duchess. Apparently, he felt beneath the big star now and had taken on some of the grievances expressed by the rest of the crew. Though he couldn't fully turn on Camilla for he still had a soft spot for the girl, fear of being perceived as a traitor and how that would affect his place among his fellow workers, persuaded Dominick to keep his distance.

In an effort to deal with the rising pressure, drinking and carousing had increased among the troupe. More money coming in meant more access to booze. The rowdiness sometimes reached the ears of villagers, who sent authorities to offer warnings. One town even forced them to leave prematurely for ignoring the town ordinance. But Camilla did not partake in any of it because she needed to stay focused, which contributed to her growing unpopularity, despite the increasing financial benefits.

Camilla would have perhaps felt these shifting attitudes more keenly had she not been so thoroughly consumed with training Duchess to improve their act. She felt a growing responsibility to keep the circus thriving. And what little spare time she had was given to Frederick. Tonight, she was excited to introduce a new addition to her nightly routine. She had taught the elephant to do a handstand—its hind legs high in the air, with Camilla sitting on its back.

She was also working with Duchess to add some comedy to the act, as inspired by Frederick and Sugar. In this routine, the two would pretend to fight over who gets the ball. After a series of back and forths, Camilla would appear to win, holding the ball high over her head, and Duchess would wrap her trunk around the girl's waist, raising her off the ground in the final victory. Being more complex, that one required a bit more work, but they were making headway.

Camilla was quite satisfied with the progress she and Duchess were making. It was as if the elephant was made to perform. There was such an understanding between them, and their bond brought much joy to Cami's heart as she dearly loved the animal. She was one of her only friends nowadays. Spending time with Duchess wasn't like work at all, but rather felt like fun and games. They had grown so fond of one another, Camilla often forgot Duchess did not belong to her. She was still the property of Maximillian Angelini, who, for the most part, showed little interest in her care—only in the money the elephant brought in.

This evening was sure to be another crowd-pleaser. Camilla was waiting in the wings, in full costume, watching each act that went before her. It was all she could do not to assess the effectiveness of each performer and the crowd's response to their feats. Some routines she had become so familiar with, they bored her now. *No wonder Max is putting the heat on. These clowns haven't come up with anything new since I got here*, she thought to herself.

Finally, Frederick was up. His act never ceased to thrill her. He was as capable as ever. Never one to be satisfied, he had pushed his troupe to add new tricks almost nightly. It was as if he had something to prove, even to himself. Tonight, he was trying a new act that he and Sugar worked out, a variation on something he had done before. Frederick would ride Sugar, then jump off the horse, running alongside her, keeping a grip on her harness, and then jump back on. Only this time, his plan was to land, do a back flip, then jump back onto Sugar's back.

Never before had Camilla seen them do this routine at such speed. And now, incorporating the somersaults, if you blinked you might miss it. Frederick was in top form! Camilla was breathless. She may have been the big star, but she knew without doubt that Frederick was far more skilled as a performer than she would ever be. It even made her embarrassed to consider herself in the same league.

She was contemplating this when suddenly everything came to a halt. Frederick, trying to mount his beloved mare after another backflip, had suddenly fallen and was on the ground, doubled over in pain. He was hurt! Camilla screamed as she saw a number of people from the troupe rush to his aid. She wanted to join them but was frozen in place. Eventually, they carried the wounded performer outside the tent, and the act continued—at Max's orders, the show must go on.

They laid Frederick down on a makeshift cot outside the tent and Camilla ran to his side. "What happened, my dear? Are you badly hurt?" she asked, kneeling beside him and grabbing his hand.

Frederick winced in pain, "Oh, it's just my damn ankle, I twisted it."

"Is it serious? Will you be okay?"

"I don't know, Camilla, please…" The pain was still too intense for him to think straight.

The circus physician rushed to Frederick's aid to get a

better look at the ankle. It was quickly swelling, so he got to work, wrapping it up in bandages. Max was soon by his side as well, checking to see how badly one of his top performers was faring. Seeing the seriousness of the injury firsthand threw him into a fit of curses. Clearly, Frederick was done for the night, so he ordered two of the crew members to carry him back to his wagon to rest.

"I'm sorry, Max," Frederick said.

Max, having genuine affection for the star, put his hand on Frederick's brow and reassured him that all would be well.

"And you," he added, turning to Camilla, "You're up next. So, get ready, because you're going to have to carry this show!"

⚜⚜⚜

Camilla did as Max instructed, though her thoughts were on Frederick the rest of the night. She felt as though she were simply going through the motions, but the cheers from the crowd told her otherwise. In her moment of distress, she found herself being more reckless than usual. Not sticking with all the safe tricks but pushing Duchess to do tricks and routines that were slightly less reliable. Duchess seemed to follow her lead and was particularly obedient. It was as if they had hit a new stride between them.

Camilla rewarded Duchess generously as a result, and Max, approaching her after the show, promised to do the same.

"You really pulled it off, kid," he said, looking her up and down with that twisted smile of his and licking his lips. "Who would have ever guessed you'd be such an asset to me when you came here? What a dirty little urchin you were, but look at you now—my biggest, brightest star. But hey, that's circus life for yeh. I guess anything is possible."

Camilla knew it to be true, but somehow hearing Max say it in this way felt degrading. She had certainly made him proud, but once again, she felt like a fraud. It's not that she wasn't willing to work hard, she always had been, but deep inside, she was still that messy little girl running barefoot on the farm. Not an object of admiration...or lust.

When the crowds had finally thinned, she walked Duchess back to its wagon for the night. She made sure there was plenty of fresh hay, then said goodnight in the usual way—rubbing her face, giving her a final treat, then placing a small peck on the base of her trunk.

It was a moonless night. Cami had difficulty locating the lock with the key, as she felt around in the dark. Once finally secured, she turned to head back to the grounds, hoping to check on Frederick before bed.

Staring at her from beneath the shadows was Wolfie. She could only tell it was him by his stature, but his expression was hidden—and so were his intentions. A chill ran down her spine, and she shivered from the cold night air. Refusing to demonstrate any signs of intimidation, she calmly walked away in the opposite direction, avoiding a possible confrontation.

Once on the main grounds, she went directly to see Frederick, who had taken some liquor to help alleviate his pain and was half asleep. She kissed his forehead and told him she would return the next day. She was thankful they would all have the day off before heading to the next town. This would give Frederick time to rest and assess his injury. She silently prayed over him as he drifted off, before leaving and heading back to her own wagon. Suddenly, she felt very small.

CHAPTER
31

C amilla checked on Frederick first thing in the morning, bringing a bit of breakfast to help nourish him. The circus physician had already beaten her there and was tending to his ankle when she entered the wagon. Seeing the ankle in the light of day was very telling. It had greatly swelled overnight and had turned various shades of purple.

The physician took hold of Frederick's ankle and carefully turned it in different directions to assess the total damage. It was all Frederick could do not to holler in pain, so he gritted his teeth and resisted the urge to the best of his ability. A couple of times, he succumbed, in spite of himself. As it turned out, the ankle was badly twisted but did not appear to be broken. This meant the performer would be laid up for a time, but the doctor didn't seem too concerned about it in the long run.

"You should be back to performing without restriction by the end of the month. You just need to take it easy in the meantime." The good doctor stated confidently.

Though the physician delivered good news overall, Frederick was none too happy. "This is impossible! How can I wait that long? I've never been out more than a day from any injury since I began."

The physician reassured him. "Not to worry, my man, you won't be laid up for long. Just rest for a few days, then slowly start to get yourself around. Don't push too hard or the damage may become permanent. You will be able to ride soon enough, but don't spend too much time on that ankle otherwise."

Frederick sighed, knowing there was nothing else to be done. The doctor rewrapped his ankle, then left the two of them to their breakfast.

"Have something to eat, my dear," Camilla said, placing a tray of food before Frederick.

He resisted. "Oh, I'm not hungry."

"But Frederick, you must eat. You need to keep up your strength. You heard the doctor—you'll be better in no time. But you have to take care of yourself, which means eating."

Frederick yielded and took a bite of some fruit, but he was in a sullen mood and said little else. Cami decided not to press the issue and instead ate with him in silence. She just wanted to be there for him. She understood his disappointment, but was ultimately encouraged to hear he would recover soon enough.

Suddenly, a knock came at the door. It was Max. He, too, had come to check up on the star performer. Camilla decided now would be a good time to feed Duchess, so she promised to return later and leave the two of them alone. Frederick seemed fine with that. Max took the seat beside Frederick, where Camilla had just risen, glad to be rid of the girl.

Once they were alone, Max finally looked at Frederick with a wink, "You sure seem into this one, Frederick, my boy. I don't recall you ever having a particular affinity for any of the girls. Yet, I never see you with anyone else."

Frederick's spirits were too low to humor the ringmaster. "Yes, well, you must know, Camilla's a special girl."

"Sure, sure, I've no doubt of it. But pretty too. She is quite the looker. I'm sure she's been a bit of fun for yeh."

Frederick sat up a bit. "She's been no such thing! I mean, yes, she is wonderful, but not in the way you mean."

Max laughed. "Oh, don't tell me there's nothing going on here. I may be old, but I'm not an old fool. No girl has ever resisted Frederick the Fantastic. No girl is that special."

"As a matter of fact—can we just change the subject, please?"

Frederick was clearly annoyed with the topic, but that didn't stop Max from pressing in. "Don't tell me you're actually serious about this one? My goodness, never did I think I'd see the day. Well, don't get too serious, if you know what I mean. I need you to keep the ladies happy. You've always been so good at that, and besides…"

"I said, can we please change the subject?"

Max didn't like being told what he could and could not talk about, but he had more pressing issues on his mind. "Okay, fine then. Tell me, what did you find out from the physician?"

Happy to turn the conversation toward something else, Frederick filled Max in on all he had learned. Max was no happier than Frederick that he would be laid up for a time, even slowed down from picking his act back up at full speed, but he knew it could be worse.

"That's fine, you're an important part of my show, Frederick. Just see to it that you're back in top shape sooner rather than later. In the meantime, I'll have Marco fill in your spot."

This did not make Frederick happy. Marco had always wanted a chance to shine, to topple the big star and grab some of the limelight for himself, but what choice did Frederick have? Marco was the next best equestrian performer, and as always, the show must go on.

⚜⚜⚜

The days went by, and Frederick's ankle started to greatly improve, and along with it, his spirits. He was still quite immobile, but the swelling in his ankle was going down, and the circus physician had assured him he would be able to get around soon with the help of a cane. He even started to enjoy the attention it garnered.

Many of the cast and crew had stopped by to see him, to offer their condolences and words of encouragement. Their many visits were evidenced by the roses and other flowers and gifts filling his wagon space. The girls were especially attentive, offering homemade goodies and blankets, along with their company, to soothe the star. Even Isabelle, Fiona's replacement, stopped by often, dressed in her most provocative costumes, as if her figure alone would bring about some miraculous healing.

Camilla was surprised by none of this, though it did trouble her inwardly. She did her best to keep her emotions in check and trust Frederick, as he never gave her any reason to be concerned. Still, he seemed to be basking in the light of all this attention, a small consolation in light of being out of commission. Meanwhile, the jealousy over her own success was growing, and the girls snubbed her brazenly.

Isabelle pretended to still be friendly toward Camilla in Frederick's presence. Her voice was laced with a sticky sweetness whenever they crossed paths, coming and going from Frederick's wagon. "You poor dear," she would coo, "How terrible you must feel having to carry so much of the show since Frederick took a fall. I am sure you must feel just sick about it. But we're all just so lucky to have you."

Frederick thought her kind, though Camilla knew better.

She refused to be rattled and would just return the fake smile, then get on with her business.

This particular evening, Camilla was glad to find Frederick alone when she entered his wagon after the show. She had not yet had a chance to change out of her costume, but went right over to see him after dropping Duchess off. She felt a bit lonely and hoped to spend some time together.

Frederick, who hoped to be further along now, was lying in bed feeling sulky. As the swelling went down, some of the pain returned, which kept him from putting much weight on his ankle. Feeling uncomfortable, even as he lay in his bed, he took some liquor to help alleviate some of the pain. It appeared he had taken more than necessary for medicinal purposes, because Camilla noticed the room reeked of alcohol when she entered the wagon.

"Hello, my sweets," he slurred as she approached. "Don't you look just lovely tonight! Did you have a good show?"

"Yes, it was a good night. We did quite well. It's just…" she wanted to pour her heart out to Frederick and tell him how she was feeling. Besides Duchess, he was her only friend in the world.

"That's good to hear. Why don't you come sit down and keep me company?"

Camilla was glad for the invitation. She went to sit beside him in the chair, but he patted for her to come sit beside him on the bed instead. She did so, glad to be near him. She began talking about the night and how some of the girls were treating her.

Frederick rubbed her arm affectionately, which felt nice.

"I'm so sorry," he said sympathetically. "Those girls are just jealous, Cami, you are so talented and beautiful. That's all it is. You have nothing to feel bad about."

It sounded good to be told these things, but somehow it didn't make Camilla feel any better. Was it worth all this to be completely alienated by everyone? Frederick continued to caress her arm and shoulder, then held her hand.

"Enough with all this talk about the show. You know how bad I feel to be left out of it right now. Why don't you lie down with me for a bit? I am so tired, and it's been a hard day. Stay here with me."

"Well, I have to go back to my wagon soon. I still haven't changed out of my costume, and I'm a little chilly." Camilla rubbed her bare arms, but it did nothing for her exposed legs.

Frederick was persistent, "Come on, I'll warm you up. Besides, we've both had a difficult time. Let's hold each other for a bit."

Camilla welcomed the invitation to lie in Frederick's arms. Even in a weakened state, he felt strong and comforting. Camilla nuzzled her head under Frederick's neck, dangerously close to falling asleep.

"You smell nice," he said finally, stirring her back to reality. "I sure miss our outings. It's been so long since we've sat like this and just talked."

As Camilla thought of it, he was right. It had been some

time since they were able to be together without distraction. "I hope we can do it again soon," she replied. "The physician says it won't be long before you should be able to start riding again. We'll be able to plan an outing before you know it."

"Well, at least we're together now."

Camilla nodded and buried her head deeper into Frederick's chest. How safe she felt in his arms. Only now did she notice she was pressed against his bare chest, something she'd never felt before. His skin, warm and inviting against her exposed flesh.

Holding each other closely, Camilla looked up to Frederick and smiled, "Thank you, somehow you always make me feel better."

"That's my job," he replied.

"Oh?"

Frederick looked into Cami's honest face. To him she looked as sweet as a child. Never before could he recall someone gazing at him so lovingly. At least not since his mother died. He brushed against her rosy lips lightly with his own. Camilla's entire body tingled with delight. She wanted more.

Sensing her desire, Frederick pressed his lips more firmly against hers with a growing hunger. The two were now tangled in a deeply passionate embrace, the heat of the moment taking them over like a fever. As the kissing increased, Frederick positioned himself to hover over Camilla, showing little restraint of his intentions as his hands caressed her body. For a time, Camilla allowed herself to be swept away by the moment, even allowing herself to respond to his touch in ways she never had before.

Frederick began kissing her neck and moving down to her shoulder when Camilla finally got a hold of her senses. "Wait," she finally said weakly. "What are we doing?"

It never occurred to Frederick that perhaps, knowing very little of the world, Camilla was ignorant about such things as this.

"I thought we were comforting each other," he replied.

"Yes, we were. I mean, we are, but perhaps this is a bit too much. Maybe I should go now."

A hint of desperation rose in Frederick's voice. "No, don't go, please. Stay here with me. Must you always leave? I want to be with you."

Camilla bit her lip. "I want to be with you too, but I'm not ready for this…"

"It's okay, little one," Frederick said with a hush. "You have nothing to fear."

Camilla swallowed. "I'm not afraid, Frederick. It's just that…"

"Yes? What is it?"

"Well, do you love me?"

Frederick didn't hesitate. "Of course, you know I do. Would I have waited so long for this if I didn't?"

"Does that mean you wish you marry me?" Camilla searched Frederick's eyes for signs of life. They were blank.

Frederick was dumbstruck. "Marriage? Why are you

bringing up marriage at a time like this?"

"Well, isn't it obvious?"

Perhaps she knew more about these things than he realized. Frederick, feeling taken off guard on the subject, quickly sobered up. He lifted himself off the girl and rolled onto his back.

Camilla, feeling unnerved by his tone and action, turned on her side to face him. "Well? Am I just another one of these girls to you?"

"No, but..."

"But what? Frederick, I love you. If you love me too, then I would think you'd want to marry me. Isn't that how this works?"

Frederick's mouth was dry. "Listen, little one..."

"Camilla." She corrected him.

"Camilla. I do love you. In fact, I'm sure I've never loved anyone before I met you. But marriage? You have to understand, I am not the marrying kind. I've never even considered it."

"You never even considered it?" Camilla's voice was rising, and her face was hot. "Then what has this all been about?"

"Honestly, I didn't think about it."

"Didn't think about it?" Tears were welling up in Camilla's eyes at the revelation. She pushed herself out of the bed, despite Frederick's pleading for her to stay. "Frederick, I really can't believe you thought I would...and without even knowing..."

"Listen—*Camilla*—this is the way things are on the road. It's no place to start a family or build a life. We live in the moment. And at this moment, I want to be with you. Isn't that enough?"

Along with the hurt, the anger inside her began to grow. "I've got to go."

Camilla rushed for the door and left, leaving Frederick speechless and unable to chase after her. He could only call her name, but she was gone.

CHAPTER
32

The next morning, Camilla woke up early, but she had not slept well. The only reason she got up at all was because Duchess needed to be fed, and they still had much work to do before debuting their new addition to the act. She wanted to speak with Frederick about all that was on her mind, but it would have to wait.

Cami knew breakfast would be mandatory if she were to make it through the day. She walked over to the food tent and grabbed a few things that would be easy to take back to her wagon. As she crossed the grounds, she ran into Isabelle, who seemed to be just emerging from her own wagon.

Catching sight of Camilla, Isabelle smiled brightly, "Good morning, Cami, how nice to see you out and about so early. I assumed you'd sleep in after the night you had."

Camilla couldn't begin to know what Isabelle was getting at, but her curiosity got the better of her, so she decided to bite. "Whatever do you mean, Isabelle?"

"I saw you leaving Frederick's wagon quite late last night. So, tell me, does he live up to his stage name—*The Elastic Fantastic?*"

Camilla was disgusted by Isabelle's coarse suggestion, and it showed on her face, "Why on earth would you ask me such a thing? As if I…"

"Oh, don't act all sanctimonious," Isabelle cut her off, scoffing. "I know how this business works. You may think yourself a big star, but you're no different than the rest of us. I can only imagine what you've done to earn that position of yours."

Camilla was incredulous at the insinuation. "I beg your pardon. I can certainly tell you I've done nothing to be ashamed of."

"Now, don't tell me, we have a Puritan in our midst? Perhaps you are the Mother Mary herself!" Isabelle's haughty laugh made Camilla want to take a swing at her.

"Not everyone needs to sink to your level, Isabelle. I think you've made it quite clear how you got here. It's no wonder I see you cozying up to Max all the time."

Isabelle pretended to yawn. "I have no shame about anything *I've* done. I know how to use what I have to get exactly what I want. But I do feel sorry for poor Frederick."

"And what's that supposed to mean?" Camilla snapped.

"Does he know he is stuck with such a saintly little prude? How awful that must be. I pity him."

Camilla's temper was beginning to flare. "If you had any sense in that frilly little brain of yours, you'd know that Frederick doesn't answer to anyone. He spends time with who he wants."

"Well, maybe he doesn't want you anymore. Perhaps it's time he considered taking up company with a real woman." Isabelle wore a self-satisfied smirk as if she knew something.

The implication cut deep. "Frederick is free to do as he pleases," was all Camilla could muster, as she held back tears.

"Indeed," was the French girl's reply before sauntering off, leaving Camilla to burn in anger.

Camilla was at a loss, her spirits low. She still didn't know what to make of her conflict with Frederick, and Isabelle only made things worse. Doubt was planted in her heart, which meant further alienation for the young girl as she had no other allies in her midst—except Duchess.

She ate what she could of her breakfast, then went out to see the dear elephant. As always, Duchess was waiting patiently for the girl and stood up at the sound of her approach. Even as Camilla worked the lock, Duchess was shifting anxiously in the wagon's limited space, anticipating release from the chamber.

Duchess exited without any prodding, having grown accustomed to their daily routine. With great affection, she approached Camilla and leaned into her with her trunk. Camilla hugged the elephant in return, glad to receive comfort from her faithful friend. And Duchess went on being particularly sympathetic this morning as if reading the girl's mood. It was the only thing that could bring Cami a hint of joy at the moment.

The training session continued as normal, though perhaps a bit more subdued. Mostly, the pair enjoyed their time together outdoors in the warm summer sun. Duchess especially seemed taken with the new fruit Camilla offered up—apricots. Cami ate a couple herself, ripe from a nearby tree.

By midday, they were running through the new comedic act smoothly. Duchess thought nothing of picking Camilla up with her trunk, even allowing her to sit in its nook while they walked around. This seemed a nice mode of transport to the young girl. Never did she imagine she would one day be an elephant's closest companion, but she loved it with all her heart. They were there for each other when they both needed a friend.

The heat of the day was getting to them both, so by late afternoon, Camilla led Duchess to a nearby creek to cool off. The elephant stepped in, but the water was only about knee high, so Cami assisted by taking a bucket, scooping up a pail full of water, and pouring it over the elephant to the best of her ability. Duchess responded by blaring happily with approval.

The best show of all was when Duchess took in water with her trunk and sprayed it over her back and all over Camilla. It made Cami feel like the young, free child she once was, with no care for her appearance or what others thought of her. She was living. This, of course, made her think of home and even dear old Griffin. A true friend to her always, she missed him now. She briefly wondered if he had gotten married, then put it out of her mind because she had enough to concern herself with at the moment.

After the training session was over, Camilla returned to her wagon to prepare for that night's show. It was all she could do to keep from thinking about Frederick and their painful encounter. She had trusted his intentions so much that it never occurred to her that he didn't intend to marry her someday. *His love seemed so real*, she thought to herself. *I have been an utter fool.*

For the first time since arriving, Camilla wondered if she wasn't cut out for circus life. Perhaps she was not as wild as she thought. She was growing weary of looking out for herself. She once believed she was up to the task, and maybe so, but it wasn't nearly as thrilling as she imagined when all was said and done. Perhaps a quiet life on the farm was enough after all. But it was too late to go back and change things. And for that ever to be a reality, she knew she'd have to keep working hard to pay off her father's land.

No, this is my life for now, and I must make the best of it with or without Frederick. But no matter the outcome, at least I have

Duchess, she sighed.

CHAPTER
33

$\mathcal{A}$nother show was about to begin, and the energy was mounting as the performers readied themselves to present their acts before an eager audience. The band played on as the start of the circus was underway. Camilla was feeling a tad distracted, but confident that she would be able to maintain enough focus to please the crowd.

Max was spirited. The Angelini Bros. Circus was bringing in more people than ever before. This, of course, was reflected in their monetary gains, which were also at an all-time high. This greatly pleased Max, but also pleased Camilla, as it meant she would pay off the farm sooner than she could have ever dreamed. She could almost taste the freedom that would come with acquiring the only land her little family had ever known.

In light of recent events, Camilla purposed in her heart to

give nearly all her earnings to ensure her freedom. She even considered selling off some of her pretty things to aid in that cause. Perhaps she would even have enough left over to purchase Duchess. She wasn't exactly sure what use an elephant would be on a farm, but with that sort of brute strength at her disposal, she would certainly figure it out.

The heat of the day had not subsided. In fact, the temperature seemed to climb well into the evening, a building storm system visible on the horizon. There was a static in the air from the dark clouds rolling in, which only added to the mounting anticipation of the night. Once Camilla and Duchess were up, they were met with many cheers. They ran through their set and then exited to the sidelines, much to the crowd's dismay.

Frederick would have been up next, but of course, was not quite ready to perform again. His absence had left a vacancy in the show, at least to Camilla. Marco was a fine fill-in but had nowhere near the charisma or agility that Frederick possessed. That kind of natural ability was rare indeed.

By the third act, the storm could be heard approaching. Thunder began to rumble, increasing its intensity with every passing minute. Benito the Fire Eater was up, and Camilla noted he was on stilts, something she had never seen before. Apparently, he had taken the pressure to up his act seriously, though to Camilla, he didn't seem altogether confident as he wobbled a bit with every step onto the main stage.

Benito's routine was not unlike his usual lineup of stunts,

though it did appear that the size of the flames increased. Those standing near him could feel the heat emanating with each flare, even from his current height.

The thunder had all but ceased as the storm continued to rapidly move over the tent, when suddenly a gigantic crack sounded over the entire circus. This caused the ground to rumble and the audience to gasp in surprise. This, too, startled Benito, and he suddenly lost his concentration and began to falter on the wooden stilts, as a large blast of fire emerged from his torch. He tried to regain his composure, but that only made the situation worse. He rocked around for mere seconds when suddenly, Benito came crashing to the ground. The audience gasped in chorus with the breath they had been holding.

The fall caused fuel to spill onto Benito's face and hands, and to the horror of all onlookers, flames quickly began to consume the fire eater. In a panic, Benito flailed his limbs and began rolling around in the sawdust, writhing as he tried to extinguish the fire. Benito was soon surrounded by crew members who draped him in heavy blankets, also attempting to put out the inferno, which was beginning to spread. All the while, the crowd shrieked at the catastrophic chain of events taking place before their eyes.

Though it felt like hours for the spectators, in reality, the flames were doused quickly, but the damage was done. Benito lay on the ground, motionless, and appeared to be burned badly by any who could get a look. The crew who helped put out the fire soon lifted him onto a stretcher and removed him from the tent quickly.

Max did all he could to calm the assembly, but it was of no use. The people were in utter shock, and soon it was evident that the show was over, and the ushers began to assist the showgoers to the exit. A low murmur among the people chattering filled the space. Though they tried to keep a professional face, even the cast couldn't contain their dismay at what had transpired.

Once the grounds were cleared of all patrons, the troupe assembled outside the main tent, awaiting news on Benito's condition. There was much discussion between them as they each shared their perspective on how the incident unfolded. Camilla was silent, a strange sense of guilt pervading her.

Even Frederick was roused by the commotion and emerged from his wagon to see what was going on. He immediately spotted Camilla and approached her to get answers. Despite their recent troubles, Cami was glad to see Frederick and hugged him tightly.

"Oh, Frederick, it was awful, just awful, poor Benito…" She then proceeded to tell him what transpired to the best of her ability. Frederick was deeply disturbed to hear of the unfortunate incident. "It's all my fault," she finally said.

"Of course, it's not," Frederick reassured her, "This is a dangerous business. We all know the risks. Sometimes accidents happen."

Wolfie, who was listening nearby, took the opportunity to

vent on the poor girl. "She's right, it is her fault. Benito would never have been out there on those stilts if it weren't for pressure from the boss man. He barely knew how to use the damn things."

Frederick quickly cut him short. "How does that make it Camilla's fault? Wouldn't that make it Max's fault if he pushed him to do the act before he was ready? But blaming her is much easier because Max would fire you in a minute if you leveled such accusations at him."

"Hey, the boss wouldn't have made him go out there if it weren't for that dirty lil' canary makin' a spectacle of herself all the time—her and that deranged elephant. She's the reason for all our problems, and you know it. Look at you, fancy boy, even *you* are out of the show on account of her antics. Why don't you wise up?"

Frederick was raging mad now, "And why don't you shut up before I silence you for good?" He raised a fist at the brutish man. "Camilla is no more responsible for my ankle than she is for Benito's foolish decision to perform an act he hadn't yet perfected. That's on him."

Wolfie growled at the star performer. "You don't intimidate me. You're a has-been. Even if you do recover, Marco is already doing a damn good job filling in, and it won't be long before Max realizes you ain't all you're cracked up to be. You don't carry this show. That girl of yours has done well to ensure that. And when the boss finally gives you the boot, well, we'll see who intimidates who."

Frederick was ready to throw punches, even with his hurt

ankle, but Camilla held him back. "Don't worry about him, Frederick, he's nothing. He's just trying to get to us. Our focus now has to be on Benito."

Frederick eased a bit but added, "Get lost, Wolfie. Camilla is still the star, as you know, and if Max comes out, we'll both see to it that you're finished here."

The surly man knew well enough that Max would be in no temper to deal with him fairly, so he left, but not before spitting in Frederick's direction and giving him a final sneer. "This isn't over."

"It's all right," Frederick finally said to Camilla, "Go back to your wagon and get some sleep. We probably won't hear anything until the morning. If I hear any news, I'll be sure to let you know. But really, you should rest. And don't let what Wolfie says bother you. He's an imbecile."

"But I really do think…"

"Hush now," he said putting a finger to her lips. "No more foolish talk. Just go get some rest."

Camilla did as she was told, feeling hopelessly dejected. But she thought perhaps Frederick was right—rest would do her good. While he had done well to reassure her that Wolfie's words were meaningless, she hoped he, too, did not take his accusations to heart. *Maybe he does blame me for his own predicament*, she thought. She wasn't sure that Wolfie wasn't right about everything.

The next morning, Camilla awoke to the news that Benito had suffered incredible burns to his face, throat, and hands. He was in bad shape, well beyond what their physician was capable of handling. They planned to have him moved to town for more medical assistance, but it proved to be unnecessary. By mid-afternoon, Benito could not withstand the pain of the burns and passed away in a state of agony. Darkness fell over the circus, and Camilla felt the accusing eyes of the entire troupe on her.

Wailing could be heard all over the circus grounds. Only Frederick could offer her comfort, but even he seemed out of sorts. Having performed with Benito for many years, Frederick had quite a fondness for the fire eater, as did everyone else.

Out of respect for his time of grieving, Camilla kept her distance and instead turned to her beloved Duchess for love and support. Not that she could understand her plight, but somehow Camilla felt a great deal of empathy from the now sweet-tempered elephant who was content to just sit with her in her time of need. And it was Camilla's turn to cry.

CHAPTER 34

*L*osing Benito in such a tragic way was a devastating loss for all. Even Max had become quite reclusive, laying off on barking his usual orders, and spending most of his time holed up in his wagon. Anyone who dared to disturb him did so at their own peril. It had better be an emergency because anything less was sure to incite his fury.

Camilla was quite content to steer clear of him. Though she might not be directly at fault for what happened to Benito, there was no telling how Max might soothe his own guilt by passing the responsibility onto the young girl, as many others had. Being the blame for so many struggles in the troupe made her an easy target.

Frederick also seemed content to be alone. She visited him a couple of times briefly, but his words were short, and the grief still hung heavy over him. To aid in his healing, Camilla decided to give him some space, knowing their problems would have to be addressed when things settled down.

Somehow, she was just fine with that. She worried about what talking things through might bring. It would perhaps finalize the deterioration of their relationship, which seemed almost inevitable without some change of heart on Frederick's part. For her part, Camilla had no intention of settling on his idea of a casual encounter. She loved him too greatly for that, and though she was downcast at the thought of losing him forever, she knew that real love could never be sustained at the sacrifice of self-dignity.

The more she thought of it, the more she concluded that circus life was ultimately not for her. She enjoyed aspects of it, to be sure, but there was much that left her longing for more stability, some certainty in life. She thought of her mother and father and their modest life. They didn't have much excitement, or much of anything at all, but they seemed content. Their undying love for one another carried them through each day.

Such love, Camilla had believed she and Frederick shared. Admittedly, she too had not thought much beyond the present, but deep down she had believed they were committed to one another and naturally assumed they would make choices about their life together. He'd never offered such assurances, but the way he had stood by her side through so many trials gave her reason to believe he was in it for the long haul. His intentions seemed noble.

Even in light of their recent altercation, Camilla could not allow herself to believe she had meant nothing to Frederick all along. *He's just confused*, she told herself. *Surely, he won't easily forget all we've shared*. But such thoughts were futile and only saddened the poor girl's heart, on top of everything else. Instead, she did her best to put it out of her mind until such a time as they could talk everything through. Then she would know for sure where they stood.

Max, eager to move on to the next town after the terrible incident with Benito, had a fast funeral and ordered the crew to pack up quickly and prepare to head out straight away. By no means was anyone sorry to go. Circus life moves fast, and it was evident that the entire troupe was ready to get on with it. There was little time for tears—theirs was a life of survival.

To survive herself, Camilla spent a great deal of time in solitude with Duchess. She couldn't escape the knowing gaze of her peers and had no desire for any encounters that might make things worse. No, Cami felt it best to keep a safe distance until the terrible incident blew over.

Having just arrived in a new town, Camilla wanted desperately to consider it a fresh start. That was the benefit of being part of a traveling circus after all, wasn't it? Each day held the promise of something new. As evidence of that, Max took no time at all to begin scouting for Benito's replacement. It wouldn't be long before some new act would join them, and new dynamics would be forged. Everyone would have to adjust or move on.

Tonight, though, Camilla was satisfied to focus on settling into their current location. Though the troupe lacked the energy of their usual triumphal entry, the parade was well received by the townsfolk, and it was clear word had not yet reached them about the preceding disaster. After completing their usual set up, the cast and crew gathered for dinner, and then each headed in their own direction to spend the evening as they wished.

Camilla talked to Frederick briefly at dinner. He was now getting around quite well with the use of a cane. He wanted to get to bed early as he planned to be up by sunrise to make his first attempt to ride Sugar since his accident. He was cordial to Camilla as he discussed his plans, though still a bit standoffish. To her, it felt as if they were mere acquaintances and never lovers.

Feeling a bit disheartened, she decided to check on Duchess. It was already getting dark, but she decided to let the elephant out of the wagon for a bit of fresh air after being on the road. Duchess seemed grateful for the opportunity to stretch her enormous legs and munch on some tree bark.

Camilla walked her over to the pen and the two of them wandered about for a while, enjoying the coolness of night. It was dark now, and the air was still. There was hardly any rustle through the trees, a far cry from the night of the storm. Camilla was feeling tired and decided it was time to walk Duchess back to her wagon.

They were just about to exit the pen when a figure emerged from the shadows—it was Wolfie. Standing behind him was his old buddy, Rocco. They approached the gate, and even in the dark of night, Camilla could recognize the look of menace on their faces.

"What are you up to there, little missy?" Wolfie sneered. His intention to make trouble was clear.

Camilla tried to play it cool. "Nothing, Wolfie, just letting Duchess out for a bit and then heading to bed. Would you please let me through?" she asked softly, nudging against the gate.

Wolfie and Rocco didn't budge but pressed further against the gate to ensure she would not escape. "Not so fast. We just want to talk to you for a minute."

"About what?" Camilla did her best to hide how uneasy she was feeling.

"Oh, just about you and pretty boy. Word has it, the two of you are through."

Camilla's heart sank as she tried to determine what started such a rumor, but she said nothing.

"Well, is it true? Is he done with you? Because we'd be happy to pick up where he left off."

The slithering tone in his voice made her skin crawl. "We?" she asked weakly.

"Yeah, Rocco and I. Yeh know, you ain't been so polite with us, but this is your chance to make it up to us. Don't you think?"

Camilla was getting a pretty good idea of what he was getting at and wanted nothing more than to run to safety. "Please get out of my way," she said sharply, then forcefully pushed against the gate once more.

"I don't think so, girly," Wolfie replied, holding her back.

Camilla knew getting through the gate was futile, so instead she turned and ran along the side of the pen and tried to climb over it quickly to make a break for it. Wolfie and Rocco were too fast for her, though, and they grabbed the girl before she could clear the railing, each grabbing hold of her arms.

"Nice try," Rocco spat.

Camilla tried to scream, but Wolfie quickly placed his rough, swollen hand over her mouth, and the two began to wrestle the girl to the ground, their sinister motives becoming increasingly clear. Camilla fought hard against their grip to no avail, but finally got an advantage when the struggle caused Wolfie's hand to slip down just far enough for her to bite him hard through his calloused fingers.

Wolfie cried out in pain from the impact of the teeth on his flesh, but Rocco had too tight a grip on the girl for her to break free. Camilla began to scream again, but Wolfie regained his composure by backhanding her across the face, nearly causing her to pass out. It was no use; she could not fight the two burly men, and she now feared she would succumb to their strength over her.

Suddenly, a blaring sound like a trumpet rang out through the night. Duchess went utterly berserk at the sight of her faithful companion in distress. The elephant rose high on its hind legs, crashing through the pen railing with ease. The two men watched helplessly as the elephant rose again and landed directly on Wolfie, knocking him to the ground. Again, Duchess rose and stomped on his lifeless body, putting an end to his tyranny.

Rocco, now aware of the danger he was in, began to scream maniacally and ran toward the circus grounds in an attempt to save his own life. The elephant was undeterred, returning to her former state as an out-of-control beast. Duchess chased the man, stomping and shaking the ground with every step, blaring all the while. The crew, whose quarters were closest to the edge of the grounds, began to emerge to see what the commotion was.

Duchess, now among the circus grounds, began crashing against anything in its way, destroying another animal pen, a tent, and a wagon. The men knew they would have to act fast. Duchess approached Rocco, who had fallen onto the ground, primed to be the next victim. The elephant once again lifted its feet high in the air when Camilla's voice shrieked "Duchess, no!!!"

The girl recovered in time to approach the unfolding scene. But it was too late. Several shots echoed, then several more, and the final result was the sound of Duchess hitting the ground with a hard thud.

Camilla ran to the lifeless elephant, sobbing hysterically over the lifeless body of her only friend. Rocco, who was still on his backside, was shaken by how close he had come to losing his life. Several of the crew tried to lift Camilla off the elephant, but she was too emotionally violent to be moved just yet.

Questions began to fly as to what caused the elephant to go into such a rampage as everyone scrambled to understand what took place. Rocco only stuttered, unable to tell how the events unfolded. He could only say "Wolfie," and point to where his cohort's mangled body lay.

This incensed Camilla greatly. "It was those two!" she screamed. "They attacked me. She was only trying to protect me from these thugs."

A crew member made another attempt to grab the girl, lifting her to her feet, but Camilla struggled free from his grip. "How could you? You monsters, she was only trying to protect me!"

Suddenly, Max emerged from his wagon, in a half-drunken stupor. His eyes widened at the sight of his prized performer and meal train lying still on the ground, along with the damage surrounding it. This sobered him up quickly as a slew of rage-induced curses flew from his mouth. "Who is responsible for this?" He roared and looked at Camilla. "You! Get over here and tell me what in God's name the meaning of all this is!"

Camilla didn't think; she only acted. The grief and fear over the situation overcame her, and all she could think about was Frederick. She turned and fled the scene as fast as she could. Only Frederick could save her now.

CHAPTER
35

The night's ruckus had only begun to reach the rest of the troupe on the other side of the grounds. They, too, heard the shots ring out and began to emerge from their quarters.

Frederick's wagon was still when Camilla approached. *The events were happening so fast that he must not have had time to react,* she thought. Without knocking, she reached for the handle, threw herself against the door, and it opened with ease. She stumbled in, lacking all composure, but rather seeming quite mad. The sound of her entry startled the star equestrian, who was currently half-dressed, clutching his cane and standing next to an equally half-dressed Isabelle, her hand resting on his arm.

"Camilla, what is going on?" He called out at the sight of the wild look in her eyes.

Those eyes widened in horror as she took in the scene,

unable to withstand one more atrocity. She couldn't remain in Frederick's presence a moment longer. She took off into the night, Frederick calling after her to come back. "What's going on?" He hollered. But she could not answer. There was no comfort to be found there.

If there was anyone else watching Camilla as she disappeared into the darkness, she was unaware of it. She was blind with madness. She ran with no sense of direction or purpose, only utter despair. She continued past the circus grounds and into a nearby field. The ground was lumpy and hard, the result of recent rainfall, and it caused her to stumble. She continued until her body could take it no longer, and she crashed to the ground, weak and in physical agony over her heartbreak. Camilla cried until her throat went dry, her eyes closed, and her body shut down and went to sleep.

The light of day had just broken the horizon when Camilla opened her eyes once again. The smell of fresh grass and the sound of birds chirping with delight were almost serene. For a moment, she didn't recall how she got into the field that was now laced in morning dew. She was damp and shivering, but confused, when suddenly the events of the night before came flooding back.

Her entire being ached at the memory she wished was somehow only a nightmare, but she knew it wasn't. A great weight came over her heart, yet she finally mustered the strength to prop herself up and look out over a misty haze toward the circus grounds. She had run further than she realized. Being so cold, she only wanted to return to her wagon to change her clothes and sleep the day away. She thought nothing of what would become of her just yet.

She rose to her feet and began the trek back to the circus, her senses returning to her. She thought it best to sneak back in before the rest of the troupe was awake, if at all possible. She didn't want to talk to anyone or answer any questions just yet. The thought of reliving the horror of the night before filled her with dread.

By the time she approached the grounds, she saw some of the crew had risen to start cleaning up some of the damage left by Duchess. She didn't dare study the area for fear of seeing the elephant's body, which she could not handle. Instead, she was careful not to be seen as she sneaked around to the cast quarters.

As she drew near to where her wagon was stationed, she could hear voices. She approached to find the door open and piles of her belongings outside the wagon. Suddenly, a crew member emerged, his arms full of more of her things, with Max following behind.

They looked up and saw the confused girl staring at them in disbelief. "What's happening?" she asked.

Max was hot. "Oh, so you decided to show your face, huh?" Turning to the crew member and another standing nearby, he said, "Get the rest of this girl's things out of here, and then make sure you remove her from the premises."

"I-I-I don't understand," Camilla choked out. "But why?" Tears were burning her tired eyes.

"Did you think I'd let you stay after what happened last night?"

"But that wasn't my fault. Wolfie and Rocco, they..."

Max huffed, "Rocco is out of here, too. And Wolfie, well, he's dead. So, I've lost two of my best crew members, and with the elephant dead, I surely have no use for you. You've caused me enough trouble, so you may as well be dead, too. You have ten minutes to grab what you can of your belongings and get the hell out of here, or I just might finish you off myself."

Camilla was in full tears now, scared, but desperate. "Max, please, don't do this to me. I can find some other work here. I'll do anything..."

Max displayed no sign of sympathy as he looked upon the pathetic creature begging before him. "No, I'm afraid it's impossible. I cannot bear to be in your presence after what you cost me last night. And you are not cut out for the kind of work you'd have to do to stay. You must leave at once."

Camilla continued to plead with the ringmaster, but he had already turned his back on her, deaf to her appeal. The two crew members dumped the last of her belongings on the pile and then urged her to grab what she wanted. They, too, had no compassion to give, but only followed orders.

Camilla had very little sense to make such a decision, but she knew enough to grab her father's old army coat, what little money she had stashed away in her purse, and a good pair of walking shoes. She could see little value in taking any of the beautiful costumes or accessories, though if she had more time, she might have tried to take them to town to sell. But as it was, she cared little about any of it.

Before being escorted from the premises, Camilla thought to say goodbye to Frederick, but as images of his betrayal flashed in her mind, she could not endure the idea of seeing him again. He had devastated her heart by revealing his true character and desecrating the love she believed they shared. She now knew she meant nothing to him, so saying goodbye would be of no value to either of them.

As Camilla stood on the edge of the circus grounds, the crew members left her with a warning not to return or Max would cause her great harm. Unbeknownst to her, Dominick watched them send her off from where he was tending to the animals. Once the crew was out of sight, he ran to the girl, startling her a bit.

"Dominick. What is it?" she asked, tears still streaking down her pitiful face.

The short man gave her a sympathetic stare. "I just couldn't let you leave without saying goodbye."

"But I thought you hated me, like the others."

Dominick looked away in shame. "I know I wasn't very kind to you these past months, but I never hated you. I guess I'm not very good with words, but the problem is, you were never like the others. You were special, and they all knew it—so did I. Not just because of Duchess, but you have something that scared the rest of us."

Now it was Camilla's turn to feel shame. "I let it go to my head, Dominick. I was a real fool. Fiona tried to tell me, but I thought I was better than that. And now I have nothing at all."

"That's not true. You have real heart—and courage. That's something Max and Fiona and the other one…well, they don't know anything about it. So, you must promise me you won't lose it on our account. Because I couldn't live with myself if…"

"Oh, Dominick, I blame you for nothing. Thank you for coming to me. I was certain I was completely friendless now, but I see at least one person still cares a little." She gave him a quick hug, which caused the coarse little man to blush.

"What will you do now?"

Camilla shrugged. "I honestly have no idea."

"What about home?"

"Home? I have no home. And Griffin, well, I'm sure he's moved on."

"Who?"

"Never mind." Camilla's mind had not yet considered where she belonged.

"What about money?"

"Oh, I have a bit." Camilla patted her pocket.

"Well, just the same, here is a little something. It's not much, but hopefully, it will give you a couple of hot meals." Dominick reached into a little money bag and pulled out a couple of hard-earned coins.

"Oh, Dominick, I couldn't—" But he shoved them into her hand and kissed it. She could feel they were wet from tears that now sprang from his hard face. "Thank you," she finally said, knowing this was more than pity but a gift of love. "I'd better go now. If Max sees us talking, there's no telling how he might take it out on you."

Dominick hung his head to hide his tears. "It won't be the same around here without you."

Camilla gave him a sad smile. "That's probably for the best." She then gave him a final embrace and was on her way. She began to head toward the nearby town, unsure where she was or what would become of her now. All she could see in her mind was the sea. That was where she must go. She didn't know how or why, but it was as if a memory was calling out to her. The sea was home; the sea was where she belonged. It didn't make sense, but it was a direction anyway. Yes, that was where she must go—to the sea.

CHAPTER
36

From her earliest memory, the sea is all Camilla ever knew. Running high atop the rugged cliffs, splashing about in the foamy surf, bobbing on the waves in the old wooden boat to haul in fish for an evening feast, and her father. Her father loved the sea. He introduced her to its wonder before she could even walk. He taught her to respect its unrelenting power, but also how to enjoy its many benefits. Her last great memory of the two of them was their time together fishing.

For that reason, her desire to go to the sea was all that drove her. Camilla had nowhere else to go. Home was not an option. She had not yet paid off the farm, she had no livestock or crops to tend to, and her mother was well cared for by her sister. She could not bear to go back to her Aunt Meredith and beg for forgiveness. Plus, she would just be another mouth to feed. And then there was Griffin.

He was probably married by now, building a life with a girl who deserved his love. She certainly didn't. And though she was certain that he would run to her aid in her time of need, Camilla couldn't interfere with that. Not only because it wasn't right, but her pride would not allow it. And so, she walked on, blinded by grief and unable to consider any other options. Somehow, she was certain that the sea was where her redemption lay.

Camilla stopped in the closest town for a bite to eat and to gather provisions for her journey, silently thanking Dominick for his generous gift. She sought directions from a local baker to ensure she was heading in the right direction and to get an idea of approximately how long it would take her to get there on foot. Turned out, the coast was some ten miles off. She figured she could make it in a day if she urged herself on, but planned for a two-day journey as it seemed a more reasonable expectation in her current state.

The pain that spread inside her was so great, Camilla was tempted to indulge in a bottle of liquor to silence the invading memories of all that transpired in the days past. But not only was she a stranger to strong drink, she thought it best to hold onto what little money she had just in case.

Besides, she thought, why shouldn't she suffer? Hadn't she been the cause of suffering for so many others? Camilla was quite sure she was responsible for all the pain and death of her loved ones. She had failed those she cherished with all her heart, so the excruciating pain she felt seemed well deserved. Now it was her turn to endure the anguish of a broken heart

Blindly, she marched on toward the western horizon. *The sea, the sea*, was all she could manage to focus on amidst the blinding fog of overwhelming grief. All other thoughts were a blur of events of the last year—those things that took place and led her to this moment. Camilla was completely destitute and devoid of any tenderness in life. Having no time to collect herself from her night in the field, she was still dirty and bedraggled so that even strangers looked upon her with pity or contempt. Her blank face was equally uninviting.

By noon, Camilla was well into the country, and her tummy rumbled with the exertion of carrying on over the varied landscape. She would have liked to deny herself the joy of a meal but knew it was needed to keep up her strength if she were ever to reach her vague destination. It was that urging alone that kept her going when it would have been easier to lie down and give up altogether.

She ate a portion of bread and nibbled some cheese and nuts. She took a ripe apricot from a nearby tree, but it only made her think of Duchess; how she had happily devoured the sweet treat. The realization once again overcame her that the poor elephant was dead on account of her.

She saved me, she died to protect me, Camilla told herself, but she didn't feel worthy of such a deed. *She would be alive if I had*

just gone to bed instead of taking her out. These feelings of regret dogged the young girl. Even though she knew there was no way of knowing what the outcome of her actions would be, nor could she go back and change them.

Taking a final look at the peach-colored fruit, she chucked it from sight. It didn't seem fair to enjoy such a delight with no one to share it with any longer. Feeling satisfied that she had received enough nourishment to continue on, Camilla proceeded to walk throughout the afternoon, eventually coming upon some tall grass that led to a wooded patch of trees. Evening would soon fall, and with such little strength left in her, Camilla decided this was as good a place as any to rest for the night. She doubted that her sleep would be peaceful, but she had no ambition to push further on.

Lying in the tall grass next to a shady tree made her think of Frederick. She closed her eyes and remembered their times together in such a setting. They would never get to do this again. She replayed those special moments in her mind, as if to torment herself purposely. It was the only thing she could do to keep his memory alive, the way she remembered him, even though it turned out to be a lie. The tears soon flowed as she recounted his tender words, his sweet kisses, and all the intimate things they shared.

With no one to hear her, Camilla fully succumbed to her tears and sobbed uncontrollably now. The realization that she had lost everything dear to her was more than she could bear. Her lungs labored from the emotional release, and her breaths began to hitch. She cried herself to exhaustion, and she soon could take no more. Camilla was overwhelmed with the pain of loss, so her mind darkened and she drifted off under the slowly setting sun.

⚜⚜⚜

Camilla awoke to rustling in the grass. She opened her eyes to pitch blackness. It was far from dawn. She heard the rustling once again, and her breath caught in her throat. Someone or something was watching her. She sat upright and looked around, but could see nothing.

The sound came nearer now. Camilla closed her eyes tightly for fear of what might take hold of her at any moment, then opened them to see a large elephant standing before her wearing a sparkling tiara.

"Duchess!" she cried out. She leapt to her feet and ran to meet her beloved friend. Duchess raised her trunk in approval. Cami threw herself against the elephant's enormous, yet familiar body, wrapping her arms around it as far as they would go. Duchess lowered her trunk and wrapped it around the girl, returning the embrace.

Camilla didn't stop to wonder how or why the elephant was there; she was only overcome with the joy of knowing her beloved companion had found her. The two friends were reunited, and no one would ever separate them again. She wasn't alone in the world, after all!

But of course, as real as this moment felt, it was nothing more than a dream. Camilla woke in the same dark of night to find all still and quiet, no Duchess to be seen. The pain returned as she lost the sweet elephant all over again.

She laid her head back down, despondent. She had no more tears left in her. Drifting off to sleep once again, Camilla awoke at the first light of day. The golden rays began to light up everything in the field around her, which brought many of the wild critters to life. Rabbits grazed, and birds began their morning chorus. None of it meant anything to her; it was only a reminder that life went on.

Camilla walked much further the day before than she had planned. She figured the sea couldn't be far off now. She could practically taste the salty air as she looked at the line of trees before her. She reached into her bag to munch on a small portion of her provisions before starting for the shore again.

Once satiated, Camilla threw her satchel over her chest and began walking toward the trees. She noticed a path that led into the wooded area and figured that it would take her where she needed to go. The air inside the trees felt cool and shady; she was glad to have her father's jacket. She saw minimal signs of life, and no other people crossed her path at any point. It was just her alone with her thoughts. She tried her best to silence them, and for a time it worked, when suddenly all would come rushing back and send her to her knees once again.

It went on like this all morning and into the early afternoon, Camilla taking a rest on the occasional log. She now saw light breaking through the trees, indicating that she had just about come to the end of the wooded portion of her journey.

As she came closer to the tree line, a notable roaring filled the air—a sound she was all too familiar with. It grew louder as she moved forward, the sea evidently not far beyond the path's exit. She continued on, picking up her pace slightly. It wouldn't be long now. And then what? She didn't know exactly, but some part of her was quite aware of the purpose in choosing this destination. She didn't dare reflect on it consciously, but a deep knowing was within her that drove her onward.

Stepping out between two tall maples, the light hit her face and blinded her momentarily. The sound of the waves was ever more present. She walked up a tall, sloping hill that revealed a slate blue sky, spattered with gray clouds which hung above her. Soon, all would be revealed.

Camilla reached the top of the hill, which turned out to be a cliff overlooking a rocky shoreline. The line of sparkling blue on the horizon was unmistakable. There was nothing but water as far as the eye could see. Looking down, she saw the source of the roaring waves, churning up the coast and crashing against the rocks below. It was quite a welcome sight—it felt like home.

Hardly able to stand, as she was overwhelmed by the

impact of her arrival, Cami placed her hand against a lone birch tree to hold herself up. But rather than feeling replenished by the moment, she felt desolate. Camilla felt small and insignificant—consumed by the vastness of the sea—alone. Max's words returned to her. "You may as well be dead too." And why not? What better place to die than this?

A sense of peace filled Camilla in the form of numbness. There was some hope in knowing she didn't have to continue suffering from such devastating losses. She could put an end to all this misery and never have to face the enveloping grief. God would forgive her, surely. He would have to understand the hopelessness she felt.

She let go of the tree, removing her satchel and shoes, and began to walk toward the cliff's edge. Once at the brink, she looked down and stared at the jagged rocks below, beckoning her to dash herself upon them and put an end to this hellish nightmare. She thought of removing her father's coat, but then decided she might perhaps want to wear it after all, as it was her only bit of comfort in remembering his love for her. She could imagine he was holding her in her final moments, and she wouldn't feel so alone.

It was only in wanting her final memory on earth to be a good one that Camilla, her father's Little Cami, yielded. She closed her eyes and allowed her mind to flash wonderful childhood memories of being in her family's cozy cottage, the warm fire, her father playing his fiddle, and her mother tending to a meal. She thought of fishing again, thought of the farm animals, and helping her father collect chicken eggs. And she thought of Griffin, barefoot with messy hair and laughing at some ridiculous inside joke they shared. She even thought of Frederick, the way she wanted to remember him—young, handsome, gentle, and kind, even if he turned out to be anything but.

Camilla inhaled deeply. The moment had come, and she was ready. Her body prepared to take the plunge, and she needed only to take a step forward to plummet into the depths of the sea, and the deed would be done. No one would miss her or ever need to know what came of her.

She lifted her foot, when suddenly a cry in the distance kept Camilla from taking that step—it sounded like a young girl. She heard nothing else but scanned the water below to see where the sound might have come from.

Looking out over the water, Camilla spotted what appeared to be a person in distress. She acted quickly, throwing off her father's coat and running down the path that led to the surf. Once there, she could see a young girl struggling against the waves. Camilla, who had always been a good swimmer, dove into the water without hesitation, heading in the direction of the child.

The girl was flailing, struggling to keep her head above water and grabbing at the slippery rocks to no avail. Camilla reached her and told the girl to climb on her back. She managed to grab a hold of Cami and did as she was told. Cami then began fighting the current and swimming her way to one of the larger rocks to get to a point of safety. She helped heave the girl onto the rock, then she, herself, got swept up in the current and began to struggle.

The child screamed further, calling for help. Camilla was losing strength. It looked like this would be her final moment after all. She gave up the fight and slipped under the cold, dark water, succumbing to her fate. That was all she remembered before her world went black.

CHAPTER
37

*C*amilla blinked her eyes awake, surprised to find herself very much alive with her head resting against a soft pillow, her body covered in a white quilt. Or perhaps this was heaven? But her head hurt. Camilla was sure she remembered a verse in the family Bible that said there would be no more pain.

She turned her head to the left and then to the right to get a better look at her surroundings. Her neck ached too. This was certainly not a place she had been before. The room was quite large, bigger than her whole cottage on the farm. There were tall wooden posters with intricate carvings on each corner of the bed, and heavy, wooden, ornate furniture throughout. A small flame was kindled in the fireplace near her, and a young girl of about seven in a yellow dress sat beside her, staring at the strange girl who had suddenly awakened.

"Where am I?" Camilla asked, her voice barely audible.

"Father," she called out, "The lady is up now. Please come quickly!"

Moments later, a tall, well-dressed man entered the room. He was not exceptionally handsome but carried himself with an air of dignity that made him appear so. His dark blonde hair was combed back neatly, and it was apparent that he was a man of good breeding.

"Hello, there, young lady," he said politely. "And how are we feeling today?"

"I'm not quite sure," Camilla replied weakly. "What happened? Where am I?"

The man stood beside her bed and tried to calm her. "You are safe, Miss. You nearly drowned saving my daughter, Tabitha. My name is Lord Edmond, and you are now resting in my home. This is all you need know for the present. Please rest, and when you are feeling better, we will discuss more of the details. Now please rest, while I get the physician."

A lady then entered, who was of middle age and wearing a plain frock with an apron. "And this is one of our servants, Dorothy. She will be sure to tend to any other needs you have."

Camilla tried to process all he had told her, but had little time to contemplate its meaning when the servant lady asked if she needed any water. Camilla was thirsty, now that she thought of it. She took some water, but it made her somewhat nauseous. She laid her head back down and drifted off to sleep again until the doctor came to see her.

The physician seemed quite convinced that Camilla was fine and would recover in no time. "Just get plenty of rest," he told her, and then went to relay his findings to Lord Edmond. Camilla, feeling secure in her surroundings, was glad to take him up on his orders.

She continued to sleep on and off throughout the day and overnight. By morning, she was feeling much better, even a tad restless. Dorothy was in again early to see if Camilla wanted breakfast brought to her or if she was feeling well enough to come down for breakfast. "Lord Edmond would like to have a word with you, if at all possible. He is quite grateful for what you did."

Camilla barely remembered the events; it was sort of a blur to her. But she was feeling much better and agreed to join him. She started to rise when it occurred to her that she was unprepared to be seen in public. She was currently wearing a long, white nightgown and was certain her own clothes were dirty from traveling the past two days and sleeping out of doors.

"Don't worry about a thing, dear," Dorothy reassured her. "We'll make sure you are quite presentable before you head down. Now how about a bath?"

It felt great to be clean and presentable. Dorothy found Camilla a simple, yet pretty dress and helped pin her hair up in a simple fashion. She felt plain, but tidy. Dorothy led her down a large winding staircase to a hall where breakfast was being served. There was a grand table that filled most of the room. Lord Edmond sat on one end, his daughter Tabitha on his right, and a fine-looking lady with soft brown curls sat to his left, who the child resembled.

"Good morning," Lord Edmund greeted Camilla, rising. "Won't you have a seat?" He gestured to a seat next to Tabitha.

"Thank you very much," was all Camilla could say.

They sat in silence as a middle-aged man in a suit and tie, whom they called Hector, began serving them. Once their meal was before them, and Hector had exited the room, Edmond began to speak.

"Please tell us, what is your name, dear creature? To whom do I owe such an incredible debt of gratitude?"

"My name is Camilla, Camilla Waller," she answered politely. "Only you owe me nothing, I am certain."

"Oh, but you are wrong. Indeed, you saved my daughter's life! This is Tabitha. She is my pride and joy. For my life, I could not imagine losing her. She is my most precious possession." Tabitha smiled brightly in response to her father's kind words.

Camilla looked around the room. It seemed he certainly had many possessions at that. It was apparent that she was in the home of someone important. "It was my pleasure, honestly. I saw the girl in distress and couldn't help but do what I could."

"Yes, but if you hadn't been there, I shudder to think what would have happened. And besides, you were magnificent. I went after you myself and found the water quite difficult to maneuver. However you managed it, I thank the Lord above!"

Lord Edmond went on to describe exactly how the events unfolded. He had been walking the grounds of his estate while his daughter played along the shore, as she often did. He had warned her that the water looked particularly rough and to steer clear of the rocks. But Tabitha did not mind her father.

"It didn't seem so bad to me. I just wanted to see the spray," Tabitha replied.

"Yes, well, now you see why you must trust your father. It almost took your life, and then what would have become of me?" Edmond continued, explaining that while the waves were mostly breaking further off, a large swell came upon the child unexpectedly and swept her off the rocky ledge she was standing on. "So, you see, that's all there was to it. How quickly things can happen in a moment if you're not careful. That was when I heard my daughter scream, and I rushed to find you struggling in the water. As I understood it, you had rescued my dear girl but got swept up in the current yourself. So, I dove in after you and managed to get us both to safety."

"So, you saved me as well. Doesn't that make us even?" Camilla replied.

The man shook his head. "Not even remotely. You certainly would not have found yourself in such a predicament had you not risked your life for the sake of my daughter. And she would have surely died without you. For that, I will forever be in your debt."

Tabitha seemed unconcerned with how close she came to drowning, but rather seemed to like the bit of excitement and attention it brought. Not to mention a fascinating new guest. "Good thing you showed up when you did. I just like seeing the waves, don't you? When that big one came over me, I sure was taken by surprise. Never saw a wave so huge in my life!"

Lord Edmond hushed his daughter. "Yes, it is a good thing indeed. But only from a safe distance, sweet pea." The lady with brown curls nodded in agreement, then Lord Edmond turned back to Camilla. "But please, tell me, how did you manage to show up at just the right time? Where did you come from? I do not think I recall any Wallers in these parts. How may I be of service in returning you to your loved ones? They must be very worried by now."

Camilla hung her head in embarrassment. "The truth is, I have no loved ones close by. I only just arrived when I saw your daughter struggling in the water. I have traveled far to get here, but I do not wish to speak about it further, if you don't mind. Please, just give me a day or so to recover, and I will move on and leave you to your family. That is, if your wife wouldn't mind so very much."

Lord Edmond wore a look of confusion. "Wife? Oh, Lady Edmond here. I am sorry, I forgot to introduce you. This is my sister, Hillary Edmond." The pretty lady smiled simply. "And my name is Jonathan. We welcome you to Mayfield Hall. It would be a pleasure to host you while you decide where it is you need to go next. I will not demand you tell us anything, but I do hope in time you will entrust us with your woes so that we may be of some assistance to you in your time of need. It is the very least we can do."

Camilla was dazed by this strange turn of events. She couldn't fathom how she ended up in this grand home among such fine people. She wondered what they would think if they knew her background. It didn't matter much what they thought, but for now, she didn't want to share such painful memories. Instead, she decided to eat of the bounty before her and enjoy the great fortune at finding herself at the mercy of such kind people.

CHAPTER 38

*A*fter breakfast, Camilla was escorted to a sitting room where she, Hillary, and Tabitha were invited to spend the rest of the morning. It included a library, with shelves on three walls containing a wealth of leatherbound books and a grand piano in the corner for entertaining.

Immediately taking a seat on the piano bench, Tabitha insisted on showing their new guest the song her music tutor had her learning. In truth, it sounded more like practice than performance. The child clumsily moved her fingers across the keys, stumbling through the difficult portion of the simple song and losing all sense of timing, but Camilla smiled at her enthusiasm to please her.

"That was very nice, I'm sure it is fun to learn such a marvelous instrument," Camilla said kindly.

"Fun? Hardly. Father makes me take piano lessons. And art. Though I do enjoy that so much more. Do you play piano?"

"I'm afraid I don't," Cami replied plainly.

"Do you paint?"

"No, I have never had the pleasure."

The look on the child's face was one of astonishment, "Oh my, I thought every lady did these things. At least that's what Father tells me. Are you not a lady?"

Hillary stepped in. "Hush, child. Your father is right to encourage you in these accomplishments, but we do not know our guest so well or what her skills may be. Now grab your schoolbook and go to work on your studies. I ask that you sit quietly at the table and leave Miss Waller to me."

Tabitha didn't hide her look of disappointment at being excluded from the conversation, but did as she was told. It was becoming increasingly clear that the child was a bit obstinate, but well-meaning overall. Camilla felt a strange kinship with the young girl.

"Now," Hillary said when Tabitha was well situated with her nose pressed firmly to her book, "What sort of things might you enjoy, my dear?"

Having no formal education, Camilla thought about what might pass for a suitable answer. "Well, I do love animals. I have worked closely with them throughout my life. I love to be outdoors. I also enjoy reading and writing a little."

"Well, that's just fine. Please feel free to indulge yourself in any of the books you see here. And I'll be sure that Dorothy includes some pen and paper in your room in case you wish to write to anyone. We send out mail every morning. Just be sure to give it to Dorothy, and she will ensure it gets taken down to the post office for you."

Camilla was grateful for the offer but was unsure how best to engage such a fine lady beyond this. What would she have to talk about that would be of interest? Lady Edmond was a lovely girl, perhaps only two or three years older than herself, but seemed much more refined. Her hair was stylish, but not showy. Her clothing was neat and elegant as she sat with an upright posture. She thought to herself that her mother would probably have been much like her if she had been raised in a similar station.

"Do you live here with your brother and niece?" Camilla finally asked.

"Yes, for the time being. My dear brother is frequently away on business and needs someone to look after Tabitha since her mother died a few years ago, so I have been living here and helping out the best I can. She needs a woman's care, as you can see."

"I'm so sorry to hear of their loss," Camilla replied sincerely.

"Yes, well, Tabitha was quite young and remembers very little of her mother, only what she hears from us or sees in her portrait in the hall. My brother, of course, was devastated. They were not married long when she became ill, only a few years. He spared no expense in getting the best doctors to care for her, but in the end, it could not be helped, and her health deteriorated. It was a dark time for Jonathan, but he is doing much better these days. And Tabitha keeps him busy enough.

"So, this is why another loss would have finished him. She is all he has left of his dear wife, and in truth, Tabitha is his only source of real joy. Even though she pushes his boundaries constantly, she brings much fun and laughter to a household that would otherwise be dreary."

Camilla's heart went out to Lord Edmond and his daughter. "I see, well, I am all the more glad I could spare him further pain. He seems a gentle man."

"Yes, he certainly is that. The kindest of men. But also taken to melancholy if not mindful. Which is again, why his daughter means so very much to him. He meant it when he said he was indebted to you. I beg you to not take advantage of his gratitude, though."

"Certainly not. I wouldn't dream—"

"I don't mean to accuse you of anything. Why, I hardly know you. It's just that many would take advantage of him if given half a chance, and as his sister, I feel it is my duty to see to it that no one does. You see, our father has amassed much wealth and has already bestowed a great portion of Jonathan's inheritance on him. He wholeheartedly trusts Jonathan in matters of business, and Jonathan is quite a natural when it comes to handling finances. He has a nose for a good investment, which has benefited my father greatly.

"But since losing his wife, Jonathan cares very little about any of it, only that he honors our family name and does some good with what he has. For that reason, he is eager to relinquish his funds to the right cause. I share this because you seem a sympathetic soul. I only ask you to be mindful of his tendencies. I am most protective of him and Tabitha and offer my counsel liberally, which, thank heavens, he is prone to take. You see, I am the sensible one. So, I can't help but exert my influence when needed. But I'd so much rather we reach some understanding to begin with. Do you understand, my dear?"

Camilla was quick to respond to these concerns. "Well, let me assure you, Lady Edmond, I came with no expectation. I am just grateful to have a place to stay for the moment. And I do not plan to stay long, so you have nothing to concern yourself with. My saving Tabitha was just fortunate timing."

Lady Edmond seemed satisfied. "Well, thank you for putting my mind at ease. I trust you are sincere. I don't want you to think me ungrateful. I, too, am indebted to you for saving my niece, and all too happy to oblige you. Though I must admit, I've never seen a lady act as you did. You were swift and heroic, traits I rarely find in the female sex. And yet, you are also quite lovely in your way. Forgive my boldness, but I observe you have a strange look in your eyes. I imagine those eyes have seen much."

Camilla turned away to hide her face from exposure. "Yes, I suppose they have. But it's not important."

"Then tell me, what *can* we do to help you and ensure my brother is satisfied? I sense you are in dire need of assistance."

"Is it that obvious?" Camilla felt exposed.

Hillary offered a knowing smile. "Women know these things. You don't have to tell me anything you don't want, only how we might best help restore you to your previous station."

"Well," Camilla began, "I suppose I just need a place to stay for a while. At least until I get settled. I need to find work so I can support myself. If you or your brother could help with that, I would be quite grateful."

"Again, I won't press you on details, but I suppose I'd be a fool not to ask that you reassure me there are no legal matters to be concerned about. I wouldn't want my brother caught up in a scandal."

Camilla replied quickly. "Absolutely not. My problems are only of a private nature. I give my word. You have nothing to worry about, scandal-wise."

Hillary breathed a sigh of relief. "Then, I'll see what I can do. In the meantime, you are free to stay here for the time being. We have plenty of room, and my brother would insist on it, I know. And I will help acclimate you to society until such a time as we can find a place for you. Does that sound good?"

"Most certainly. But first, I need to go retrieve my things. You see, when I ran down the hillside, I left my belongings behind."

"Not a problem, I will send Hector to gather them for

you..."

"No," Camilla interrupted. "I will get them myself. I just need to be told the way, as I don't have any idea what direction I was carried in."

Hillary seemed concerned. "But dear, you have suffered quite a trauma. Surely you are too weak to make the trek back up there. No, please let us send Hector."

But Camilla was insistent. "I really would like to go myself. Besides, I could use the fresh air."

"Suit yourself, I will have Hector tell you the way. Only wait until after lunch, will you? My brother likes to spend his mornings in peace, and any sudden activity would certainly alarm him."

Camilla agreed and then decided to settle in with a book. Despite such a large library, she found little that would calm her overactive mind, but finally settled on an intriguing mystery to keep her occupied until lunch.

CHAPTER 39

*L*unch was quite pleasant, but like Lady Edmond, Lord Edmond had concerns about Camilla going up the cliff after all she had physically endured. "At least let me accompany you," he offered.

Camilla had planned to go alone and spend some time collecting her thoughts, but she did not want to appear ungracious, plus the chance to get to know her benefactor proved tempting, so she finally agreed.

It was a beautiful summer day, picturesque in every way. The sun was shining brightly while fluffy clouds drifted lazily in the sky. The temperature was moderate with very little humidity—perfect for a stroll.

Once outdoors, Camilla felt unreasonably shy being alone with Lord Edmond. She said little as they headed toward the coast together. The property stretched quite far, and it took some time to walk back to where she had first rescued Tabitha from the rough sea. Once a fair distance from the house, Camilla got a better look at the abode she would call home for the time being.

Mayfield Hall was a sprawling estate, which she already sensed from her limited scope of being relegated to only a handful of rooms thus far. From what she could assess looking out the windows, it appeared grand in stature, but only now could she fully grasp the size and vastness in its entirety. Stone-clad and ivy-draped, the stately manor had an air of nobility, standing tall among green rolling hills in solemn grandeur. Its many gables and mullioned windows gazed out across the gentle swell of the countryside like an old and dreaming sentinel, giving an impression of permanence and stability.

The grounds were neatly landscaped with gravel paths that meandered through the velvet green lawn to a hidden fortress on the west end lined with clipped boxwoods. Camilla assumed these must border a garden, and she secretly hoped she might have the pleasure of exploring these grounds during her stay.

Lord Edmond, noticing the girl surveying the property, asked, "Do you like it?"

"Like what?"

"Mayfield Hall." Lord Edmond stated, waving his hand to indicate the entire estate.

"What's not to like? It's breathtaking. I can't imagine living in a home so grand."

"Yes, well, I do have a fondness for it, but it has its drawbacks too."

"I can't imagine…"

"Memories."

Camilla nodded silently; certain he was referring to his late wife.

"Did my sister fill you in on my background?"

"Yes, a little. She told me you lost your wife some years back. I am sorry for that."

"I have to tell you, Camilla, it is no great privilege to always be known as the guy who lost his wife. I'm sure she told you I took it quite badly, but we've been doing well here for some time. You needn't concern yourself over that. Plenty have, and I've grown tired of their sorrowful looks. The best part about making new acquaintances is that you get to start fresh on what impression you make. And I would like very much not to be seen in a pitiable light, if you can oblige me on this one matter."

Camilla smiled warmly at Lord Edmond. "You got it. Sounds like we could both use a fresh start."

"Indeed. I hope I might aid in that cause. It appears as though you'll be staying with us a while."

"Did Hillary inform you of our discussion earlier today?"

"Yes, I'm afraid she did. Knowing my sister, she may have said other things to you as well. She is quite protective of Tabitha and me but never mind her. She really has a very generous nature and is eager to know you better. We all are."

This was reassuring to Camilla. "And I would like to know all of you as well. I am very grateful, Lord Edmond, for your kindness in allowing me to stay while I figure out what to do next. I really can't thank you enough."

"Think nothing of it, we are glad to help," Lord Edmond replied simply.

It was then that Camilla spotted her satchel, shoes, and her father's old army coat. "There are my things!" She cried and began running to claim the items.

Lord Edmond trotted up the hill alongside her, happy that the task was successfully accomplished. When they reached the top of the cliff, Camilla looked out at the familiar skyline. She thought of her mental state when she was last in this place and felt the familiar pang of grief that led her to the moment when she almost ended her life.

Lord Edmond couldn't help but notice the pained expression on her face as she gazed out at the sea. "Are you quite all right, Miss Waller?" he asked.

Camilla looked up, taken off guard by the question. She hadn't realized how transparent her emotions were. "Yes, I am fine. I'm just feeling a little tired now."

Lord Edmond took her hand. "I imagine so, you have been through quite an ordeal. Let me take you back to the house so you may rest for the afternoon. I'll call on the doctor."

Camilla shook her head. "A doctor won't be necessary, but I would very much like to rest." She then allowed Lord Edmond to lead her down the cliff and back toward the sprawling manor. They spoke only in generalities, commenting on the weather, the rose bushes, which were in full bloom, and what meal was planned for supper.

"I hope roast duck is to your liking?" he asked as they approached the front door.

"I wouldn't know," Camilla answered honestly.

"Well, then, you are in for a real treat. It's my favorite. In the meantime, please get the rest you need. I'll make sure Dorothy gets you up in time to dine with us."

Camilla looked down at her dress. "I'm afraid I don't have anything suitable for dining. Even this dress was lent to me."

"Nothing to concern yourself over. Dorothy will make sure you are taken care of. Only think about feeling better. And if you're up for it, I would love it if you would join me for a ride in the morning. My sister tells me you are quite fond of animals, and I am sure you will find we have a nice variety of fillies to ride."

Riding with Lord Edmond sounded fine, but Camilla knew it would bring back memories of her time with Frederick. She thanked him and told him she would let him know. Then headed up the stairs to lie down for a while.

Dorothy came to check on Camilla an hour before supper, just as Lord Edmond promised. She brought her a new dress to wear and offered to fix her hair, which had come loose from the activities of the day. The new dress was slightly more formal, yet unlike what she was used to wearing in the circus. It seemed odd to wear a fine dress and not be expected to wear makeup, but Camilla didn't wish to make a fuss.

She looked herself over in the full-length mirror, located in the corner of the room. She appeared quite elegant, though not at all how she had grown accustomed to seeing her reflection. She appeared more grown-up, refined, ladylike even. Having someone help you dress for dinner was bound to do that to a person. Even in the circus, they had assistants but there was something different about the type of service Dorothy offered. Much more proper than the young, silly girls they hired for the performers.

Dinner turned out to be another pleasant affair. Not only did she find she enjoyed duck after all, but this time Camilla got to speak to Tabitha a little more. Mostly she listened as the child told her all about her life, her studies, and what it was like growing up as the daughter of Lord Edmond.

Tabitha motioned for Camilla to lean in and whispered loud enough for everyone to hear. "Now that you're going to be here a while, I think there are things you ought to know. If you have any questions, be sure to ask me. I'll give you the real low down."

Camilla thought it humorous how the young girl spoke so

informally compared to her father and aunt. If not for the striking family resemblance, she would have thought the girl was related to someone else altogether. But she could see why Hillary informed her of the importance she held for Lord Edmond, as she was full of energy and said unexpected things, often causing him to laugh out loud—a sight not too often seen otherwise. Camilla found herself taking great delight in the young girl as well.

When supper was over, Lord Edmond rose to retire to his study for the evening, but not before approaching Camilla. "I have some work to do, but this is usually when the ladies take tea in the sitting room. You are welcome to join them. And I trust you did not forget my invitation for tomorrow morning?" he added.

Camilla shook her head. "No, I didn't forget."

"Well, if you don't mind, please inform Dorothy first thing tomorrow morning if you are able to join me. And I do hope you will." He then took Camilla's hand and kissed it, as was a mode of convention. Still, Hillary gazed at the pair with watchful eyes.

Camilla did not accept the invitation to take tea in the sitting room but informed Lady Edmond that she was quite fatigued and would like to rest. Hillary, of course, understood and bid her goodnight, then followed her brother to his study instead.

CHAPTER 40

*A*fter receiving plenty of rest, Camilla decided to accept Lord Edmond's invitation to go riding the next morning. She informed Dorothy of her decision, so the maid left to tell her master and then returned with a green riding habit, complete with undergarments. Camilla wondered how the woman seemed to easily find apparel to suit her size, though perhaps not her usual taste.

She worked her way into the costume, with Dorothy's assistance, who then went to work on her hair. It seemed an awful fuss just to go riding.

The idea was to go for a jaunt through the countryside and then return for breakfast. As it turned out, Hillary and Tabitha would also be joining them, which made Camilla a tad less nervous. She was escorted down to the stables, where Lord

Edmond was already waiting. The early morning haze had not quite worn off, making the air cool and damp.

"Now then," he began, "Which horse would suit our lovely guest?"

Camilla looked down the line at all the prized ponies and couldn't tell one from another. "They all look like they come from excellent stock. I suppose I'll let you choose."

Lord Edmond already seemed to have the perfect filly in mind, a speckled pony with a grey mane named Gypsy. Camilla thought it suitable and mounted it in her usual way—one leg on each side. It took her a moment to adjust with the abundance of fabric from the skirt of her dress getting in the way.

Hillary and Tabitha arrived shortly thereafter and seemed to have horses of their own that they preferred. Camilla couldn't help but notice that they mounted them quite differently, choosing to ride side saddle. She had never attempted to ride a horse that way, as it seemed most inconvenient. She thought it would feel even more awkward to try and make the change now, so she acted as though nothing was unusual about her sitting position.

It didn't stop Tabitha from noticing. "See, even Camilla rides her horse astride! It seems so much easier. Why can't we all ride that way?"

"Quiet now," Hillary said.

Camilla blushed with embarrassment but was grateful that Lord Edmond seemed to pay no attention. Once they got moving, the whole incident passed from her mind. Her horse was quite obedient and easy to direct. That gave her at least an advantage to demonstrate her proficiency, if not her ladylike attributes.

Still, Lord Edmond addressed her as a lady, never talking down to her or treating her as if she were beneath him. She felt honored in his presence. They rode as one unit for a while, moving along with an easy gait, before finally breaking up into two groups, with Hillary and Tabitha going further ahead due to Tabitha's penchant for trotting.

Camilla and Lord Edmond began by discussing the weather again, a common topic to fall back on whenever an awkward moment presented itself. Eventually, he got onto more pressing topics. "My sister and I had a discussion last evening, regarding your situation. I hope I might be of assistance to you in making an offer that could satisfy all parties."

Camilla nodded, unsure of what to expect. She was getting comfortable with her environment, but was eager to find out the decision that would determine her ultimate fate.

"As you know, my sister is here frequently to help with Tabitha, but this is not her permanent home. My mother needs her often, and so she travels back and forth more frequently than she should. It occurred to me that perhaps we might help each other out, considering this unexpected circumstance.

"How would you feel about being a governess to my Tabitha? The child seems to have taken quite a liking to you, and it is apparent to us both that you have a nurturing nature. Is this something you might consider to satisfy your need for a proper placement? May I further note that you would not be treated as mere help, you can expect to be regarded with the utmost respect in my household as the caretaker of my beloved daughter."

Camilla was stunned by the offer but was by no means disappointed. She indeed had a natural affection for the child. "Yes, I would be happy to take on the role if you feel I am qualified," she answered decidedly.

"Well, you have nothing to concern yourself with in terms of qualifications. She has tutors to assist in her education. Your greatest responsibility would be in keeping an eye on her and ensuring she minds her superiors, especially while I am away. It would give me great peace of mind knowing that she is looked after, and I believe you could do her a world of good to that end. Does that answer your question?"

"Yes, I suppose it does. You truly have a wonderful daughter, and based on what you've described, I believe I am up to the task. It would be an honor to be of help to you and your sister as well. Although I must say, you haven't known me for long. I am flattered you trust me with such a critical undertaking."

"I can't imagine anyone more suitable for the role than one who thought nothing of risking her own life for the sake of my girl. That tells me all I need to know of your character. And some things a person can just tell. There is a pure and genuine quality about you. I felt it right from the beginning. In you, I sense no deceit."

Camilla turned to face Lord Edmond. "And does Hillary share your good opinion of my character?"

"Hillary will always be protective of me, but she does admit there is some logic in making the offer. If she seems cautious, it is because she, too, senses something different in you. In truth, you are not like anyone either of us has ever known. I hope you will beg my pardon, but it seems clear you are not familiar with the rules and etiquette we are accustomed to, and yet you do not seem to be associated with the lower classes either. There is something almost otherworldly about your demeanor. I can't quite place your society, but I don't think I'd be half-surprised to learn you came from another realm altogether. Yet I do not find it alarming. It's honestly most becoming. You remind me of someone I once knew, and yet, altogether different at the same time."

Camilla was flattered by his words, though she found his assessment of her intriguing, considering her origins and recent life experience. "Well, I assure you, Lord Emond, I am quite human. You can be sure of that. And I will accept your kind offer and do my best to put your mind at ease where your daughter's care is concerned."

Lord Edmond smiled warmly at Camilla and thanked her for her swift answer. "Now, let's see if we can't deliver the good news to Tabitha. How do you feel about picking up speed a bit?"

Camilla did not hesitate. "You're on!" she said with a

playful grin, and she and Lord Edmond raced to where his sister and daughter were, a short way off. Tabitha received the news with much enthusiasm. Hillary, however, displayed little reaction at all, so Camilla could not tell whether she was pleased or not. She liked Hillary and understood her hesitancy but wanted her approval all the same.

I am going to have to get to know her better and, hopefully, that will put her mind at ease, she told herself. But she wasn't quite ready to talk about all she had gone through. Being a circus performer would probably not secure anyone's peace of mind where she was concerned. No, those things she would keep to herself until the time felt appropriate to share her past. For now, her focus would be on proving her worth to these fine people who had given her a new chance at life.

It thrilled Camilla to know she would be able to go on paying for the farm and that her mother would have even less to worry about once she was informed of her new position. All in all, it was a delightful morning, and the thought of Frederick barely crossed her mind. Well, almost.

CHAPTER 41

*T*abitha's excitement made Camilla far less intimidated to take on the new role as her governess. After all, it couldn't be any more demanding than working for Fiona. She was given a full rundown of what her duties would include and the weekly rate of pay for the position—it was as much as she made at the circus in a month. Hillary was to stay through the week and see to it that the child was acclimating to the new change before heading back to tend to her mother's needs.

Camilla's first order of business was to write her own mother regarding the new position, which she hoped would give her the assurance that the farm would be paid off in no time. She gave the letter to Dorothy to mail first thing in the morning. She was sure it would make her mother glad to find she was no longer working for the circus but was now in a respectable position in the house of a Lord. She left out the details of what led to this sudden change of events, unwilling to recount the terrible memory.

If there was one thing Camilla had done since coming to live with Lord Edmond, it was to make an effort to push away all unpleasant thoughts of the past. To her, dredging it up would be akin to looking into the sun—completely unbearable. Her only hope of survival was to focus on the here and now. Something she was able to do most of the time, except at night, when lying in bed. Then her thoughts would drift to moments with Frederick, Duchess, and life with the circus, even against her will. It relentlessly invaded her dreams. Sometimes she awoke deep in the night, panting and thinking she'd never really gone. Echoes of cheers from the audience still reverberated in the recesses of her mind. This was always followed by a deep realization of what she had endured and lost. Then she would lie awake in the dark for a time, aching from missing it all.

But going back was not an option. Max had made it perfectly clear she was no longer welcome, not to mention she had nothing to offer the circus without Duchess. Perhaps she could have taken to training some other exotic animal, but after the tragic loss of lives, Frederick's bitter betrayal with Isabelle, and the resentment from the troupe, it made it impossible to seriously contemplate. Caring for the child was the sensible thing to do. Besides, she had never been treated so generously, and she couldn't abandon her benefactors in their time of need. So, these thoughts quickly dissipated with the light of day.

With all the preparations being made for the transition, it was decided that a new wardrobe would be supplied to Camilla. Hillary offered to aid in choosing just the right clothing to suit her needs as governess. Camilla was also given a spacious room with a large window overlooking the grounds that led out to the sea—a room carefully selected by Lord Edmond himself. For all she knew of life, she may as well be living in a palace.

Hillary, though somewhat standoffish, began to warm up to Camilla in the days that followed. They spent much time together, sharing meals, having tea, and reading books. Life in the manor was slow-paced, so reading seemed to be an appropriate pastime, which suited Camilla just fine. She felt she could use less excitement for the time being to heal and work toward restoring her spirits. At least she hoped one day that would be possible.

Today, Camilla was being given a tour of the entire estate so that she would be able to make her way around with ease. So far, she had seen very little and was curious as the outside indicated a much greater size than she had explored. Lord Edmond wanted to do the honors, but was called away suddenly, so Hillary picked up the mantle.

She was first shown the entire main floor, including the rooms she was already familiar with. She was then taken down one hall that led to another sitting room she had not seen, presumably Lord Edmond's. Hanging proudly at the end of the hall was a large portrait of Tabitha's mother, the one Hillary alluded to when Camilla first arrived. She took a moment to look it over; she was a lovely woman with fair hair, set in ringlets, and bright eyes. She appeared to be a lady, without question, but something in her smile hinted at mischief—an indication of where Tabitha inherited it from.

She was then led down into the kitchen and the servants' quarters and introduced to all the staff so they would know who to regard as being in charge of the young Miss Edmond. To Camilla, the size of the staff seemed almost as numerous as the people who lived in her little village.

Following the introduction, she was shown a series of bedrooms on three separate floors, including Lord Edmond's sleeping quarters. They entered it briefly, as one of the servants had just finished tending to it. It was as Camilla expected— simple, yet regal and fitting for a gentleman. A smaller portrait of the late Lady Edmond hung there as well, but appeared more recent. She wondered how soon the painting was done before her passing, but didn't dare ask.

Attached to Lord Edmond's room was another that remained locked. Hillary regarded it as Lady Edmond's dressing room. She explained how it was only opened to be cleaned once a week, but had largely remained untouched all these years. "Tabitha may want to visit this room, but we ask that you please allow only Lord Edmond to do that honor. He is quite specific about this particular request." Camilla understood.

Lastly, Hillary took Camilla to Tabitha's room. It was an enchanting room, the sort of every little girl's dream, and decorated by Lady Edmond herself shortly after giving birth to her daughter. The bed contained four slender posts dressed in a frilly, pink and white canopy stretched across the top, tied at each end with large pink satin bows. The bedding complemented the look of soft pink and white tones, lined with ruffled edges. A few stuffed animals rested at the head, completing the tidy, charming setup.

Matching, billowy drapes hung from the windows and were tied with the same satin ribbon. Sitting in the corner was an ornate rocking horse next to a large, white toy box with whimsical hand-carvings of stars and moons. Sitting on the toybox were an assortment of elegant porcelain dolls and more plush animals.

Along the adjacent wall was a white fireplace, and next to it, two small armchairs seated in front of a rounded wooden table adorned with a charming miniature tea set speckled in dainty rosebuds. Camilla couldn't imagine having such a luxurious room as a child. But she couldn't prepare herself for what came next.

Turning around to survey the room at all angles, Camilla's breath caught in her chest. On the wall was a giant mural of a circus scene, an elephant front and center, standing on a platform and balancing a ball on the tip of its trunk. Her reaction was something of a gasp, which even caught Hillary's attention, who had been talking endlessly about Tabitha's morning and evening schedule. She stopped and caught sight of the young girl's face, which had gone pale.

Without realizing it, Camilla's bottom lip began to

quiver, and tears welled up in her eyes. Memories of Duchess came flooding back without warning. The loss of her life returned like a fresh wound. It was all Camilla could do not to break down in front of her host.

"What is it, my dear? Are you not feeling well?" Lady Edmond asked.

"I'm afraid not," Camilla replied. "I'm feeling a bit dizzy. I'd like to go lie down for a bit if you don't mind. I do apologize; you must think me such a fragile creature. But I assure you this is not usual for me." She had never been prone to such weakness before, but suddenly she could barely manage the will to hold herself up. All efforts to push the past aside came crumbling down on her at the sight of the colorful mural.

Hillary approached Camilla, placing her hand on her back to steady her body so she wouldn't take a fall. "Well, you have recently been through an ordeal. Come, dear, I'll get Dorothy to help you."

They exited the room, and Hillary called for help. Dorothy was close by and assisted in taking the young girl back to her room, which was just a short walk down the hall. After fetching a glass of water and helping Camilla to the bed, Dorothy said, "Lie down a while, Miss, and I'll be sure to check on you in a bit. It might be this sudden heat wave we're having. I'm sure you'll feel better soon."

Camilla nodded, knowing her grief alone was to blame for her sudden turn. But she couldn't tell anyone that. Who would understand her great loss? Even though she knew she had done nothing wrong, once again, she felt like a fraud. But the problem was, she didn't know who she was at all anymore. She certainly wasn't that girl on the farm. And some part of her still regarded the circus as home, though she could never go back.

This must be my new life now, she told herself before drifting off, her mind no longer able to process the pain of missing Duchess.

CHAPTER 42

*M*onths passed, and Camilla had settled nicely into her position as Tabitha's governess. The child kept her on her toes, to be sure, but there was a great affection developing between them, and the girl did make great efforts to mind. In many ways, she craved structure, but Camilla didn't wish to kill her spirit altogether and would take Tabitha on little adventures to let her run free with little restriction. This seemed to give her the energy release she craved and helped her to settle down when she needed to focus on her studies.

Sometimes Camilla liked to sit in on the tutoring lessons, eager to learn herself, especially History, English, and the Arts. She even tried her hand at painting for the first time, but found she was not a natural. Tabitha, who was much more proficient with a brush, even for her age, was blunt in letting Camilla know she wasn't very good, but Camilla took no offense. She appreciated the child's honesty and praised her for it. But also took the opportunity to teach the girl how best to express her opinions in a way that would show delicacy to the feelings of others who might not be quite so appreciative.

Lord Edmond was away often, as he claimed he would be, but when he was home, he took great joy in his daughter, as well as in Camilla. He invited them both to dine with him nightly and took them on afternoon outings into town in his carriage. And he always returned bearing gifts for his dear child. He even brought home the occasional trinket for Camilla, which she accepted gracefully. Toward her, he was always kind and considerate, showing his gratitude at every opportunity.

Hillary also left shortly after Camilla took on the role of governess, but was planning to return soon. Camilla was both excited and nervous, as she did like Hillary, though she still wasn't positive if the feeling was mutual. She was certain Lady Edmond wrote to Dorothy regularly to request updates on how everything was managing. The last thing she wanted was to give her any reason for concern, so she was careful to fulfill all the duties assigned to her and not to overstep any boundaries given.

But all in all, Camilla was feeling quite content with life at Mayfield Hall, despite the dull ache she carried deep inside. Though she desired to put the past behind her, it haunted her memories and was easily dredged up by a simple word, a song, or a picture. Sometimes on her outings with Tabitha, Camilla would find herself reclining beneath a tree and thinking about the past, recalling the excitement of performing for an audience, the lights, and the applause. She also wondered what had become of all the people in the circus. Though she had few friends near the end, she loved them just the same. She even wondered what came of Fiona and longed for her friendship, shallow as it was.

And then there was Frederick. The pain was too great to ruminate on him for very long. It didn't take much for that sharp dagger-like sensation to return to her heart when she remembered how much they shared and how quickly it was taken from her. She wondered if it might not be the kind of wound one never fully recovers from.

But she wasn't altogether unhappy, though. And that was more than what she could hope for when she considered how close she came to ending it all. The hopelessness she once felt had been replaced with hope for the future. Still, she sometimes wished she had a friend to confide in with all these things. But as time went on, she guarded these secrets as hers alone. For some inexplicable reason, she didn't want to let the Edmonds in on her past and felt it best never to speak of it. And in short order, they too seemed uninterested in her origins and focused solely on the present.

Yes, the present was all that mattered, and Lord Edmond was set to return home shortly. He had been gone for an especially long duration, attending to some business affair his father had given him charge over. This meant the whole house would soon be abuzz with preparations. Tabitha was even more excitable than usual and could speak of almost nothing else. It was a lonely life without her father, and though Camilla did her best to fill that space, anyone was a poor substitute by comparison.

Camilla found that even she was excited regarding his return, as well as Hillary's, and took to doing what she could to prepare for it. She wanted Tabitha to remain in good spirits and to be presented as her best and most well-behaved self. She would often remind her to be a good girl and make Father and Aunt Hillary proud. Tabitha would promise and then find herself getting up to a little mischief, but nothing overly concerning.

The week passed quickly, and the evening of Lord Edmond's homecoming had arrived. Tabitha was dressed in a pretty yellow frock and donning a large white bow to secure her braid in the back. She was the picture of a demure, well-mannered child, though it took only seeing her father's face to bring her true spirit to life. She cried out joyfully at the sight of him, running toward him with abandon, wrapping her arms around his neck, and peppering him with many kisses. Camilla thought it sweet how much Tabitha utterly adored her father, and it made her miss her own dear Papa.

The three of them went into the sitting room to take tea and wait for Hillary's arrival before going into the dining hall for supper. When Hillary entered, it was with equal fanfare. Tabitha displayed almost as much affection for her aunt, who had been a caretaker to her since the loss of her mother. Hillary, too, betrayed her usual decorum and shed tears of joy at the sight of her beloved niece. Camilla thought her even more beautiful at this moment.

It wasn't long before Tabitha began speaking at an enormous rate of speed to fill her aunt in on all she missed since her departure some months back. She told her about her schooling and the daily outings, even including Camilla's unfortunate attempt at painting. Hillary was quick to correct Tabitha's lack of kindness in making such remarks, but it seemed to please the girl to recount the funny incident, so Camilla took it in stride and, with good humor, agreed that she really was no good at all.

"Well, perhaps I could help with that," Hillary said kindly.

Camilla was touched by the offer and thanked her. "That would be very nice. I have so much to learn."

Being they had a late supper that went long, Camilla offered to take Tabitha back up to her room so that Lord Edmond and his sister could have some time to catch up. Lord Edmond begged her not to go just yet, but Camilla could see that Hillary appreciated the suggestion, so she went without haste. But not before Lord Edmond added that he hoped they would all join him the following afternoon for a luncheon by the shore.

Tabitha squealed with delight at the suggestion. The weather had just begun warming up again, and she longed to go for a swim. Once upstairs, she spoke incessantly, this time about which bathing suit she might wear for such an occasion.

"How about your new one?" Camilla suggested. Her father had picked it up during one of his recent travels.

"Oh yes, that's probably a good idea. But too bad there won't be more people to see it."

"Well, bathing suits are not for showing off, Tabitha, they are for bathing."

The child nodded, then attempted to remove her dress to get into her nightgown. Camilla came to assist, always making sure not to look at the mural on the back wall. "Did you see what Father got me this time?" she asked while dressing.

"No, what did he get you?" Camilla humored the child.

"Don't know. He said it's to be a surprise! And he said he had a surprise for you, too."

Camilla blushed. "Well, I can't imagine what on earth it would be."

"He said we'll know soon enough. I love surprises. Don't you, Camilla?"

Camilla did enjoy surprises, though nothing she ever received felt like it was hers. In a strange way, she felt it all truly belonged to Lord Edmond. "Your father is very kind," she responded.

"Yeah, especially when he really likes someone. He really likes you. I can tell. He smiles more since you came here. Even more than just being with me. I think Father needs more things to smile about, don't you?"

"Get into bed," Camilla said, pulling back the covers. Tabitha jumped in quickly, and Camilla covered her snuggly.

"You like Father too, don't you?" Tabitha asked

innocently.

"Of course, I do. He is a very kind man, as I said."

Tabitha seemed content with the answer and flipped on her side to go to sleep. Camilla kissed her gently on the temple, then turned down her lamp and headed back to her own room to read. Except that she knew she wouldn't be able to focus on the book. Tabitha's words were pressing at the forefront of her mind.

CHAPTER 43

I t couldn't have been a more ideal day for an afternoon by the sea. The weather was moderately warm with just a hint of humidity in the air and accompanied by a soft breeze. After a quick breakfast, Camilla took Tabitha up to her room to prepare for their outing. She helped Tabitha select a bathing suit—she went with the new one after all—and packed up a change of clothing, a linen towel, a shovel, and a metal pail splashed with a playful print of sailboats. She then helped Tabitha dress for their luncheon and called on Dorothy to do the child's hair while she tended to her own preparations.

Camilla perused her wardrobe, which contained a selection of simple, yet elegant, dresses to pick from, all of which had been chosen for her by Hillary during their shopping excursion when she first arrived. She didn't have much opinion of them, but they seemed to suit her needs and figure. She chose a white linen dress with a sage green accent at the waist and collar. She had no bathing suit for herself, but she rightly assumed the adults would not be joining Tabitha in the water anyway.

Considering the seaside was in close proximity to the house, planning the luncheon seemed an unnecessarily complicated ordeal. The servants packed up chairs, tables, linens, dishes, and more. The food was prepared ahead of time and brought down in silver trays. It all seemed like a lot of fuss, especially compared to the picnic lunches Camilla and Frederick threw together in haste. Yet it never felt like anything was missing.

But this was the way of the wealthy, and such luxury could hardly be refused when the resources were at your disposal. And anyway, Lord Edmond, being away so much, rarely had the pleasure of indulging Tabitha in such activities, so when he got the opportunity, he went all out.

Camilla had to admit to herself that the setup was beautiful. The table and chairs were nestled under a large white canopy to keep them shaded from the sun. The table was covered in a white tablecloth and set up as any meal would be in the house, complete with tapered candles. The meal consisted of cold ham, sweet rolls, a potato casserole, and fresh fruit. For dessert, they were served a slice of strawberry cake and tea.

After a thoroughly enjoyable meal, they moved to the sun to bask in its glorious rays. The sound of the ocean roaring was enough to lull Camilla to sleep if it weren't for the sudden announcement from Lord Edmond.

"I have some exciting news," he began with a sparkle in his eyes like that of a child. "I've been speaking with my sister, and we both think it's time we plan a dinner party for the local society. And we'd like to start by inviting you and Tabitha," he said to Camilla.

Tabitha did her usual squeal and thanked her father enthusiastically. She was all too thrilled at the thought of attending her first grown-up dinner party, while Camilla felt a tad stunned by the invitation. "Me? But I'm not part of any society. I'm just the governess."

"Nonsense," Hillary chimed in. "You will be our own special guest. It is time we began introducing you to society. People are dying to meet you. And it will be good for you to get out and meet some of the locals—including the gentlemen."

Camilla wondered if she hadn't felt Hillary nudge her every so lightly.

Lord Edmond frowned at the last comment but continued, "Yes, well, it is certainly high time you met some of our acquaintances. You live here with us now, and there's no reason you shouldn't integrate into our circle. And besides, it's been quite some time since we've planned such an event at Mayfield. It is long overdue."

Tabitha was overjoyed and already talking about what she might wear. Her father continued, "As for you, you can only stay through supper, but you have no need to worry about what you will wear. It has been taken care of. And for you as well," he added, turning back to Camilla.

"So that was your surprise? A new dress for my first grown-up party?" Tabitha cried.

"Indeed. And I will show it to you at once when we get back up to the house, but for now, go and play," he urged her on.

Tabitha quickly changed into her new bathing suit behind a changing curtain, which was already set up by the staff before they arrived. The suit was blue with white stripes, like a sailor's uniform, complete with a giant bow in front and ruffled pantaloons on the bottom. Lord Edmond commented on how becoming it looked, which made the child happy. She gave him a quick peck on the cheek before heading out to the cold, shallow waters to splash about.

He then turned to Camilla once again and added, "As for you, I hope you too will be pleased by my surprise."

Camilla blushed. "I'm sure anything you chose is just fine."

Hillary, once again, kept a watchful eye on them both. It did not escape her attention that her brother's eyes shone in Camilla's presence or that he took great delight in watching her play with his dear Tabitha. He was amused by her charms, no question about it.

Shortly upon returning from their seaside afternoon, Lord Edmond ordered the dresses he had purchased to be taken out. Tabitha's was frilly Pink with white lace, much like her bedding. She adored it and ran to her room to try it on at once.

Camilla's was a shimmery cerulean blue, which suggested ocean waters, and was accented with an intricate beadwork of pearls. Even with her wardrobe of fancy costumes for the circus, she had never owned anything close to being this elegant in her life—she was certain it would make her feel more like a queen than a governess.

"It's quite lovely," Hillary admitted. "I should have to ensure that my own dress is its equal if we are to be hosts."

Once again, Camilla couldn't quite tell if Hillary didn't possess a hint of ire toward her. The remarks were so subtle and proper that it was difficult to decipher the meaning behind her words, but it made her uneasy just the same.

"I'm sure whatever you choose will be most elegant, Lady Edmond," Camilla replied, hoping to ease any perceived tension.

"I doubt I will come across anything so fine in these parts. My brother no doubt had this dress imported from Italy or France, by the looks of it."

"Never you mind," Lord Edmond interrupted. "I simply wanted Miss Waller to have a suitable gown for a social event. Something a little less plain than the frocks you provided, I should imagine."

Hillary gave her brother a wicked glare. "I do not believe

I have done wrong by Miss Waller. I did my best to help select a fine wardrobe so that she would be able to properly care for your daughter, not for entertaining. I give you, my taste is not so fanciful as yours on any given day, but I think all would agree I always choose attire in good taste."

"Indeed, you do, dear sister. Let's not quarrel. The fact is, Miss Waller needed a dress, and so I provided one while doing the same for my daughter. It is the least I could do under the circumstance, being such short notice and all."

All Camilla could say was, "I am happy with anything, really." But the words were lost on both Lord Edmond and his sister, who had already set their minds to whatever opinion they would hold. And Lord Edmond was certainly not going to apologize for purchasing the latest fashion for his guest. He then excused himself to his study, leaving Camilla and Hillary alone.

Camilla sat quietly, but the awkward silence was soon broken. "I do apologize for my brother and me," Hillary said. "I know he intends well."

"By no means do I want to be the source of strife between the two of you. And by no means do I wish to make you believe I would take advantage of his kindness. I assure you, I remember what we spoke about, and I have been mindful to be considerate of your concerns."

Hillary sighed, "I believe you, Camilla, I do. It's just that I'm afraid my brother is not being sensible. For whatever reason, he has developed a great interest in your well-being, and I just want to make sure he does as is proper."

"Well, I certainly have not encouraged anything improper. I am fond of your brother but would never wish to cause harm to any of you."

Hillary gave Camilla a reassuring smile. "I realize I can be a bit overprotective. And the truth is, I was concerned when you first came, just because we didn't know you or where you came from. But I do admit, I have heard great things about how you have attended to my niece, and there is no denying she has developed a real fondness for you. And if I'm honest, she is excelling under your care. I just have a hard time letting go after seeing all Jonathan went through after his wife died. I thought he might never recover. And here he is, the happiest I've seen him in ages, and for some reason, I feel uneasy about it."

Camilla wanted more than anything to put Hillary's concerns to rest, but she didn't know how except to assure her of her intentions once again. "I do appreciate your kind words. I ask that you please trust me. I desperately wish only to do right by Lord Edmond and Tabitha—and you. I only hope we can be friends. I don't have many, you know."

"But that's just it, why don't you have many friends? A delightful person such as yourself should have many. Isn't there anything you can tell us of your past or where you came from? That might help put my mind at ease."

Camilla looked down. "I'm afraid I'd rather not talk about such things, except to tell you this. My father died a couple of years ago, and it devastated me. So, I understand what Lord Edmond and Tabitha have gone through. My mother is still alive, but she lives with her sister. I only left her so that I could find work to help out with my father gone. I hope that will satisfy."

Hillary wanted to know more, but decided not to press Camilla further. "That will do, thank you for sharing this, it does much in helping me understand your predicament. I hope you will forgive any unpleasantness on my end. It's never been personal, but I do so love my brother, you understand."

"Of course," Camilla replied. "I truly appreciate your concern for him. But I have no designs on him whatsoever." And that was the truth. She was still too grieved to entertain possibilities beyond securing a safe environment far from the tragedy of circus life. The idea of ever opening her heart again was really quite impossible.

CHAPTER 44

*I*t was the day of the dinner party and Mayfield Hall was buzzing with last-minute preparations. Since their discussion, Hillary and Camilla grew closer, spending much time together and enjoying each other's company. Hillary taught Camilla to paint a little, as promised. And though she showed some improvement, Camilla was still no good at all. Even so, it was fun to have some activity to keep her mind occupied while she waited for the night of the dinner party.

In truth, Camilla was nervous at the prospect of meeting so many new people. What did she know about pleasing the upper crust? She had grown safe and comfortable among those in Lord Edmond's household, but these were friends—equal in status and breeding. Still, she would attempt to remain optimistic.

Even as the day of the party drew closer, the more she

found herself daydreaming of how she would look in the beautiful gown Lord Edmond had brought her. It amused her to realize she was really no better than Tabitha. Dressing quite plain most of the time, she forgot what it felt like to be done up and was looking forward to wearing the breathtaking cerulean gown.

Now that the highly anticipated evening had arrived, Hillary joined Camilla in her room after tending to Tabitha. Hillary was already in her own gown, a rich crimson and gold, complete with a jeweled ornamental brooch nestled in the front to match her dress, also a deep crimson red, and her hair done up in beautiful, shiny curls. She was quite unlike her normal, sensibly dressed self, but rather wore the look of a young girl, pink with possibilities. It appeared all the ladies of the household were full of joyful anticipation.

Camilla was still in her undergarments when Hillary entered. She was initially expecting Dorothy to assist her, but was relieved to see Lady Edmond's face. With her, she could be honest about the nerves mounting inside.

"You'll do just fine, Camilla. You are a lovely girl. Everyone is just excited to meet you. They've heard much about you."

Camilla was stunned. "They have? Well, that makes it worse!"

"Naturally, my brother and I have shared your many wonderful qualities with our friends. They are glad to see Jonathan faring better than he has in ages, and Tabitha as well."

The effort to quiet her concerns didn't make Camilla any less nervous.

Hillary continued with a new approach, "If you don't know what to say, just ask questions. People around here love to be asked about themselves. That will take any unwanted attention away from you."

"That's actually very helpful," Camilla replied, sitting down at her vanity to apply some makeup—something she had not done since leaving the circus. She looked closely at her reflection. She didn't recognize herself or even know for certain who she was.

She began applying the rouge in the usual way, but Hillary stopped her. "That's far too much. You'll look like a French girl if you do it that way." Camilla turned a crimson color that rivaled Lady Edmond's dress. "Let me help you…"

Camilla turned to face Hillary as she removed the rouge with a towel and then showed Camilla how to apply it sparingly in a way that would flatter her bone structure. She went on to help make up the rest of her face, all in ways much different than how Fiona had taught her.

Hillary then walked behind her to help tighten the corset wrapped loosely around her mid-section. She hadn't worn a corset in months and was reminded of how uncomfortable they were, but knew she would become accustomed to it as the night went on. She was now ready to slip on the cerulean gown. It slid over her body easily and fit as though it were custom-tailored for her.

Hillary helped finalize the ensemble by adding a small tiara that Lord Edmond had gifted Camilla to complement the dress.

Once secure, Camilla turned to look at herself in the full-length mirror and gasped at the lady she saw before her. *Could that really be me?* She had asked herself this question before, and once again images of the messy girl she once was came rushing to her mind. But now, she was even a far cry from the glamorous circus performer she believed herself to be. She could pass as being of royal blood. The contrast was stunning, but Hillary wouldn't know that. No one did—or could.

Hillary herself couldn't help commenting on the exceptional transformation, even from her limited perspective. Looking the part certainly made Camilla less concerned about blending into society, though her behavior was still something altogether different than the upper set. She felt confident that she could fake it well enough to get through the night and was now ready to head down and face the guests that awaited them.

She and Hillary descended the staircase together, Camilla holding her breath with every step. Waiting near the bottom was Lord Edmond, who was engaged in conversation with an elegant couple. Hearing their approach, he trailed off mid-sentence and stared in awe, captivated as Camilla made her way to him. Anyone in the room could not mistake the look of admiration in his eyes.

Lord Edmond gave his excuses and departed from the couple, approaching the threshold of the stairs. He first took his sister's hand and helped her off the last step, then did the same for

Camilla, allowing his hand to linger on hers.

"You're radiant," he said without shame, lifting her hand to kiss it lightly.

Camilla's crimson returned. "Then it turned out all right? I must admit, I feel a little out of place," she said softly, so that only Lord Edmond could hear.

"Better than all right, I've never seen your equal. You are sure to dazzle them all, just as you have dazzled me."

Camilla's head lifted as they entered the dining hall. Many people were already congregated and stopped to see the arrival of the girl they'd heard so much about. Lord Edmond introduced her to this one and that one, each greeting her politely, giving the occasional compliment. Some whispering to Lord Edmond, "Wherever did you find such an enchanting creature?"

Tabitha soon came running up with Hillary, grabbing hold of her hand in hopes of leading her, but finding the task impossible. "Oh Father," she cried, "Isn't it just lovely? My very first dinner party. And Camilla—she looks like a real live princess, doesn't she? I can hardly recognize her."

Lord Edmond reached down and lifted his daughter, a task he wouldn't handle with such ease for much longer at her rate of growth. "Yes, it is a lovely party at that. And I do agree, Miss Waller looks like a real live princess." He kissed his little girl's forehead and then set her back down. She ran off to say hello to the other guests, Hillary following helplessly behind.

They soon sat for dinner, Lord Edmond at the head,

Tabitha on his left. Hillary sat at the other end of the table, specifically requesting that Camilla sit beside her so that she might offer guidance. As the meal was served, Camilla found herself at a loss for words as the company spoke of things she knew nothing about, regarding people they knew, their positions in society, and political matters.

One conversation nearby turned to a more general topic about literature. Even Camilla could follow this discussion. A Sir Wesley seemed to have some very particular opinions regarding the work of Dickens. "How about you, Miss Waller, are you a Dickens fan?"

Camilla admitted she was not a huge fan of his work overall, though she did enjoy David Copperfield quite a bit, as well as Oliver Twist.

"I say, I must agree, I do find Dickens to be a bit of a bore at times. That damned Tale of Two Cities nearly put me to sleep."

Camilla laughed to humor the man, though she had never read it herself.

"I do say, what kind of name is Waller?" He continued, changing the subject to one about Camilla. "I don't recall knowing any myself, though my wife is much more acquainted with folks than I."

"Miss Waller is not from around here," Hillary kindly interjected.

"Well, if you don't mind me asking, did I hear the child call you Camilla?"

"Yes," Camilla answered. "That is my name."

"Damned unusual name at that. I've not met many named Camilla, but it does have a familiar ring, though, for the life of me, I can't recall why."

Camilla thought the man had been at the wine a bit too much. For someone of his class, he did seem to have a devil-may-care attitude that everyone seemed to think nothing of. He was clearly a mainstay, with everyone in attendance, used to his ways.

Another gentleman spoke up, "You old loon, you're thinking of Lady Allen's niece."

Someone else, the wife of another Lord, chimed in, "No, that would be Charlotte. I don't recall any Camillas in these parts. You'd have to ask Harry."

Camilla was lost again and hoped the focus on her would end. To her great relief, someone began to talk about a nice bit of gossip regarding Lady Allen's niece, who had recently become engaged to a naval officer from a questionable family. To Camilla's relief, this moved the conversation onto entirely new topics.

Dinner wrapped up, which meant it was time for Tabitha to say good night and for the guests to move into the hall for further entertaining. Tabitha was disappointed, insisting she was not yet sleepy, but a yawn gave her away. Dorothy was nowhere in view, so Hillary offered to take her upstairs to make sure he was properly put to bed.

"I'll be back soon," she said to Camilla. "My brother will

keep you company in the meantime." Lord Edmond approached and gave his word to ensure she would be well taken care of.

As everyone filtered into the hall, more people approached Lord Edmond, who had not yet made Camilla's acquaintance. They, too, were taken with her beauty and charm, which made Lord Edmond beam proudly.

Within a short time, music began playing, and Lord Edmond was quick to ensure he would be Camilla's first dance partner. Camilla knew nothing of dancing, only what she observed from Fiona's perfect pirouetting and the little Hillary had taught her in a short period of time. But she did her best to follow Lord Edmond's lead. He swept her across the floor, and her feet felt light, as if she were nothing more than a feather in his arms.

"Well, it appears your first introduction into society is a great success, wouldn't you agree?" Lord Edmond asked.

"I suppose, at least I'll be glad to get it over with."

"Nonsense, you must enjoy every minute. That's what this night is all about. I planned this for you, you know."

Camilla did not know. "You didn't have to…"

"I know, but I wanted to. You've been so good to my Tabitha and have had so little society for yourself. It seemed only right to allow you an opportunity to shine. And you do, you know."

Camilla was beside herself at such a grand gesture. Never had she been treated with such generosity. "What can I say? Thank you doesn't seem to be enough for your goodness to me since I came here. I truly feel unworthy."

"I meant it when I said I owed you such a debt of gratitude for saving my daughter, but it's not been a burden to be so indebted. I have loved every minute of it."

"Lord Edmond, I—"

Lord Edmond cut her off. "Please, Camilla, I wish you would from this day forward call me Jonathan. In fact, I wondered if you would step out into the garden with me. There's something I'd very much like to discuss with you."

Camilla nodded and followed him out the double doors onto a terrace surrounded by perfectly manicured hedges and plants bursting with flowers, whose fragrance filled the night air. Camilla looked up at the clear sky above her and noted the bright stars that twinkled like diamonds in the heavens. The orchestra wafted gently through the doorway, breaking up the silence.

They walked without speaking until Lord Edmond finally stopped and gently turned Camilla to face him. "There's something I need to ask you, but first, let me say that whatever your answer is, I don't want it to change your situation here."

Camilla was confused. "Why should anything change?"

"It's not that it will, but it might after you hear what I have to say." Lord Edmond swallowed hard before commencing with the speech he had prepared in his head. "Camilla, as you know, I've been alone for a long time now. I never thought I would love again after my wife died, and then you came along. Like bright sunshine, you came out of nowhere and brought me back to life. I hadn't felt that in so long." Lord Edmond grabbed Camilla's trembling hands and held them close to his chest. "I don't want to go back to the man I was before you came. Can you understand what I'm saying? I'm asking you to marry me."

Camilla's world began spinning. She cared for Lord Edmond a great deal, but after her discussions with Hillary, she had not considered marriage a real option. This all came as such a surprise. Still, she knew he was waiting for her response.

"Lord Edmond—" she began.

"Jonathan, please."

"Jonathan—I think…"

But before Camilla could give an answer, Sir Wesley came stumbling through the doors, unaware of the delicate moment he was interrupting, and yelled out, "I remember!" You're that circus dame! Yeah, I remember you…what did they call you? Camilla the Great? Your poster was everywhere. Who knew we had a star performer among us? Hey, where's that damned elephant of yours? Quite a spectacle, as I recall…"

Camilla went white.

Lord Edmond thought little of the man's outburst, except that he was annoyed by the interruption to the answer he was waiting breathlessly for. "Whatever are you talking about, you fool? Go back into the house and lie down in the study. I'll send your wife to check on you in a bit."

But there was no stopping it. A crowd was beginning to gather to find out what the commotion was.

"I'm telling you—that's her! I saw her performance myself. Magnificent she was…and wearing a lot less than she is now." He chortled, the wine getting the better of him so that he lost all sense of decorum.

"What is the meaning of this?" Hillary called out among the crowd, but Camilla didn't stop to answer. She ran past Sir Wesley, pushing past the crowd, and up the stairs, a flood of tears pouring from her eyes.

CHAPTER 45

*T*he damage was done—Camilla's secret was out. Surely, she would bring shame upon the entire Edmond house. Camilla lay on her bed, weeping when there was a soft knock at the door.

"Camilla, please," the voice of Lord Edmond on the other side called out. "Open up. I'd like to speak with you."

Camilla was certain that if she opened the door, he, too, would send her packing as Max had. And then what would become of her? How had such a beautiful night turned into such a disaster? "I can't..." was all she could manage.

Lord Edmond knocked once again, this time with a bit more intensity. "Please, I must see you. Won't you talk to me?"

His pleading touched Camilla's heart, and she couldn't refuse him this simple request, whatever the consequences might be. She rose and walked over to the door, opening it slowly. Standing on the other side was Lord Edmond with a look of great concern on his face.

Camilla hung her head shamefully. "Well, now you know. What I am—who I am."

"I don't understand. Whatever was Sir Wesley talking about? Please, don't be afraid. You can tell me anything," Lord Edmond replied.

Camilla knew she had nowhere else to hide, and it was time to tell the whole truth about that day they met by the shore. She started by explaining how her father had died, how she needed to find a way to make money to pay for the land, how she ended up in the circus and became an elephant trainer, how she saved the circus from ruin, and how everything came crashing down around her. The only thing she didn't mention was Frederick and how he had left her utterly broken-hearted.

"So, you see," she concluded. "That's how I ended up here. I didn't know where else to go. I was hopeless as there was nothing left for me. I wanted to put an end to it all when I saw your daughter struggling in the water."

Lord Edmond grabbed Camilla by the arms. "Why didn't you tell us all this before?"

"Because I was far too overcome with grief to share such terrible things with complete strangers. And by the time I settled in, well, you treated me with such honor. I've never received such kindness, and I worried, or I suppose, I believed you might come to think less of me."

"Less of you for what?" He asked, gazing earnestly into Camilla's face.

"That I was a circus performer and not the fine lady you had come to see me as."

Lord Edmond pulled her close, somewhat chuckling at the revelation. "Oh no, you have nothing to be concerned about, my love. I think it explains everything." He pulled away, looking into her face again. "I believe it was quite clear you weren't one of us, but you see, that's what made you so fascinating. So, you understand, you have nothing to concern yourself with. To me, you are every bit as much of a lady as ever."

Camilla brushed her tears away as her worst fears dissipated. "So, you don't despise me? You don't wish me to leave?"

"Heaven's no! Not a single thing has changed. I'm actually quite relieved. My sister and I couldn't imagine what could be so terrible that you were hiding from us, and I do admit, my imagination ran away with me at times. So, you see, I am just glad to have the mystery solved, and what's more, I am thankful for everything that led to this moment. It brought you here—to me."

Camilla showed a small smile, which gave Lord Edmond the courage to continue, "You never answered my question, you know." He tenderly brushed a loose curl from Camilla's face as he stared into her eyes, awaiting her answer.

"You still wish to marry me? Even after all of this?"

"Indeed. I told you; nothing has changed." There was a silence that hung in the air as Camilla considered how best to answer. As if sensing her inner conflict, Lord Edmond rescued her by saying, "I'll tell you what, this has been quite a night. Do not give me an answer under such conditions. Why don't you rest, and we'll discuss all these matters when things have settled down a bit. Does that sound good to you?"

Camilla nodded. "Yes, thank you, I am quite fatigued. I wonder what Lady Edmond thinks of all this too."

"Don't worry about my sister, I will handle her. For now, just take it easy. I'll send Dorothy up to tend to you, and all will be well."

"What about your guests?"

Lord Edmond smiled reassuringly. "I'll handle them too. The locals like a bit of excitement now and again. You have nothing to concern yourself with." He placed a kiss on her forehead and then shut the door gently behind him, leaving Camilla to her thoughts.

⚜ ⚜ ⚜

Camilla awoke the next morning feeling groggy. She had done a fair share of tossing and turning as she contemplated Lord Edmond's proposal, along with the events that unfolded the night before. She hoped all would become clear in the light of day.

She crept down the stairs to breakfast with an air of hesitancy. She still didn't know how Hillary would take the news of her past. Perhaps she had convinced Lord Edmond that it was much too scandalous to have her stay. When she entered the dining room, only Hillary and Tabitha were present. Lord Edmond had evidently been called away and left Camilla a note saying he would return that afternoon and hoped she would join him for a walk in the garden.

Camilla was a bit relieved, not knowing yet how to behave in his presence with such a big question still hanging in the air. Seeing Hillary, however, unnerved her a bit as she looked for signs of how she might feel about her now. But Hillary gave little away. She seemed cool and collected. She was back to her usual self. She greeted Camilla cordially and engaged in some light conversation to start, mostly regarding the fair weather and the lovely arrangement of flowers that were on the table.

But all that came to a halt when Tabitha began to talk about the dinner party and how it was the most exciting thing that ever happened in her life. Of course, she had gone to bed long before the dramatic announcement from Lord Wesley, so she knew nothing except what took place up until dinner. Still, it awakened a new tension in the room that had not been there before. Hillary responded to the child by keeping things short and impersonal, as if to dissuade the conversation from continuing.

Once Tabitha was finished eating, Lady Hillary sent her

to get started on her studies and then invited Camilla into the sitting room. Camilla had little excuse not to accept, so she followed along quietly, unsure of what would happen next.

"Have a seat, my dear," Hillary offered, waving her hand in the direction of the settee in front of the fireplace. Camilla sat down on one end and Hillary on the other. "Of course, I was hoping we could speak about what happened last night. I hope that's all right."

Camilla nodded. "I figured you would want to."

"Yes, well, I spoke to my brother after he went to see you. He told me as much as he could about your past, and I do understand that Lord Wesley's announcement was likely most distressing to you. I would have much preferred it if you had told us these things in your own time. Though I must admit, it does seem unlikely you would have stayed hidden for long. It appears you are quite well-known throughout the county. Several of our acquaintances confessed to having seen your act, something most polite society would be discreet about. But under the circumstances, well, I'm sure you understand why they would set aside any concerns of their own reputation."

Camilla nodded. "If I'm honest, I just assumed the chances of anyone you knew attending our circus would be unlikely. But I see now that was naïve of me. If I had thought it was possible, I would have saved you and your brother the embarrassment of my public exposure."

"I believe you, but the truth is, my dear, it's not quite the scandal you might imagine it to be. Certainly, everyone was surprised to find that you were the girl with the elephant, but more than anything, they just hoped you would come down as they were eager to ask you questions about your life in the circus. It may sound strange to you, knowing so little of the company we keep, but there is less snobbery and more curiosity about them. They enjoy a little excitement from time to time. Don't get me wrong, people will certainly talk and form opinions, but not anyone you need worry about. As for my brother and me, the most embarrassment we suffered was in being unaware of your identity, but even that will soon blow over."

Camilla felt terrible for that. "I am sorry and do hope you will forgive me," she pleaded. "Your friendship has been so valuable to me. I will gladly tell you anything you'd like to know now."

Hillary waved her off. "No need to apologize, we can talk more about that later, but my concern is of a much more serious nature."

"Oh?"

"Yes, I have thought continuously about the scene I walked in on when Sir Wesley made his announcement. You and my brother were on the terrace alone. I asked him about it myself, but he would confess to nothing. Still, I suspect it was not altogether insignificant. Tell me, is there something I should know about his intentions?"

Camilla's loyalties were torn. "I do not feel it is my right to speak on your brother's behalf," was all she could think to reply.

"Well, how about on your own behalf? What are your intentions where he is concerned?"

"My intentions?" Camilla swallowed hard.

"Yes. Do you love him? Would you intend to marry him if he were to ask you?"

Camilla hardly knew herself what the answer was. She did care a great deal for Lord Edmond but had not yet had the chance to sort out her feelings. She certainly couldn't speak of the heartache she still suffered for Frederick. Still, she knew she had to say something that would appease Lady Edmond, but all she could manage was, "I don't know."

"You don't know? Have you not even thought of it?" Hillary pressed.

"Honestly, I haven't. I wanted to honor your wishes where your brother is concerned and did not even want to entertain the possibility of having such feelings for him. Now, everything is happening so fast. And when I think of causing more damage than is already done, well, I wouldn't want to upset you, Hillary."

Hillary eased up at this. "Listen, my dear, I know what I have told you in the past. My concern was very real, but I have also witnessed a great change in this house. And for that, I can't be completely ungrateful. My brother is the most at peace that I have ever seen in ages. And Tabitha is truly a happy child and has been behaving quite well since I returned. You owe me no explanation. I only wished to express that if such a question were to be asked, you would have my blessing."

Camilla was stunned by this sudden change of heart on Hillary's behalf. Only mere hours ago, she felt her whole world was certain to come crashing in around her once again, and now she found herself made more secure both by Lord Edmond's repeated proposal and Hillary's approval should she choose to accept. These new variables added to the many questions weighing on the young girl's mind. She needed time to sort this out before Lord Edmond returned this afternoon. It didn't seem right to keep him waiting.

Camilla replied, "I hope you will forgive me then. I don't know how to answer your question except to say that I am deeply touched by your generosity towards me. It's all I need for now. And I promise, I will do right by you both to the best of my ability, whatever may come about. But for now, I need some time alone. I hope you will understand."

Hillary was satisfied to end the conversation and speak of it another time. But before leaving the sitting room, she did an uncommon thing and embraced Camilla. "I'm sorry for all you've been through, but I wanted you to know you will always have a home among us."

CHAPTER 46

*A*s intended, Camilla spent the rest of the morning in deep contemplation. She remained in her room going over every variable until Dorothy came in to announce that Lord Edmond had returned and wished her to join him for a turn in the garden in fifteen minutes if it pleased her to do so.

Camilla's insides felt unsettled, but she was as ready as she was going to be. She entered the foyer to find Lord Edmond waiting for her, dressed for an afternoon stroll. She thought he looked quite handsome in a white, linen, button-up shirt, and beige trousers. His dark blonde hair was not combed back as neatly as usual but rather fell forward slightly over his brow. He looked younger, more vulnerable. He offered his arm and together they strolled toward the back of the house.

Finding themselves a short way into the garden, Camilla

wasted no time speaking up. "I think we should have our talk now," she began bluntly. "I do not wish to keep you waiting for an answer longer than necessary. I've been thinking of your offer, and I must start by saying I am deeply flattered, but—"

"So, you refuse me?" He interrupted.

"It's not as simple as that. I do care for you, Lord Ed— Jonathan, more than I believe I even realized. It's just that, with my past being brought to light, it has forced me to face it head-on. I believe I have been putting it off for far too long, and there is still much that is unresolved. I don't think it would be right to accept your proposal when I still feel I am not free."

"Does that mean there is someone else?" Lord Edmond asked, showing concern on his brow.

"Not exactly, but there are matters that must be put to rest. You may recall that I left home to find work so I could earn the money to pay off my father's farm so that we could own the land outright. Well, I am getting close, thanks in large part to the position you've provided me with, but I still have a ways to go. I think it would be best if I continue as Tabitha's governess until it is paid in full. And my mother. I have written to her, but she has not had the opportunity to communicate with me, and I think it's only right that I go to her when we can purchase the farm. Until that time, I couldn't possibly consider my own happiness. I hope you understand."

Lord Edmond gave Camilla a tender smile. "Did you not think that being my wife would put an end to all these concerns?

What need do you have of a farm as mistress of my estate? As for your mother, you could bring her here to live with us. So, you see, all is settled on that account."

Camilla had not thought of that, but even now, when presented with such an offer, she resisted. "Certainly, being the mistress of your estate would be a great honor, but this is my father's land. I cannot let it go into the hands of strangers. The landowner would certainly not care for it, as it is only one of many properties he owns. I must not lose sight of why I left my home and all my loved ones in the first place. I almost did so once, and it cost me dearly. I cannot abandon my mission."

"And once you pay off your farm, would you then wish to accept my offer?"

This was the hardest part of all for Camilla. "I don't know," she answered honestly. "Only when I have faced my past can I consider my future. And as I said, it's still a ways off. It doesn't seem right to ask you to wait."

Lord Edmond took a moment to take in all that Camilla had communicated. It was clear she was at a crossroads in her life, and he didn't wish to pressure her before her time. "I'll tell you what," he began, "I have an offer for you. Tell me what you owe on this land, and I will give you whatever is necessary to satisfy the debt, along with a suitable sum for you to travel home to get your affairs in order. This should help settle the matter so you may decide what course of action you wish to choose."

Camilla shook her head. "Oh no, I couldn't accept such

an offer. The debt is mine. I couldn't take advantage of your kindness to me."

But Lord Edmond was resolute. "I've told you before that I owed you a debt of gratitude. Well, let me do this and consider us even. If you return, it will be of your own accord. That should give you the freedom to choose the life that suits you best, and I will know for certain what your answer is based on that decision. I hope you will agree that it is a fair offer?"

"Oh, Jonathan, it is more than fair. I feel I have already received so much from you as it is. But I can't deny it would be a step in the right direction to figuring out where my future lies. It's quite hard to resist your offer, only I'm scared. Really scared, Jonathan. I have come to regard this as my home and have felt safe and cared for. Such a journey consists of so many unknowns. And the thought of never seeing any of you again…"

Lord Edmond grabbed Camilla by the hand delicately. "You have nothing to fear, my love. I will send my own coachman to take you wherever you need to go. He will ensure your safety and that you are returned to Mayfield when you are ready—if that is what you wish."

Camilla squeezed his hand in return, courage flooding her heart. "This is more than I could hope for, and I thank you for it from the bottom of my heart. Tell me what I must do, and I will set the plans in motion."

Lord Edmond lifted Camilla's hand to kiss it lightly, then looked up into the sun shining down upon them. "Let's start by paying off this damned farm once and for all."

Within ten days' time, Camilla was ready to set off for home and reclaim the land that seemed as good as lost the day her father died. She was dressed and packed, waiting by the front entrance for the carriage to come and whisk her away. It turned out, home was a day's journey in a northern direction. She couldn't believe that at that same time tomorrow, she would be in the place where she spent her entire childhood. It didn't seem possible that she was finally ready to reclaim the land, just as she promised the day she left her childhood home.

But she was no longer the same child who set out for parts unknown. Now that she thought of it, she couldn't even recall the last time someone referred to her as Cami. No, that little girl was long gone, lost in the annals of time where once a circus procession was enough to thrill her heart. Though she was setting off for a place she knew well, her future couldn't be less certain than the day she left.

Lord Edmond, Hillary, and Tabitha waited with Camilla to see her off. Many tears were shed over her departure. Tabitha had cried through the night, causing Dorothy to tend to her more than once to calm the poor child.

"Why is she leaving?" She wailed. "Doesn't she love us?"

Then she would be reassured once again that Camilla adored her, but that she must leave for a while to attend to some business back home. Only, to Tabitha, it was like losing yet another parental figure.

"Why does everyone have to go away? Can't we just all stay together?" she asked while sipping warm milk. Dorothy soothed her with promises that all would turn out for the best.

Even with her lack of sleep and bout of melancholy, Tabitha awoke early, was properly dressed, and present for Camilla's big send-off.

Lord Edmond seemed to have come down with a bit of melancholy himself. Though he did his best to appear strong and supportive, his eyes held deep sadness at the realization that he may, in fact, never see his beloved Camilla again. There were no guarantees. They all knew that, yet they regarded each other as if she would only be gone a little while.

The carriage pulled up, and Camilla gave Hillary and Tabitha a final embrace before approaching her ride. Lord Edmond grabbed her bags and gave them to the coachman to load up for her. He then helped Camilla into the carriage, but not before saying his own goodbye. A part of her hoped he would beg her to stay and that she wouldn't have to go after all.

Instead, he merely kissed her forehead and whispered, "I'll be waiting." He closed the door and off they went, into the dewy morning haze. Camilla couldn't resist turning around for one last look at the people she had grown to love in the month's past. They stood waving until she was out of view. Only then could Camilla turn around and settle into the carriage seat. The sadness consuming her thoughts was more than she could bear, so she soon drifted off. It would be a long day.

CHAPTER 47

*I*t was close to midnight when the carriage stopped at the inn where she and the coachman would be staying for the night. Camilla was travel-weary and ready to lay her head down on a soft pillow. She knew she wouldn't have much time to sleep because they planned to depart first thing in the morning, and it would only be a short ride to her father's farm. Even in the dark, she was familiar with her surroundings. She walked this distance often as a child, so it was tempting to run straight home. But Camilla thought better of it and decided rest was necessary to keep up her strength for all that must be done the following day.

Her first order of business was to stop at the farm. There she would meet with the landowner to sign the final paperwork to switch the deed to her name. Camilla could hardly believe such a day had all but arrived. It seemed like such a foolish notion when she first set out to make it happen. She was sure everyone had thought she'd gone quite mad. And she wasn't positive she hadn't, in the wake of losing her father so suddenly. But through it all, she never lost her resolve, and in just a few hours, it would be a done deal.

Afterward, she planned to ride up to see her mother to collect her and bring her home—their home. With some of the other money Lord Edmond gave her, she knew she could set her mother up quite nicely in the old cottage and have plenty left over to boot. Lord Edmond had been quite generous indeed. He sent her off with what amounted to a small fortune, something he did not disclose, but gave to the coachman to give her at the first stop. Camilla was beside herself, but there was no way to refuse, so she only thought of how best to put it to good use.

She couldn't think of a better cause than to provide a comfortable life for her dear mother. *Perhaps I'll even give some to Griffin. I'm sure his old farm would benefit from some updating as well*, she thought. *Griffin.* She hadn't considered him much until now and she began to wonder what became of him. She contemplated the real possibility that he might be married with a child or one on the way. The thought of such a scenario was difficult to imagine, yet it seemed likely after what he told her the last time they met. And so, she prepared her heart for the possibility.

She couldn't make plans beyond that, though. She wasn't sure how she would feel until those tasks were complete. Then she would have a better idea of what cards she held in her hands at the end of it all. She didn't even write to let her mother know she was coming; she was afraid of getting her hopes up in case something went awry. In her heart, Camilla wasn't certain she dared to go through with the plans, so she wanted to leave an opening to back out in case she changed her mind. Leaving the love and comfort of Lord Edmond's house was a serious risk. But here she was. She had made it, and in the morning, all would be set right with her father's farm once and for all.

Camilla fell asleep quickly, but it didn't last. She was up before the crow. Yet, she wasn't tired. She got herself around, making sure to look respectable when she went to sign the paperwork—she was leaving nothing to chance.

The carriage was ready for departure at exactly 7 am, as planned. The ride through town and up the hill to her home would take less than an hour. She gave the coachman clear directions, which allowed her to sit back and drink everything in as they passed all the familiar sights. As they drove through town, she found herself looking back at the now-empty space where the circus was once set up and recalled the excitement she felt as her and Griffin watched the procession and all the excitement and wonder it held.

She then remembered the first time she laid eyes on Frederick as he passed her, performing a sample of his act. How he made her heart flutter from the start. Even now, the thought of him still had a potent effect, but she pushed those feelings away as they were laced with much painful history. Her good memories could not be savored due to his betrayal.

The path that went by the sea and wound its way up the hillside looked untouched. It was rugged and wild, just as she once was. It was as if she never left—the waves continued to roll in and out without a single hesitation on who had come or gone. Memories of climbing up and down those cliffs returned as she inhaled the salty North Sea air. She looked to see if she could spot the tide pools she and Griffin often explored for clams, but the morning mist was too heavy yet to get a good view.

Once the carriage reached a higher elevation, the scene became much clearer, and Camilla was able to spot the old cottage even from a ways off. She wanted to jump out of the carriage, run to it, and throw open the door, as she always had, but she knew there would be no one there waiting to greet her. Pa would not be sitting by the fire sipping black coffee, and Ma would not be preparing breakfast for the family. The thought of the empty cabin kept her still. Instead, she sat patiently, the suspense of the moment building.

When the carriage finally pulled up to the cottage door, the coachman hopped off his seat to help Camilla out. She looked over her childhood home, and it felt strange suddenly, unfamiliar. The cottage appeared shabbier and in disrepair than she ever recalled. She wasn't sure if it was due to being abandoned for these many months or if it always looked that way and she simply never took notice. It was quiet and lonely on that hill, and the cool morning breeze made her shiver.

"Will you be needing your belongings?" The coachman asked formally.

"Not yet, I don't know how long I'll be staying. Would you mind hanging around while I wait for the landowner to arrive? Then I'll have a better idea of my plans."

"At your service, Miss," was his reply.

Another carriage soon approached, which she assumed was the one she was waiting for. She was certain she had never even met the man who owned the deed to their farm. His carriage was not nearly as luxurious as the one Lord Edmond owned, but it was certainly far and away nicer than anything her family and friends could ever afford.

When the man got out of the carriage, she noted his age and dress. He was likely around fifty, fat, and dressed in a dark suit that indicated he was a well-fed man of importance. Another man got out with him, who he claimed was his lawyer. This man was taller and thinner, with a sullen face elongated by his top hat. He seemed quite cheerless, and both were eager to get down to business.

The lawyer spoke first. "I received the letter from Lord Jonathan Edmond's lawyer, with all the necessary arrangements to purchase the land. We only need your signature and to sign everything over to you, Miss Camilla Waller. He was quite explicit that it should all be put in your name, is that correct?"

Camilla nodded, then proceeded to sign where she was

told. Everything looked quite formal. She knew little of business, but she trusted Lord Edmond was more than capable of arranging things properly, based on his sister's account of him and his reputation as a great businessman.

Quicker than she could imagine, the deed was handed over to her, and the two men turned to re-enter their carriage. "So, that's it?" She called out as they were getting in.

"Yes, that's it," The lawyer answered. "The land now belongs to you and your family. Good day, Miss, it was a pleasure doing business with you." He tipped his hat, and the two were on their way. The landowner said very little, as if it were nothing more than a business exchange and not a beloved property containing many precious family memories.

Despite the lack of fanfare, Camilla was not sad to see them go. She held the deed in her hands, a sense of pride welling up inside her at the accomplishment of redeeming her father's land once and for all. Never again would she suffer a sleepless night over it or concern herself with how she would keep up with the payments. She was free and clear, just like Jonathan said. And most of all, she knew her father would be proud.

"If you don't mind, I'd like to look around a while before we leave," she said to the coachman, who was unperturbed.

Camilla approached the cottage door and pushed it open easily. A dusty, yet familiar smell assaulted her nostrils. Being shut up for some time made the usual scent much more pungent, and a flood of memories came to her. She looked upon the old fire stove that her mother would cook family meals, and the modest furnishings, including her father's favorite hand-carved wooden chair. His fiddle was still propped against it where he had last laid it down. She stopped to take in her mother's handmade art that hung on the walls, including the cross her grandmother made of tiny stones and dried vines. All was as she had remembered it, but there was no one to share in the moment of her return.

She lay in her old bed, covered with the quilt that her mother also had as a child. She remembered now what it was like to lie there so many nights, trying to fall asleep while her mother and father talked to each other in low, soft tones. She even recalled the glow of lamplight flickering on the walls and how she would imagine the shadows it cast on the wall were of large and unknown beasts.

The cabin was smaller than she remembered, no larger than the room she now occupied at Mayfield Hall. She cried for the loss of those precious moments in their modest abode, knowing they were gone forever. But being there now made it feel like she could bring them back, even if only briefly, so she basked in the memory until it faded from her.

Camilla finally got up and decided to have a look around the property. Griffin had told her it had not been tended to, so she wasn't surprised to see there were no crops or livestock in the barns. She spotted her father's old fishing pole and wooden boat. The boat was quite weather-worn, and she figured there was little possibility of repair. Still, she didn't dare move it.

The thought of Griffin made her look in the direction of where his old house lay. She longed to go see him but was frozen in place by fear of what she might find or how he might react. Maybe he didn't want to see her again after how badly she treated him. Perhaps it would bring back too many painful memories to relive the past again. But she and Griffin had known each other their whole lives. He was like a brother to her. Surely, he wouldn't spurn her after such a significant history together.

Camilla finally got up the courage to start making her way toward the Griffin family farm. She wondered if she would be spotted before she even got to the door. Would she first come across Mr. or Mrs. Felix or Griffin himself? As she made her approach, she heard the unfamiliar sound of two children, their laughter carrying over the hill. She doubted very much that Mrs. Felix had borne more children. Her only conclusion was that it must be Griffin's new family.

The children she heard soon came into view and were seen running to the barn. She thought they seemed a bit old to be Griffin's, but there was little other explanation. She approached the cottage, but things looked different somehow. The old rocking chair his father would sit and read in was gone, and two stools were in its place. She noticed window boxes now in the sills, full of fresh spring flowers—something she had never known Mrs. Felix to tend to.

She heard nothing inside to give her any forewarning of what she might expect, but she swallowed hard and then knocked, allowing the exchange to play out as fate would have it. A dog began barking until finally she heard someone approaching. She braced herself with anticipation of who might greet her, but the face was not one she had ever laid eyes on. It was a young woman in an apron, covered in flour from preparing some sort of pastry.

"Hello, may I help you?" she asked.

Camilla looked over her shoulder to see if anyone was behind her that she might recognize, but she was alone. "Yes, my name is Camilla, Camilla Waller. My family used to live in the cottage at the top of the hill. I was wondering if Mr. or Mrs. Felix was in. Or Griffin Felix perhaps?"

The woman looked a bit perplexed. "I don't recall ever having known of any residents on the hill."

"Yes, well, my family moved out some time ago, but we own the property and are just returning. The Felixes are old friends, so I wanted to stop by and give my regards," she explained.

The lady shook her head. "I'm very sorry to inform you, the Felixes no longer live here. They sold their farm sometime back, and my husband and I moved in with our family shortly thereafter. I am afraid you missed them."

Camilla was perplexed to think the Felixes would sell their land. Surely Griffin would have done everything in his power to ensure things continued to run, even if his father was incapable of doing so himself. Nothing made sense. "Can you please tell me where they went? I would very much like to look them up if possible."

The lady thought about it and then said, "Yes, I believe I heard the young Felix, their son, moved them to the next town over to become a bookkeeper of sorts. You might consider looking him up there, but that's all I know."

Camilla thanked the woman for her kindness and complimented her on the pretty flowers, which seemed to make the lady happy. She then headed back to her own farm. Emptiness consumed her as she realized how many things had been completely altered in her absence.

When she got back to the cottage, she saw the coachman was resting and had drifted off. She figured it was just as well, as it allowed her to do all that was necessary before moving on to their next destination. When the man heard her coming, he sat up with a start and apologized for falling asleep.

"It's quite all right," Camilla assured him. "I think I'm ready to go now. I need to see my mother."

CHAPTER 48

*M*rs. Waller could not have been more thrilled to see her baby girl. This unexpected arrival brought about an emotional reaction Camilla did not recall ever witnessing in her mother. Under normal circumstances, she was exceptionally reserved and sensible, but in this case, she did little to hold back her joyful tears.

Camilla was just glad that when she knocked on the door, her mother was the one to answer. Being so thoroughly transformed in appearance since leaving home, it took her mother a moment to recognize her own daughter. It was only when Camilla said, "Hello, Mama," that the woman fully realized who it was that stood before her.

It was then that Mrs. Waller opened the floodgates. She cried out at the sight of her child. It was as if it were a great release after years of living in a constant state of fear that the daughter who left home wouldn't make it in the world on her own. It couldn't have been a happier reunion. But there was a brokenness of spirit in her mother that Camilla didn't recall. She knew she was partly to blame.

They didn't speak right away. They simply embraced and held onto each other to make up for lost time. Camilla was thoroughly relieved to see her dear mother once again and was reminded how much she missed her maternal care and comfort. But now, having wiped the tears of joy away, Mrs. Waller got a chance to truly behold her little girl and was in awe.

The ruckus had startled her mother's sister, Meredith, who made her way to the door to find out what all the fuss was about. Meredith, who until now was a mere spectator, spoke up first, "My, my, what a lady you have become. However did you manage it?" She then looked over Camilla's shoulder at the horse and carriage. "And I see you travel in similar style."

"It's a long story," Camilla replied, "But Mother, I am here with a purpose. I hope you will be pleased with my reason for coming so unexpectedly. Come, let's talk."

Camilla sent the coachman on to town to spend the rest of the night, requesting he return first thing in the morning. Then Mrs. Waller invited Camilla in to catch up. Camilla had only vague memories of her Aunt Meredith's home. Though she didn't live a far distance from their farm, just one town over, the two sisters rarely got together over the years, but communicated regularly by mail. She recalled visiting once as a very young child, but the memory of her aunt's home did not leave a lasting impression.

It was twice the size of their old cottage and was made up of several rooms, a luxury the Waller family did not have. They took a seat at a round oak table while Meredith offered to put on some tea.

"So, what's happened to you?" Mrs. Waller began, eager to know all the details of Camilla's life since she left home.

"We'll talk about all that soon, but first, I need to tell you why I came."

"Well, do tell, child!" Her mother replied. Even Aunt Meredith was listening intently.

"Oh, Mama, I did it." Camilla smiled brightly.

"Did what?"

"The farm. I paid it off. It's ours, free and clear."

Mrs. Waller appeared uninterested. "Oh, I see."

"Don't you understand what I'm saying, Mama? The land—Papa's land—it's all ours. I have the deed. We can go back first thing in the morning if you wish. I know the cottage needs fixing up a bit, but I have plenty to cover it. It will be nicer than ever, and we can even build on to it. You'll have a room of your very own. And then I'll get the livestock back. Everything will be as it was, only better. So much better."

Camilla was surprised to see that her mother still showed no signs of joy at the news. "What's wrong? Aren't you excited?

Do you know what this means?"

But Mrs. Waller did not respond in the way Camilla had hoped or expected. "Yes, dear, I do understand. But did it ever occur to you that perhaps I don't wish to go back to the old farm?"

"Honestly, no. What's wrong with you, Mama? I thought you'd be overjoyed to go home. After all I've been through—after all we've been through," she corrected herself.

"That's just it, Cami, this was never about me. I know how much your father's land meant to you, and it meant a great deal to me at one time as well. But since he died, well, I see little use in going back. I'm too old to work a farm. I have no husband, no sons. I am content here, with my sister."

Camilla couldn't believe her response but tried to reassure her, "Mama, you don't need to work the farm. I am here, and besides, I have money now to hire help. We will live quite comfortably. I thought this is what you'd want."

But Mrs. Waller was firm. "Cami, I sincerely appreciate what you are trying to do. I know how hard you've worked for this, and you have my blessing. But I must stress once again, I do not wish to go back to the old farm. Without my husband, I would be lonely, don't you see? And the memories…" She trailed. "If only there had been some way of reaching you, I would have told you as much."

"But Mama," Camilla pressed, "You'd have me. Isn't that enough?"

"It's not the same. You—you have your whole life ahead

of you. Just look at you! You are certain to marry, and then what would become of me? No, my place is here, with my sister. Please understand, but that is final."

Camilla was beside herself. For every dollar she earned to pay off the farm, it never occurred to her that her mother would not want it every bit as much as she did. It was in part for her mother that she went to such lengths. Or was it? She was no longer certain.

Thinking back on the empty farm, she wondered what would become of it now. Would she live there alone? Once again, she realized she had some very big decisions to make about her life.

Her mother, sensing the disappointment Camilla was experiencing over this revelation, tried to change the subject. "Come now, my dear, be at peace once and for all. The land is yours to do with what you will. I am well taken care of here. My sister needs me, and I need her. You can do as you wish. But what's more, I would very much like it if you would tell me all you've been up to since you left. I should be angry with you, I know, but seeing you as you are, I have nothing left in me to be bitter or sad about. I am only glad to see my daughter is well off and I want to hear about her many adventures."

Camilla surrendered. She knew her mother was a determined woman, and once she made up her mind, there was little hope of changing it. Ultimately, she wanted her mother's happiness, and it was clear that returning to the farm was not in her best interest. So instead, she spent the evening regaling both her and Aunt Meredith with all the tales of circus life and how she had come to live with the Edmonds. It was a long story, and by nightfall, she had grown very tired and yearned to sleep after such an eventful day.

She knew the coachman was set to return in the morning, but offered to stay a few more days, which pleased her mother greatly. Still, Camilla knew that when her time there was over, she must set her mind to figuring out what to do about the farm. And there was one more order of business to attend to in the meantime—she must go see Griffin.

CHAPTER 49

$\mathcal{C}$amilla enjoyed the time she spent with her mother and Aunt Meredith. She could see they had a cozy routine they had settled into, and they got on quite well. After five days of close observation, she felt content that her mother had made the best decision for herself by remaining there. Camilla remembered what Griffin had said about her mother's suffering health, but seeing her daughter again and knowing she was safe seemed to bring a glow to her cheeks she probably hadn't felt since the day her husband died.

Saying goodbye would be difficult though. Those five days brought about so many wonderful moments together, catching up, recounting all the good memories of the past, and spending time outdoors together, basking in the sun on the cobblestone porch her uncle had custom-built. She forgot the warmth of her mother's presence and would miss it dearly.

As for sustenance, Camilla found there was enough to feed them all, but she could tell that provisions were low. Both Aunt Meredith and her mother spoke of a recent drought that caused many crops in the region to fail. Some people went hungry over the winter as a result. This made Camilla all the more glad she continuously sent her mother money, which apparently helped sustain them.

During her stay, she walked to the market and gathered supplies to ensure they would be stocked with plenty of food and other resources for the time being. Before leaving, she took her mother aside and gave her a sizeable portion of the money she received from Lord Edmond.

"Mother, I want you to take this and use what you need for repairs around here. This should cover any expenses. I also want to make sure you have plenty of everything else until you hear from me again. I promise I will send more."

Mrs. Waller was astonished by the sum of money placed in her hands. She was certain she and her husband had never accumulated as much over a lifetime. "My goodness, child, this is more than enough," was all she could manage.

"Exactly. Keep it well guarded, and it will last you for some time. I need to know you are taken care of if I can't be with you. Aunt Meredith will help you decide how best to use it."

She then held her mother, kissed her on the cheek, then did the same to Aunt Meredith before stepping into the carriage to head into town in search of Griffin. Though she would miss her mother dearly, it did give her much peace to know she was well provided for, was settled in comfortably with her sister, and that they finally had a proper goodbye.

⚜ ⚜ ⚜

When Camilla entered town, she immediately sought out some of the locals to ask if they knew a Griffin Felix and where she might find him. Not having spent much time around other people since beginning her travels, she was taken aback by how she was regarded. The townsfolk stared, and when she approached a man and his wife to inquire after the Felixes, they treated her as if she were someone of great importance. All the men tipped their hats in her direction, and she heard a child ask its mother, "Is she a princess?"

Camilla was not dressed in what she considered especially fancy attire, but it did have a simple elegance and was the latest fashion—one of Hillary's choices. The couple did not seem familiar with the name, so she tried another angle, "Do you know where I could find the local bookkeeper, please?" They seemed to know that at the very least, and they pointed her to the other side of town to a Mr. Butterfield's.

Heading in that direction, Camilla suddenly felt self-conscious. Although she and Griffin had seen each other once over the last year, when he surprised her after the circus performance in another town, she realized she might be even more altered than he recalled. But inside, she still felt like Little Cami.

As the carriage approached the Butterfield place, Camilla took a moment to consider what she might say. What if she had gotten poor information and he wasn't here? What would she do next? She finally decided it best to take her chances and let the chips fall where they may.

As she opened the shop door, a little bell jangled to alert the clerk of a customer entering. Only there was no need. Sitting at a desk, in deep concentration, was a mop of copper locks she recognized immediately. "Griffin!" she called out excitedly, all concerns of the meeting melting away.

Griffin looked up. He was wearing a dress shirt with the sleeves rolled up, a vest, and black spectacles. He was frowning, to begin with, but when he saw the face of his childhood friend, his eyes grew wide with excitement. But they appeared fearful.

"Camilla! What are you doing here?" He asked, his voice quaking. "You must leave at once." He rose to escort her out the door, looking behind him as if concerned about who might see her.

Camilla's heart sank, her worst fears realized, "You do not wish to see me? Your oldest and dearest friend?"

"It's not that Cami, I am very happy to see you, it's just that, you must go. Right away, please."

Just then an older gentleman emerged from the back room. He had hard lines on his face, held a cane, and wore a suit that appeared two decades old. His bushy, unkempt eyebrows rose in surprise. "Who do we have here and how may we help you, young lady?"

"I was just asking her to leave, Mr. Butterfield."

"And for what purpose? Perhaps we can be of service to her." Then turning to Camilla, the old man added, "You must forgive my young apprentice here, he's not too bright as you can see. What is it you came to inquire about?"

Camilla's eyes narrowed, and Griffin hung his head in shame, bracing for whatever would come next. "Excuse me, sir, I only wished to inquire after my old friend, Griffin here. We have been long parted, and I wished to say hello while I am in town visiting family."

"So, then you are in no need of our services? Well, then I can't help you. Griffin here is working, so I must ask that you leave at once." He waved his cane toward the exit.

"I am sorry, but..." Camilla began, before being interrupted by Griffin.

"It's okay, just go. We are quite busy." Camilla looked around but it didn't seem like much was going on at all. As if reading her mind, Griffin only pressed harder. "I will meet you outside after I get out of work this evening. Five o'clock. I will see you then." And with that, he all but pushed her out the door.

Camilla found the entire exchange rather concerning but

thought better of going back inside for answers. She trusted her friend would explain everything to her later, so she decided not to make another attempt to see him before five o'clock. Instead, she asked the coachman to take her to the inn where she had a bit to eat, then settled in with a book for the rest of the afternoon. But she had difficulty concentrating on the novel she hoped would distract her. All she could do was recall the fear in Griffin's eyes and wonder what it was all about.

When five o'clock rolled around, she walked back into town toward the bookkeeper's shop, not bothering to enlist the assistance of the coachman. She found a little bench on the side of the street that seemed as ideal a place to wait as any. She did her best to be patient, but time seemed to move slowly. Fifteen minutes passed, but she figured Griffin was only getting out late. Another fifteen minutes, and then half an hour passed. Before she knew it, the time was six o'clock, and still no signs of Griffin. Camilla wondered if she shouldn't check in on him, but then she remembered the harsh manner in which Mr. Butterfield responded to her. The last thing she wanted was to cause Griffin any trouble where his employment was concerned.

She kept a close watch on the door and saw no signs of stirring. She wondered if perhaps she had missed him, but doubted very much he would have left early and not been there to meet her on time. So, she continued to wait until it was seven o'clock. A part of her began to wonder if he hadn't stood her up after all. It was getting dark now, and Camilla was just about ready to give up any hope of seeing Griffin that day. So, she rose from the bench to head back to the inn when the door to the bookkeeper's shop opened, and the two men emerged.

Mr. Butterfield seemed very much unconcerned with the hour, but Griffin wore a look of weariness. Mr. Butterfield said some words to Griffin that she could not hear, then turned to walk in the opposite direction. Whatever was said appeared to bring no joy to Griffin's already dejected disposition.

Camilla stood up and waved to her friend. "Hey, Griff, over here!" Hardly a refined greeting from one who appeared to be a lady, but she didn't care.

Griffin looked up, his eyes widening once again at the sight of her. He ran to meet her at the bench where she stood.

"I didn't think you'd wait," he began. "I'm really sorry it took so long. The owner, Mr. Butterfield, well, he needed me to work late tonight."

Even in the dimming light of the setting sun, Camilla could see the red mark on his arm and another on his collarbone. "Are you okay?" she asked, reaching out to touch the fresh wounds.

Griffin pulled away. "It's nothing." Camilla withdrew her hand and stared at him. "How did you find me anyway?" He asked. It wasn't exactly an ideal opening for two old friends who hadn't seen each other in a long time, but it couldn't be helped.

"The lady who lives on your old farm told me. I didn't know you and your family had moved. It came as quite a surprise."

"Yes, it all happened very suddenly," Griffin replied, rubbing the mark on his arm.

"Can you tell me about it?"

"Why were you there anyway?" He snapped back. This was definitely not going the way Camilla had hoped. Her face communicated surprise at being treated so harshly that Griffin finally said, "I'm sorry, Cami, I don't mean to be so severe. It's just been a rough day. Will you forgive me?"

"Of course I forgive you." Camilla tried to hide the hurt she felt and wished to move past the unsavory beginning.

Griffin attempted to correct course with a lighter tone. "Please, tell me, what brought you here?"

Camilla softened at the return of the friend she knew. "The land. My father's farm. I paid it off. So, I went to check on it. Naturally, I attempted to see you and your family as well, so imagine my surprise when I found you had all gone. I was very confused to think you would give up your farm so easily…"

Griffin's irritation returned. "You think it was easy? Some things can't be helped, Camilla. Not everyone has the luxury of running away from their problems. If you must know, we're lucky we survived at all."

Camilla frowned. "I'm sorry, Griff, I didn't mean to insinuate—anyway, I just meant it didn't seem like you. I just wanted to know what happened. Why are you 'lucky'?"

Griffin eased up once again. "We had a terrible drought last year, hardly any rain to speak of."

"I heard."

"Well, our crops didn't survive. They produced only enough for us to live on. Certainly not enough to sell, so we couldn't keep up with the payments. Anyway, you may remember when I came to see you that I had been apprenticing to be a bookkeeper. It was only meant as a backup, but when the crops failed, we had no choice but to leave the farm, and my only hope was that Mr. Butterfield offered me a job. It was all I could do to keep my parents from starving through the winter."

Camilla's heart ached as Griffin told her what happened. "I'm so very sorry, Griff. I can't imagine what a difficult decision that must have been for you."

"It wasn't difficult at all, because the truth is, we had no choice. Do I wish things were different? Of course. But there's nothing I can do about it now. My only hope is that I can find work somewhere else in the next couple of years."

"What's wrong with Mr. Butterfield? Do you not like working for him?"

"The man is a tyrant, as I'm sure you could guess. But again, what choice do I have? He knows I have nowhere to go at this time. So, I have no option but to endure his cruelty." Griffin was silent as Camilla looked upon him with pity. He resented it, but added bitterly, "You can be thankful you didn't take me up on my offer of marriage after all. Where would that have gotten you? It appears you've done much better for yourself on your own."

Camilla's eyes began to water as she was filled with sorrow

for all her friend had endured. "Griffin, I never wanted it to be this way. I want the best for you, always. If I thought my coming here would make things worse, I never would have."

"It's all just as well in the end. I'm glad you came. I just wish I had better news. But as for you, how did you manage all this? You are even more improved from our last meeting. Did you marry that Frederick fellow after all?"

Camilla shook her head. "No, I'm afraid not. It didn't end so well. I am no longer with the circus. I have a new situation, a much better one. Or at least, I did. I'm not sure what I'll do next. But it's the reason I was able to purchase my father's farm. And what about you? Did you marry the young lady you spoke of? I figured you might have a couple of kids on the way by now."

"No," he replied simply.

"May I ask, why not?"

Griffin turned away, unable to look into his old friend's eyes. "I couldn't. Not when I knew that…perhaps…you were still out there. I'm sorry things didn't work out with that Frederick fellow. Though if I'm honest, I'm not altogether surprised to hear it. I spoke to him briefly before I left, and he did not make his intentions clear where you were concerned. I suppose as long as I thought there was a chance you might return, I couldn't marry another."

Regaining his composure and able to look at Camilla once again, he added, "I know now you were right all along to refuse me. I would have been no help to you at all. And seeing you now,

I couldn't be more convinced of that fact. My only consolation is knowing you are doing well. I'm sorry that I ever doubted you. I should have known better than to underestimate 'Camilla the Great.'"

"Please don't call me that. I'd rather forget the whole thing."

"Camilla, your greatness is not bound by some traveling circus. It is a title you have earned for all time."

Camilla didn't know how to respond except to say thank you and that she hoped Griffin would be able to meet with her again the following day. "I have so much to think over, I hope you will forgive me for leaving so soon, but it is much later than I expected to be out. I left the coachman behind at the inn, so I have a ways to walk."

Griffin understood and apologized once again for being late and making her wait so long. "Let me walk you back to the Inn. It's the least I can do for keeping you out, and a lady such as yourself should not be seen walking around after dark alone. I can meet you first thing in the morning if that suits you better. I have a bit of time before I have to get to work. I know Ma and Pa would love to see you too, if you're going to be in town for a while."

Camilla wasn't sure just yet what her plans were, but she committed to the morning meeting for now. One day at a time was all she could manage.

CHAPTER
SIX

After a night of endless tossing and turning, it was obvious to Camilla what she must do. She was anxious for her meeting with Griffin and wasted no time heading to the spot they had met the day before. To her surprise, Griffin was already there waiting for her. He, too, had trouble sleeping and thought the morning air might help him clear his thoughts.

Unlike the day before, this time he greeted her with an embrace. He apologized once again for his confusing behavior. He explained that he had been taken off guard by her sudden arrival and promised to behave better this time.

"Don't make promises you can't keep," Camilla laughed. "But I do understand. I'm sure it's all been overwhelming, the move, the new job, and having to be the man of the house now."

"We've just not had an easy go of it," he explained. "My

ma and pa are grateful for this opportunity, that we have a roof over our heads and food on the table, but I think we would all agree it has been less than ideal. But that's life for you. There are just no guarantees of how things will work out."

Camilla saw her opening. "So, tell me then, if life were different, what would be ideal? Do you like being a bookkeeper? I mean, aside from old Mr. Butterfield."

Griffin kicked his head back and laughed out loud. "Oh no, you heard the man, I'm no good at it really. I just wanted to please my father. He always felt guilty that he wasn't able to provide me with a better education. But the truth is, I was made to work with my hands. Who knows, maybe I'll join the circus someday and buy back our land. What would you think of that?"

Camilla grinned and playfully punched her old friend in the arm. "I believe there are much easier ways of going about it. I can honestly say I don't recommend it."

"So, you didn't enjoy circus life at all? You seemed to be when I last saw you."

"Oh, I suppose it had its moments. It was fun and exciting—I'll give you that. And there is something intoxicating about hearing a crowd cheer your name. It's the reason so many stay. However, the cost was much greater than I ever anticipated. I'm just fortunate things turned out for me as well as they did. I'm finally starting to see how much so."

This piqued Griffin's curiosity, so Camilla filled him in on how she came to Lord Edmond's house and became the governess for Tabitha. She expressed her desperation when she made her way to the sea, but left out the part about her plans to end her life. That was a part of the story she'd rather forget. But the rest was as accurate as time would allow, including Lord Edmond's proposal.

"That's some story," he whistled. "Never a dull moment for you, that's for sure. I believe you could write a book about this someday."

Camilla laughed. "My story's not over yet…but yours could have a happy ending."

"Oh?" Griffin asked, raising an eyebrow.

"I've been thinking. I mean, I've reached a conclusion in light of everything I've learned since coming home. Griffin, I want to give you my farm. I came this morning to sign the deed over to you. I can think of no one's hands I'd rather turn it over to."

Griffin reacted swiftly. "No, no, no, I couldn't. Not after all you have been through to possess it, free and clear. I absolutely cannot bear it, Cami. Please, this land is yours and no one else's."

"But Griffin," she insisted, "I have no use for it. My mother doesn't want it, and I can't run it on my own. But you. This could mean your freedom. You would never have to worry about leaving again. You are my dearest friend, and I believe with all my heart that you would have done the same for me. So let me do this for you. Please."

Griffin was emphatic, "No, I won't hear of it, I simply can't—"

Just then, old Mr. Butterfield approached the couple, unaware. "Mr. Felix," he bellowed. "What in the blazes are you doing? Get over to this door at once and let me in!"

Griffin only now realized how much time had passed since they met up. "I am so sorry, Mr. Butterfield," he said, shaking. "I'll be there right away, just let me say goodbye to my friend here."

"Did I not make myself clear, Mr. Felix? I have no time for your foolishness. Now get over here at once and unlock this door!"

Camilla was getting hot. "Excuse me, sir," she said sharply. "But my friend Griffin here and I were just about to say our farewells. Do be kind enough to give us a moment?"

The man showed no signs of backing down. Instead, he began marching toward them as if he might yank Griffin away. "I don't think this is any of your affair, Missy. If Mr. Felix wishes to keep his employment, he will come with me at once. Do you understand me, Mr. Felix?"

Griffin looked utterly terrified by the man. "I'm sorry, Camilla, I must go, but let's try to meet up later if possible."

The man laughed wickedly. "Oh no, you don't. I'm having you work a long shift today. Just for your insolence. As for this young lady, she'll have to come look for you on your own time."

Camilla was hot. "It doesn't sound like he has any of his *own* time, if you ask me. What's your problem anyway? How dare you treat my friend so dreadfully!"

All of Mr. Butterfield's attention was now on Camilla. "And just who do you think you are? Sounds like you are even more foolish than ol' Griffin here. Well, not to worry, his time is all his own now. I have plenty of young lads just like him lined up to take his position. You're fired, Mr. Felix, so don't bother coming in at all. You can tell those parents of yours, I am sorry I wasted my time on employing their ungrateful son."

Griffin was beside himself with the events unfolding beyond his power. He suddenly became desperate. "Please, Mr. Butterfield, I do apologize for my friend here. She means well, but I ask that you not let me go. You know I need this job. Please, reconsider," he begged.

But there was no sign of Mr. Butterfield relenting. "You should have thought about that before letting your little tramp here speak on your behalf. You are through!"

Griffin grabbed the man's arm and continued pleading, which only made him all the more angry. He finally lifted his cane to hit the boy. Griffin instinctively shielded himself from the blow, something he had seemingly done many times, from the location of the marks on his arm.

Camilla screamed and jumped in to intervene, causing the crusty old man to turn and raise his cane in her direction. A newfound strength welled up in Griffin as he saw Camilla come under threat of physical harm by this monster. He yelled at the old devil to stop, then put his hands out to stop the rod from bearing down on the young girl. Mr. Butterfield fell back but did not appear injured.

"Get out of here at once! Before I call the police!" Mr. Butterfield hollered. "I never want to see your face again! Do you understand me? You are finished!"

And before Mr. Butterfield could finish his ranting, Camilla and Griffin ran from his presence. First in a state of frenzy, then in a state of hysteria as they recollected the look on the man's face as he came crashing down on his behind. They finally ended up behind the bakery within a small patch of trees.

"I'm sorry, I know I shouldn't laugh," Camilla howled, "But could you believe it?"

Griffin could hardly catch his breath. "I would pay money if I could go back in time and see it happen all over again."

Camilla finally calmed down enough to say, "Thank you, Griffin, for protecting me."

"Of course."

"How did you ever work for someone so cruel?"

Griffin quickly sobered up with the realization of what had transpired. "I had no choice. I just tried to keep my head down. My father went through a lot of trouble to land me that job. I don't know what I'm going to do now. There's so little work around here and—"

"You know exactly what you're going to do." Camilla handed Griffin the deed to the farm. "Take it. You have no choice now. It's yours. And I know you will care for it just as I would have."

Griffin grabbed the deed reluctantly. "Cami, your father's farm…you worked so hard for this. How can you just give it up?"

"I know it's hard to believe, but I realize it was never meant to be mine. Griffin, you are like a brother to me, so I know you will love and care for it as a brother would."

Griffin didn't know what to say. It was so much more than anything he could have ever dreamed. "Thank you," he finally managed. "I promise I won't let you down." As if Camilla had any doubt.

Camilla stayed for dinner and was present when Griffin delivered the news to his parents. There was much celebrating in the Felix household that night, and once again, Gerald Felix repeated the words he once said to Camilla so long ago, "You're a remarkable young woman."

"So, I'm told," Camilla echoed once again with a childish grin. It filled her with gladness to know that the Felix family would be well taken care of and that Griffin's dreams for the future were restored. He would raise a family on that farm and possibly pass it down to a son one day. Something about that thought warmed her heart, and she knew it would have pleased her Pa, as he always had such great affection for the boy.

After dinner, she and Griffin decided to take a walk outside. "So, what will you do now?" He asked.

"I'm not sure. I suppose I'll start by going back to the Edmonds and figure it out from there."

"This Lord Edmond, is he only the girl's father, or does he mean something more to you?"

Camilla felt no reason to lie. "Yes, he means a great deal to me. He has been exceptionally kind, and he's a wonderful man. I am lucky to have fallen at his mercy."

"But you said so yourself, you are a free woman, correct?"

Camilla nodded. "I suppose I am."

"And what of Frederick? Is it done for good?"

Camilla nodded again. "Yes, I'm afraid it is. I don't think he ever really cared for me after all. I was a silly girl, Griffin. I'm embarrassed when I think of how naïve I was."

A silence hung in the air as they continued to walk, when finally, Griffin spoke up, "He came to see me, you know."

"Who?" Camilla asked.

"Frederick. He was looking for you."

Camilla's heart began thumping like a drum in her chest. "What do you mean? When? Why?"

"He only told me he needed to find you. He said he'd been looking everywhere. Of course, I didn't know where you were, and he didn't tell me his reasons for trying to find you. He just left. I was a bit concerned because he didn't seem well, mentally. But I thought you should know."

The impact of this revelation was difficult to measure. Camilla walked on silently, pondering why Frederick might have come looking for her. Griffin understood her need to process this new piece of information and was considerate not to interrupt her thoughts.

When they returned to the house, Camilla informed Griffin that she would be leaving in the morning. The old friends held each other for a long while, knowing it would be some time before they would see each other again, if ever. Camilla promised to write and let him know where she ended up.

"You know, Camilla, I'm not going to be free forever," Griffin said playfully, giving her a toothy grin. There were tears in his eyes despite the familiar smile on his face.

For a brief moment, Camilla tried to imagine building a life with Griffin. She cared for him as much as she ever cared for anyone, but deep down she knew they were only ever meant to be friends. "I'm sure whatever girl is lucky enough to land you will have her work cut out for her. You do talk incessantly, and she should know how competitive you can be. Though I must admit you are a better runner than me now. Even Mr. Butterfield had to see that," she teased.

Griffin looked into Camilla's eyes tenderly, finally accepting this as her final goodbye, and replied, "I envy whoever wins you. Just remember, I knew you were 'great' before anyone else."

CHAPTER 51

*A*nother long day of travel gave Camilla time to think. What led her to this moment, what she had experienced, what it was she wanted for the future. She thought about Griffin—she wondered if she really made the right choice in refusing him from the beginning. She thought about how much her stubborn pride caused many of her problems. And she was surprised by how much peace she had in letting go of her father's farm. If that was no longer her dream, what was?

She thought about Frederick—how he captivated her the very first time she laid eyes on him. How he had confided in her all the hurts of his past. Their first kiss. Those tender moments in the country. His encouragement when she needed a friend. But also, his betrayal. He had shattered her heart and her innocence. But the biggest question pressing on her mind of all—*Why did he go and see Griffin?*

And lastly, she thought about Lord Edmond; sweet, tender, and generous Jonathan—how good and patient he was with her. How kind he was to everyone he met. How much she loved his daughter, Tabitha. How she found a sister and friend in Hillary. And all the things that had to take place to lead her to them. It seemed like fate.

But she still had the feeling deep down that something was unresolved. With her future wide open, it seemed necessary to figure out what that was so she could finally decide where she truly belonged. No more running, no more striving. She needed a place to call home and build roots without fear of tomorrow or being at the mercy of cruel people. She longed for stability again—the kind her father once offered her. As a child, she never worried about tomorrow. His love ensured that she was always taken care of and as a family, they took care of each other. She longed for that kind of life once again. She longed for love. Real love.

As the carriage ambled on, she pondered all these things. She wasn't sure it wouldn't take a lifetime to sort it all out. All she knew was that she was returning to Mayfield Hall—to the Edmonds. And somehow that gave her significant peace. It had to mean something.

The coach arrived just as the final light of day was fading in the sky. She looked up at the manor she called home now and wondered how she might be received. In a flash, Lord Edmond was at the door, anxiously awaiting news, trembling.

The coachman had hardly come down from the carriage before the questions began. "Did everything go all right? Is Miss Waller okay? Did she decide to stay a while?"

The coachman only replied, "Why don't you ask her yourself?" Then he opened the carriage door, and Camilla stepped out with his assistance.

Lord Edmond's hands flew to his face, covering his mouth in surprise. He lost control of his dignity, his emotions laid bare for all to see. "You've returned to me," he cried.

She had finally made it, and seeing Lord Edmond at that moment sent a surge of great affection through Camilla's heart, and she longed to be in his arms. Jonathan scooped her up as if she were nothing more than a child, tears pouring from her eyes with the release of all she had seen and done during her travels.

He kissed her tears away as he eagerly pelted her face. Camilla took pleasure in allowing the great show of affection. It was nice to be loved without abandon. "Does this mean your answer is yes?" he asked earnestly.

Camilla was overjoyed in the moment. "Yes—my answer is yes." Their lips finally met, Jonathan now certain that Camilla was his and that she had come home to him of her own free will.

The next day, there was much excitement as both Jonathan and Camilla happily shared the news with the rest of the family. Tabitha couldn't have been more thrilled to see Camilla and to know she would soon call her 'mother'. Even Hillary could not hide her delight over the future union.

"We will truly be sisters now," she said, embracing the young girl.

The thought of having a family made Camilla feel that she finally belonged somewhere in this world. She knew she was blessed beyond measure. She felt it was so much more than she ever deserved. Lord Edmond felt quite differently. He spoke of almost nothing else except how he planned to spoil her endlessly. Though Lord Edmond was a conservative man, she knew he would spare no expense where she was concerned. That included their wedding.

"We must make the announcement right away," he remarked. "The sooner we settle on a date, the better. How does two weeks' time sound to you?"

"Brother, that is so soon!" Hillary exclaimed. "The girl only just accepted your proposal. How on earth do you plan to arrange a suitable wedding in such little time?"

"That's what you're here for," Jonathan smirked. "What do you think, my love?" he asked, turning to Camilla.

Camilla was too travel-weary to think about making any plans just yet, but was pleased to see Jonathan eager to do so. "Whatever you think is best," she said with a smile.

"All I need know is that you will be my bride." He cradled both her hands in his. "The future Lady Edmond. And what a great lady you will be. It was as if you were destined for such a station. I assure you, everyone will see you exactly as I do."

Camilla believed he thought far too well of her, but it was nice to be doted on so. The idea of being "the future Lady Edmond" was slightly daunting. Though she was sure it was only a title and required few duties, what did she know about such things? *Will I have to host parties?* She wondered, thinking of all the people who attended the previous dinner party, including Sir Wesley. She was certain she would, but she would worry about all of those details another time.

As if reading her mind, Hillary assured Camilla that she would be there to help her every step of the way, both in the planning of the wedding and when it came to adjusting to her new life as Lady Edmond. Camilla expressed her undying gratitude, but then added, "Would it be okay if I picked out my own clothing though?"

The two had a good laugh. In truth, Camilla was getting used to Hillary's choices, but she did wish to add a little of her own flair to her wardrobe. Even if only to feel like something was truly hers and not on loan. She had never felt like her own person, so she was eager at the prospect of taking hold of her own life for a change. Clothing seemed a trivial way to begin doing so, but it was something.

"We'll go shopping first thing this week, and you can pick

out whatever you wish. I will only offer my opinion when asked," Hillary promised.

Camilla hugged her sister-in-law to be. It was nice that they were getting so comfortable around each other that they could be honest and even tease a little—just like real sisters.

Lord Edmond assumed he would have to play the mediator from now on in a house full of women, a role he didn't relish, but he couldn't be happier. It made him glad to see how thoroughly Hillary adored Camilla now. And Tabitha loved her so much that she boasted to everyone in the house that she was going to have a new mother soon. For the third time that day, she asked her father if it was too soon to start calling her mother. "Do I have to wait? Why not just begin right away?" She grinned.

"All in good time," he assured his daughter, touching her lightly on the nose with his index finger.

Camilla embraced the child and kissed her on the head. "I am very much looking forward to being your mother as well. I couldn't be more proud to have a daughter as sweet and lovely as you."

The idea of being a mother was still very foreign to Camilla, but she felt privileged to have the opportunity. *Who knows, perhaps it won't be long before I have children of my own.* That was something she'd not yet thought of, but the realization, along with Jonathan's loving gaze, made her all warm inside.

CHAPTER
52

There was little talk of anything besides the wedding over the next two weeks. Lord Edmond was quick to set things in motion and hired a small army to help with the preparations, but much required Camilla's input and approval. Things were moving along so rapidly that she barely had time to stop and reflect on the major event ready to take place that would change her life forever.

Lord Edmond had been away with his own preparations. He only hinted that he had some special plans that he needed to personally tend to. Hillary was put in charge of helping Camilla manage things until he returned. Separating again so soon was difficult, but afforded Camilla time to get things done.

More than the wedding, she was nervous about meeting Jonathan's parents. He had gone to see them himself to break the news. He didn't tell her much about their reaction, though she could only imagine how concerned they probably were to think their son was marrying some vagabond who had emerged from the trees and had a background in a traveling circus. Assuming this to be the case, she hoped that, like Hillary, she would be able to ease their minds in time.

The type of society Camilla was now to become a part of was foreign to anything she or her family had ever known. She wondered what her father would think of what had become of his scrappy, freckle-faced little girl. She didn't doubt he would like Lord Edmond very much, considering how good he had been to her. He was a true gentleman, as was her father, though perhaps slightly less proper in his demeanor.

The wedding was in two days, and most of the arrangements were finalized so that Camilla could rest without ruminating on dresses, cakes, flowers, and other decisions that needed to be made. Lord Edmond would be home that evening, and he would bring his parents with him, so that weighed most heavily on Camilla's mind.

She couldn't help but confess her nerves to Hillary, who did her best to reassure Camilla. "If I'm honest, my father can appear to be a severe man, but he is not so bad as he seems. Also, he trusts Jonathan's judgment implicitly. No doubt he has already accepted you as a daughter, knowing that Jonathan would never do anything truly irresponsible. As for my mother, she is preoccupied with her own affairs regarding the many causes she takes up. She has little time to worry over Jonathan. And besides, they both know that I, too, approve of his choice and that even Tabitha loves you. So, they will love you in time as well."

This made Camilla feel a bit more at ease, though she would be happy to get the meeting over and done with. In the meantime, she thought of taking a walk to clear her head of all the activity swirling around her. The idea of some alone time appealed to her a great deal.

Camilla stepped outdoors and walked the grounds that she would soon be mistress of. She couldn't comprehend it. After all, it wasn't something she sought after. In fact, she avoided any appearance of such, so it was amazing to find herself in such a position. She wondered how often she might walk these very grounds in the years to come and, in time, become completely familiar with them. For now, she was content to explore. The estate was always in view from every angle, so she didn't fear getting lost.

For some reason, Camilla suddenly felt pulled in the direction of the place where she had first come upon the Edmonds. It was a warm, but breezy day, which only added to the enticement of heading toward the seashore. Having taken Tabitha to the sea often over the past months, she knew the way well.

It wasn't long before Camilla came upon the incline that led to the cliff where she had first stood on the fateful day she saved Tabitha's life. Making her way up the slope, she relished the sensation of the wind caressing her skin. She reached the top and looked out, noting how much her disposition had improved since the time of her first arrival. Now, there was everything to hope for, and the sorrow she once held in her heart had dulled considerably. Some days, there were no thoughts of her past at all. For the first time in years, she was at complete peace with her life.

Camilla stood gazing out at the horizon for some time, noting that the sun was beginning to fall from the sky. Jonathan would be home soon, which meant dining with his parents, so she thought it probably best to head back now to prepare for their arrival.

As she made her way toward the bottom of the cliff, Camilla noticed a figure sitting on a horse, waiting for her at the bottom. It appeared Lord Edmond had come home and was out looking for her, but upon closer examination, she realized it was someone else altogether. In fact, she did recognize the horse, but it was not one of Jonathan's prized fillies. The while coat and mane were all too familiar to her, as was the dark gypsy-like figure who was riding it.

Camilla froze in place as she was flooded with a range of emotions at once, so that the hair on her arms stood on end and she suddenly stopped breathing. Dismounting from the horse was Frederick. He ran in her direction just as she was standing at the base of the hillside.

Still unable to move, Camilla blinked twice to make sure she wasn't hallucinating. Was it really the man she had given her heart to so long ago? How was that possible, and why had he come now?

When he finally approached her, Camilla could feel herself buckling under the heat of the midday sun. Frederick caught her in his arms, calling out, "Camilla, are you okay? It's me, Frederick. Please tell me you are all right."

Camilla could hear his words but felt too faint to respond. He helped her to a tree stump she could sit on beneath the shade of a nearby oak. He then walked over to his horse, Sugar, to get some water for her to drink. When he returned, Camilla was coming to her senses, but she took the water from him as an act of gratitude. Only then could she process the reality that Frederick was in her presence once again and not some hallucination.

He kneeled beside her as she took another drink and asked once more if she was all right. "Do I need to get help?"

"No, I am okay," she replied faintly. "I think the sun just got to me." Frederick waited to speak, allowing Camilla to collect her thoughts. Finally, she managed to say, "What are you doing here, Frederick? I honestly never thought I'd see you again."

"Ever since you left the circus, I've been looking for you. I didn't even know where to begin. I wasn't even sure if you were alive."

"I don't understand. How did you find me?"

"The wedding announcement. It's been in all the papers. When I saw it, I came at once," Frederick explained.

"I can't begin to imagine why you even cared."

Frederick positioned himself to look into Camilla's face.

"Are you kidding me? Of course, I cared. I've thought of nothing else. I was so worried about you, after all that happened…"

"Yes, exactly, after all that happened." Camilla's strength was returning to her now, along with her pride.

Frederick looked confused. "You don't think I wanted you to lose Duchess, do you? I was brokenhearted for you. I was devastated when I heard—"

"No," Camilla snapped back. "You made it quite clear how little regard you had for me. You led me on for months. You made me believe you loved me. And then to find you with Isabelle. How could you?" Tears began to pool in Camilla's eyes at the pain of the memory it spawned.

"Isabelle? She was nothing to me. You misunderstood completely, but you were gone before I even had a chance to explain."

"I know what I saw," Camilla replied coolly, turning her face away from him.

Frederick grabbed her arms. "Will you let me explain, please? You owe me that much."

"I owe you nothing!" Camilla exclaimed. "I gave you everything, my very heart, and you treated it with contempt."

"That's not true!" Frederick cried out in desperation. "Now will you let me explain, *please*?"

Camilla said nothing, but her silence was enough to give Frederick the permission needed to continue. "I was in my wagon that night and had gone to bed after a long day of trying to ride

Sugar again with my ankle and all. As I was sleeping, Isabelle came into my wagon without my knowing it, wearing as little as you can imagine, climbed into my bed, and tried to seduce me. I demanded she leave at once when multiple gunshots were heard. Naturally, we were stunned and wondered what was going on—if it was even safe to exit the wagon—especially with my ankle affecting my mobility. That was when you came busting in, you looked so frantic, but you didn't stay long enough for me to find out what was happening or to even explain.

"Camilla, I tried to stop you, but by the time I was able to exit the wagon, you had disappeared. I had no idea where you went. I searched the entire grounds, but you were nowhere to be found. I stayed up all night trying to understand what happened, hoping you'd come back, before finally passing out in my wagon. By the time I woke up, I found out you'd been removed from the circus and were long gone. I've been searching for you ever since."

Camilla was beside herself as the realization of Frederick's story sank in. Even with such an elaborate story, she was skeptical. "How do I know you are telling the truth?" she asked, afraid of falling prey to his charms all over again.

"I'm here, aren't I? Camilla, I know I was a fool. I never should have made you doubt me, but honestly, I was afraid. I've been on my own since I was a kid. You know that. I never loved anyone before you came along, and I felt unworthy, I suppose. I never wanted to hurt you. I just needed time to think. But I never betrayed you, I promise. Once you were gone, I realized how stupid I'd been, and the only thought on my mind was making sure you were safe."

Camilla's mind continued to reel. Had he loved her after all? Why had she not trusted he would do right by her? How different things would be now if she had, if what he said were true. In what ways, she wasn't certain, but she wondered if she'd cheated herself of the chance to find out.

"I'm sorry," she replied softly. "I really believed you didn't love me."

"I loved you, Camilla, I do love you. I always will." He hugged her close to him now, and though she embraced him in return, Camilla stopped him short of kissing her. Something still didn't feel right to her about his story.

"What is it? Don't you love me anymore?" he asked, "I thought you'd be pleased to see me."

"Frederick, it's not that. I'm just very confused. I need time to think all this through. You saw the papers. I'm getting married in two days."

Frederick pulled away. "You wouldn't still think of marrying this guy, would you? Not after all we've been through. I finally found you. I can't just let you go off and get married."

"I'm sorry, Frederick, but it's not as simple as that. I need time to process all of this." Camilla asserted herself further. "In the meantime, I must go."

"How much time do you need? You said so yourself, you are to be married in two days!"

Camilla understood the pressure she was under, but she knew she must get back before Jonathan arrived with his parents. He would surely be worried if she were nowhere to be found. "This is all very sudden, but I can't discuss this right now. I'll meet you back here tomorrow, okay? I have a few things to do in the morning, but then I should be free while Lord Edmond goes hunting with his father. It will have to do."

Frederick would have protested, but was now in a helpless state and knew he had little other choice. "Please, do make sure to be here. I can't lose you again. Not like this."

Camilla stood up to leave. "I really do have to go." Her stance was resolute.

"I understand," Frederick relented, "But just in case I never get a chance to tell you again, I love you."

Camilla wanted to return the sentiments, but she was far too overcome by emotion to say more. She had to leave before she lost the will to make a well-thought-out decision. She was no longer a child, and it was time to start behaving as a grown-up, which meant counting the cost. And though she took some pride in knowing she had the sense to take control of the situation, in her heart, Camilla knew that if she lingered one moment longer, she would run off with Frederick and never look back.

CHAPTER 53

*C*amilla had just enough time to get ready for dinner before Lord Edmond returned with his parents. Hillary had inquired after her whereabouts, but Camila simply said she had gone for a walk and lost track of time. Though she did nothing wrong, she felt guilty sneaking around with Frederick, but it wasn't the kind of thing she could divulge at that time.

Even as she dressed, Camilla's heart raced at the thought of Frederick's declaration that he still loved her. Feelings she had long put to rest began to resurface, and she was seeing her entire past in a whole new light. She felt robbed, but she only had herself to blame. No, Frederick shared some of the blame, too. If he had not given her reason to doubt his love to begin with, none of this would have happened. And what made Isabelle think her advances would be welcome? She wanted to believe Frederick, but these questions troubled her. And regardless, no amount of blame would allow her to go back and do things differently.

Even as she was alone with her thoughts, she flashed to memories of those dark eyes penetrating her soul. She thought of the hundreds of passionate kisses they shared and how he caused such a stir within her from the start. How had she gotten herself into such a mess? In just a short while, she was to become Lady Edmond, but now her heart revived fresh feelings of love for the man she worked so hard to forget.

Lord Edmond returned in a happy mood. Despite a long day of travel, he was eager to return to his future bride and for his parents to finally meet the lady who had completely altered his existence. They were as Hillary described—polite and proper. But at no point did Camilla feel slighted by either their mother or father. Though their demeanor was naturally reserved, they seemed eager to accept her.

Perhaps the most difficult part of all was that they asked many questions, and Camilla had difficulty focusing on their inquiries. Her thoughts continually wandered back to Frederick and how he would be waiting to meet her again the next day. It felt strange to hold such a secret from those whom she had entrusted with her future and wished so badly to think well of her.

If she hadn't hidden her distraction well, Lord Edmond didn't seem to notice. It was the most talkative she'd ever seen him. Hillary was more upbeat than usual, too. But no one had Tabitha beat. The eager child had a million and one things to tell her grandparents since she last saw them, including the many fun adventures Camilla took her on and how excited she was at the prospect of acquiring a new mother. Camilla was thankful that they were able to fill in much of the void, as her mind turned endlessly.

After dinner was through, the entire party moved to the sitting room to spend the rest of the evening. Tabitha was permitted to join them and entertain by demonstrating her progress on piano. Camilla had to admit, her latest piece, Minuets in G major, was quite an improvement from the first time she heard her play. There was more small talk, which only made Camilla restless. She wanted to be alone with her thoughts, so she let Jonathan know she was heading to bed early. Thankfully, she had a good excuse for wanting additional rest, as the ladies were planning to tend to some last-minute wedding preparations first thing in the morning, not to mention the general activities of the days ahead.

Lord Edmond's parents understood and admitted they, too, were eager to retreat to their bedchamber, but Camilla ducked out before anyone else could, with Lord Edmond escorting her to the hall.

"I do hope you get some rest, my love," he said tenderly. "I did notice you seemed a bit tired this evening. I don't want you to overexert yourself."

"Thank you, Jonathan," Camilla replied. "These last two weeks have taken their toll, I'm afraid. Although I was enjoying getting acquainted with your parents very much, I knew it was the responsible thing to do to turn in early."

"Indeed. How very wise of you. And you were fantastic tonight. I have no doubt they will love you every bit as much as I do." He kissed her on the cheek, adding, "Sleep well, my love. It will all soon be over, and then we'll have plenty of time relax— together. I wanted to surprise you, but I'm afraid now is as good a time as any to tell you what I've been up to. I have arranged for us to board a ship the day after our wedding. I want to show you all of Europe. Oh, I do hope you are pleased."

Camilla never considered going far from home. What an adventure it would be to sail to lands unknown with her husband at her side. Only she was still deeply conflicted and didn't know how to rightly respond except to say, "Thank you. I can think of no grander wedding gift. You really are too good to me." She returned his kiss, then headed off to her bedroom for the night.

⚜⚜⚜

The activities of the morning were all but torment for Camilla as she thought of nothing but seeing Frederick again. All the girlhood fantasies of passion and romance had returned to her in the night. At first opportunity, she broke free and fled to her room to prepare for their meeting. She touched up her hair and makeup, feeling elegant—quite different from when she was a flashy circus performer.

As she was leaving, she saw Tabitha dancing through the lawn, singing and seemingly off in a make-believe world that only children have access to. She sprinted past her in hopes she would not be seen, afraid to face the child who had come to put so much faith in the knowledge that she would soon be able to call her mother.

She ran on to the spot where she had met Frederick the day before and found him waiting in the grass with Sugar. From a distance, he looked as handsome as ever. A thought flashed in her mind that they could mount sugar now and leave exactly the same way she came, and never look back. She could live the life she once dreamed of with the one who held her heart captive for so long. But something held her in place.

With the shock of their sudden meeting out of the way, she could see something was different about Frederick. As she drew closer, he somehow seemed less extraordinary in the light of day—older, tired. It was as if she were looking upon a stranger. Or was it she who changed? She couldn't be sure.

"You came," he said breathlessly, rising to meet her.

"Were you waiting long?' she asked.

"Not very. Maybe an hour."

Frederick seemed intent on embracing her, but she was still too nervous to invite his affections. He picked up on the cue and shoved his hand in his pockets instead.

"Do you want to walk?" He asked her.

"Yes, please."

A bit of tension hung in the air. The anticipation of seeing Frederick again dissipated, and Camilla suddenly felt strangely subdued. To her relief, Frederick spoke first.

"I must say, you are even more becoming than when I last knew you. I didn't know it was possible. You look like a real lady."

"Thank you," Camilla replied softly.

"So, how did it happen anyway?"

"How did what happen?"

"All of this?" Frederick's hand gestured at her being. "I just mean, your current circumstance seems a far cry from circus life."

Camilla went on to explain to Frederick all that transpired that fateful night when Duchess was shot, how she had fled the circus and ended up by the sea, saved the young girl, which led to her becoming the governess, and how she had managed to rebuild her life with the Edmonds. Pride welled up in her as she spoke of Jonathan and his sister, the kind people they were, and how highly she regarded them.

Frederick listened intently to all she told him and was glad it had worked out for her, but also seemed sad. "I'm sorry I wasn't able to be there for you. It should have been me who was there for you in such a tragic circumstance."

Camilla didn't disagree but said, "It's funny, you know, because I saved the little girl, but when you think of it, she saved me." This truth hit deep within.

Frederick nodded as they continued to walk.

Curiosity got the best of Camilla, and she finally asked, "So, where is the circus set up now?"

"I wouldn't know. I left soon after you did."

"Oh?"

"Camilla, how could I continue working for Max after how he treated you? If you must know, I gave him a good punch to the nose after he told me."

"You did?" Camilla wished she had seen that for herself.

"Yeah, he had it coming for a long time. I had had enough, so I gave it to him good. They threw me out, of course, but it was worth it."

Camilla laughed. Max had once scared her and caused her much pain, but somehow the thought of him now was only as a crusty old circus bum. He had no power over her at all. "So, are you with a new circus then?"

"No, I'm through with that life. After I was unable to find you, I couldn't think of going back to it."

This surprised Camilla greatly. "But you are a great performer! How could you give it all up? I'm sure any circus would be more than glad to take you on."

"That life is no good. It will only get you so far. Yeah, it's thrilling at times, but I knew I was just running. It was like I never really got away from my father. I ran from you too. I guess I figured it was time to try to make a life for myself."

Camilla suddenly noticed that Frederick was limping as they walked along. "How is your foot? Did it heal after all?"

Frederick stopped walking and turned red. "Oh yes, it's fine. It's giving me a little problem today, but it's no problem."

Camilla suspected this was the real reason Frederick left the circus, but thought it unnecessary to confront him about it. "Oh? So, what is it you're doing now?"

"I work at a horse ranch. I figured that's where my passion truly lies. And who knows, maybe someday I'll own my very own ranch. That's the dream anyway."

Camilla was now concerned and genuinely wanted the best for him, but her heart was far from him. "That actually makes a lot of sense. I think you'll do quite well at it. I'm truly happy for you, Frederick. I hope you build a good life as a rancher."

Facing her, he said, "We could do it together, Camilla. I know I could never offer you anything so grand as all this, but I'd work hard to build us a good life."

She finally got the proposal she longed for, but Camilla's heart was no longer torn. The young girl in her would have loved to be a part of making Frederick's dreams come true, but the lady she had become was being pulled in another direction. "I wish things had worked out back then," she replied honestly.

"But?"

"Lord Edmond, I gave him my promise. He is a good man, and he needs me now. And so does Tabitha. I don't think I could disappoint them after how kind they've been to me."

"But Camilla, this is *your* life, it's your opportunity to make a choice for yourself. Don't you see? It's up to you, not me, and not him."

Camilla thought about her father and the kind of man he was. The way he had loved her mother, and what a good father he was. How much she learned from him. She thought of their last time together fishing and how he had told her to "cast the net." That was much like life. No one knows what the future holds. You can only cast the net and see what you catch. Sometimes you get nothing, sometimes you get a little, and sometimes you get lucky, and you get to feast. But you must cast the net to find out, or you're guaranteed to come up with nothing. Camilla had cast her net, and it brought her right here—where she truly belonged.

Suddenly, Camilla heard Tabitha's musical laughter echoing over the grounds. It occurred to her that beautiful laughter was a gift from on high, and she knew she got lucky. She was needed here, and it was where she found belonging. This was the stability and security of home she longed for. So, today, and for the rest of her life, she would feast. She had found love. Real love. Lord Edmond had ultimately won her heart and was waiting for her.

Camilla looked out at the sea, and it brought to mind the day she and Griffin sat and watched the sunset on their last day as children. How simple life was then, yet how rich. This was who she was. This was the life she wanted. And now her resolution was firm.

"Goodbye, Frederick," she said, kissing him for the final time. "I wish you all the best, but I have a wedding to attend." And with that, Camilla disappeared over the hill, never to doubt the life she chose as the future Lady Edmond.

Check out these other titles by Jakki Jelene:

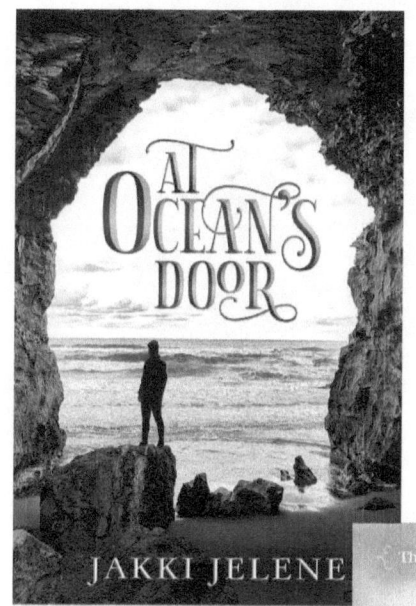

About the Author

Jakki Jelene is a lover of literature and the sea. Whether cozying up with a classic novel or a book of poetry, immersive storytelling has inspired her to express her thoughts in writing for most of her life. Jakki currently resides in beautiful West Michigan with her husband and furry companions.

www.jakkijelene.com